SHADOWS RISING

Published by Dark Nebula Publishing 2017

This book is a work of fiction. Names, characters, places and incidents either are products of the author's imagination or are used fictitiously. Any resemblance to actual persons, living or dead, events, or locales is entirely coincidental.

First published in Great Britain in 2017 by Dark Nebula Publishing

www.darknebulapublishing.com

A CIP Catalogue record for this book is available from the British Library

Paperback ISBN: 978-0-9930202-4-7

Also, available as an eBook

ePub: 978-0-9930202-5-4 Mobipocket: ISBN: 978-0-9930202-7-8

Based in Scotland Andy Malone is a popular international speaker and technology instructor with more than 21 years' experience. Since winning the Microsoft 2006 TechEd Speaker Idol contest Andy has delivered technical and security content to thousands of delegates worldwide. His passionate style of delivery, combined with a sense of fun, has become his trademark and has won him great acclaim with large international audiences.

In recent years Andy's international travels have also ignited another passion, writing. Having already written articles for magazines, websites and blogs, Andy has enjoyed great success with his debut novel, The Seventh Day, which won an acclaimed IPPY award in 2015 and was also nominated for the Peoples Book Prize. Having made the decision to create an exciting trilogy, Shadows Rising is the second instalment. Enjoy!

Follow Andy on Twitter @AndyMalone

ALSO BY ANDY MALONE

THE SEVENTH DAY

Runner Up:
Best Original Science Fiction 2015

Available from all good book stores and online retailers in both Paperback & eBook format.

Paperback: 978-0-9930202-0-9 & ePub: 978-0-9930202-2-3

ALSO BY ANDY MALONE

THE SEVENTH DAY

From a small eighteenth century Scottish village, comes the story of an ordinary man who makes a discovery so shocking that it will change the very foundation of life on Earth. Dougie Allan, a local silver miner, accidentally unearths a terrifying secret and is catapulted 300 years through time. Arriving in the modern world, amidst a backdrop of catastrophic natural disasters, Dougie must forge new alliances if he is to battle his unfolding nightmare.
Befriending a local man, Tom Duncan, and a feisty reporter, Kate Harding, they soon find themselves entangled with the authorities in a deadly race against time. However, they are not the only group interested in the mysterious goings on ...

As a conspiracy unfolds, the trio find themselves pursued by a ruthless assassin. One who seems determined to stop at nothing to protect a secret so shocking that it lies at the very heart of world power itself. As humanity teeters on the brink of disaster and with time running out, Dougie must convince the authorities that a force of unimaginable power is preparing for Armageddon.

Available from all good book stores and online retailers in both Paperback & eBook format.

Paperback: 978-0-9930202-0-9 & ePub: 978-0-9930202-2-3

ACKNOWLEDGMENTS

A huge thank you to everyone involved in the production of Shadows Rising.

Thank you so much to my amazing daughter, Amy, who did a great job as copy editor and to my wonderful wife, Patricia, for putting up with endless hours of me being huddled away in front of a desk.

I would also like to thank my friends Denise McLaughlin, Julie Leverton and Thirza Karsen, for their inspiring words of wisdom and proofreading skills.

Special thanks also to my great friend, Sasa Kranjac, for his wonderful translation services. The richness of his work really brought my Italian and Croatian characters to life.

Finally, I would also like to thank the nice folks from the Excavations Department at The Holy See in Italy for allowing me access to the amazing Vatican Necropolis and grounds. It was a truly inspiring experience.

This is the second book of my trilogy featuring the Scotsman, Dougie Allan, and his friends. I hope you enjoy the story and that it fires your imagination.

As with my first book, all the locations are real and you can visit them today.

SOME SECRETS ARE BETTER LEFT UNDISCOVERED ...

SHADOWS RISING

ANDY MALONE

For my Mum, Rita

Gone but never forgotten…

And he had power to give life unto the image of the beast so that, the image of the beast should both speak and cause that as many as would not worship the image of the beast should be killed.

Revelations 13 - 15

PROLOGUE

Location – Unknown. Date - Unknown.

LAST NIGHT, AS with every other night, he came again to torture my dreams. But who he is, or what he wants is unclear. He is cloaked… he is always cloaked, with hair as black as night and eyes as bright as two silvery moons. As he speaks I struggle to understand.

A moment later the others arrive. Although similar they are different from him, calmer, more composed.

Then the music begins, the sweetest of tunes that has ever seduced my ears. Now, I begin to understand. As the tones echo throughout my consciousness, I begin to float; to drift away into a slumber beyond sleep… beyond life. Then I realize it's not music at all, but whispering. Then during my dream, his message becomes clear. Alas it is not the song of an angel that I hear, but the howl of a beast. I have been seduced by a fiend whom is both a master of lies and a king of deceit. For me it's too late now and I fear I shall never wake again.

1

Saturday 15th October - 10.55pm EST - 65 miles east of Sable Island

FOR JACOB LARSEN, there was no way he could have predicted the storm's ferocity. The fisherman simply looked on in awe at the increasingly turbulent waters below, and darkening skies above. Pale and trembling, he stood on the deck of the "Sea Mist." A 65' steel hull twin-screw fishing vessel built in 1984. As the boat rolled between the waves, he barked out orders as his crew battled the elements. Desperate to keep the Halifax bound fishing vessel afloat.

As another colossal wave crashed mercilessly onto the deck of the boat, Jacob's stomach sank. Not with a sense of nausea, but for the first time in fear. As a fisherman, he was no stranger to bad weather. But in over fifteen years at sea, he had never known such cruelty from a storm. Turning towards the wheel house, the face of a soaked youngster echoed his own look of concern. Determined to be heard above the roar of the storm, he yelled out "Nick, ten degrees to port… quickly now."

Wiping water from his face, the young deckhand shouted "Aye" as he gripped the small wooden wheel and turned it with all his strength. As the vessel began to change course another wave struck. This time with such viciousness, it sent Jacob careering backwards onto the steel deck of the boat. As the wall of water crashed down upon him, the deckhand darted out from the wheelhouse and screamed out "Skipper!"

Panic turned to relief for the youngster as he watched the water eventually subside, revealing a dazed but bruised Larsen sitting on his backside, clinging to a rope for dear life.

Spotting the kid away from his post and gasping for air, Jacob slowly pulled himself up and yelled out, "What are you doing? Get back to that goddam wheel and hold her steady."

Without questioning the order, the teenager turned heel and bolted back towards the wheel house.

"Jacob… look at that!"

"What?"

Now on his feet Jacob glanced across to where his brother and first mate Alistair was pointing. At first Jacob couldn't make anything out, other than the white foam of the crashing waves hitting the hull. But as the moments passed he caught a glimpse of a small but powerful bright light emanating from beneath the darkness below. His elder brother jumped down from a nearby ladder and was now standing adjacent to his younger sibling, Alistair suddenly shouted out in alarm. "What the hell. Is that a submarine?"

At first glance Jakob thought that his brother was right. However, upon closer scrutiny, he concluded that there was something unnatural about the light. It appeared to remain static for too long, which is impossible for a surfacing submarine.

"I don't think so…"

At first, the light was small and unfocused; then as the seconds ticked by, it's intensity grew and within moments the waters surrounding the "Sea Mist" exploded in a blaze of brilliant white light. As another wave crashed onto the deck, the vessel began to list dangerously to the left and Jacob gazed backwards at the terrified youngster in the wheelhouse. Then wiping a trickle of blood from his forehead and gasping heavily, he turned to his brother. "Alistair… you'd best put out a distress call."

"What?"

"You heard me… go now, before it's too late."

Without another word, the storm battered fisherman made his way awkwardly past the young deckhand into the main cabin. With shaking hands, he proceeded to tune the VHF radio transmitter to the emergency channel and pushed the red "DSC", or Digital Select Calling button which immediately began to transmit the boat's GPS coordinates to the coastguard.

"Mayday, mayday. This is the Sea Mist. We are 65 miles east of Sable Island and are taking on water. As well as the storm, we have encountered unexplained lights from below. Possibly a submerged vessel. We require immediate assistance."

"Again, this is the Sea Mist…"

As another wave came brutally smashing down onto the deck, the boat suddenly began to vibrate with a low rhythmic sensation. Struggling to remain upright, Jacob turned to face his brother who emerged from the main cabin with a look of bewilderment.

"Do you feel that, what the hell is that?"

Before Jacob could respond, the shuddering became so violent that inside the main cabin, equipment and crockery began to fall, smashing onto the floor with such force that it drove the young deckhand to move quickly out of the way in order to avoid injury. But as he emerged from the cabin, another enormous wave struck the vessel and literally lifted the teenager off his feet and flung him up into the air. Looking on in horror, Jacob and his elder brother watched helplessly as the youngster's head struck a protruding metal pole. The impact was so devastating that the metal literally tore through the back of the teenager's skull.

"Nick!… Jesus Christ."

All the men could do was look on in horror at the grotesque scene which left the youngster lying dead on the deck. His eyes fixed wide in terror and his blood-soaked head left with a gaping hole because of the injury.

"Oh my god… Jacob, what are we going to do?"

"Get the men to the life raft… now!"

For a moment, Alistair just stood, soaked and dumbfounded at his brother's apparently brutal reaction. "What?… Jesus Christ Jacob, y… you just can't leave him like that."

As the shaking increased, the intensity of light blazed around the vessel. Another wave crashed down onto the hull.

Turning away, Alistair stepped across the deck towards the dead teenager. But before he could kneel, Jacob suddenly seized his arm and roared, "Don't be a fool Alistair. Do as I say and launch the raft… otherwise we'll all end up like him."

Tearing his arm free Alistair turned and hissed in seething anger, "Aye Captain."

Then as he grudgingly moved away to muster the men, there was an abrupt and almighty jolt almost as if the vessel had been gripped by some unknown force. The impact caught Alistair off guard and he lost his footing. As he hit the floor, another wave crashed down on him, tossing him mercilessly along the deck as if he was nothing more than a child's plaything.

"Alistair!"

Even as Jacob moved to somehow save his brother, the sheer force of the water hitting the deck was so unbearable, that in a single horrific moment, the last he saw of Alistair, was his contorted, terrified face as he tumbled over the rear rail of the "Sea Mist" and down into the icy depths of the North Atlantic.

"No…"

As he opened his mouth to scream, he experienced a sudden and remarkable moment of calmness. Gazing across the deck he looked on as the remainder of his terrified crew frantically climbed aboard a life raft to escape.

"Jacob… Come on, get in, hurry!"

However, it was too late; the deafening roar of the crashing waves and screams for help were replaced by a sudden and unexpected eerie silence. Then for a moment, the blinding white light turned night into day and for Jacob Larsen and his crew, the "Sea Mist" was no more.

2

Monday 17th October - 6.40pm EST - Central Intelligence Agency - Langley, Virginia

PRIOR TO JOINING the United States Secret Service, special agent Mark Reynolds was a navy man. In fact, he was part of a long-distinguished line of Reynolds men, who could trace their seagoing past back to the 1800's. His own father, Frank James Reynolds, had served with distinction in Vietnam and his great grandfather was one of thousands of sailors unfortunately killed at Pearl Harbour during that fateful Japanese attack in December 1941.

So, it was with a heavy heart that he informed his father of his decision to quit the navy and seek a career as an agent in the United States Secret Service. Of course, that was six years ago and no one could have predicted the calamitous spate of events which caused so much destruction and took so many innocent lives. Until that fateful day in Iceland, he was just like everyone else; ordinary, normal. Now though, times were different. People were different… he was different.

He wished that he hadn't witnessed what he did. But

the fact is he did and now no amount of backtracking or remorse could change those events. Two years earlier he had been assigned to the US Presidential detail in Reykjavik and when the President himself hand picked him for a clandestine task, he jumped at the opportunity. But to allow the President to drive off unaccompanied into the Icelandic countryside in the dead of night, was one order he couldn't obey. If anything had happened to the man, he couldn't have lived with himself.

But after following the President to Midlina Bridge, or as it's known locally *The Bridge between two Continents*, he was astonished to discover that Richard Bryant, The President of the United States and a man whom he would've given his life for, was not a man at all; but some hideous cloaked creature.

Watching unseen from a safe distance, Reynolds recalled looking on in horror as a tartan clad Scotsman was thrown viciously to the ground like a rag doll. Afterwards Reynolds remembered being stunned as mortal combat ensued with an equally sinister counterpart. As the ground shook and a nearby volcano spewed out it's deadly innards, a lethal battle commenced on the bridge. Whilst attempting to move into a better viewing position, a chasm unexpectedly opened beneath Reynolds's feet, sending him hurtling backwards and disorientated onto the uneven ground. Although temporarily knocked out, he did eventually regain consciousness. Unfortunately, and despite his best efforts, there was no sign of the tartan clad Scotsman and the two deadly figures. In the weeks and months that followed, many ridiculed his story as being both outrageous and absurd. Finally, it was recommended that Reynolds should be *reassigned* as soon as possible.

Standing opposite the Kryptos sculpture in the northwest corner of grounds within the George Bush Center for Intelligence, the forty-something Reynolds sighed and took a sip of his hot milky latte. Dressed in his favourite dark blue navy suit, Reynolds swallowed the hot liquid and continued gazing up and down at the four large copper plates in a vain attempt to somehow make sense of its hidden secrets.

It had taken many years and many attempts by individuals, far more gifted than him, to decipher three out of its four plates. But for crypto analysts worldwide, the fourth remained an on-going mystery. Taking another sip of coffee, he shrugged inwardly and shook his head. For all he knew, or even cared, it could be a recipe for chocolate chip cookies.

"Have you managed to solve our puzzle Mr Reynolds?"

"Huh..."

Turning, Reynolds was greeted by a tall, but physically fit looking elderly man in his sixties, stepping into the sunlight from within a nearby cafeteria. The smartly dressed man spoke with a soft southern drawl.

"The Kryptos Mr Reynolds. I'll be honest, it's kept me awake for more than a few nights, I can tell you. I'm David Tyler, deputy director of operations here at Langley. Thank you for agreeing to meet with us."

"Us? But I thought that..."

"No Mr Reynolds... For future reference, when you attend an appointment at Langley, it's actually code for a meeting."

Suddenly the agent's relaxed expression fell away and was replaced by a more anxious look. "Meeting, but I…"

Opening the door to the cafeteria. Tyler grinned and ushered Reynolds inside. Then, after a short walk through the busy cafeteria, the two men emerged into a large hallway adjacent to a set of three elevators. As Tyler pushed a button, the elevator pinged and the doors hissed open.

"Relax Mark, everything will be explained."

3

11.45pm CET - Copenhagen International Airport - Terminal 1

FIDGETING PROFUSELY, PROFESSOR Helen Moore was not just uncomfortable, but in unmistakeable pain. After being stuck on a plane for five unpleasant hours in an unbelievably unforgiving economy seat, her back and legs ached. So, when the Scandinavian Airlines Airbus A340 finally drew in at terminal 1, Helen sighed in relief at the prospect of finally being able to move around.

As the captain switched off the seatbelt sign, there was a loud ping and a sudden rush of passengers as they leapt out of their seats and hurriedly crammed into the tiny aisle, all in apparent haste to exit the aircraft. As the aisle began to clear, Helen collected her belongings, thanked the stewardess and made her way out onto the corresponding air bridge and then up a short flight of stairs into the main building. The terminal itself was unlike any other she'd visited before. To say it was grand was an understatement. Painted stark white, the almost cathedral like building was both enormously tall and very long. For Helen, gazing down the vast corridor reminded her of a church complete with its small windows: deliberately placed every few meters to help distribute light.

To her right, a solitary figure sat waiting for a flight, seemingly engrossed in the pages of a crime thriller and to her left, the start of what appeared to be an insanely long moving walkway carrying multitudes of people towards what seemed to be the very popular destination of "*Baggage Claim.*"

As the throng of passengers pushed past, her concentration was momentarily interrupted as her cell phone began to ring.

"Oh Christ, not now…"

Stepping aside, she stopped by a small row of seats and tutted to herself in annoyance. Placing her coat and bag down on the seat, she glanced up frustratingly, as the flight's remaining passengers scurried away down the long moving walkway like a giant centipede. After a few moments of fumbling with her bag, she finally retrieved her cell phone and pushed the answer button.

"This is Helen Moore, hello."

"Helen, its Richard. I'm sorry to bother you…"

Rolling her eyes in apparent displeasure, she groaned. "Richard, you always manage to call at the most inopportune moments. I've just got off a flight and I was…"

"I know, I'm sorry. But that's why I had to call. I need you to come to Rome."

"Rome?… Richard I've just arrived in Copenhagen and…"

"Like I said, I'm sorry but this is important. You see I've received a message from Demarco."

"Who?"

"Father Antonio Demarco, remember? He was the priest who deciphered Dougie's symbols."

For a moment, Helen shivered as she recollected her first encounter with the Scotsman, Dougie Allan two years previously. Despite her initial scepticism during their first meeting, his tales of time travel and plots by sinister creatures mesmerised her. Tragically though, most of his revelations appeared to ring true, as a series of devastating events struck, causing billions to be killed and in the aftermath millions more displaced.

As cities crumbled, it was Dougie Allan who finally stepped forward with an apparent olive branch from one of the creatures. A branch in the form of a cryptic message. Containing a series of symbols, which if deciphered, would offer mankind a reprieve and a second chance. But as Demarco solved the mystery and world leaders met in Iceland. The Scotsman, the President of the United States and several others mysteriously disappeared without a trace.

For Helen, time had passed and the nightmares had eventually stopped. She was finally in a place where she could sleep at night. Now, all she wanted was her life back. She wanted to move on and she wanted to forget.

Massaging her temple, she frowned, "Of course I remember Richard, but that was two years ago, I don't see how…"

Suddenly a frustrated Quest interrupted.

"Helen… you don't understand; Demarco's discovered additional symbols which were hidden discreetly within the original message."

Moore's eyes widened, "Really? Has he deciphered them?"

"Not yet, but per Demarco these are totally new and considerably more elaborate."

Helen sighed and rubbed her tired eyes. "Well I suppose I could try and arrange something for tomorrow morning."

"That's great Helen..."

As Quest Paused awkwardly, Helen sensed that the message from Demarco was not the only reason for his call.

"What else is it Richard?"

"Hmm..."

"I've known you for too long now. What else are you not telling me?"

"Well... I received another call yesterday afternoon. It was from the team in Scotland. They appeared to have made an interesting discovery, inside the entrance to the Alva mine."

"I don't understand. You told me that site had been sealed."

"It was, but the government are looking for more and..."

"Just cut to the chase Richard. What was found?"

For a moment, there was an awkward pause then Quest responded, "Tom's watch."

Suddenly Helen's eyes widened in surprise. "What?"

"You heard me right. Tom Duncan's watch along with an apparent message carved onto a nearby rock adjacent to the entrance."

Taking a deep breath, Moore glanced up to notice

that the gate area was now almost clear. Apart from a few remaining crew members hurriedly making their way towards the main terminal, she was now almost alone. Glancing across to her right, she caught sight of one lone passenger, apparently still engrossed in the pages of his book.

"What did it say?"

"Just two words: *I'm Alive.*"

Suddenly Moore's eyebrow's rose.

"Alive? Richard, does that mean… he emerged somewhere else?

For a moment, Quest paused and then responded. "No… don't you see? Not where… but when."

4

Tuesday 11th February 1710 - Alva, Scotland

AS GOLDEN RAYS of afternoon sunlight trickled majestically over the snow-capped tops of the Ochil hills, a lone rider approached the village of Alva from the west. Riding with a profound sense of purpose, James Ritchie drove his black fell pony hard through deep snow, pushing it almost to its limit. Having ridden non-stop for over an hour, The Hardies of Falkirk employee was in no mood for an animal with attitude. So, when the horse objected to yet another request for an increase in speed, Ritchie ignored it and kicked the beast as an incentive for it to keep up the momentum.

For Ritchie, passing the now familiar sight of three derelict farmhouses signalled his arrival in Alva. Minutes later he stopped outside the Allan's modest cottage and climbed down from his horse. Sighing in genuine relief, not just for having made it one piece, but also at being able to finally take a respite for his sore backside.

Then, after tying up the animal, Ritchie walked across to the now familiar cottage door and rapped three times.

After a few moments and with no answer he exhaled disappointingly and turned back towards his pony, untied it and climbed back into the saddle.

"If you're lookin' fae Mary, she's gone o'er tae the mine."

Turning his head towards the voice, Ritchie was confronted by an elderly man, perhaps in his sixties, grasping a large basket of vegetables.

"The mine?"

"Aye, apparently, there's a wee bit of a commotion and…"

Without warning, Ritchie suddenly re-mounted his horse, yanked its reins and was already galloping away as the bewildered man simply stood mumbling

"Aye, well you're welcome I'm sure."

Silhouetted against the icy brilliance like a great black bird, Ritchie drove the pony harder through the snow-covered glen, until at last, the entrance to the Erskine silver mine was visible. After coming to a halt, he leapt off the horse and quickly tethered it to a nearby post.

Up ahead, an angry crowd of men stood by the mine entrance, jeering like a pack of wild dogs. At first, Ritchie couldn't source the cause of the commotion. But as he forced his way through the crowd, he caught a glimpse of a screaming Mary Allan, Robert McRae and a furious looking Fraser McAndrew kicking what appeared to be a wounded man on the ground. Forcing his way to the front of the group, Ritchie gazed on in dismay as an almost possessed looking McAndrew placed a length of rope around the blooded man's neck and began to drag him kicking and choking across to a nearby tree.

Stepping forward, Ritchie had seen enough.

"Whit the hell is goin' on here?"

Wiping his forehead, the powerful looking McAndrew glanced across at Mary and then to Ritchie shouting, "This has nothing tae do with ye Ritchie, we'll deal with this our way."

"Nothing tae do with me. Best ye remember who ye work fae… I'm sure Sir John would hae somethin' tae say aboot murder."

Releasing the rope, a blooded and terrified Tom Duncan gasped desperately for air and McAndrew turned towards a now nervous looking Ritchie and gritted his teeth.

"Listen laddie I never cared for that Jacobite lovin' bastard. So, less you want tae join this witch at the end of a rope, you'd best be on yer way."

As McAndrew turned back towards his snivelling victim, Ritchie un-hilted his broadsword and stepped menacingly forward. "Step back Fraser, I'm warning ye. I won't ask ye again."

Facing Ritchie once more, McAndrew sneered and edged closer, towards a nearby axe embedded in a block of wood.

"Warning me are ye? Laddie, you havenae got the balls…"

"Dinnae test me McAndrew. I dinnae want to be the one tae tell her missus why yer nae coming home tonight."

"For Christ sake, will you twa just stop it…"

Running forward, Mary grabbed MacAndrew's arm before he could reach the axe handle. "He's right Fraser, listen tae him. This is all wrang. Dougie wouldn't have wanted this."

Gazing around at the multitude of anxious faces, McAndrew sighed and hesitantly took a step back.

"Aye... Mary, well I suppose yer right of course."

Turning to face the rest of the workforce, McAndrew gave a reluctant nod and motioned the men to return to work. "Come on lads, let's get back tae work."

With a unanimous and genuine sense of relief, the entire group shouted "Aye."

Re-hilting his sword, Ritchie looked on as the men picked up their tools and returned to work. Stepping across to where the blood-soaked stranger lay, he knelt, carefully removed the rope from around his neck and looked up at Mary in obvious concern. "Missus Allan, this man is in dire need off some kindness, will ye help me with him please?"

After stepping across to where the blooded stranger lay, Mary drew a deep breath and sighed. "Aye, Mr Ritchie Sir, I will."

5

Monday 17th October - 6.45pm EST - Central Intelligence Agency, Langley, Virginia

ENTERING THE LARGE, fourth floor conference room, Mark Reynolds was now in no doubt that this was not the small meeting that he had been expecting, nor been promised. Seated around a large oval table, was assembled a group of twenty or so sombre faced individuals, both civilian and military, judging by their appearance. Although Reynolds didn't recognise everyone, he did manage to pick out a few familiar faces. Jack Nelson; Chief of staff to the President and senior army General Mark Gates. As he took his place in an empty seat, CIA deputy director Tyler patted him on the shoulder and stepped across to a nearby lectern and cleared his throat.

As the ambient noise level fell away, the room came to an ordered hush.

"Good afternoon. Firstly, thank you for taking time out of your busy schedules to join us here today. Before we commence, I'd like to remind you that the contents of this meeting are classified. As you are all aware, two years ago, our planet encountered a series of catastrophic and unprecedented events, accumulating with an enormous loss of life, as well as the near destruction of many of the world's great cities."

"As far as the general population are concerned, these events, as tragic as they were, appear to be nothing more than a series of unfortunate and unrelated incidents. The reality is of course, quite different. The disappearances of former President Bryant, news editor Kate Harding, British agent Robert Wilkes and the mysterious Scotsman, known as Dougie Allan now appear to be only part of a much larger mystery."

"I'd like to introduce Special Agent Mark Reynolds from the United States secret service. Mark has... well, what I consider to be a... unique perspective on the matter."

As Tyler stepped aside, he motioned Reynolds across to the lectern and sat down on an empty seat. As he rose, Reynolds sheepishly walked across to the podium and coughed, more out of nervousness than necessity.

"Thank you, Mr Tyler. I... er, well I didn't really plan on giving any kind of presentation..."

Leaning forward in his black leather chair, General Mark Gates cleared his throat. A serious faced, middle aged Texan who addressed Reynolds almost as a teacher would sternly address a child.

"That's alright son, just give it to us straight. No bullshit, just tell us what you know. That's all we want."

For a moment, Reynolds simply stared at the faces around the table before taking a deep breath. "Well... I'm sure you've read my initial report, but now I stand before you feeling conflicted at not being well… entirely honest."

"What do you mean?"

"Well General, after being summoned to the president's hotel suite, he instructed me to covertly monitor the movements of Kate Harding, the newspaper editor from *The Daily Chronicle* and…"

"Harding?"

"Yes General."

Reynolds continued. "He appeared to show a lot of interest in the woman, although at first I wasn't sure why. He seemed pretty insistent that the operation was just to be one of surveillance and emphasised that no contact was to be made."

"Did you learn why?"

"Sir?"

The interruption came from Nelson. Younger and distinctly more handsome than his predecessor, Ethel O'Brien. He was light haired, in his mid-forties and originating from Seattle, Washington. Nelson always dreamed of being in politics. After serving in the air force for five years, he gained a degree in political studies at Yale and later became a prominent member of the Democratic Party. His appointment as White House Chief of Staff would have been the pinnacle of his career. However, the loss of his parents during the quakes two years earlier, had somewhat soured his appointment.

"I asked, did you discover why she was of such interest to the president?"

"Partly. We've managed to connect a few pieces together. During an investigation of the *Daily Chronicle,* an MI5 analyst discovered the real Harding's body, murdered in her home and consequently alerted an agent in Reykjavik."

"The agent, Robert Wilkes was then ordered to take the Harding imposter into custody. Unfortunately, it appears that she was never apprehended… the post incident review revealed CCTV footage from the hotel showing Wilkes entering the suspect's room, but he never re-emerged. Afterwards it was assumed that she had killed him… but to this day, his body was never discovered."

Reynolds took a deep breath and continued.

"It was then that I telephoned the President and informed him that Harding had left the hotel along with, Dougie Allan."

"Dougie Allan?"

Turning to the General, Reynolds acknowledged the statement with a nod. "Yes, General and that's when things began to get even more bizarre. The President left the hotel to follow them and was pretty adamant that I should not escort him…"

For twenty minutes the group listened intently as Reynolds barely stopped for breath. Meticulously explaining every aspect of the events in Reykjavik, from his initial briefing with the President, to witnessing the battle between the two creatures known as Bryant or Alexander McArthur, and Caius. Finally, as he ended, he described his accident and how, when he regained consciousness, Dougie Allan and the two creatures were nowhere to be seen, leaving himself alone to walk back to civilisation.

Pausing for a moment, Reynolds picked up a glass of orange juice, took a sip and returned the glass to the table.

Sitting forward, Gates sniggered and cleared his throat. "So, Mr Reynolds… what you're saying is you believe this woman… this Harding and President Bryant are perhaps some kind of shape shifting aliens… is that right?"

For a moment, Reynolds paused and shook his head. "No… not exactly General. Something else perhaps, I'm not sure what precisely. But from what I saw and heard, these creatures have abilities far beyond ours."

"Really in what way?"

This time, the question came from Tyler.

"Well, from what I witnessed, they appear to have skills far beyond humans. I also believe that the two individuals were perhaps from separate factions, and that we, er well, humans have somehow been caught up in the middle of…"

"The middle of what son… just spit it out."

"A war, general."

6

Monday 17th October - 11.52pm CET - Copenhagen International Airport - Terminal 1

PRETENDING TO READ his book, Gabriel Quinn was what you would call a specialist. A forty-eight year-old Irishman who knew how to get a job done without asking too many questions. Born in Belfast in the early sixties, his rise to notoriety came at the tender age of fifteen, when he was abandoned by his foster parents after he shot and murdered two unarmed police officers during a foiled IRA bank raid on the Falls Road. In a bid to avoid prosecution, he fled Northern Ireland for the United States, where he resurfaced years later as an army sniper. After being dishonourably discharged for "*accidentally*" shooting an unarmed group of civilians in 1998, he vanished again, only to appear again in 2002, as a mercenary in Northern Iraq.

After the quakes, Gabriel returned to Europe and formed *The Red Club,* a sinister underground outfit, which had but one grotesque purpose. For a mere one-million-pound fee, he would personally guarantee the clinical and professional disposal of any enemies of his selective and anonymous list of clienteles. So far, he was key suspect in at least thirty-seven murders worldwide.

Today, his target was a woman, a science advisor to the British Government named Professor Helen Moore. Who she was or what she had done, was in his opinion, irrelevant. He never asked questions and always preferred to keep a professional distance.

With 50% of his fee already deposited in a Swiss bank account, his coded instructions were clear: eliminate anyone with prior knowledge of a piece of ancient Scottish parchment. Once all the names on the list had been eliminated and the parchment safely in his hands, he was instructed to deposit the item into a safe deposit box in Zurich within fourteen days. Once deposited, he would then receive the remainder of his fee.

*

Call it almost a sixth sense, but from the moment Helen ended her phone call with Richard Quest, she felt uneasy. Placing her phone back inside her small brown leather rucksack, she zipped it shut, pulled it onto her right shoulder and again glimpsed down the deserted, stark white corridor towards her perceived salvation of the baggage reclaim.

At first, everything appeared normal. But after glancing across once more at the waiting passenger, who was still immersed in his book, she began to feel mildly uncomfortable and somewhat vulnerable. Then, in an instant, she understood why. The gates information screen above his head displayed the message "Gate Closed."

"If the gate's closed… who was he waiting for? There's nobody else here."

As small icy shivers of electricity began to tingle the tip of her spine, she quickly gathered her belongings and moved smartly towards the moving walkway. As her feet came down on the slowly moving metal plates, she knew from the increasingly nauseating feeling in her stomach exactly who he had been waiting for.

From somewhere inside her head, she heard Quest's voice repeating over and over "*Helen, don't be ridiculous. You're just being paranoid.*" At first, she didn't want to look… or couldn't look. At this point, she wasn't exactly sure which. But plucking up the courage, she gradually turned her head back towards the seating area and in one alarming moment, their eyes met and she knew she was right.

Gazing back at her with steely blue eyes, the muscular, greasy haired figure licked his lips in anticipation. Glaring at her almost like a cat, as it stares at a mouse just before it pounces.

For an instant, Helen froze in surreal disbelief. Fear rolling over her like waves, lapping across a distant shore. Her eyes darting around, desperately trying to find a way out, but there was none. The vast cathedral like emptiness was absolute and in one terrible moment, Helen knew that for her, there was now only one possible course of action.

Breathing heavily and with her heart pounding, she began to walk purposely forward, albeit sluggishly at first, like a train pulling out of a station. But as she turned to confront her nightmare again, their eyes collided. No longer pretending to read, the greasy haired figure was now on his feet and gazing back at her with a cold callous stare. Then to her horror, he stood and began to move towards the moving catwalk. As panic began to take hold, Helen knew in her heart what she had to do. So, plucking up her courage, she dropped her case and tore off down the seemingly endless walkway towards the main terminal.

Grinning like a Cheshire cat, Gabriel stood for a moment at the beginning of the walkway. Then reaching inside his jacket pocket, he pulled out a highly-polished knife with a distinctive black, almost marblesque handle. Gazing at its sharp jagged edge, he caressed it momentarily, almost as if it were his lover. Then, watching the woman flee, he took a deep breath and with his eyes firmly fixed on his target, raced off after his prey.

7

Saturday 15th February 1710 - Alva, Scotland

"CORPORAL… IS THAT you?"

His voice reverberated eerily off the mine's stone walls. Tom swallowed nervously, desperately trying to relocate the others through the overpowering darkness. But his efforts were in vain. Jarvis and the others were nowhere to be seen. With each passing moment, anxiety began to coil itself around him. Smothering him almost as if a hand had been placed over his mouth. Standing in the cold damp silence, Tom now realised that he was completely alone and that if he had any chance of finding his way back to his family, he had to somehow trace his steps back to the entrance.

Fumbling awkwardly inside his jacket pocket, he suddenly remembered that he still possessed an emergency torch, given to him by his wife only days earlier. To be fair it was no bigger than an average pen. But under these circumstances, it was perfect.

Once retrieved and switched on. The slim torch sent out a small, but intense beam of white light, which tore through the darkness like a fine blade. As he breathed out in relief, he began to move forward again and as he did, the beam of light began to dance erratically off the cold damp walls. Minutes later and to Tom's further relief, the blackness surrounding him began to ease as strands of daylight began to ooze their way through the cavern, almost like blood gushing through a man's veins.

Suddenly stopping dead in his tracks, Tom thought that he had caught sight of a figure just up ahead. Initially thinking that it was perhaps Corporal Jarvis or another member of the survey team, he opened his mouth to call out. However, he suddenly stopped himself and retreated backwards, crouching down low behind a nearby rock. Realising that it was not Jarvis, he switched off his torch and remained still, he shivered as the mine was again plunged into near darkness.

After a few moments, he slowly edged his head outwards, peering over the top of the protruding rock to peer out in the direction of the intruder. Almost instantly he froze, as only meters away, a fearsome figure emerged out of the darkness and stepped into the half-light. Although barely visible through the gloom, Tom knew exactly what it was. Roughly six feet tall and cloaked in a long-hooded robe, it matched exactly the description given by Dougie. It's face pale and gaunt, with eyes blazing like a wolf.

However, this was no animal. At first, Tom wasn't entirely sure if the figure had seen him. To his alarm, it suddenly turned and glided towards him, almost like a shark that had detected a faint but unmistakable drop of blood in water.

"Do you think me so blind, as not to see you human?… I see everything and I see you!"

It was too late to run. The speed and prowess of the creature was so overpowering that before he could even scream out, a terrifying pale hand reached menacingly towards Tom's throat. In a moment of sheer panic Tom shrieked and stumbled backwards, falling clumsily onto the rocky ground in a desperate, but vain attempt to escape.

"NO!"

"Mr Duncan…Tom can you hear me?… Wake up."

"Huh… what?"

As the nightmarish image of the creature dissolved into a whispery blue haze, Tom's eyes slowly flickered open.

"Can you hear me?"

Opening his eyes, Tom struggled for a moment to work out where he was. But as the Allan's simple cottage slowly came into focus, the stark realisation of his situation became all too clear.

"What… yes, who, who are you?"

Looking down upon her patient, Mary stepped aside and the young James Ritchie moved forward. Raising his head to look around, Tom winced as a sharp pain travelled through his right shoulder. "Argh…"

"Easy now, you took quite a beating. It'll take a few days for ye tae recover."

"Recover?"

"Aye, Mr Duncan, isn't it?" If I hadn't come along so smartly, McAndrew and the lads would have killed you fae being a witch fae sure."

"Witch…"

With his grogginess clearing, Tom found himself in the small room composed of a simple stone, complete with a thatched roof. The room itself appeared to be separated in two, divided by a large woollen tartan blanket. Lying flat in a basic, but comfortable, wooden bed he recognised the familiar faces of Mary Allan and the man who had somehow pulled him to safety from the angry mob.

"I'm James Ritchie, Mr Duncan… or can I call ye Tom?"

Nodding, Tom attempted to sit only to find himself wincing in more pain.

"Yes… Mrs Allan… Mary I'm sorry, I…"

Stepping forward Mary shook her head and softly responded,

"Easy Mr Duncan, you need to tak it easy. You've been oot o it now for about four days."

"Four days!"

"Aye."

"But I need to tell you about your husband…"

"It's alright Mr Duncan, you dinnae need to explain. I understand everything now."

"What… you don't understand… I…"

Tom suddenly fell silent as another voice spoke out from behind the blanket. This time however, it was not only vaguely familiar, it was a voice that he had heard many times before, but not one that he ever imagined he would hear again.

"You should listen to her lad, she ken's what she's talkin aboot."

8

Monday 17th October -11.56pm CET Copenhagen International Airport - Terminal 1

WITH HER HEART pounding and shoes clattering along the long metal walkway, Helen moved as quickly as she could through the bleak emptiness of the terminal. As she ran, her cries for help echoed through the nothingness in vain, as there was no one to help her. No passengers, no flight crew, not even cleaning staff. In fact, there was no one except for herself and the terrifying stranger who now pursued her.

Approaching the end of the third walkway, Helen suddenly tripped and cried out in pain as one of her shoe heels snapped off, causing her to slip and crash uncontrollably on the highly-polished floor of the terminal. Momentarily stunned, but wasting no time, she pulled herself back up on to her feet, removed her remaining shoe and sped off barefooted towards the main building.

"Shit!" Gabriel muttered in annoyance, as his prize tore away. Glancing briefly upwards, he took a mental note of

a passing gate numbers as he ran by. "*Gate A15*" He had pre-calculated that he had approximately two minutes of pursuit time before she'd emerge into a populated area of the airport. That was something he couldn't allow. Just up ahead he watched as his target suddenly stopped running and leapt over the railing of the moving walkway and was running towards a nearby elevator.

Now just thirty meters away, Gabriel gave a cruel smirk as he too leapt over a nearby barrier and rushed towards his prize. He knew through painstaking reconnaissance that this elevator was rarely used and that this was the opportunity he had been waiting for.

Hysterical and gasping profusely, Helen lunged desperately towards the sleek metal doors of the elevator. As she made contact, she slammed her sweat-covered palm against the nearby call button and proceeded to frantically hit it repeatedly with her thumb, in a desperate bid to seek escape.

"Help… Oh Christ, someone help me please."

But it was too late. Her greasy haired assailant had finally caught up and as she turned to run, she felt the sudden yank of a powerful hand from behind as the hunter seized a clump of her hair. Despite screaming and thrashing her arms wildly, the thug's grip was just too overpowering and as she crumpled to the ground, her small leather handbag slid off her shoulder, spilling out its contents onto the floor of the terminal in all directions.

Licking his lips in quiet anticipation, Gabriel readied himself for the moment. He had slain so many that the actual task itself had become, for the most part, mundane. This was certainly true for most political or religious assassinations. These were mostly old men who had pissed off their superiors or owed vast sums of money. Either way, it didn't matter to him; the solution was always the same, quick and clinical. Two in the chest and one in the head.

Occasionally though a job would arise, which called for a little more finesse and he did enjoy those. So, like today, when she ran, he had a habit of letting them go, at least for a while anyway. This one could run and he enjoyed her for that. But now the game was over. He had been in the terminal for far too long and eventually he would draw attention to himself.

Releasing Helen's hair, he grabbed her arm, hauled her over onto her back and then grasped her throat. With his grip tightening he raised the glimmering blade upwards and drew a deep breath… "Time to die."

Choking and thrashing her arms wildly, Helen glared into the man's cold unemotional eyes in utter disbelief as she caught sight of the blade.

In that single moment, time appeared to freeze and as she closed her eyes, she now prepared herself for what she saw at the inevitable.

"Where is it?

"Huh…"

The voice that spoke was Irish and to Helen's surprise remarkably calm.

"The parchment, give it to me."

Momentarily confused as to why she was still alive, Helen opened her eyes. Above, glaring down with a cold unemotional gaze, the predator suddenly thrust the knife to her throat.

"No... Please, don't."

"Then tell me where it is. The parchment from the Scotsman?"

Helen's expression turned to one of confusion. How on earth could this man, this stranger, possibly know about the parchment, given to her and Richard Quest two years earlier by Dougie Allan.

"Wh... what parchment? What are you talking about?"

Suddenly the man's calm expression transformed, from one of quiet calm into one of sheer anger. Tightening his grip, he thrust the blade to her jugular and gritted his teeth.

"Don't lie to me you bitch. I'll ask you one last time. Where is the parchment?"

Choking and barely able to breathe, Helen was suddenly aware that her right hand had come into contact with an object on the ground. Groping at it for a moment, she realised that it was her bottle of perfume, which had fallen from her bag during the struggle. With the glass container now firmly in her hand and in sheer desperation, she flipped the lid off, held it up to the man's face and proceeded to unload its contents directly into his eyes.

"Arghhh."

The unexpected shock of the stinging liquid in his eyes, sent Gabriel reeling backwards, howling in pain. Temporarily blinded and somewhat disorientated, he raised the jagged blade and lunged instinctively towards the woman. This time however, instead of plunging into the chest of his victim, the blade merely clumsily brushed off the ground and sent the knife spinning out of his hand with a dull clatter.

For Helen, this was the opportunity she had been waiting for.

Writhing wildly and pulling herself free, she raised her foot and with all her strength lashed out with the back of her heel. For the greasy haired Irishman, the impact was devastating. Striking him firmly on the cheek. The blow caused his nose to explode like a child's balloon, sending blood and mucus flying across the crisp white floor of the terminal, almost like a grotesque mural. As Gabriel reeled backwards howling in pain, there was a sudden ping behind and for Professor Helen Moore it appeared that for a single instant in time, salvation itself had arrived. As the elevator doors hissed open she clambered to her feet and leapt forward, towards the open doors.

Now back on his feet and struggling to see through stinging eyes, Gabriel gasped as he watched helplessly as the beleaguered woman breathed in relief as the elevator doors hissed closed. With his prize now gone, he raced up to the closed doors and hammered with rage against the metal with his fists, howling with rage, "No…"

9

Saturday 15th February 1710 - Alva, Scotland

"NO, IT CAN'T be… this is impossible."

As the segregating tartan blanket was flung aside, Tom stood wide eyed, as the instantly recognisable shape of his friend, Dougie Allan, appeared. Climbing to his feet, Tom rushed forwards and without thinking, embraced his friend warmly.

"Dougie… I, I can't believe it's you. You're alive."

"Easy lad… everything's all right. If you'll give me a chance tae explain. There are things… important things that I need tae tell ye."

Turning to face his wife and a somewhat bewildered looking James Ritchie, Dougie lowered his voice.

"If ye twa wouldn't mind. I'd appreciate a moment alone with my friend."

As instructed, Mary nodded curtly. "Of course, my love… Come awa Mister Ritchie Sir, let me offer ye a wee dram and we'll leave these twa gents tae their business."

Nodding, Ritchie turned and followed the young woman into the adjacent room, where after taking a seat by the fireplace, he was offered a glass of familiar looking amber liquid.

Now alone, Dougie motioned the bruised and battered Tom to take a seat on a nearby stool. Once seated, Dougie perched down onto a second stool and leaned in closer to Tom, in order to talk privately.

"Dougie, what the hell is going on? How did you make it back?"

Dougie gave a heavy sigh. "It's a long story lad. I'm nae exactly sure where to start."

"It's alright, just start at the beginning. The last time we saw each other. You, Kate and Mr Wilkes were heading for the lighthouse. Are they okay, did you make it?"

For a moment, Dougie fell silent.

"Dougie what is it? Are they okay?"

"Nae really lad. I'm afraid that back in Alva, I was tricked… coerced, somehow into helping them."

"Them?"

"Aye, the creatures Tom. McArthur… It was all a trick. He wasn't the real enemy, she was."

Tom's face turned to one of confusion, "What you're talking about. Where's Kate?"

"Kate? I'm afraid, Kate's dead."

"Dead!… But how?"

"Killed and probably replaced by one of those creatures from the mine."

The look of confusion on Tom's face transformed rapidly into one of horror.

"What?"

"I ken how it sounds Tom, but you have to trust me. In Iceland… I saw her for what she really was…"

"And just what was that Dougie?"

Dougie momentarily fell silent, trying to find the right word. Then, after taking another breath, he whispered: "A monster."

For over fifteen minutes Tom sat engrossed, listening intently as Dougie described in detail his recent adventure in Iceland and of his encounter with the terrifying creature known as Caius.

As Dougie paused for breath, Tom shook his head in disbelief at what he was hearing.

"So, all along it was this key that he was after?"

"Aye."

"For what purpose? I mean as powerful as these creatures appear to be, why the deception? Why not just kill us and be done with it all?"

"Don't you see?… Its nae destruction he wants. That's too easy; besides that's what the others want. For him it's simply about power… and the only way for him to achieve that is through complete control."

For a moment, both men sat in silence and stared into nothingness, each contemplating his own future.

"So, what now?"

Dougie sighed, "Now! Well, firstly you need to get yourself well. Then I'll need your help.

I overheard one of them talking about a second key… If that's true and another does exist, then we have tae find it and destroy it before he can get his hands on it."

Tom took a deep breath, "And then?"

"Then… we need to work out how exactly it was that I made it back here and if we can use the same method tae get ye hame tae that good wife of yours."

10

Monday 17th October - 740pm EST - Central Intelligence Agency, Langley, Virginia

AS A QUARTER moon began to rise in the evening sky, the meeting ended and the last of the tired attendees filed out of the conference room, Deputy Director David Tyler motioned Mark Reynolds to remain seated. As the door closed, the two men were left sitting alone at opposite ends of the large, oval conference table. As they stared at each other in silence, Tyler finally reached for a nearby cup of coffee, took a sip and broke the silence. "So, what do you think?"

"About what Sir?"

"Why… the job of course?"

"Job?"

"Mark no one knows this stuff more than you. Other than the Scot, you're the only one who's seen one of these creatures. The agency needs a man like you."

Reynolds leaned his head back and gave an exasperated laugh. "Now just wait a minute… are you asking me if I want to work for the CIA?"

"Of course, but before you answer, I've something I'd like to show you… Something that will hopefully convince you to make the right choice."

Reaching across the table, Tyler picked up a slim remote control and pointed it towards a large flat panelled monitor, mounted on a nearby wall. As Tyler glanced uncomfortably at the monitor he took a deep breath.

"I hope you understand, but I didn't want to share this with the others, as I believe it would have caused a bit of a stir."

After gulping down the remainder of the coffee, Reynolds placed the empty cup down and continued to listen intently.

"Mark, we believe that the creatures you encountered can somehow masquerade themselves to look human and as such blend into our society unnoticed: almost like a chameleon. This of course leaves us in danger of being er… Well shall we say, infiltrated."

Suddenly the large wall monitor flickered into life, displaying now what appeared to be the interior of a large hotel reception area.

"This is a security tape from the Hilton in Reykjavik for the morning that President Bryant disappeared. Other than myself, the President, the British Prime Minister, the Secretary General of the United Nations and now you, no one has seen this tape."

Watching closely, the pair looked on as a lobby elevator opened and Bryant stepped out, followed moments later by Ethel O'Brien, the previous White House's chief of staff, who emerged from an adjacent elevator.

Suddenly Reynolds gasped as O'Brien appeared to

uncontrollably drop to the floor, along with the other bystanders and security staff in the lobby. For a moment, Mark sat stunned as he watched Bryant move towards the hotel doorway and eventually disappear through the exit before the screen turned to static and finally faded to black.

"Jesus…"

Sitting in silence the two men stared at the blackness of the screen before Director Tyler spoke again. "Now, given your… *experience* in this area, I hope you can appreciate why I called on you."

Shaking his head in apparent disbelief, Reynolds continued to sit in silence for a moment before turning back to face Tyler and exhaling. "Yes… Yes, of course I understand. But I have to tell you that after meeting with the man you would never have guessed that he wasn't… er"

"What?"

"Well… You know… Human."

At this point, Tyler exhaled, pushed back his chair and stood up. He then proceeded to walk slowly around the perimeter of the large table. "Mark, no one could have predicted this one. If these creatures can disguise themselves as humans, let alone pass themselves off as the President of the United States… Well to be honest, it's pretty much game over. What chance do we have?"

Leaning forward, Reynolds rubbed his tiring eyes and glanced up at the Deputy Director. "What exactly is it you're asking of me Sir?"

"Join us… I know you can make a difference. I believe that whatever this is, it's not over."

"Sir?"

"Have you read the papers today?"

"Er, no… not really."

Walking to the opposite side of the room, Tyler picked up a blue A4 folder lying on the table. After opening it, he took out a single, typed document, paced back and handed it to Reynolds. "Here. Read this."

The Halifax Herald

HALIFAX BOUND FISHING VESSEL SINKS WITH THE LOSS OF ALL CREW.

Sunday 16th October: Halifax, Nova Scotia: The fishing community of Halifax was in shock this morning as it mourned the loss of The Sea Mist. A 65' steel hull, twin screw fishing vessel, which disappeared in stormy seas east of Sable Island on Saturday evening. Despite an extensive search by the Canadian Coastguard, no trace of the vessel or its eight-man crew could be found. Continued Page 4…

Placing the sheet of paper down onto the table, Reynolds leaned back and returned his gaze to Director Tyler.

"This is a tragedy for sure, but I don't see the connection."

Picking up the paper, Tyler placed it back into the folder and took out a second sheet and handed to Reynolds.

"Okay now look at this one."

"What is it?"

"It's a copy of the log from the Canadian coastguard, I think you'll find it interesting."

Picking up the sheet as instructed, Reynolds took a deep breath and began to read.

The Joint Rescue Co-ordination Centre (JRCC), Halifax, Nova Scotia:

Sunday 16th October: Log entry pertaining to Loss of Fishing Vessel "The Sea Mist" near or around Sable Island on Saturday 15th October. Time: 11.04pm: MESSAGE BEGINS: "Mayday, mayday. This is the Sea Mist. We are 65 miles east of Sable Island and are taking on water… As well as the storm, we have encountered unexplained lights from below. Possibly a submerged vessel. We require immediate assistance… Again, this is the Sea Mist…" MESSAGE ENDS.

Reynolds eyes widened as he gazed up at Tyler with a look of concern. "Lights? The report never mentioned anything about lights."

Tyler smiled and shook his head, "No. That's because this version of the message was never made public. As far as the media are concerned this was just another awful shipping tragedy."

"And what of the reality?"

Tyler frowned and sat down opposite. "The reality Mark, is that we've thoroughly checked our sources and the lights were definitely not from one of our boats, or anyone else's for that matter. Whatever this was, it was not of our making."

Gazing at Tyler, Reynolds cleared his throat. "So, you called me in?"

Tyler reached across the table, took another sip of water and nodded.

"That's right… like I said, no one knows this better than you. If this is the beginning of another *event*, then the president wants to be ready. I'm sure you understand?"

Reynolds gave a nod and deep sigh "I think I do Sir… I think I do."

For a moment, Tyler remained silent before eventually pushing back his chair and standing up. "So, what do you think Agent Reynolds? Will you help us fight the good fight?"

At this point, Reynolds stood, straightened his tie and extended his hand. "Yes Sir, of course. It would be an honour."

11

Tuesday 18th October - 11.05am CET - Rome - Italy

AS AN EARLY morning rain shower finally cleared, Professor Helen Moore fidgeted nervously in the back seat of an unmarked, black Mercedes Police car, as it sped through narrow crumbling streets, surrounded by what appeared to be a constant stream of building sites.

Two years earlier, the damage to the city caused by the quake had been catastrophic, the loss of life almost incalculable. The aftermath for many was almost unbearable, as the once great epicentre of Roman imperialistic architecture lay in ruins. But that was then; now, like many of the other great European cities, Rome had found its feet again and was hard at work rebuilding its infrastructure. Political and religious leaders from all sides had come together, united in their passion and determination to restore the city to its former greatness.

One of the most generous financiers of the project was *The Holy See*. Per the new Pope, Julius IV, "*It was the church's duty to not only invest in its flock, but also in its infrastructure.*" The result had been truly inspiring, as builders and tradesmen from across Italy had come to help lift Rome, literally out of the ashes almost like a phoenix had risen from a flame. The success of the project could not simply be attributed to the skill of the tradesmen, but also to the sheer dedication of the pontiff himself. In just two short years, he had put Rome back on the map as the nucleus of the Roman Catholic Church.

Staring blankly through tired bloodshot eyes, Professor Helen Moore shook her head in quiet disbelief at how lucky she had been in escaping the vile clutches of the grotesque Irishman in Copenhagen. Unfortunately, despite a thorough police search of the airport terminal, the callous and brutal intruder had made good his escape.

Once the Danish authorities had contacted the British consulate, Helen had been immediately collected by armed embassy personnel and whisked away to a safe location, before being escorted, the next morning, onto an almost empty diplomatic flight to Rome.

Now back on the ground and in the apparent safe hands of the British government, Helen sped through the streets of Rome towards Vatican City in an unmarked police car, where she anticipated an emotional reunion with her long-time colleague, Doctor Richard Quest.

The car passed *Piazza San Pietro*, but this was not the St Peter's Square that she remembered visiting with her parents so many years ago, today there were no tourists, no buses and no rows of seats for the thousands of believers who came to catch a glimpse of the Holy Father. Today the square was one enormous building site, complete with a multitude of tradesmen and machines of all types and sizes. All with a single purpose, to restore Bernini's once great vision and ensure its grand re-opening in just under a month's time.

The black Mercedes finally came to a halt outside a small hotel opposite the entrance to the *Musei Vaticani.* Normally Helen would have found a trip to Rome exciting and somewhat romantic, but not today, not after almost being brutally murdered by a maniac.

Without uttering a word, the front-seated passenger opened his door, leapt out onto the street and after a moment, approached the back of the car and opened the passenger door.

"Here you are professor the *Hotel Alimandi Vaticano*. It's perhaps not as grand as what you may be used to… but I think you'll be comfortable here."

Still jittery after her somewhat unorthodox flight to Rome, Helen's eyes darted around apprehensively as she climbed out from the safety of the black Mercedes.

"And what of security?"

The tall dark suited man glanced at her as he lifted her small suitcase out of the trunk and smiled reassuringly.

"Professor… I assure you that every precaution has been taken. The hotel, staff and surrounding area have all been thoroughly checked. I myself, have been placed in the room adjacent to yours to ensure your safety."

"You?"

The man smiled. "Forgive me… of course we haven't been formally introduced. My name's David Shaw. I am a security liaison officer based out of our Rome office."

Moore's face relaxed and she nodded. Closing the car's trunk, Shaw motioned Helen forward, towards the hotel's main entrance.

"Please professor, if you'll follow me this way. We'll get you checked in. I know that Doctor Quest will have just finished his meeting at the Vatican and is keen to see you. He shouldn't be too long."

"Yes… Of course."

Helen swallowed and followed the officer sheepishly into the main lobby of the hotel. Once inside, the pair made their way to the small but elegantly decorated reception area where a smartly dressed male receptionist greeted them.

"Buona mattina, vuole fare il check-in?"

Stepping forward, Shaw cleared his throat.

"Sì, ma solo la signora. Io ho gie fatto il check-in. Credo che avete una camera riservata per la Professoressa Helen Moore?"

"Ah, sì, certamente… Welcome to the *Hotel Alimandi Vaticano* Professor. We have you in room 220 next door to your colleague Dr Quest."

"Thank you."

After picking up her room key and completing a hotel registration form, Helen gave the receptionist a weak, but warm, smile of thanks as Shaw escorted her to her room.

Walking past an un-stocked lobby bar, covered in plastic sheeting, gave Helen the feeling that she wasn't exactly seeing the hotel at its best.

"That's not a good sign…"

"Sorry Professor?"

"No bar… and for once I could really use a drink."

Shaw smiled. "My apologies, but hotel choices in Rome are limited now, I…"

Suddenly, Helen realised how pathetic and somewhat

arrogant her last statement must have sounded. What these people must have gone through the destruction of so many magnificent buildings, as well as the colossal loss of life. Given her own circumstances, she abruptly realised how lucky she was.

As the hotel's, small elevator door opened, she stepped inside and cleared her throat.

"I… I'm sorry Mr Shaw. That must have sounded terribly ungrateful. I… didn't mean to…"

As the elevator door closed and the elevator began its journey upwards, Shaw smiled, "Don't worry about it Professor. If I'd experienced what happened to you, then I'd probably need a drink as well."

The door again hissed open and the pair exited the elevator and turned left. Finally stopping outside room 220. The door swung open and to Helen's delight, the room's decor oozed with an airy sophistication that most western hotels simply could not achieve.

"Here you are Professor…"

Almost like a bellboy and partly through habit, the agent walked through the apartment and checked that everything was in order.

"Your bathroom…"

To Helen's relief he also opened an elegant oak fronted cabinet to reveal a fully stocked minibar.

"You'll even get that drink after all."

Helen gave a forced smile, "Thank you."

Finally, Shaw placed Helen's small bag on top of the room's large double bed and reversed back out towards the door.

"Well. I'll let you get some rest. If there's anything you need. I'm in the room 223, just down the hall."

Shaw left and the door closed leaving her alone. She exhaled and awkwardly strode across to the minibar. Then, with a shaking hand, opened its oak door and took out a miniature bottle of *Vecchia Romagna* Italian Brandy. Without the bother of looking for a glass, she unscrewed its flimsy plastic cap and proceeded to drink the entire contents directly from the bottle.

Once empty, she placed the bottle down, exhaled and walked across to the room's large window. Then, with a heavy heart, she found her thoughts again being tainted as disturbing images of the assassin flashed before her eyes. It was almost as if her thoughts were a school of fish swimming in a pond, thrashing wildly in desperation to reach a morsel of food. But in such situations, there is always one who makes it first. Today, like the fish, it was one singular thought that surfaced to the top of her troubled consciousness *"Why?"*

12

Monday 18th February 1710 - Alva, Scotland

TOM MOANED, AS he looked awkwardly at his reflection in the small cracked mirror. Dressed in one of Dougie's white ruffled shirts, bottle green waistcoat and a pair of dark tanned breeches. He then turned to Dougie and shook his head.

"You can't be serious… Look at me, I look bloody ridiculous!"

Dougie glanced across at Mary for encouragement, but only found embarrassment, when she smirked.

"Mary…"

"Oh… er aye Mr Duncan Sir… ye look grand Sir."

Raising his eyebrows in apparent annoyance, Dougie stepped forward and slapped his friend encouragingly on the back.

"Dinnae listen to her lad, she doesn't ken what she's talking aboot. You look just fine and besides, unless you want tae find yourself at the end of another rope. You can't go walking around in those futuristic clothes. It's too dangerous."

Returning his gaze to the matter at hand, Tom straightened himself up, adjusted the slightly oversized waistcoat and exhaled.

"Well… perhaps you're right. After all I did the same for you… right?"

For a moment, Dougie looked puzzled, almost as if he had forgotten his shopping experience with Tom in Stirling. Then, as an awkward grin replaced his confused look, Dougie stepped backwards and snapped his fingers.

"Of course, my apologies lad. I can't believe I forgot that."

For a moment, Tom felt slightly hurt at Dougie's sudden attack of amnesia, but decided to brush it off as nothing more than an innocent error. After all, there was no damage done and after considering what both men had been through, it wasn't entirely surprising.

"Now lad, if you'll forgive me I have tae get back tae work."

"Work?"

For a moment, Tom stood dumbfounded at the thought of Dougie allowing the men back into the mine.

"Dougie, you can't be serious! You can't possibly let those men back inside that mine. What if they discover…"

Stepping forward the big man raised his hand to alleviate Tom's concerns.

"Easy lad… dinnae worry aboot it. That entrance is well sealed. When that tunnel collapsed and young Mr McRae died, Sir John ordered that entrance be sealed on safety grounds. So, you can rest easy, our wee secret is safe… at least for the moment."

"But what about the entrance we came out of, what if…"

"Like I said lad, dinnae worry aboot it. I've taken care of everything."

Tom breathed in a sigh of relief.

"Aye… well then, I suppose…"

Dougie walked forward and swung open the door to the cottage and turned back to Tom with a reassuring smile.

"Ye have tae understand Tom, that we lead a simple life and like all men we have tae earn a living. So, if you'll excuse me, I need tae put food on the table."

As Dougie stepped outside into the cold morning air and began closing the door, Tom yelled out, "What about me… what should I do?"

As the door closed, Dougie shouted back, "I dinnae ken, go for a walk. But for God's sake try tae keep oot of trouble."

Tuesday 18th October - 11.40am CET - Copenhagen, Denmark

Having narrowly escaped the Danish authorities and still seething with anger at his failure to kill Professor Helen Moore, Gabriel Quinn gazed on with contempt at the badly bruised face, which stared back at him from his bathroom mirror. Having used an alternate passport, Quinn had checked himself into the city's *Copenhagen Island* hotel under the pseudonym *Johan Schmidt.* Strategically located on the *Kalvebod Brygge,* the hotel was situated close to the city's Central Station and the one major road out of the city. If he needed to make a quick departure, this was his best option.

Rinsing soap off his face with cold water, Quinn muttered, "*Bitch*" as he wiped the tender spot where Moore's heel had struck his cheek only a few hours earlier.

After drying his face, he stepped through the doorway into the brightness of his hotel room, changed into a pair of black jeans, a grey shirt and black leather boots. Then, after placing his old clothes into a rucksack, he sat down on a nearby chair and reached across to retrieve his smartphone.

With a sense of nervous trepidation, he stared momentarily at the blank screen before finally taking a deep breath and dialling. As the line began to ring, there was a click and then a male voice answered. "Si…"

"It's me…"

"Si, Gabriel, we were becoming concerned. Is it done?"

For a moment, the greasy haired Irishman was lost for words. He had never failed in a task before and now found himself in uncharted territory at having to admit failure.

"There were complications…"

"Complications? Don't you mean incompetence?"

For a moment, Gabriel remained silent, then after drawing breath he sneered.

"The target was just lucky today, that's all. You don't need to worry."

"I'm not worried Gabriel. However, you should be, he is displeased. You were supposed to clean this mess up. But now we have the added complication that she's met the others in Rome!"

For a moment, the Irishman almost choked. "R… Rome, but how?"

Although he couldn't see the man on the other end of the line, Gabriel knew what the man's next comment would be.

"We know everything my friend, never forget that."

"But, wait… this is perfect. If they're all together then surely that simplifies matters.,"

"*Si, precisamente*… however you must be careful. He is concerned that your methods are attracting… shall we say, unwanted attention."

At this point, Gabriel relaxed back into the chair and smirked.

"Tell him not to worry. I'm on my way and this time I promise; they'll never see me coming."

13

Tuesday 18th October - 2.40pm CET - Vatican City, Italy

AFTER AN EARLY morning meeting with Dr Richard Quest, Father Antonio Demarco decided that he needed to gather his thoughts. As such, he chose to visit what he often referred to as his own personal sanctuary within the walls of Vatican City. Although many of his colleagues preferred the grandeur of St Peter's Basilica or the marvel of the Sistine Chapel, he considered himself a simple man when it came to prayer. He favoured *Vignola's* sixteenth century masterpiece, *The Church of Sant'Anna dei Palafrenieri.*

For Antonio, it wasn't because it was the largest or the grandest of the Vatican basilicas; it simply held a special place in his heart. As a child, he came to visit with his father Peitro on his tenth birthday. The visit had such a profound effect on the youngster that in later life it turned out to be the catalyst for his decision to join the church. Indeed, it was poignant that years later, this basilica would become his first appointment as a parish priest.

Strolling through the afternoon sunshine past the Porta Sant'Anna gate, Antonio smiled as a young, colourfully dressed Swiss Guard clicked his heels and offered a polite salute.

"Buon pomeriggio, padre."

As he strode past the guard's position, Antonio acknowledged the young man's politeness with a warm smile and a nod of gratitude. *"Grazie e buon pomeriggio anche a lei."*

Moments later he was climbing up stone steps of the church towards its main entrance. Once inside, he carefully ducked past a large scaffold, which adorned the main entranceway and proceeded inside to the main basilica. Normally when visitors came to worship, they would separate and pass through a thick, red velvet pediment, which hung over each of the buildings four doorways.

Today however, and for the past two years, those drapes were missing. Replaced with a thick plastic sheeting, designed to protect the building's priceless sculptures, artwork and décor from further damage whilst repairs were being carried out.

Entering the empty church, Antonio walked quietly down its centre aisle and came to a stop adjacent to its large marble altar. After genuflecting, he took a seat on one of the plush red velvet pews and gazed up in awe at its central dome and lantern, the buildings only source of natural light. Today it provided the most wonderful display of angel rays.

Taking a deep breath, Antonio knelt and gazed through the beams of twinkling sunlight as they glistened against the dove of the Holy Spirit. From where Antonio knelt, the circular rays of gold looked even more magnificent than ever. After uttering a few words of prayer, the young priest glanced briefly around the empty church before closing his eyes and continuing to pray.

"Buon pomeriggio, amico mio."

"Che cosa… Gesù!"

Antonio jumped with a start, as a hand was placed on his shoulder from behind. Opening his eyes, he looked up to see his friend, Cardinal Jean Louis Bouchard. Jumping to his feet, he quickly apologised. *"La prego, mi perdoni, Sua Eminenza,* but I did not hear you come in."

The cardinal, dressed in traditional red and white robes, patted Antonio on the shoulder once more and motioned him to take a seat.

"No, ti prego, perdonami, amico mio. I didn't mean to startle you, let alone disturb you at prayer."

Antonio momentarily collected his thoughts and smiled at his mentor. "That's alright your Eminence. Is there something I can do for you?"

Bouchard smiled and began to slowly walk around the church. "*No… no davvero*. To be honest I was simply looking for an excuse to escape a meeting with Cardinal Ponti and, like you, this place is one of my favourites."

Antonio nodded, "*Sì,* I meant to congratulate you on your new post Eminence, but it's been difficult to see you. You appear to be a very busy man."

Bouchard turned to face the young priest and his expression turned to one of mild guilt. "*Perdonami amico mio*, but I'm still adjusting to my new role. That combined with the holy father's continued illness, means that any free time I have is limited, to say the least. That said, I will try… I promise."

"Grazie, Sua Eminenza."

"And what of you Antonio? Still solving puzzles?"

For a moment, Antonio fell silent and returned his gaze upwards towards the light filled dome. Then taking a deep breath, he reached into his jacket pocket and took out a piece of A4 paper, unfolded it and handed it to the Cardinal. "*Sì*. Well… I'm trying."

Taking the sheet, Bouchard nodded with a sense of familiarity. "Ah, sì, I've seen this before, remember?"

Antonio shook his head, "*No, Sua Eminenza*, I solved that puzzle. It was numeric remember. This one however, is quite different… look closer."

Antonio placed his index finger on the top of the sheet and pointed to a small symbol integrated inside the larger symbol. The faint, almost watermarked image depicted three closely interlocked circles with two horizontal lines passing through the centre. "Do you see it?… It's very subtle, I almost missed it."

Bouchard looked at the symbol and shrugged his shoulders as he passed the sheet back to the young priest. "*Sì, lo vedo Antonio*, but what does it mean?"

Antonio's expression turned to one of puzzlement and he sighed. "*Non lo so*, I feel like I've seen this before, but I can't quite place it. I showed it to Dr Quest and he suggested that we do as he did before; send it out to a small number of scientists and mathematicians."

"I see…"

"He also suggested that we bring it to the attention

of the authorities, just in case it yields something of significance."

Bouchard smiled warmly. "Well, my friend, if anyone can find the answer, it's you. I shall pray for your success."

"*La ringrazio, Sua Eminenza*, I appreciate that."

Placing a hand on the young priest's shoulder, the cardinal smiled once more and cleared his throat. "Now Antonio, if you'll excuse me. I believe that meeting with Cardinal Ponti beckons."

As Bouchard turned to leave, the main door of the basilica was suddenly flung open and a young, grim faced Swiss Guard rushed in. Pale and sweating profusely, he ran up to a concerned looking Antonio and Cardinal Bouchard.

"*Eminenza, Padre…*"

Standing, Antonio moved quickly to stand beside his mentor and the approaching guard. "*Calmati figlio mio, cosa c'è? Cosa succede?*"

Breathing heavily and with his eyes filled with tears, the young guard swallowed hard before grasping Antonio's arm and uttering one single word. "*V… Vesuvio!*"

14

Tuesday 18th October - 10.55pm EST - Central Intelligence Agency, Langley, Virginia

The Joint Rescue Coordination Centre (JRCC), Halifax, Nova Scotia:

SUNDAY 16TH OCTOBER: Log entry pertaining to Loss of Fishing Vessel *"The Sea Mist"* near or around Sable Island on Saturday 15th October. Time: 11.04pm: *MESSAGE BEGINS: "Mayday, mayday. This is the Sea Mist. We are 65 miles east of Sable Island and are taking on water… as well as the storm we have encountered unexplained lights from below. Possibly a submerged vessel. We require immediate assistance… Again, this is the Sea Mist…" MESSAGE ENDS.*

Gazing solemnly at his computer screen and despite having read the same report six times, Agent Mark Reynolds felt no closer to explaining his continuing and overpowering sense of unease. Despite no reports of submerged submarines, stealth boats, missing planes or even little green men for that matter, he was at a loss to explain the cause of the mysterious lights as reported by the crew of the *Sea Mist.* Although he had only been in his new role for a matter of hours, Reynolds already felt an enormous burden to find answers. But with so many questions, he wasn't entirely sure where to start.

Gazing once more at the report on screen, he was sure about one thing; his experiences in Iceland were unquestionably related to the disappearance of ex-President Richard Bryant and the tragic events of two years earlier.

"Mr Reynolds…"

"Huh…"

For a moment, the CIA's newest recruit didn't hear the woman knock on his door, let alone enter the room.

"Mr Reynolds… I'm sorry to disturb you Sir but…"

Shaking himself back to the moment, Reynolds raised his eyes upwards from his screen and turned to face his somewhat grim-faced support co-ordinator and smiled. "I'm sorry Laura I didn't hear you come in…"

Within a moment however, his smile evaporated as he realised there was something terribly wrong. Pushing his brown leather chair backward he got to his feet and walked across to where the tearful twenty-something year old was standing. Expecting bad news, Reynolds drew a breath and swallowed hard. "Are you alright? Is there something wrong?"

"It might be easier if you just go into the hallway sir."

After giving the young woman a gentle nod, he turned and stepped through the doorway into the starkly decorated hallway and walked across to where a group of office staff were huddled around a flat screen television. Pushing his way to the front, Reynolds looked on in disbelief at the distressing images of a blooded and bruised reporter standing amidst a backdrop of utter devastation.

"Again… this is Richard Delany reporting live for CNN. This is just incredible… I can't believe what I'm seeing. Only two years after a series of catastrophic events rocked the world and killed so many. It appears that we must again endure another wave of heartbreak and pain. This morning, Vesuvius, the world's most infamous volcano has again erupted leaving a cataclysmic trail of death and destruction in its wake. Just under an hour ago, and with very little warning, it has utterly devastated the Mediterranean city of Naples and the surrounding areas. Although it's still far too early to speculate the exact number of fatalities, it's expected that the death toll could eventually run into the tens of thousands…

Without listening to the remainder of the report, Reynolds immediately turned heel and sped off back towards his office. Once inside he ran across to his desk, picked up the phone and proceeded to dial. Moments later the call was answered by a woman's voice.

"Director Tyler's Office. Jess Marshalll speaking."

"Yes, this is Mark Reynolds in operations, I need to speak with the Director urgently…"

"I'm sorry Mr Reynolds, I'm afraid he's busy and can't be disturbed."

"What? But please I need to…"

"I'm sorry; like I said he's on an important call and can't be interrupted…"

With images of the devastation still imprinted on his mind and with frustration boiling over into anger,

Reynolds uncharacteristically slammed his hand down onto his desk and screamed into the mouthpiece. "Look lady, I don't give a shit if he's speaking with God. This is matter of national security, so for Christ's sake put me through now!"

*

Tuesday 18th October - 16.10pm CET - Bavaria, Germany

Thundering through the magnificent Bavarian countryside, the sleek white ICE train, number 681 from Copenhagen, sped its way smoothly and efficiently towards Munich at an impressive 180 miles per hour. On board, Irishman Gabriel Quinn relaxed in an empty first-class compartment. After finishing a dinner of a blood rare steak, green beans, mashed potatoes and black coffee, he stood for a moment to stretch his arms before pulling down a black medium sized rucksack from the luggage rack above his seat.

After glancing cautiously around to ensure that the carriage was free of prying eyes, he unzipped the bag and checked that its contents were in order. Inside were various items of spare clothing, jeans, sweaters and so on. However, these did not appear to provide any interest. What caught his eye, was a sleek black leather pouch. Which, when opened, revealed a polished silver Beretta semi-automatic pistol with accompanying silencer. Quinn stroked the weapon, almost with a sense of admiration before he closed the case, zipped the bag shut and placed it back into the luggage rack. As he retook his seat, a door hissed open from behind and a smartly dressed attendant approached.

"Are you finished Sir? Was everything to your satisfaction?"

At first Quinn didn't answer but as the man picked up the dirty dishes he took a deep sigh and then gave a confident, almost sly sneer.

"Yes, thank you… everything is just perfect."

15

Monday 18th February 1710 - Alva, Scotland

AFTER RESTING FOR what now felt like an eternity, Tom concluded that if he didn't get fresh air soon, he would probably go insane. So, dressed in his borrowed attire, including an old woollen coat, breeches and ruffled white shirt he decided to take Dougie's advice and go for a walk. After allaying Mary's concerns for his safety, he assured her that he felt much better and that after a lunch of her home-made broth, some fresh air would do him the world of good.

As he edged towards the doorway, Tom drew breath and lifted the doors heavy metal bolt upwards. As the door swung open, an icy blast of cold February air hit him in the face, and after exhaling, he stepped anxiously out into the afternoon sunshine. As his eyes slowly adjusted to the glare, Tom almost expected to see the familiar village that he knew so well. However, the stark reality was entirely different. Today there were no tarmacked roads, no shops, no schools nor even a church for that matter. There were just five or six small-scattered stone buildings with thatched roofs, along with one or two others at various stages of construction.

To Tom's relief though, familiar landmarks were still there. The snow-covered peak of Dumyat to his left and the foreboding rocky faces of Craigleith could be seen just above where he was standing. In fact, from his current position and elevation, Tom estimated that he was, in fact, standing on familiar ground. A spot that had, or rather would become the village's *Cochrane Park* in about 180 years' time.

Despite the air being bitterly cold, most of the weekend's heavy snow had melted away, leaving the ground wet, but firm to walk on. Turning to his right, Tom decided that a walk to a familiar spot would be a good place to start. So, after a momentary glance back towards the safety of the cottage, he turned and continued upwards towards Alva Glen.

Striding past a clump of young rowan trees, Tom smiled to himself in mild familiarity as he watched a flock of starlings circling and swooping gracefully in unison overhead. Then, moving onwards, he suddenly experienced a flashback of long walks up the glen with his wife and daughter. It was then, in that single moment that his smile evaporated away as Tom felt the awful realisation that he was now alone and might never see them again.

It was also in this moment that he glanced at his arm and he realised that in his haste to get dressed, he'd forgotten to remove his wristwatch. Taking a deep breath, he gazed at the watch for a moment, acknowledging that by continuing to wear it, he might attract further unwanted attention. As he unstrapped the timepiece, he had the sudden revelation that he could perhaps use it to send a message to the future, possibly even a message home.

Turning swiftly eastwards, rather than continuing up, Tom now marched towards what would eventually become Silver Glen. He did this for three reasons. Firstly, it was the mine entrance where he'd emerged from just a few days earlier. Secondly, accordingly to Dougie, the entrance was sealed off and finally, it was also the entrance that he, Dougie, Dr Quest and Professor Moore would come to explore in the future.

There is an old Scottish saying, *"Blink and the weather will change."* For Tom, that was certainly true today. As he arrived at the mouth of the mine, heavy clouds had appeared overhead from the north and what had been a cold but promising morning had now been replaced with a cold, sleety snow.

After surveying the entrance, he concluded that if he were going to leave his watch along with a message, it would be best left just inside the opening. So, walking forward he took the watch out of his pocket and slowly edged inside the mine. After spotting what he considered to be a suitable location, he placed the watch on a raised ledge behind a large boulder and proceeded to pack the surrounding area with smaller rocks. Once satisfied that it would not easily be discovered, he picked up a sharp stone and began to engrave the words *"I'm alive"* into a smooth area of rock.

"Daddy…"

"Huh!"

Suddenly Tom froze in disbelief at the sound of a child's voice as it reverberated eerily from deep within the mine.

"Daddy…"

This time there was no mistake, it was the voice of a child, a young girl perhaps. Tom immediately dropped the stone and turned inwards to investigate.

"Hello... is there someone there?"

"Daddy is that you?"

Suddenly, disbelief turned to icy fear as up ahead a faint blue mist was beginning to form. A mist that as it moved closer, began to glow brighter, until to Tom's dismay the mist slowly morphed itself into the image of his six-year-old daughter, Amy.

On seeing this spectre, this ghostly apparition of his daughter, Tom's world collapsed and he fell to his knees and burst into tears.

"Oh Amy... yes it's me, its daddy. I'm here baby..."

"Daddy where are you? Why don't you come home?"

"I'm trying baby, I really am."

Now fully formed, the eerie, glowing figure now stopped directly in front of Tom.

"Find the key Daddy... Find the key and it will bring you home..."

Wiping a tear away, Tom suddenly looked up in surprise and any fear that he had been experiencing was instantly transformed into sceptical curiosity. How could she know that he and Dougie were planning a search for a key?

As he raised his head, he looked directly into the apparition's face and a chill ran down his spine. Now realising that what he was looking at was not his daughter at all, merely a projection, a facsimile of someone who he loved. Remembering Dougie's similar experience in Alva, he stepped back and took a deep breath.

"You're not my daughter… who are you and what do you want?"

At first the spectre didn't answer, but then after a short pause she gave Tom an unnerving smile as she began to softly hum to herself, almost as if she was a real child trying to remember the words of an old nursery rhyme. Tom was about to interrupt when she began to sing…

"At Pilate's birthplace on ancient lands
A tree grows strong on ancient sands
In its roots lies an ominous key
That can control mankind for eternity
But should its secrets be uncovered
Then all our souls will be recovered"

The creature repeated the rhyme multiple times and then whilst in mid song, it suddenly began to lose its cohesion and dissolved into nothingness. Leaping forward Tom raised his hand, "No wait! Please don't leave me…"

It was too late, before he could complete his sentence, the blue whispery shape of his daughter was gone and was again replaced by cold damp air.

"I knew it…"

"Huh…"

Suddenly, turning heel Tom looked on in disbelief, as now standing about ten meters outside the mine entrance was a furious looking Fraser McAndrew wielding what was unmistakably a long and deadly broadsword.

"You bastard, I was right all along. You are a bloody witch after all."

16

Tuesday 18th October - 4.30pm CET - Vatican City, Italy

"HELEN… ARE YOU ok?"

As a second knock reverberated against her hotel room door, Professor Helen's Moore's eyes slowly flickered open, and after sighing with annoyance at being disturbed, she turned towards the small bedside table and reached out in an attempt to pick up her watch. After a few moments of fumbling, she finally grasped hold the timepiece and immediately sat up in surprise at the time. Then swinging herself out of bed, she placed her feet firmly down onto the cold wooden floor.

"Helen, are you in there? It's Richard, are you alright?"

"Huh… Yes, I'm coming. Just give me a moment."

As she attempted to make herself look semi-presentable, the sound of clattering glass caused her to stop and look down. With a look of surprise, she discovered that the glass in question was in fact the remains of nine or ten empty miniature bottles of liquor that she had unwittingly consumed before falling asleep.

Now groggy and somewhat unfocussed she got to her feet and awkwardly crossed to the main door of her hotel room. After taking a deep breath, she turned the handle and the door swung open to reveal a concerned looking Doctor Richard Quest.

"Helen, are you alright? Why didn't you answer?"

Overcome with relief to see her co-worker and friend, she suddenly lost control, burst into tears and flung herself into his arms.

"Oh Richard, I… I thought I was going to die. He… he tried to kill me…"

"Hey, easy. It's okay, you're safe now and everything's going to be alright."

Gently supporting her weight, Quest moved his distraught colleague back inside, closed the door and sat her down on the edge of the large double bed. As she flopped down, Quest shook his head disapprovingly as he spotted the small pile of empty glass bottles on the floor.

"Oh Helen, what happened?"

As the distraught Moore raised her head, she wiped her face with her sleeve and gazed upwards, desperately trying to compose herself.

"It… it was just after we spoke. He was waiting for me."

"Who was Helen, do you know?"

"I… I don't know, I've never seen him before. He had an accent, Irish I think. He kept asking about the parchment. You know the one that Dougie Allan gave you?"

Quest's eye widened, "Parchment?"

"He was crazy, he seemed to know all about me Richard. Everything. I mean… how's that possible?"

Standing, Quest exhaled and began to pace around,

"I don't know… but we need to find out that's for sure. I think I should have a word with our consulate friend and make him aware of the situation, he'll want to contact London."

Pausing for a moment, Helen glanced down at her watch and immediately got to her feet.

"Richard. Look at the time, where the hell have you been? The last thing I remember was Shaw telling me that you were on your way back."

Suddenly Quest's head dropped and he gave a deep sigh.

"I'm sorry Helen, but there's something you should know."

"What?"

"There's been another incident. An eruption here in Italy."

"Oh God… Where?"

For a moment, Quest, didn't answer, he simply turned to face the window and took a deep breath.

"Vesuvius."

Helen suddenly ran across and pulled him around to face her.

"What!… Richard we have to go. Perhaps we can help…"

As Helen moved towards the door, Quest grasped her arm and sat her down on the corner of the bed and shook his head.

"It's too late… there's just too much devastation…"

"You can't be serious Richard, how could you just…"

"Helen, our duty is to find out what's happening and

why. Once we know that, perhaps we might have a chance of stopping it"

"Just how do you propose we do that Richard?"

"We need to speak with Demarco."

"Father Demarco? I don't see how…"

Helen's voice suddenly faded away as another sharp knock sounded on the hotel room door. With a look of concern, she glanced at Quest and shouted out "Who's there?"

After a brief pause, the familiar voice of security liaison officer, David Shaw, spoke out.

"It's David Shaw Professor, I need to speak with both of you please."

Gasping a sigh of relief, Helen stood and walked across to the entrance, unhooked the chain, grasped the handle and swung the door open to reveal a smartly dressed but somewhat flustered looking officer.

Glancing ominously across at Quest, Helen stepped back in preparation herself, almost as if she was expecting the worst.

"Is everything alright Mr Shaw?"

Stepping into the room, Shaw exhaled and closed the door.

"Professor, Doctor. I'm afraid I've received some disturbing news from the authorities in Denmark. Apparently, they've identified the assailant who attacked the Professor."

Quest smiled with relief,

"There you are Helen; that's good news, isn't it?"

Shaw's expression turned solemn.

"No Doctor, I'm afraid to say. It appears that the man

who attacked the Professor is a professional. His name is Gabriel Quinn and to be frank, he's not the kind of chap who leaves a job unfinished, so I…"

As Shaw spoke, Helen's eyes widened in alarm.

"What! Y…You don't think he'll come, here do you?"

Turning to face the nervous couple Shaw shook his head,

"Probably not. However, at this stage I feel it prudent that we prepare ourselves for any eventuality, just to be on the safe side."

Suddenly, Quest got to his feet and began pacing.

"Forgive me for saying so Mr Shaw, but it doesn't sound like you have much of a plan."

Stepping across to the room's large bay window, Shaw glanced down into the street below, before focussing his attention towards the towering walls of the Vatican.

"I'm sorry Doctor, but perhaps we could find you both a place to stay, that's maybe a little more… secure."

17

Tuesday 18th October - 1.20pm EST - Central Intelligence Agency, Langley, Virginia

HAVING BEEN KEPT waiting for over an hour for his hurriedly arranged appointment with Director Tyler, Mark Reynolds sat frustrated on a small brown leather couch outside the Director's office. Sitting opposite with a smug look of satisfaction on her face, was Tyler's personal assistant, Jess Marshall. Glancing at the woman with a sense of mild guilt, Reynolds knew, that keeping him waiting so long was her revenge for his unorthodox outburst earlier.

As he was about to stand and enquire as to how much longer he would be forced to wait, the thirty something blonde looked up.

"The Director will see you now Mr Reynolds."

"Thanks."

Gritting his teeth, Reynolds stood and gave the woman a forced smile. Then walking forward, he knocked on Tyler's door and proceeded inside.

"Ah, Mark. Please come on in."

As Reynolds entered, Tyler closed a brown A4 folder, pushed his chair back and got to his feet.

"Take a seat. Can I offer you a drink?"

"No thank you."

As instructed Reynolds strode across the office, pulled out a seat and sat down, while Tyler poured himself a glass of orange juice and returned to his desk.

"Well… congratulations appear to be in in order."

"Sir?"

"You appear to have made quite a first impression with my assistant. I have to wonder if every day will be this interesting."

"No Sir… My apologies, I…"

Interrupting the agent in mid flow, Tyler leaned back and took a deep breath. "So, tell me Mark, what was so important that I had to be pulled away from a conference call with the President?"

"Sir, I was going over the *"Sea Mist"* report and I just couldn't shake off the feeling that this must be somehow connected to the events of two years ago, forgive me for saying so, but these lights don't just sound like a natural phenomenon. Just as I thought I was losing my mind, CNN reports of another massive eruption in Italy. I just feel that we're seeing history repeat itself and if that's the case, we need to be ready."

For a moment, Tyler remained silent and then sitting up, he reached across to the brown A4 folder that he had been reading. After opening he took out a series of photographs and slid them across the desk to Reynolds. "Do you recognise these people?"

Looking over the pictures Reynolds nodded. "Yes Sir,

this is the Scotsman, Dougie Allan and these… others. Forgive me, I've seen them before but I don't know their names."

"They're both science advisors for the British Government. Doctor Richard Quest and Professor Helen Moore. They were involved in the initial investigation of the Scotsman, Dougie Allan."

"I see."

"Mark, the President and the British PM both feel that because of the three of your collective experiences, it would be in everyone's best interests if we were to work together to solve this little mystery."

Giving a sigh, Reynolds nodded in agreement. "Yes Sir… perhaps it would."

"Good. That's settled then. We'll get you on the next flight to Rome. Jess will…"

"Rome?"

With a look of shock on his face, Reynolds almost choked at the thought of travelling out of the United States. He'd only been in his new post for a matter of hours. Before he had chance to object, Tyler was already on his feet. "Yes, as it happens Quest and Moore are both on assignment in Rome and unfortunately travel comes with the turf I'm afraid. In this brave new world, we must act and react quickly. I hope you're up to the challenge Agent Reynolds?"

Pushing his chair back and rising to his feet, Reynolds stood to attention and nodded enthusiastically.

"I am Sir."

Smiling, Tyler extended his hand and the two men shook in agreement. "Excellent. I'll have Jess book you on the next flight out. Take this file; it's everything we have from the British. Oh, and Mark…"

"Yes Sir?"

"Take a diplomatic bag and a weapon… just in case."

"Of course, Thank you Sir."

As Reynolds turned heel and left the office, Tyler walked slowly back towards his desk and smiled inwardly, his face suddenly beginning to change, to morph into something different, something inhuman. His normally handsome appearance replaced by a hideous pale expression, with unnaturally bright blue eyes and jet-black hair. Turning to face the office's small glazed drinks cabinet he gazed at his changing reflection through the glass and watched as his normally smart grey suit was replaced with a fearsome long black cloak. At first, the creature didn't speak. But when it did, it was not the voice of a man, but the whisper of a serpent. "Finally, everything is in place my brothers. Now it can begin."

18

Monday 18th February 1710 - Alva Glen, Scotland

OUTSIDE THE MINE entrance, Dougie and his men had finished lunch and were preparing to return to work. Overhead, the once promising blue skies over the Ochil Hills had darkened and had become heavy, as large snowflakes began to slowly turn the ground white, almost as if a silk white sheet and been thrown down.

"Alright lads, there's work tae be done. Let's be having ye."

With little argument, the men rose to their feet, picked up their tools and dutifully headed back to work. Once satisfied that all was well, Dougie collected a nearby shovel and turned to join his men.

Glancing around, Dougie suddenly became aware that he was a man short. Indeed, worse than that, the missing man happened to be none other than Fraser McAndrew, the very man who had so viciously attacked his friend only days earlier.

Standing motionless for a moment, Dougie swiftly

reached out and grabbed hold of the first man at the back of the line. "Alistair…"

The youngster, who was no older than 14, immediately stopped in his tracks, turned to face Dougie and stared at the big man with a look of concern.

"Aye Mr Allan."

"Where's Fraser?"

"I… I'm not sure…I"

As the teenager's head dropped, Dougie knew in that moment that the youngster, like the rest of his men weren't being as forthcoming as they should be.

With frustration now turning to anger, Dougie grabbed the teenager by the scruff of the neck and barked at him angrily, "Don't lie to me laddie, now tell me where he is."

"Th… the witch. He's awa to take care o the witch."

"Oh, for Christ's sake…"

Suddenly Dougie exploded with anger, released the boy and stormed away to where a nearby horse was tethered to a post.

"Get back tae work, I'll deal with this."

After mounting the beast, he took hold of its reins and kicked the animal to a full gallop and sped downwards, thundering through the snow-covered glen towards home.

*

For a moment, Tom simply stood frozen with fear. Staring wide-eyed in disbelief at the powerful looking McAndrew now standing just meters away. The man's face: white with fury and his eyes filled with a hatred that sent a chill down Tom's spine. As the seconds ticked away, Tom thought that he could perhaps somehow reason with the man and attempt to provide him with a reasonable explanation as to whom he was conversing with.

However, as he looked on, the thought evaporated almost as quickly as it had come. In its place now surfaced one of pure instinct. In this case, it was to flee. But after briefly turning his head inwards, he realised that any effort on his part would be pointless as there was nowhere to run to.

"Please wait. I'm not a witch, I can explain…"

The big man shook his head and growled, "Dinnae lie tae me ye Sassenach bastard. I'm nae interested in yer excuses; I saw ye with my ane eyes. Now, are ye coming oot or do I have tae come in and get ye?"

With his heart pounding, Tom desperately looked around for something, anything that he could use for defence. But as his eyes swept over the ground, his heart sank as their seemed to be nothing. As he turned to confront his fate, he suddenly spotted a heavy looking pickaxe leaning against a nearby wall. Moving swiftly, Tom grasped hold of its handle and with his hands still shaking, raised the heavy tool upwards into a defensive posture before reluctantly stepping out to face McAndrew.

*

As the door to the Allan's small cottage was suddenly flung open, Mary dropped her basket of washing; staggered backwards and shrieked out in alarm as her somewhat flustered looking husband now stood panting heavily in the doorway.

"Jesus Dougie, you gave me a start. What is it, Whit's wrang?"

Sweating profusely and still shaking with anger, Dougie didn't say anything at first. He simply glanced around the room in silence before walking briskly past Mary and stopping beside the fireplace. Taking a deep breath, he leaned over and grasped hold of a large broadsword sat against the wall, next to a basket of logs.

"Tom… Is he here?

"No…"

As Dougie picked up the weapon, Mary stepped closer with a look of concern and grasped hold of her husband's arm. "Dougie… why do you need your sword, whit's wrang?"

"Where did he go lass, think?"

"He… he went fae a walk, headin' oot towards Silver Glen I think. But whit is it? Whit's wrang?"

As he hauled himself free from her grasp, Dougie rushed forwards towards the doorway. Then, after swinging the wooden door open, he returned his gaze inwards towards Mary and grimaced. "McAndrew…"

*

Tom sheepishly emerged from the mouth of the mine and as he did, McAndrew suddenly rushed forward, his eyes filled with fury. Raising his broadsword menacingly, he lunged like a hawk about to strike its prey. For Tom, watching the Scotsman move almost seemed like a scene from a movie, one in which the action is slowed to a point where the characters hardly appear to be moving.

But this was no movie and for Tom, it was blind luck that when McAndrew's blade fell, it missed him by a hair and clanged harmlessly off a nearby rock.

For an instant, Tom couldn't believe his luck as the Scotsman suddenly lost his balance and tumbled to the ground. It was in that moment that Tom saw an opportunity to make his escape. So, taking a deep breath, he mustered all his courage, dropped the pickaxe and set off at speed towards the opening. However, as he ran past the stunned McAndrew, he shrieked out in alarm as McAndrew suddenly raised himself up and grabbed hold of his foot.

Unable to maintain his balance, Tom yelled out in alarm as he stumbled forwards. As solid ground was replaced by air, Tom lost his footing, only to come crashing down onto his knees.

"Arghhh…."

The impact of the fall was overwhelming. Landing face down in a pile of freezing snow, McAndrew let go of his ankle, leaving Tom writhing on the ground like a wounded animal. But in one final bid to secure freedom, he gritted his teeth and glanced back towards his attacker. To his horror, he could see that McAndrew was already back on his feet and in the process of retrieving his weapon.

Whimpering and gasping heavily Tom fell forward onto his stomach and attempted to drag himself away, but it was too late. The enraged Scotsman moved like a shot and to Tom's dismay, was now standing above him with his sword poised to strike a fatal blow.

19

Wednesday 19th October - 10.10am CET - Vatican City, Italy

SITTING IN A small waiting room, adjacent to the *Archivio Segreto Vaticano*, Richard Quest, Helen Moore and British Embassy Security Officer, David Shaw, waited patiently for their morning appointment with Father Antonio Demarco. They stared solemnly at a small television set in the corner of the room. Its screen flashing image upon image of devastation and a news reporter, who appeared to be as traumatised as many of the victims in his report.

"*As the world again comes to terms with the cruelty of Mother Nature, CNN has been informed that United States President, George Hillary, and British Prime Minister, James Walton, are to host an emergency meeting of World representatives next week at the United Nations in New York. It's expected that more details on the event will become available during the coming days. I'll be back with more on this later in the programme, but for now I'll hand you back to Kate in the studio, for the day's other news. For now, this is Richard Delany reporting live for CNN."*

As the screen flickered, the picture changed to a brightly lit studio and a smartly dressed middle-aged woman sitting behind a news desk.

"Thank you, Richard, now to the day's other news.

Reports are coming in from the Canadian Government about the sinking of a second fishing vessel off the coast of Nova Scotia. This comes just days after of the tragic loss of the Sea Mist, a similar fishing boat. With authorities at a loss as to the cause of the disaster, the Canadian Prime Minister has ordered a full investigation. We will of course bring you further details on this story as we get them.

Finally, "UNITY" has announced an unprecedented rise in its membership. Launched less than two years ago, with a mere handful of members, the religious groups numbers have now swelled to an unprecedented one billion plus worldwide. With followers coming from all levels of society and faiths, the group appears to be capturing the hearts and minds of people everywhere.

As for the church's leadership: the order's *mysterious and elusive leader known only as "Michael" continues to spread his word of peace and global unity. However, as no one has seen Michael, many sceptics, including an increasing number of renowned religious leaders, have expressed concerns regarding the group's rapid and somewhat unnatural rise to power. Despite this however, the lure for potential followers seems stronger than ever..."*

As the door to the waiting room suddenly opened, the group shifted their attention away from the television news reporter and rose to their feet as a smiling Father

Demarco stepped inside the room. Dressed in a black raincoat, trousers, black shirt and sporting a familiar white collar. Demarco Said warmly. "*Buongiorno a tutti*, I'm sorry to have kept you waiting."

The thirty-something year old priest smiled kindly and extended his hand. Shaking Quest's hand first, before moving on in turn to Helen and finally to Shaw.

"Father, if you'll allow me. I'd like to introduce my colleague Professor Helen Moore and from the British Embassy, Security Officer; David Shaw."

"*Sì, Professoressa* I've heard so much about you. Welcome to the Vatican… All of you."

"Thank you, Father."

With a nod towards Shaw, the priest then turned and beckoned the group out into the corridor.

"Please, if you'll follow me, I've reserved a meeting room for our discussion."

As instructed, the trio exited the small room and followed the priest as he escorted them through the building and into the library's great hall. Walking through the stunning picture gallery, Helen gasped in awe at the elaborately decorated ceilings and walls. Each adorned with magnificent images of saints, philosophers and scribes from ages past.

"This is just incredible…"

Turning to Helen, Demarco smiled, "Isn't it? In fact, every time I walk through these halls I can't help but feel in awe of the work that has been done. One might almost call it an archive of devotion."

As they continued past beautifully painted depictions of ancient Babylon, Athens and Alexandria the group entered the main library, complete with its shelves upon shelves of priceless books, artefacts and portraits dating back thousands of years.

"Father, it seems such a shame that all of this is locked away. Almost a waste..."

"*Niente affatto Professoressa*, scholars and academics have complete access here, by appointment of course."

Helen smiled, "Of course."

Finally arriving at the end of the corridor, Demarco turned to his left and opened the door into a small study room. "Professor did you know that there is actually only one authorised person who can take books out of the library."

"Really, who's that?"

Ushering the group inside the room, Demarco smiled, "Why, his holiness of course."

Once inside, Demarco closed the door and steered the group across to a large desk, which was laden with various books, papers and diagrams. "Now as you know, I've been working on the symbols and..."

Suddenly, Shaw's cell phone burst abruptly into life. Demarco fell silent whilst the agent reached into his pocket and quickly silenced the device with a look of mild embarrassment. After recognising the number as coming from his office he began to make his way towards the door.

"*Chiedo scusa Padre* but it's my office. If you'll excuse me, I need to take this call."

"*Certo Mr Shaw.*"

As the agent left the room, Demarco returned his attention to the two scientists and continued.

"*Dunque, dov'ero?*... Ah yes, as you can see, this

document is the one you emailed me and contains the original symbols which we now know were a series of numbers."

Glancing across at his colleague, Quest smiled and gave a nod. "Correct."

"So, the reason I called you both here today is this..."

Picking up a magnifying glass Demarco stepped closer and focussed the glass onto the centre of one of the strange symbols.

"*Vedete qui?*"

Helen squinted and tilted her head. "What am I supposed to be looking at Father? I don't see anything."

Slowly moving his hand onto the page, Demarco stopped and tapped his index finger.

"*Guardi qui,* do you see them? The three circles?" "Oh yeah... I see them. It has two lines through the centre."

"*Molto bene Professoressa.*"

"But what are they? What do they mean?"

Demarco sighed. "*Purtroppo,* we don't know yet. I thought that perhaps, like it's mother puzzle, it was simply a binary number, but I've now discounted that theory. I then began to look through as many books on symbols to see if I could find a match, but so far, I've had no luck I'm afraid.

I must admit though that my knowledge in this area is somewhat limited. I've taken the liberty of contacting an old teacher of mine in Dubrovnik. Father Vladimir Palovic. He's an abbot at the Dominican priory there. But don't let that put you off, he's actually a very knowledgeable man and I'm sure he can help. Here, let me give you his details..."

Suddenly the conversation was interrupted as Agent Shaw re-entered the room and cleared his throat. "*Mi scusi Padre, posso interromperla per un momento.*"

"Sì, certamente."

"Doctor, Professor forgive me but it seems you have a visitor."

Helen stepped forward with a look of surprise. "A visitor?"

"*Sì,* er I mean yes. A Mark Reynolds, apparently, he's an agent with the CIA and per London you have a history together."

"History, what are you talking about?"

"All three of you were in Iceland… two years ago,"

"Iceland?"

"Indeed, it would appear that he's been authorised by the Prime Minister to work with you on this case."

Suddenly Quest stepped forward and raised his voice. "Now just wait a minute Shaw, please tell them that this is completely improper and we have no intention of…"

Shaw raised his hand, cutting the Doctor off mid-sentence. "I'm sorry to interrupt Doctor, but you don't understand. He's just landed in Rome and I've been asked to go to the hotel. So, if you don't have any objections, I'll leave you in the capable hands of the good father here, whilst I collect him."

Turning to Helen, Quest shrugged his shoulders and gave a deep sigh. "Well, it looks as if we don't really have much of a choice, do we?"

As Shaw left the room Helen dropped her head and she turned to Quest with a look as if she was reliving a bad memory. Then taking a deep breath, she turned to

Demarco. "Father, Richard, would you mind if I excused myself? At least for a short while…."

"Helen, are you okay?"

"It's just bad memories and I… Well, it's been a rough couple of days and I feel that…"

Demarco raised his hand and smiled. "*Sì Professoressa*, of course, I know just the place."

*

10.10am CET - Rome Termini Train Station, Rome

Outside Rome's central railway station, early morning drizzle had turned into a heavy and persistent rain shower. In a desperate bid to avoid being soaked in the morning deluge, many pedestrians could be seen running for cover or struggling with umbrellas. Amongst the chaos, a foreboding figure emerged from the mouth of the station's entrance. But for Irishman Gabriel Quinn, stepping out into the coolness of the morning rain was a welcome relief after having been cooped up in a stuffy train for so long.

Reaching inside his jacket pocket, he pulled out a cell phone. After dialling a number, he placed the phone to his ear and waited patiently for it to be answered. As the line clicked, a man with a strong Italian accent answered the call. "*Sì*…"

"I've arrived. So, tell me, what do you need?"

"Go to The *Hotel Alimandi Vaticano*. You'll find them there."

"Then?"

"Find out what they know and bring me everything about the Scotsman."

"And afterwards?"

For a moment, the voice on the line fell silent and then Quinn heard the man let out a heavy breath. "Do what it is that you do best."

"I understand."

As the call ended, Quinn returned the phone to his pocket, stepped across the street to where a nearby taxi was parked. After climbing inside he slammed the door shut, leaned across to the driver and sneered. *"Hotel Alimandi Vaticano."*

20

Monday 18th February 1710 - Alva Glen, Scotland

"MCANDREW!"

Sweating profusely and in a frantic bid to save his friend's life. Dougie leapt down from his horse, trudged slowly and carefully forward through the deepening snow, his voice booming through the glen to distract McAndrew from thrusting a blade into his cowering friend's back.

"McAndrew!"

As the furious Scotsman caught sight of Dougie, he cautiously lowered his weapon and turned to face him. Then, as Dougie continued his approach, he jeered and raised his hand as a signal for him to halt his advance.

"That's far enough Dougie..."

"Now Fraser, whit's all this aboot lad. Surely we can talk aboot this like men?"

Without warning, McAndrew suddenly spun around and seized hold of the terrified looking Tom Duncan by his hair and thrust his deadly sword against his throat.

"Dinnae come any closer Dougie... I'm warnin' ye. Otherwise you'll be picking this bastard up in pieces."

"Whit are ye talking aboot lad…"

Tom let out a cry as McAndrew tightened his grip and yanked his head violently to the side.

"Dinnae gie me all that innocent talk, he's in league with Lucifer and ye ken it. Talkin awa tae a spirit, as if they were best friends. I saw it with my ane eyes. Now if ye ken whits good fae ye, you'll just turn around and walk awa."

"Now Fraser, you ken I cannae do that, so why don't ye just put that blade down and…"

"Stay oot of this ye Jacobite bastard. He's mine and there's nothin ye can do aboot it."

Dougie shook his head and gave a disappointing sigh. Then, slowly edging his way backwards, he concluded that any further words between the two men would be futile. McAndrew had clearly made his mind up and no amount of discussion would change that now. Despite his best efforts, it seemed to Dougie that a conflict between the two men was now unavoidable.

With his horse now parallel to his left shoulder, Dougie sighed, reached up, took hold of his broadsword and drew it slowly out of its leather scabbard. As the polished blade glistened in the daylight, Dougie raised the weapon with deadly intent and reluctantly snuck forward towards McAndrew's position. "Alright Fraser, if that's the way ye want it…"

*

Wednesday 19th October 11.05am CET - Vatican City, Italy

Having picked up the somewhat exhausted looking CIA Agent, Mark Reynolds, from Rome's *Fiumicino - Leonardo da Vinci airport*, Shaw's black Mercedes made its way back through Rome's narrow side streets towards the *Hotel Alimandi Vaticano*. Inside, Agent David Shaw attempted to bring his American colleague up to speed with recent events.

"...And you have no idea as to why the Irishman should want to target the Professor?"

"Other than his interest in the Scotsman's cryptic message, no."

Reynolds yawned, "Forgive me Mr Shaw, it was a long flight."

Shaw smiled, "No problem, my office has arranged a room for you at the hotel. Professor Moore and Doctor Quest should be finished their meeting in about an hour. I'll collect them and once you've had a chance to rest, perhaps we could meet up for dinner this evening?"

Reynolds gave a tired but enthusiastic nod, "Sure, that sounds great."

Reaching into his pocket, Shaw pulled out a white business card and handed it to Reynolds.

"That's the office details in Rome. If you need anything just give them a call."

Taking the card, Reynolds placed it in his jacket pocket, smiled and thanked his driver.

By the time the Mercedes had pulled up outside the *Hotel Alimandi Vaticano,* the heavy rain had eased and chinks of golden sunshine began to trickle through the heavy clouds. After collecting his bags from the trunk of the car, Reynolds followed Shaw into the lobby of the hotel.

"It looks like a building site, are you sure it's open?"

"Don't worry Mr Reynolds, it might look a little chaotic but I can assure you, you'll be comfortable here."

Stepping across to the elegant front desk. Shaw gave a cough and pressed a call bell. "Good morning, hello. Is there anyone around?"

After a few moments of silence, Shaw pushed the bell again.

"Hello… Marco… Maria are you there?"

Turning to Reynolds, he shrugged his shoulders. "Strange… I'm sorry about this, they must be cleaning rooms. If you'll just take a seat, I'll pop upstairs and see if I can find someone to help."

"Sure."

Shaw turned away towards a nearby elevator. Reynolds took a seat on a comfortable looking white leather couch. Although intending it to be only for a moment, he soon found his eyes becoming heavier and one moment soon became several minutes.

*

Upstairs, on the hotel's second floor landing, Shaw emerged out from the small elevator, turned left and paused outside Professor Moore's room. After briefly twisting the polished brass doorknob, he was satisfied that the door was still locked and the room secure. After pausing for a moment, he then continued onwards, to his own neighbouring room.

As the door swung open, he suddenly stumbled back in shock, as sitting in one of the room's two large leather armchairs was the sneering Irishman, Gabriel Quinn.

As Shaw reached for his weapon, Quinn was already one step ahead.

"Now then. Mr Shaw, isn't it? I wouldn't do that if I were you."

Gazing at the cold arrogant face, it was then that he spotted his gun, an automatic complete with silencer, pointing straight at him. Shaw took a deep breath, desperately trying to think of something, anything that might offer a chance for him to walk away from this with his life

"How do you know who I am?"

"Why, the receptionist of course. She was very helpful."

"What the hell do you want?"

"First things first Mr Shaw: Lose the gun."

As ordered, Shaw reached inside his jacket, unclipped his gun belt and carefully pulled out his own weapon. Once visible, he then tossed it onto the ground and it hit with a loud clunk.

After kicking it towards the intruder's chair, he carefully stepped backwards a few paces.

For a moment, Quinn remained stationary and silent, watching with interest as Shaw's facial expression transformed from one of apprehension to one of fear. For Quinn, this was his favourite part, right here, right now. Watching his prey squirming, as he slowly toyed with it;

as it pleaded for mercy. Something of course that he never gave. "Close the door."

As instructed Shaw slowly stepped forward and closed the door behind him.

"So, what now? You're just going to shoot me, is that it?"

Quinn answered the statement by taking a slow deep breath. "You look tired Mr Shaw. Why don't you have a seat?"

"What?"

"Sit down."

Keeping his eyes firmly fixed on the slim stone faced figure, Shaw did as he was ordered and walked across the room and took a seat opposite. "So, Gabriel... that is your name, right?"

Quinn gave a callous smile."Ah... an informed policeman."

"At least it's better than being a crazed fanatic."

Quinn's smirk fell away and was replaced with an icy, solemn look. "Fanatic? I'm not a fanatic, just a businessman and be assured, this is just business."

"What do you want?"

"You know what I want."

"No, I don't...

"Don't lie to me. If you didn't know her then why did you try her door?"

"I... Don't..."

Suddenly, the Irishman was up on his feet and now standing directly above him with the gun pointing at his head. Looking on in fear, Shaw felt his blood suddenly run cold as Quinn reached inside his pocket and pulled out a knife with an unusual black handle. "I'll ask you one more time. Where is Professor Moore?"

Although his spoken words were soft and calm, Shaw knew in his heart that Quinn's serenity was nothing more than an act. The man was an animal and as he glimpsed a sudden flash of steel, he knew in that moment that the animal was about to attack.

The blade fell with such force that as it slammed into Shaw's right thigh, he screamed in agony as it tore through muscle and shattered bone.

"Arghhh."

The pain was excruciating, rolling over him in waves of agony. As Quinn pulled out the blade blood began to gush onto the polished floor.

"Y… You bastard…"

"Not at all Mr Shaw… Like I said, this is just business. Now for the last time, tell me where Professor Moore is?"

With tears rolling down his face, Shaw's head dropped in defeat. "The Va… The Vatican."

Being cautious as not to step in an increasingly vast pool of blood now collecting beneath Shaw's feet, Quinn smirked and walked calmly back across the room and retook his seat opposite.

"Who's she meeting?"

"I… I don't know…"

At this point, Quinn's smirk fell away and he lost patience completely. Raising his weapon towards Shaw's head, he gave a bear like snarl. "Who is she meeting?"

"Q… Quest and a priest, Demarco."

The bullet hit Shaw like a thunderbolt. Striking his temple with such force that the back of his skull exploded, sending a shower of blood and bone across the room. His body slumped forward in the chair, Quinn sneered in mild satisfaction at a job well done.

"Thank you, Mr Shaw, you've been very helpful."

21

Monday 18th February 1710 - Alva Glen, Scotland

FOR A MOMENT, the two men simply stared each other down, standing adjacent in the freezing cold like a pair of wild dogs preparing to fight over the last few morsels of food. As McAndrew mocked Dougie, he released his grip on Tom's hair and shoved him so he fell forward, face-first into a pile of freezing snow.

"Tom… are ye alright lad?"

Shivering in the bitter cold, Tom looked up at McAndrew and glanced across at Dougie with a look of apprehension. "Yes, but you don't have to do this Dougie."

"Ah, I'm sorry lad, but I do…"

For McAndrew, the attack came quickly and with such brutality that it took him completely by surprise. As Tom watched the event unfold, he couldn't quite believe what he was seeing. The sudden change in Dougie's behaviour was astonishing, almost as if he had become temporarily possessed. His face turned white with rage, his nostrils flared like an angry bull, with its eyes bulging wide with fury. As Dougie brought his blade down on McAndrew with an incredible force, his opponent swiftly raised his own weapon in defence, which, on this occasion, successfully deflected the blow.

As the two blades clashed, the force of the impact sent sparks and a loud clanging sound echoing through the glen. But as McAndrew repositioned for his own attack, Dougie was already one step ahead and unfortunately for his opponent, this second blow would have devastating consequences. Dougie's blade struck him directly below the shoulder, plunging directly into his muscle.

"Arghhh…"

Reeling backwards in agony and bleeding copiously, the man had barely enough time to raise his weapon in a meek defence, before Dougie struck again. However, this assault was different. For the first time while staring at the man, a shiver ran down his spine and McAndrew felt fear. Not just at the ferociousness and skill of Dougie's battering, but also at the chilling smirk which was now beginning to appear on his face, almost as if the giant was enjoying himself.

For Tom, watching Dougie repeatedly strike McAndrew with such brutality was extraordinary, especially as it was coming from a man that he thought of as a friend.

As McAndrew moved into position for a counterattack, Dougie quickly stepped sideways to avoid being hit by his blade. Then, as McAndrew's shoulder flashed past Dougie's line of sight, he suddenly flipped his wrist over to expose the sword's large hilt and proceeded to thrust it upwards, towards McAndrew's face. The impact was catastrophic; smashing into his nose with such force that it sent the Scot bloodied and bruised, whirling backwards onto the icy ground.

As McAndrew lay whimpering on the ground, nursing his blood-soaked face, Tom watched in horror as Dougie, enraged and wide eyed, suddenly moved forward to deliver what would undoubtedly be the final blow. Observing his friend mercilessly raise his weapon above McAndrew's chest Tom couldn't believe what he was witnessing. "*He's going to kill him… he's actually going to do it.*"

"Dougie, enough!… For God's sake stop."

Panting heavily, Dougie's relaxed his arm and slowly lowered his weapon. Then glancing firstly at Tom and then down at the trembling McAndrew, he nodded. "Aye lad… yer right."

"Fraser, yer finished here and you've him tae thank for it. Next time we meet, you won't be so lucky, understand?"

Dropping his weapon, the snivelling and beaten McAndrew slowly raised his head, coughed up a mouthful of blood and nodded in humiliating defeat.

22

Wednesday 19th October - 11.55am CET - Vatican City, Italy

OPENING THE LARGE wooden door to the empty *Church of Sant'Anna dei Palafrenieri*, Father Antonio Demarco led Richard Quest into the Basilica's simple entrance hall. After carefully manoeuvring past the building's large, temporary scaffolding, the two men proceeded quietly inside the entranceway towards the main basilica.

"She's in here Doctor… would you like me to have a quiet word?"

Quest pursed his lips and nodded. "Would you?… Faith is not my thing I'm afraid."

Demarco smiled and nodded. "Ah, as a friend once told me, faith comes to all of us eventually my son. Of course, I'll speak with her. If you'll kindly wait here for a moment.,"

"Yes, of course."

While Quest took a seat by the door, Demarco turned and continued down the basilica's centre aisle then stopped adjacent to its sole occupant. Professor Helen Moore, who was kneeling in apparent prayer below the basilicas magnificent central dome. "Are you all right Professor?"

Glancing up at Demarco, Helen gave a weak smile. "Do you really think he hears our prayers, Father?"

Placing a hand on her shoulder Demarco smiled. "God moves in mysterious ways my child. It's in those quiet moments, when you're alone and at peace that you will truly know."

"I'm sorry Father, I didn't mean to wonder off. It's just that the past few days have been… difficult."

Demarco smiled. "So I've been hearing. May I sit with you for a moment."

"Of course."

As Helen shuffled across, Demarco genuflected and took a seat next to her on one of the plush red velvet pews. Gazing up at the basilicas central dome, Demarco sighed. "Did you know I was just ten years old when my father first brought me inside this church."

"Really?"

"Oh yes. We came into the church and sat down just over there."

Pointing with his index finger, Antonio indicated to a seat, two or three rows back from where they were sitting. "It was then I knew…"

"Knew what Father?"

"That I was destined to serve God, although I must confess that the path has been difficult at times."

"How come?"

Taking another breath, Antonio gazed up at the altar and to the dove of the Holy Spirit and nodded. "My father was… a difficult man. He was a Professor at the University, and from a very young age insisted that I followed in his footsteps. He thought that my calling to the church was a waste of time. To make matters worse, the year I joined the church, my mother died from a heart attack. He always blamed me for that. He said I broke her heart."

Helen turned towards the Priest and her expression softened. "How awful. I'm so sorry."

Antonio then gave her a reassuring smile. "Don't be. If it weren't for him, we would've never solved your little puzzle. Besides, the important thing was that even in his final moments God brought us together again and that's something I'll always be grateful for. Like I said, God moves in mysterious ways."

Helen's expression suddenly changed to one of sadness.

"What is it, what's wrong my child?"

"Everything Father, I'm so afraid. The world seems to be falling apart. Disaster after disaster and I just feel that there's not a damn thing I can do about it."

Softly clasping her hand Antonio nodded. "It's true, we do live in challenging times and I'm sure that there will be battles to face in the days to come, but I think that a little faith may just be the answer."

"Do you honestly think so Father?"

Rising to his feet Antonio gave a reassuring smile. "I do, now come my child. I also have a feeling that a nice cup of tea may be just what you need."

*

In the lobby of the *Hotel Alimandi Vaticano*, Agent

Mark Reynolds took a deep breath as his eyes flickered slowly open. He wasn't exactly sure what or why, but he had the distinct feeling that there was something out of place. Somewhere off in the distance he began to hear strange muffled sounds. Noises that could only be defined as a crying baby, combined with something or someone slurping water. As he drifted slowly back into consciousness, he raised himself up. As he did, the sounds became louder and noticeably closer. Only now, the baby sounded almost like an animal… a dog perhaps.

Yes, that was it. It was a dog and yet there was something else, drinking water perhaps.

Now fully awake, Reynolds could tell that the sounds were coming from what he assumed was a small office, just to the left of the reception area.

"Hello, is someone there?"

With no answer, he stood and walked cautiously across to the side door and knocked.

"Hello, are you okay in there?"

As he turned the brass handle, the whimpering sound suddenly changed pitch into a distinct growl and as Reynolds opened the door, he realised that whatever lay inside, was not going to be pleasant.

As the door swung open, Reynolds suddenly recoiled backwards in horror. Placing his hand over his mouth in disgust, his stomach churned at the room's grisly scene. Lying on the ground were the two blood soaked bodies of a porter in his forties and a receptionist in her twenties. From his vantage point, it looked as if the couple had been shot several times, including a single kill shot to each of their heads.

To make matters worse, Reynolds was even more horrified to discover that the source of the unusual slurping sound was the hotel owner's pet terrier, lapping up a pool of blood on the floor by the porter's head. It's face now blood soaked as it then began to franticly gnaw at one of the man's chest wounds.

"Jesus Christ… "

After kicking the growling, snapping animal away from the bodies, Reynolds reeled backwards out of the office, closed the door and ran across the lobby towards his luggage. Reaching for his jacket he pulled out his cell phone, glanced quickly around and took out the business card handed to him earlier by Agent Shaw. Realising that this could only be the work of one man, he punched in the number indicated on the front of the card and waited as the line began to ring.

"Good morning this is the British Embassy, how may I direct your call?"

"Security please"

"Certainly, one moment please."

After a brief pause the call was connected and answered by a woman.

"This is Security. Melissa Giles speaking."

"Miss Giles, this is Agent Mark Reynolds of the CIA, I'm at the *Hotel Alimandi Vaticano*. There's been an incident. Agent Shaw appears to be missing and two members of the hotel staff have been shot dead. I believe the primary suspect may be Gabriel Quinn who may be searching for Professor Moore. Can you send a backup team immediately?"

Ending the call, Reynolds placed the phone into his

front trouser pocket and opened a small black leather briefcase sitting by his foot. Once opened, he took out a black GLOCK G23 pistol and a spare magazine. After checking the weapon. He placed the spare ordnance into his free pocket and headed off vigilantly up the hotel's elegant staircase.

Arriving onto the first-floor landing, Reynolds silently and methodically edged forward, glancing up and down the length of the corridor for any signs of disturbance. Satisfied that all was clear, he moved onwards to the next staircase.

Anxious and increasingly concerned about Shaw's fate, he raised his weapon, flipped off the safety and edged cautiously upwards. Arriving on the second-floor landing, Reynolds immediately noticed an open door about half way down the hallway. But before he had the opportunity to investigate, the silence was shattered as a figure suddenly emerged out from the shadows and fired two shots, each missing him by a hair. Quickly returning fire, he then darted sideways out of the shooter's line of sight.

Poised, ready and waiting for the assailant to make his next move, the quiet was again broken. This time however, it was not a gunshot, but the unmistakeable crash of a window smashing. Suspecting an escape attempt, Reynolds quickly abandoned his position of safety and bolted down the corridor towards the only open door. Upon entering the empty room, he ran across to the broken window and gazed out.

Unfortunately, the smirking predator had already stepped out from behind the door's shadow, delighted that his ruse of a broken window had worked. Raising his knife in anticipation of a quick kill, Reynolds suddenly caught a glimpse of the blade and in an instant, gritted his teeth, fell backwards and in one swift move, looked up and head butted the attacker directly on the cheek with the back of his skull.

As Quinn tumbled backwards, disorientated and confused. Reynolds rushed forward, suddenly dropped to the ground, flipped over and fired off two more rounds. But as the bullets slammed without meeting their target into a plasterboard wall, Reynolds cursed himself as he stared at the empty spot where Quinn had been previously standing.

Moments later and back on his feet and amidst the faint sounds of approaching Police sirens. He checked his weapon and moved swiftly towards the doorway. However, before he could make it out into the corridor, another almighty crash assaulted his eardrums. This time, there could be no mistake. From the end of the hallway he heard the unmistakable sound of another window being shattered.

Wary of falling for Quinn's ruse a second time, Reynolds raised his weapon and leapt out into the corridor. With no apparent resistance, he ran towards the staircase. Unfortunately, by the time he arrived at the broken window, it appeared that Quinn had made his getaway by climbing out onto a fire escape and subsequently jumping down into the street below.

"Shit!"

As a line of Police cars arrived and screeched to halt outside the hotel, Reynolds gave a sigh of relief, tinged with a sense of disappointment. Firstly, at his failure to kill the assassin and secondly, that the blood-soaked body in the adjacent room, was unfortunately that of British Embassy Security Officer, David Shaw.

23

Monday 18th February 1710 - Alva, Scotland

AS THE LAST remaining gleams of sunlight slipped slowly beneath a wintery evening sky, darkness crawled its way across the Ochil hills like a huge flock of angry ravens taking flight. Standing in the open doorway of his cottage, Dougie Allan stared solemnly out into the approaching gloom and gave a heavy sigh.

"For goodness sake man, will ye come awa in. It's hard enough tae keep this place warm, never mind ye standin' oot there with the door wide open."

"Aye lass, I'm sorry."

As instructed, Dougie closed the door and turned inward. Then, walking across to the small fireplace, he picked up two logs and placed them carefully onto the open fire and took a seat opposite Tom.

As the flames began to lick the surface of the damp wood, both men stared, fixated, at the display of orange sparks as the logs began to slowly pop and hiss in the semi-darkness. Finally, Dougie exhaled and leaned forward. "Ye must ken I didn't hae a choice, Tom."

Sitting forward, Tom turned towards Dougie and grimaced. "I understand, it's just that... Well, I didn't think you would actually try to kill the man, that's all. It just took me by surprise."

Dougie nodded and pursed his lips, "I ken how it looked. But he would've killed ye and I had tae stop him. Surely ye must see that?"

Tom nodded, "Of course, but I never thought that..."

Suddenly the two men were interrupted by a concerned looking Mary Allan. "Tom, are ye sure ye dinnae want anything tae eat? Ye've hardly touched your food."

"Huh, um no thank you Mary. Perhaps in the morning."

"Aye. Well then..."

Picking up Tom's plate, Mary stepped across to Dougie and kissed her husband on the forehead. "Well then, if ye twa dinnae mind I'll leave ye tae talk. Tom, I'm sorry aboot the makeshift bed, I hope it's not been too uncomfortable."

Tom nodded gratefully, "No, it's fine, thank you."

"Well, goodnight then. I'll see ye in the morning."

As Mary disappeared behind the large woollen blanket dividing the room, Dougie turned to Tom with a look of concern and lowered his voice to whisper. "Ye ken there's just one thing I dinnae understand though."

"What's that?"

"Just whit the hell was it that drove McAndrew tae show such anger in the first place. Ranting on aboot ye talkin' tae a spirit, whit was all that aboot?"

At this point, Tom's head dropped and he began to whisper. "It's true..."

"Whit?"

"Well... that day when you returned from the cemetery... in the future, remember?"

"Aye, of course."

"Well, it was you that turned up at our doorstep, ranting on about seeing one of those creatures. But in your vision, the spirit resembled Mary, right?"

Dougie swallowed hard and nodded. "Aye, how could I forget that..."

"Well in my vision it was my daughter, Amy."

"Amy? What did she... I mean what did it say?"

In trying to remember, Tom fell silent for a moment before continuing. "Well, at first it appeared just to be Amy asking me to come home, but then... Then it changed. She began to rhyme or sing, I suppose. Almost as if she, or whoever, was trying to send a message."

Standing up, Dougie began to slowly pace up and down.

"What was the message, do ye ken?"

"Let me think. Yes, it went like this...

At Pilate's birthplace on ancient lands
A tree grows strong on ancient sands
In its roots lies an ominous key
That can control mankind for eternity
But should its secrets be uncovered
Then all our souls will be recovered"

As Tom finished, Dougie spun around to face him and clapped his hands, his eyes bulging in excitement. "Ominous key? That has tae be it lad. The key I mentioned." Dougie's voice suddenly tailed off as his excitement appeared to weaken and his expression became sombre.

"But, as for the rest of the poem, I have no idea where to start. I mean..."

Now it was Tom who become enthusiastic as he rose to his feet, quickly walked across to his friend and slapped him on the shoulder. "Well I do."

"Whit?

"Pontius Pilate, you know the Roman governor who gave up Jesus to the Jews for crucifixion."

Dougie shook his head blankly, uncertain as to what the connection was between Pilate and the key was. "I... I don't understand."

Tom smiled. "Dougie, you really need to learn more about history. It's a story, or myth I suppose. In the early years of the Roman incursion into Britain, Emperor Augustus sent a delegation to Glen Lyon to negotiate with a Caledonian chieftain called Metellanus. The myth is that a member of the delegation fathered a child with a local woman and it was this child that was subsequently returned to Rome, to be brought up as Pontius Pilate."

"Really? How come ye ken all this stuff Tom?"

Tom gave a sigh and laughed. "My wife I guess. You see Jane's a bit of an amateur historian. During our walks, she would often tell me stories about famous Scottish characters and historical battles. It was on one of these trips to Loch Tay that she..."

Suddenly Tom fell silent mid-sentence and his eyes widened. "Tom... whit is it lad?"

"Th... The poem. I think I know what it means."

"Whit?"

"I… I'm not sure, but I think you'll find what you're looking for in Fortingall."

At the mention of Fortingall, Dougie's face lit up in anticipation. "That's great news lad. We should leave as soon as possible…"

"We? Now wait a minute Dougie. I can't come with you. You promised you'd help me get back, I have a family to think about."

Placing a firm hand on Tom's shoulder, Dougie scowled. "Laddie, we have tae stop this Caius bastard from getting his hands on that key, for if he does, it would be disastrous. Now I promised I'd help ye get hame and I will, but for now I need your help. Can I count on ye Tom?"

Tom sighed and gave a reluctant nod. "Yes, of course I'll help."

Dougie grinned as he turned his gaze back to the dancing orange sparks and the glow of the open fire.

"Dinnae worry lad. We'll soon hae that key and then all your troubles will be over."

24

Wednesday 19th October - 12.40pm CET - Vatican City, Italy

AMIDST THE WAIL of approaching emergency vehicles, agent Mark Reynolds waved down a second unmarked black Mercedes as it screeched to a halt outside the *Hotel Alimandi Vaticano*. Once stopped, all four of its doors were suddenly flung open and three heavily armed security officers, followed by a smartly dressed woman, ran across to where a panting Reynolds stood waiting.

"Agent Reynolds?"

"Yes."

"Melisa Giles, British Embassy Security. We spoke earlier. What's the situation?"

Reynolds motioned towards the hotel and took a deep breath. "Three dead inside, two staff and Agent Shaw… I'm sorry, I couldn't do anything."

"And the intruder?"

"Gone, I'm afraid. I got off a couple of rounds, but unfortunately I missed."

"You're armed?"

"Of course, standard procedure."

Reynolds took a deep breath and continued. "Have you secured Professor Moore and Doctor Quest from the Vatican?"

"Not yet I wanted…"

"What?"

"Well I wanted to assess the situation first."

Reynolds shook his head in disbelief and began to run across the tarmac towards the empty Mercedes. "Oh, for Christ's sake, he'll try there next."

"Reynolds please wait. I can't have you running around Rome with a gun. Please, I…"

Before Giles should could finish, Reynolds was already climbing into the driver's seat.

"Reynolds, please… wait. Oh shit, alright but forget the car you'll be quicker on foot."

"What?"

Reynolds climbed out of the car as Giles pointed across the street.

"Look, that street is *Plaza Del Risorgimento*. It's mostly one way, it'll take too long by car. But if you cross over here and go down that street two blocks, you'll come to Porta Sant'Anna gate. Demarco's church, the *Church of Sant'Anna dei Palafrenieri,* is right there. It's a good bet that you'll find Quest and Moore there. Here, take this."

Reaching into her pocket she took out and handed a spare identity card to Reynolds and continued. "Show this to the Swiss Guard at the gate. We have a good relationship. Tell them what's happened and let them know that we're sending a car to collect Quest and Moore and Reynolds."

"What?"

"Guns make these people nervous, so don't be a cowboy, understand?"

Reynolds took a deep breath, checked that his pistol was adequately hidden from view and gave a nod. "Sure. I understand."

"Good. Well then, we'll be right behind you."

With that, Reynolds turned and bolted across the busy street and, as instructed, turned right and headed off down Via *Porta Angelica* towards *Porta Sant'Anna gate.*

*

After running through Rome's narrow side streets, Gabriel Quinn finally emerged onto an unusually quiet St Peter's Square. Although normally packed with tourists, the square was now filled with a mass of cranes, scaffolding and maintenance vehicles. Pausing for a moment, Quinn took a deep breath, headed off left, past the colonnade, towards the *Via Paolo VI* security entrance. Upon arrival he was met by two colourfully dressed Swiss guards.

"Buon pomeriggio Signore, ha un appuntamento?"

Deciding that diplomacy was probably his best course of action, Quinn smiled and nodded curtly. "I'm sorry, I don't speak Italian."

At his words, the youngster immediately switched into fluent English.

"*Nessun problema*, but I'm afraid this entrance is closed to the public, unless you have an appointment?"

"No, I'm simply looking to leave a message for someone, if that's possible?"

The guard smiled and gave a polite nod. "*Certamente*, who is it you're looking for?"

"A priest, Father Demarco."

"Just one moment, I'll check for you."

Turning to his colleague, the youngster nodded and the second guard began to enter Demarco's details into a small laptop computer inside the security booth. Seconds later he nodded as the result flashed up on screen. "Lui è qui, *Sant'Anna dei Palafrenieri.*"

As the first guard turned back to relay the message, Quinn smirked and immediately turned heel and began to walk away. "*Ma Signore*...your message."

Without looking back, Quinn simply cried out. "It's okay, I'll contact him myself, I'm sorry to trouble you."

Leaving the young Swiss guard somewhat perplexed, Quinn was satisfied that he had what he came for. As he strode away, he slipped quietly into the shadows of a narrow side street and, before the guard had an opportunity to call out again, he was gone.

*

Stepping out into the afternoon sunshine. Helen Moore took a deep breath and smiled at Father Demarco as he escorted her and Richard Quest through the narrow maze of cobbled streets in the Vatican towards their agreed pickup point with Shaw at the *Porta Sant'Anna gate.* Although their meeting had been brief, Helen enjoyed her time with the priest and had welcomed the opportunity to talk.

"Thank you so much for your time and effort Father. The British government really appreciates your assistance.

Demarco turned to Quest and smiled. "It's not a problem Doctor, in fact it's been a welcome break from my daily routine. I just pray we can get these symbols successfully translated for you. But as I said, Father Palovic is your man. If anyone can translate them, it's him."

As the group walked through the small security gate, the young Swiss guard stood to attention and gave a polite salute.

After nodding in acknowledgment, Demarco turned to Helen. "If I hear anything I'll be sure to pass it along."

"Thank you for all your advice and for the tea, of course."

"It was a pleasure."

Suddenly Demarco's words fell away as the Swiss guard unexpectedly shouted out, *"Padre, guarda…"*

As the group shook hands, Helen and Father Demarco suddenly turned towards the entrance of the *Church of Sant'Anna dei Palafrenieri* to see a flustered, but smartly dressed man in his thirties approaching.

"Padre, torna indietro."

Suddenly, the Swiss guard raised his spear, stepped forward with a look of concern and shouted out, *"Alt!"*

Raising his hands, the approaching figure did as he was instructed and stopped dead, just short of the entrance gate. Breathing heavily and sweating profusely, he glanced first at Demarco and then across at Quest and Moore.

"Doctor… Professor, I'm sorry."

Grabbing Helen's arm in attempt to protect her, Quest pulled her aside and stepped forward.

"What the hell is this, who are you?"

Catching his breath, the man nodded, "I'm Agent Mark Reynolds Doctor."

Stepping forward, Helen nodded, "I remember you, but where's Shaw? He was sup…"

Raising his hand and his voice, Reynolds interrupted, "I'm sorry to tell that Agent Shaw's dead, we have to get you…"

Suddenly Helen's face turned white and she began to shake uncontrollably. "No. He can't be."

Reaching into his pocket Reynolds pulled out the identity card provided by Giles and approached the Swiss guard. "I was told to hand this to you. These two are in danger I need your help."

Satisfied with the agent's explanation, the youngster nodded and turned toward a neighbouring security booth. "*Sì, sicuramente,* please wait a moment. I'll see what I can arrange."

As the guard stepped into the booth, Reynolds exhaled in relief as he heard the comforting sounds of approaching sirens. But for Helen, it was all too much and she began to sob uncontrollably. "Oh my God he's here, isn't he? I just knew he would come."

Taking Helen's hand, Quest turned to Reynolds and then to Demarco. "Father, perhaps there is a more secure area that we could wait in?"

Nodding in agreement, Demarco replied, *"Sì, certo."*

A moment later, the phone call was over and the guard re-emerged, but before Demarco had a chance to speak, he'd already stepped out of the booth and was in the process of ushering the group to a nearby building.

*

As Gabriel Quinn slid out from the shadows of a narrow side street into eyeshot of the Porta Sant'Anna gate, he gazed in disbelief at the group of people now standing only meters away. This was the moment he had been waiting for and to be offered not just one target but all three in the same location was almost unheard of in his line of business. Moving with the prowess and the skill of a predator, he quickly positioned himself into a nearby alleyway, pulled out his Beretta and took aim.

When the attack came, it was swift and brutal. A single shot rang out and struck the young guard directly in the forehead. As Helen shrieked in alarm, the youngster reeled backwards and his lifeless body crumpled onto the ground like a discarded rag doll.

Moving quickly, Reynolds pushed the priest out of the way and barked out to the others, "Get down…"

As another shot ricocheted off a nearby wall, Quest pulled a hysterical Helen Moore closer to him and yelled out, "Reynolds what do we do?"

*

With the guard lying dead on the ground, the assassin emerged from the shadows with a cold, steely look of determination on his face. As his targets clambered behind the church wall for safety, Quinn suddenly caught a glimpse of the familiar. The bitch from the airport, Helen Moore. As flashbacks of the airport came rushing back, he decided that she should be the first to die. Not simply because she'd been the first on his list, but because in his opinion, she had humiliated him and he didn't like that.

*

With the sound of wailing sirens approaching, Reynolds took out his GLOCK pistol, flicked off the safety and signalled to the group to stay down. As he leaned carefully out to take a shot, he suddenly recoiled backwards in surprise as a bullet struck a wall only meters from his head.

"Jesus..."

*

Laughing out loud at the pathetic efforts of the agent to put him down, Quinn continued to fire in the direction of the group, determined to ensure that they remained trapped and unable to escape.

"Come on, is that the best you can do?"

*

Sweating and becoming increasingly concerned for the safety of the three civilians, Reynolds was about to pick up and throw a rock to divert Quinn's attention. But before he could, two Swiss guards came running out from a nearby building. But unlike the youngster at the gate, these two were armed with deadly Steyr Machine Pistols. Unfortunately, before Reynolds had an opportunity to shout a warning, the predator had already moved to intercept them.

*

Scowling like a cat, Quinn sneered to himself.

"Now this is more like it,"

"Stop, put your weapon down."

"Huh..."

Suddenly and with a look of surprise, Quinn turned

to his left as a black Mercedes pulled up and three of its occupants spilled out onto the street and raised their weapons.

"No."

Glancing at the two approaching Swiss guards, Quinn surmised that his window of opportunity to carry out his mission was rapidly closing, so taking a split-second decision, he moved with incredible speed, raised his weapon and shot out wildly at both approaching men. As one fell dead, the other screamed out in agony as a bullet shattered his leg.

*

As the second guard collapsed, the machine pistol that he had been holding fell from his hands and bounced onto the concrete pavement adjacent to where Demarco and the two scientists were huddled. Meanwhile, Reynolds suddenly sprang in action. Rolling onto the ground he raised his pistol and fired two shots towards their attacker. Unfortunately, as before, he gritted his teeth in frustration as Quinn had already vanished. Meanwhile outside the the church, Mellissa Giles was accompanied by two heavily armed agents that had emerged from the Mercedes and were currently taking up a defensive position behind the car.

*

Huddled in a nearby restaurant doorway, Quinn glanced cautiously out towards the church and then across at the parked Mercedes. Suddenly, he spotted one of the armed officers attempting to shift position. Although only for a split second, it was all the time Quinn needed. Crouching low, he suddenly leapt out from behind the wall and fired two shots in quick succession. Reeling himself back into the safety of the doorway, he cackled inwardly as his adrenaline levels began to rise and as a volley of machine gun bullets suddenly whizzed past his ear and struck a nearby door, he felt confident that at least one of his bullets had struck a target.

"Alright, come on. This is more like it."

*

For a second, Giles simply gazed at the spatters of blood on her clothing and at the body of her dead colleague in disbelief. Although she had trained for field work four years ago, her job today was generally consulate support. She was an administrator and certainty not ready for this.

"Giles, are you okay? We need to call in support."

Swallowing hard, she gave a nod and the remaining officer pushed his radio call button.

"This is Carter, we're a man down here. We need backup now."

After a short pause, the radio crackled a response. "Roger Carter, ETA one minute."

Gazing into the worried face of her partner, Giles knew that she had to make a call one way or another. She needed a diversion, something to give them her an opportunity to either move the civilians to safety or pursue Quinn.

*

Across the street outside the *Church of Sant'Anna dei Palafrenieri,* Demarco, Quest and a distraught Helen Moore cowered behind the stone walls of the Basilica.

"Mr Reynolds, we have to get these people to safety."

Turning his head towards Quest, Reynolds nodded in annoyance. “Yes Doctor. I’m doing my best.”

Returning his attention towards the parked car across the street, Reynolds suddenly had an idea and yelled out. “Giles… Giles are you okay?”

After a brief silence the woman shouted out. “Yes, I’m okay. But we’re pinned down here.”

“Hang on.”

On the far side of St Peter’s Square, Reynolds caught a welcomed glimpse of three approaching police vehicles and sighed. “Giles, it’s okay. The cavalry’s here.”

Suddenly Reynolds whirled back in alarm as another fierce volley of shots rang out and to his horror he realised that the suspect was now on the move.

*

With the screech of Police vehicles coming to a halt and shots coming at him from the Mercedes, Quinn was conscious that for him, time had run out. Now on his feet, gun in hand and with gritted teeth, he suddenly bolted across the street at full speed, only to come to a halt a few meters away from a horrified looking Quest, Moore and Father Demarco.

With his adrenaline spiking, Quinn viciously leapt at Reynolds like an animal. As the American readied his weapon to fire, Quinn suddenly ducked and lashed out wildly, hitting him and causing the agent’s gun to fly out of his hand.

In what appeared to be Quinn’s final assault, Quest and Demarco watched in horror as he abruptly raised his Beretta towards Reynolds’ head and laughed menacingly.

"Now I have them and it appears that I've you to thank for it."

Taking a deep breath, Reynolds closed his eyes in the grim anticipation that this moment would probably be his last. But if he was to die here, he was determined that the last image in his mind would not be that of a cold grinning hitman. It would be something more meaningful, like a childhood memory.

"Get away from him, you bastard."

"What?"

Suddenly Quinn turned and Reynolds opened his eyes in astonishment, as standing behind him was not the cringing, frightened professor that he had been expecting, but a stone faced Helen Moore, armed with one of the Swiss guard's deadly machine pistols.

"What the hell are you doing Helen?"

"Shut up Richard. Just get to the car, all of you."

Grinning like a Cheshire cat, Quinn eyed the woman in a combination of frustration and admiration. The latter for being one of the only targets to have eluded him twice.

As Reynolds stepped forward to pick up his gun, Quinn smirked. "You see, I knew it. You're my kind of woman… Ballsy, I like that."

As Demarco and Quest stood and ran across the street to the waiting Mercedes, Helen stepped forward and gritted her teeth.

"You're an animal."

As Reynolds stepped forward to pick up his weapon, Quinn suddenly lashed out with his fist and struck Helen on the cheek. As she fell, four heavily armed Swiss Guards unexpectedly appeared from a nearby building and

Quinn knew that it was time to leave. Gazing down at a whimpering Helen Moore, he laughed.

"Stupid bitch. Couldn't you see that the safety was on."

As three shots suddenly ricocheted off a nearby wall, Quinn quickly turned heel and bolted away into a nearby side street.

"This isn't over. We'll see each other again…"

25

Wednesday 19th October - 2.55pm EST - The White House, Washington DC

SITTING ALONE BEHIND the elegance of the Resolute desk in the Oval office, President George Hillary stared intently at a wall mounted television on the far side of the room. Although somewhat uncommon for a President to watch television in the afternoon, he liked to keep his "*finger on the pulse of the ordinary man.*" As such, and only if time permitted, he would insist on being left undisturbed for at least thirty minutes after lunch with a cup of Earl Grey tea so he could watch the lunchtime news. His wife Caroline, called this his "*assimilation time.*"

Today it was the turn of CNN and a report on the growing popularity of an influential religious organisation called "UNITY." Taking another sip of tea, the President watched and listened with interest.

"What began two years ago, with a mere handful of followers, has today become a worldwide phenomenon which now boasts over a billion members in over 100 countries worldwide. With followers ranging from students, to

policemen, to scientists and politicians, the simple question is: just what's the attraction of this church and, more importantly, what is the secret of its success?

I'm Karen McDonald and today I'm joined in the studio with two special guests. Brother Thomas Weyn from the UNITY church's New York diocese and one of its newest members, a second-year business student from Yale University, Jennifer Adams.

Jennifer if I may begin with you. What was it that influenced your decision to join the church?"

Taking a deep breath, the blonde teen smiled and leaned forward.

"Oh, that was an easy decision. It seemed ridiculous to me that we have so many religious organisations which often appeared so fragmented. Catholics, Jews, Muslims, Buddhists and so on. I just got to thinking there must be a better way. After the quakes left so many dead I found the idea of a single faith, a single church, to be a breath of fresh air."

"In what way?"

"If you look back throughout history, religion has often played a major factor in so many world conflicts. What ironically promotes itself as peaceful, often ends up being twisted into another excuse for conquest."

"I understand. Brother Weyn, but how do you respond to the critics who accuse your faith of being just another cult that's riding on the back of disaster?"

Dressed in a sober navy blue suit, the blue-eyed, middle-aged Brother Thomas smiled warmly at the interviewer as he sat forward to respond.

"It's simple, our faith is the reason for our success. It's alive, and I do mean that quite literally. The other religions Jennifer

mentioned centre on the doctrine of the past. Our faith, on the other hand, focuses on the present and on the future. Our leader is our faith and we worship him without question, fully in the knowledge that one day he'll deliver us into a better world."

"I'm still puzzled though. How can you blindly follow this man? This leader who has never been seen in the flesh?"

"I'm sorry…"

"This Michael, isn't it? Don't you think it's strange that he's never been seen? Indeed, many observers are now beginning to question whether he actually exists at all."

For a moment, Brother Thomas remained silent. He smiled again, this time with a sense of increased confidence.

"I completely understand your scepticism Miss McDonald, but can assure you that he's already planning to address the United Nations conference of world leaders, scientists and religious organisations next week. Then you, and the rest of the world, will witness his glory and power."

The President's attention was suddenly diverted away from the interview as a knock sounded on the office door.

"Come in."

As the door swung open, a middle-aged woman entered along with the older but, familiar, CIA Deputy Director, David Tyler.

"Mr President… Mr Tyler for you Sir."

"Dave come in. Nice to see you."

As his assistant departed, the door was closed, and the two men were left alone. The President smiled and shook hands warmly with Director Tyler, before gesturing for him to take a seat. Once both seated, the President took a deep breath and restored his attention to the television on the wall. "Can you believe this?"

"Mr. President?"

"This UNITY church. How on earth have they become so powerful?"

Tyler frowned. "Well, they've been on the go for a couple of years now, ever since…"

Appearing somewhat edgy, the President nodded impatiently. "Yes, I know that, but I had no idea that they had become so big."

Tyler paused for a moment and then took a breath. "Mr. President, I'm assured by my team that all the usual background checks have been done. The organisation appears to be as you see… benign. I could dig a little deeper if you are concerned?"

Without responding Hillary returned to the Resolute desk, reached across and picked up two glasses and a decanter of whisky.

"Drink?"

Tyler nodded enthusiastically. "Please."

After pouring two glasses, the President handed one to Tyler who immediately took a sip and placed the glass down onto the desk. Taking his own glass with him, Hillary began to walk around the Oval office, and after pausing for a sip of the amber liquid, he finally came to a halt opposite a large portrait of Abraham Lincoln, painted by the artist George Henry Story. After gazing at the painting's backdrop of foreboding storm clouds, he then turned his attention to the image of Lincoln itself and exhaled. "I wonder what he would've done?"

"Mr President?"

"Lincoln. I wonder how he would have handled all of this."

Tyler smiled. "Mr President, I'm sure he would have handled it with the same level of confidence and grace as yourself Sir."

Turning his head towards Tyler, the President laughed loudly.

"Way to go Dave, that's how to suck up to your President."

Awkwardly fidgeting with his hands, the elderly man blushed. "I… I didn't mean to."

"It's okay. The situation could use a little humour anyway."

"Yes Sir."

Returning to his desk, the President retook his seat and placed his glass down. "You know, perhaps that's not a bad idea. I want to know more about this Michael character. It's a little unusual that he's never been seen, don't you think?"

Tyler nodded in agreement. "I do Sir, yes. I'll ask around and report back to you once I know more."

The President sat forward, leaned in closer to Tyler and lowered his voice. "Any news from our friends in Italy?"

Drawing breath, Tyler nodded. "Yes, they're safe Mr. President. Agent Reynolds, Quest and Professor Moore have been safely delivered to our embassy in Rome."

"What about the perpetrator, has he been apprehended?"

Tyler shook his head. "No Sir… the Brits are working with the Swiss Guard to locate him. But so far he appears to have slipped away."

Leaning back in his seat, the President picked up his glass, took another sip of whisky and returned the glass to the polished desk.

“Do you think Quest and Moore will agree to help us?”

“I hope so Sir. I believe that Agent Reynolds was planning to discuss it with them. So, I guess we’ll know soon enough.”

Taking a slow deep breath, the President clasped his hands and nodded. “So, do I Mr Tyler, so do I.”

26

Tuesday 19th February 1710 - Alva, Scotland

AS THE REMNANTS of the previous evening's full moon slipped slowly beneath an early morning sky, a watery sun, struggled to emerge over the Ochil Hills. Lying low, its rays battled for survival amidst a blanket of overnight snow and persistent fog. Dressed in a warm woollen red dress and matching shawl, Mary Allan shivered in the doorway of the Allan's simple cottage. Her eyes wide, with a combination of anger and disbelief at her husband's foolhardy decision to travel northwards with Tom to Fortingall in Perthshire.

Despite the poor weather conditions, Dougie continued to irrationally load provisions onto two horses, whilst Tom stood shivering nearby in one of Dougie's woollen coats. His face red and somewhat bemused at the prospect of riding out into a snow storm.

"Are ye no blind husband? Do ye nae see the storm? Ye must be daft going oot in this. Please come awa back inside and reconsider. At least wait until it clears."

Dressed in a heavy black woollen coat, Dougie walked

across to his horse, lifted a flap on the saddle and thrust a large broadsword inside its leather scabbard. Then, turning to Mary, he grimaced and shook his head. "I canne do that lass. I'm sorry but you'll just hae tae trust. me. I ken whit I'm doing."

"But you'll bloody freeze tae death oot there and then where will I be?"

With her eye's filling with tears, Mary suddenly turned heel and bolted back inside the cottage. For a moment, Dougie said nothing. Then glancing across at Tom he shrugged his shoulders and sighed. "Women. Come awa lad, get ready tae leave. This'll tak but a moment."

As Dougie plodded away towards the open doorway, Tom watched with interest as his friend trudged through the soft snow, listening as his feet made soft crumping sounds with every step he took.

Once inside, Dougie kicked the snow off his boots by the door and strode across to where his distraught looking wife was sitting with her head in her hands. Placing a comforting hand on her shoulder, Dougie lowered himself onto one knee and spoke softly. "Now come awa lass. Dinnae get yoursel all worked up o'er nothing. We'll be back in a week, I promise."

Gently lifting her chin with his large hand, Dougie then softly wiped a tear away from her cheek. "Have I ever let you down?"

Mary shook her head. "No… I suppose not."

Dougie gave her a reassuring smile. "Then, give me some credit. Let me do this. I promise I'll be back, okay?"

Wiping her tears away, Mary grasped his hand and gave a reluctant nod. "Aye… very well. But be careful."

"I will."

After kissing Mary one final time, the Scotsman rose to his feet and headed for the door. Once outside his warm smile quickly evaporated. He clumped back through the snow with a Resolute expression towards Tom and the awaiting horses.

"Right lad… are you ready?"

Tom nodded reluctantly. "I guess so, but I should tell you that I've never actually ridden a horse before."

Dougie sniggered as he lumbered across to where Tom was standing.

Constructing his hands into a makeshift stirrup, he hoisted Tom upwards into position. Once safely in the saddle, Tom attempted to make himself as comfortable as he could. Despite the circumstances, he trusted Dougie and valued his friendship. More importantly, if Dougie could indeed deliver on his promise to get him home, then this short-lived nightmare would perhaps be a small price to pay.

Confident that Tom was secure and would not fall, Dougie attached one end of a rope to his horse's collar. Then with the other end, he clomped back through the snow and climbed up onto his own horse before glancing back at Tom with a broad grin. "Dinnae worry lad, by the time we reach Fortingall, I'm guessing that ye'll be quite the expert."

As Dougie kicked his own animal into motion, the rope's slack was taken up and Tom's horse began to plod slowly forward through the bleakness. With the horses in motion, Tom instinctively glanced back towards the cottage. Spotting Mary's sombre face at the door suddenly brought home the seriousness of his situation, along with the thoughts of the unknown future that they faced, a future in which he may never see his own family again.

*

Thursday 20th October - 09.30pm CET - US Embassy, Villa Domiziana, Vatican City

Sitting alone in a quiet, unobtrusive coffee shop in a fashionable area off Leonida Bissolati street, Gabriel Quinn drained the last drops of his third espresso and gazed out, frustrated, towards Rome's US Embassy. Having followed professor Helen Moore and her companions to the British Embassy, Quinn was intrigued to discover why it was that the pair were so suddenly and subtly moved to the American Embassy in the middle of the night.

Placing his cup down, Quinn found himself facing his own personal dilemma. Whilst they were inside such a fortified building, there was little or no chance of him completing his mission. So, he began to ask, should he wait, or should he go?

If he stayed, there would be no guarantee of success. They could be flown out by helicopter or escorted out under heavily armed guard. Either way, he felt he'd wasted enough time and had to start looking at alternatives.

Reaching into his pocket, he pulled out his cell phone, punched in a few numbers and waited for the call to be answered. After a few moments, the call was picked up by a man with a familiar, but gruff, Italian accent.

"*Si.*"

"There's a problem."

"Another one, Gabriel?"

"I've tracked Moore and Quest to the US Embassy but unfortunately they're under heavy guard. I anticipate that it will be difficult to complete my task."

"This is disappointing. Things are not going as smoothly as you led us to believe. He's going to be disappointed."

"I understand and… I'm sorry. Do you want me to make another attempt?"

For a second, the line simply crackled and the voice on the other end remained silent.

"No. You'll get another chance at the proper time. Besides, I may have another task for you."

As the call ended Gabriel returned the phone to his pocket and, after climbing to his feet, settled the bill with a nearby waiter and left the coffee shop without leaving a tip. Once outside, he slipped discretely away down a narrow side street and, within moments, was gone.

27

EVEN AS A child, Helen sensed that she would eventually take up a career in the sciences. But, if asked at the age seven which subject she favoured, she would simply respond, "*All of them.*"

However, by the time she reached her teens, the choice was clear. On her 14th Christmas her father, William who was a part time tutor in Cambridge, managed to obtain two tickets for himself and Helen to attend a Christmas cosmology lecture presented by Professor Stephen Hawking. It was right there, in that lecture theatre, that she sat beside her father, mesmerised as the wheelchair bound prodigy delivered a truly spellbinding lecture on the relationship between quantum physics and the possibilities of time travel.

So, years later when her colleague, Richard Quest, informed her that the authorities in Scotland had uncovered an extraordinary underground labyrinth in the small Scottish village of Alva, the memories of Hawking's lecture came flooding back. Although, if asked at the time if she believed the outlandish story, she would've probably responded with a high degree of cynicism. However once introduced to Dougie Allan, any doubts she had quickly faded, as the man's story was told. Unfortunately, in the aftermath, excitement was traded for fear as the world endured a seemingly endless series of catastrophic natural disasters. That was until the unexplained disappearance of the Scotsman, along with the former US President Richard Bryant.

Indeed, when she and Quest put forward a proposal for an investigation, her request was unexpectedly refused and a veil of silence appeared to fall over the whole affair.

But that was then, today as she gazed out across Rome's distinctive skyline, she nodded inwardly to herself. Now more convinced than ever that something was going on, it couldn't simply be a coincidence that the very day she was attacked in Copenhagen; Father Demarco discovered another set of cryptic symbols. Not to mention the discovery of Tom Duncan's watch in Alva. No... Something was going on and she was determined to find out what.

Inside the US embassy, Helen sat quietly opposite her colleague, Richard Quest, on an ageing, but comfortable, brown leather sofa. Staring out of the room's single window with a sense of unease she groaned as she turned to face her colleague. "Why are we here, Richard?"

"What?"

Turning her head back towards her partner, Helen sat forward and repeated the question. "I said why are we here? Why the secrecy?"

Quest ran his fingers through his hair and frowned. "I don't know Helen, but I'm sure it must be for a good reason."

Suddenly the conversation was cut short, as a door swung open and Agent Reynolds entered carrying a navy-blue folder. Dressed in grey trousers, white shirt and a black sweater, Reynolds proceeded to walk across to where the pair were sitting and sat down next to Quest.

"I'm sorry to have kept you waiting."

"Why are we here Mr Reynolds? I mean, why move us from our embassy in the middle of the night? What's the mystery?"

Reynolds smiled.

"There's no mystery Professor, I can assure you. It's all legitimate and was undertaken with the full approval of your government."

For a moment, Reynolds paused and took a breath. "But if you need a reason, I can give you two: firstly, it was done primarily for your safety. It's no secret that your embassy has limited security personnel. It was felt that it would be best to air on the side of caution."

"And the second?"

Placing the folder down onto a small glass table, Reynolds took a deep breath and turned to Moore. "Secondly Professor, it's because we need your help."

Helen's eyes widened. "Our help?"

"It appears that it's no coincidence that we've been brought together."

"Oh really?"

For a moment, Reynolds dropped his gaze and he sighed awkwardly. "Professor. I was there in Reykjavik two years ago, I… I followed them out to Midlina and I saw them for what they really are."

Before Helen could continue, Quest sat forward and interrupted. "What exactly do you mean Mr Reynolds?"

Pushing the folder across to Quest, Reynolds sat back. "Here, look."

Leaning over, Quest picked up and opened the binder. Inside there were numerous documents, newspaper clippings and photos. One of which immediately caught the doctor's attention. A familiar drawing of a sinister, cloaked figure. As Quest pondered the picture, he remembered the first time he and Helen had seen it. It was drawn by a young police officer back in Alva under the direction of the mysterious Scotsman, Dougie Allan.

"You see, I've seen them."

Suddenly Quest's face turned serious. "I don't understand how that's possible."

Reynolds sighed and shrugged his shoulders. "It's difficult to explain, but it's the truth."

As the agent spoke, Helen got to her feet and walked across to the window, took an uneasy glance outside and returned her gaze towards the two men with a look of scepticism. "If you'll forgive me Mr Reynolds it all seems a bit of a coincidence, don't you think? I mean, you turn up the very day after I'm almost killed in Copenhagen and then we're caught in a firefight in St Peter's Square."

Reynolds contemplated Helen's statement and nodded in agreement. "I suppose when you put it like that, it does seem odd. If this was any other day I'd be happy to discuss it, but it's not and frankly our Government needs your help. So please, look at the headline on the next page."

As instructed, Quest flipped the page over to reveal a newspaper clipping. After reading the headline, he shrugged his shoulders and passed it across to Helen, who retook her seat opposite and began to read.

The Halifax Herald

HALIFAX BOUND FISHING VESSEL SINKS WITH THE LOSS OF ALL HANDS.

Halifax, Nova Scotia: Sunday 16th October: The fishing community of Halifax was in shock this morning as it mourned the loss of "The Sea Mist." A 65' steel hull twin screw fishing vessel, which disappeared in stormy seas, east of Sable Island on Saturday evening. Despite an extensive search by the Canadian Coastguard, no trace of the vessel, or its eight-man crew, could be found. Continued on Page 4…

Glancing blankly at Quest, she then handed the sheet back to Reynolds. "I don't see how we can help. Fishing boats get lost all the time."

The agent smiled, recalling his own similar reaction only days before. "True, but look at the coastguard report on the preceding page."

As instructed, Quest turned the page and began to read.

The Joint Rescue Coordination Centre (JRCC) Halifax, Nova Scotia:

Sunday 16th October: Log entry pertaining to Loss of Fishing Vessel "The Sea Mist" near or around Sable Island on Saturday 15th October. Time: 11.04pm: MESSAGE BEGINS:

"Mayday, mayday. This is the Sea Mist. We are 65 miles east of Sable Island and are taking on water…

As well as the storm, we have encountered unexplained lights from below. Possibly a submerged vessel. We require immediate assistance… Again, this is the Sea Mist…" MESSAGE ENDS.

"Jesus…"

As Helen's eyes widened, she passed the sheet to Richard, who after a moment returned his gaze to Reynolds.

"Now you understand. Both our governments believe that these events are related to the disasters two years ago, but to prove that, we need your help. Would you be interested?"

For a moment, the two scientists glanced across at each other before Helen nodded first and then Quest looked up at Reynolds and smiled. "What can I say, we'll never say no to a good mystery Mr Reynolds."

Smiling with a sense of relief, Reynolds clapped his hands. "That's excellent news Doctor."

As the agent rose to his feet, his expression changed to one of concern. "What is it? Is there something wrong?"

Reynolds shook his head, almost with a sense of mild embarrassment. "No Professor, there was just one thing that I forgot to ask you."

"Oh, what's that?"

Reynolds smiled. "I was wondering… how do you feel about, submarines?"

28

Thursday 21st February 1710 - Kenmore, Highland Perthshire, Scotland

AS A BANK of low cloud settled low over the dark waters of the River Tay, two figures on horseback emerged over the brow of a grassy hill and began to slowly wind their way down towards an eerie looking pebbled shoreline. With the last remnants of the day's light slipping away, Tom was delighted that Dougie had made the decision not to attempt the final leg of the journey to Fortingall in darkness, but to rest and continue the following morning.

Fortune had also seen a change in the weather. Light rain and warmer temperatures had replaced the harsh snow and strong winds of Alva. Thus, it meant that they wouldn't have to seek refuge in the nearby Balloch castle; they could settle down by the beach, free of awkward questions and unwanted attention. For Tom, looking at the familiar shoreline of Loch Tay brought back fond memories of past holidays to the region. Especially because in years to come, this would be the location where he would ask Jane for her hand in marriage.

As the horses came to a halt, Tom closed his eyes, drew breath and imagined that when he re- opened them, everything would be back to normal. The reality however was not to be. When he had last stepped onto this pebbled beach, he visited the restored remains of an iron age crannog, or water house on stilts. Today though, all he could see was a veil of heavy mist sitting atop the waterline, creating an atmospheric, but unwelcoming effect.

"Are ye alright lad?"

Climbing down, Dougie strode over to Tom's horse, briskly rubbed his hands and took hold of the rope which connected the two animals together.

"Yes, but my backside is killing me."

Giving a hollow laugh, Dougie motioned Tom to climb down from his horse.

"Aye, well a sore arse is all part of the experience."

"Landing on his feet, Tom responded with a wry smile. "So now what?"

Walking back to his own horse, Dougie unpacked two large blankets, a bundle of food and pointed to a clump of nearby trees.

"Now we need tae get a fire started. It's too late to carry on tonight. So, we'll rest here and move on at first light. You go ahead and collect some firewood."

As Dougie tied up the horses, Tom nodded and, as instructed, stomped across towards a clump of nearby trees and began to collect timber.

Forty minutes later, Dougie and Tom had finished

eating and were now sitting around the campfire listening to the hypnotic sounds of the water as it gently lapped against the nearby shoreline. Tom looked outwards with a sense of mounting apprehension as Dougie stared into the firelight, seemingly mesmerised by small orange sparks as they crackled and popped out into the night sky like miniature fireworks.

After such an unorthodox departure from Alva, Tom was now convinced more than ever that something was out of place with Dougie, but what it was, he wasn't entirely sure.

During the journey, Dougie had been unusually quiet, which was uncommon as he was normally so jovial. In addition, Tom pondered what on earth could have transformed such a seemingly kind and warm person into such an impatient and obsessive individual. A man, who seemed prepared to go to great lengths to find a mysterious and elusive key. Even if it meant potentially damaging his own marriage.

Watching Dougie in the semi-darkness, Tom wanted answers. No, it was more than that, he needed answers. He was desperate to ask questions. Like what had happened to Kate in Iceland and why Dougie seemed so reluctant to talk.

Tom rubbed his eyes and recalled how an unfortunate accident had originally thrust the pair into an unlikely adventure which led to the discovery of a black marble pyramid in an abandoned Alva silver mine. But that was only the beginning. After the authorities had become involved, the pair were forced into an unlikely partnership with a nosey London newspaper editor, Kate

Harding. To the annoyance of Tom and his family, the Police insisted that the three of them be placed together in protective custody. Unfortunately for Tom, Kate had unwittingly drawn her newspaper to the attention of a crazed gunman. This regrettably placed his own family in grave danger.

After the decision was taken to protect Dougie and Kate, the pair were whisked away by the authorities to a remote lighthouse on the west coast of Scotland and, for Tom, that was supposed to be the last of his involvement. That was, of course, until he was approached by the military who asked for his assistance in one last excursion into the mysterious silver mine. Once inside, he'd regrettably become separated from the group. When he finally emerged, he found himself 300 years in the past.

"Dougie… Can I ask you something?"

"Aye, of course ye can lad. What is it?"

"You've been very quiet recently, is everything okay?"

For a moment, Dougie didn't respond. Then, a moment later, he shrugged his shoulders and gave a nod. "Aye I'm fine lad, dinnae worry aboot me."

"But I am worried Dougie. What happened to you in Iceland, really? I mean, I know you told me but I sense you're holding back."

Rolling his eyes in annoyance, Dougie's expression suddenly turned to one of anger. "Look laddie, are you accusing me of being a liar?"

Tom shook his head.

"No. Of course not. It's just that."

"Well leave it alone then. I've already told you everything."

Leaning across to his left, Dougie reached down and grabbed a bundle of blankets. After separating them, he tossed one at Tom before stomping away towards a mound of grass.

"You should get some sleep. Tomorrow will be a busy day…"

29

Friday 21st October - 3.40pm GMT – London, UK

STEPPING OUT INTO the afternoon sunshine from the back seat of a black Government Range Rover, British Prime Minister James Walton, took a deep breath and nodded curtly to his security officer before walking across to nearby podium adjacent to the familiar black glossed front door of number 10 Downing Street.

For the past two years, the seat of British power had been temporarily located in Edinburgh, home to the Scottish Government. To some, it almost seemed satirical that the once mighty English Parliament had been forced to flee London with its tail between its legs. But after a devastating tsunami left hundreds of thousands dead, any perceived humiliation became inconsequential.

However, that was two years ago. Today Walton stared out at a large group of unusually quiet reporters, he felt an enormous sense of pride at how the British people had placed their petty differences aside and laboured to restore the once great city of London.

"Welcome home Prime Minister."

Before Walton could respond another reporter shouted out, "How does it feel to be back in Downing Street Prime Minister?"

With a broad smile, Walton raised his hand and addressed the throng. "It feels good thank you. Two years ago, this city and this country endured a cruel and devastating event that not only killed billions of people around the globe, but also laid waste too much of our beautiful country. Even now, many parts of our once great city lie in ruins. But we did not turn our backs on it. We regrouped and joined forces to restore London and this nation to greatness once more.

I would personally like to thank Scotland's First Minister and the wonderful Scottish people for taking us in during what were terrible and difficult times."

"Now it's with God's grace that I stand here this morning. For me, walking through that door doesn't just symbolize a return to work. It embellishes everything that this country stands for. For that, I thank you from the bottom of my heart."

Stepping back from the microphone, Walton turned heel and walked towards the entrance towards the smiling face of the Home Secretary, Anne Petrie. Shaking hands, the pair waved, continued through the iconic front door and made their way inside as the press clapped and cheered.

*

Friday 21st October - 4.50pm CET - Vatican City, Italy

Feeling shaken by the violent events of the previous day, Father Antonio Demarco had retreated inside to *the safety* of the Church of *Sant'Anna dei Palafrenieri* to find solace. As the basilica was currently closed to the public, Antonio felt the seclusion and silence would be perfect for his needs. After climbing up the church's iconic stone steps, Antonio made his way through the building's temporarily covered doorway and continued inside the basilica, eventually stopping next to its large marble altar. After genuflecting, he took a seat on one of the red velvet pews and gazed upwards towards the magnificent central dome, before taking a deep breath and closing his eyes in preparation to pray.

"*Antonio…*"

The voice that spoke, came from the back of the basilica. As Antonio opened his eyes, he turned to see the familiar shape of Cardinal Jean Louis Bouchard standing at the rear of the church. Tutting to himself in mild annoyance at being disturbed, Antonio respectfully stood and faced his mentor, who was, by now, making his way briskly down the centre aisle with an anxious look

"*Ho appena saputo cos'è successo…* Is everything alright my friend? Are you injured?"

Raising his hand to allay his friend's fears, Antonio shook his head.

"*No Sua Eminenza*, don't worry I'm fine. Just a little shaken, that's all."

After patting his friend on the shoulder, both men sat down opposite each other.

"I'm not surprised after what happened. Did the Police catch the perpetrator?"

Antonio again shook his head. "No Eminenza. According to the Swiss Guard, it appears that he has made good his escape."

"*Lo vedo* and your British friends? I hope they're safe?"

Nodding with relief, Antonio smiled. "*Sì, sono al sicuro, grazie*. But for their own safety, they've been airlifted out of Rome. I'm not sure where to. I'm not purvey to that kind of information I'm afraid."

Bouchard smiled. "*Certamente…* the important thing is that they are safe."

"*Sì Eminenza.*"

"*E per quanto riguarda te amico mio*, I've spoken with the other Cardinals and we want to assure you that Vatican security has been tightened. You are safe here."

Antonio nodded in appreciation.

"*Grazie Eminenza.*"

"È il minimo che possiamo fare. Now unfortunately, if you don't mind. I have a service to prepare for. I just wanted to check in on you and see how you were doing. I'll call by tomorrow."

As Bouchard got to his feet, Antonio suddenly interrupted the cardinal before he could leave. "*Eminenza*, is it true?"

For a moment, Bouchard paused and looked puzzled. "È la verità – che cosa Antonio?"

Dropping his gaze for a moment, Demarco glanced nervously around the Basilica before continuing. "I've heard rumors that many of our colleagues are abandoning the church to join this new UNITY cult. Surely that can't be true."

Bouchard's reassuring smile fell away and his voice sank to a whisper. "*Sì... sembrerebbe che è vero*. An internal investigation has been ordered, but don't worry about that right now. Let's get you well first. Besides, you've your own puzzles to solve. If I hear anything at all, I promise I'll keep you informed, alright?"

Antonio nodded and gave a weak smile. "*Sì, c?rto.*"

Rising to his feet, Bouchard patted his friend on the back and walked softly away.

Now alone once more, Antonio knelt, took a deep breath, closed his eyes and returned to his meditation.

*

Friday 21st October - 3.50pm - London, UK

The last time that James Walton had stood in his office, number 10 like much of London had been heavily flood damaged, almost to the point of no repair, but standing here now that seemed almost surreal for the 52-year-old Prime Minister. Originally from Reading and educated at St Andrews, Walton had never anticipated serving a third term, however after those terrible events, parliament invoked a series of extraordinary measures which would allow him to continue until as such a time as a general election could be organised.

Now standing by the drawing room's large bay window, Walton stared down below as the thong of television crews and reporters began to slowly disappear. Inside, he turned his attention to the room's walls which had, only recently, been repainted in a soft, apple white, a far cry from their once famous shades of canary yellow.

Unfortunately, many of the building's art treasures had been lost. However, as the Prime Minister turned to face the Home Secretary, he suddenly smiled as he noticed an all too familiar portrait of Winston Churchill dressed in a smart grey suit hanging on the wall behind her. "Oh my God, it survived."

"Prime Minister?"

"The portrait of Winston Churchill, of all the things."

Petrie quickly turned and glanced at the picture. "Yes, I know. In fact, I believe it was one of only a handful of paintings to survive the floods. Quite fortuitous really."

"Indeed."

Gazing at Churchill's image in admiration, Walton took a deep breath and his smile faded. "This feels strange…"

"Why's that?"

Walton returned his attention to his Home Secretary before slowly treading back across the floor to where she was sitting. Taking a seat opposite her on a plush green leather couch, he sat back and rolled his eyes.

"Being back here in Downing Street and you calling me Sir again."

Petrie smiled. "James we're back on familiar ground. It wouldn't be appropriate for me to address you by your first name whilst in the office of Prime Minister."

Not wishing to argue such a fair point, Walton conceded with a smile and leaned back against the couch.

"Well alright then Madam Secretary, what business do we have this morning?"

Reaching across to a cream A4 folder, Petrie opened it and cleared her throat. "Well firstly, we've heard from Italy. Doctor Quest and Professor Moore have agreed to assist the Americans with their investigation of the lost fishing vessel and as I speak they're being airlifted out of Rome. They're scheduled to catch a flight to Boston this evening, where they'll rendezvous with the US Navy sometime tomorrow evening."

"I see and are we any further to discovering why they were attacked in Rome?"

Petrie shook her head. "I'm afraid not and unfortunately the search for the assailant has drawn a blank. He seems to have eluded the authorities for now."

"Well, please ensure our people in Rome offer their full support to the Vatican authorities."

Petrie nodded firmly. "Of course, Prime Minister."

Leaning across to a nearby table, Walton picked up a glass of brandy, took a sip and returned the glass to the table.

"Anything else?"

"Only on a personal note…"

'What is it?"

"The invitation Sir, UNITY is still waiting for your response."

"Anne…"

For a moment, Walton grimaced and gave an uncomfortable sigh.

"Anne as I told you before, my position on UNITY remains the unchanged. Britain is predominantly a

Christian country; it wouldn't be publically correct for the Prime Minister to accept requests from what is, still generally perceived, as a cult faith."

Petrie's tone suddenly changed from being one of defence to one of offense. "I understand, but if you only knew..."

"Please Anne, I said no and let that be the end of it. I understand that this newly found faith of yours is important and I've already agreed to attend the United Nations event next week in New York, so please don't press me any further on this matter, understand?"

For a moment, Petrie gritted her teeth in frustration before finally succumbing to Walton's request with a gentle nod. "Of course, Prime Minister I apologise."

Walton smiled reassuringly. "Thank you, Now, what else do you have for us to discuss?"

30

Saturday 22nd October - 2.25am CET - Rome, Italy

UNDER THE COVER of darkness and with a quarter moon sitting high in the early morning sky, Gabriel Quinn slipped out from the shadows and moved quietly towards the agreed meeting point ten minutes ahead of schedule. The text message from the client had been blunt and straight to the point. *"Meet me at Castel Sant'Angelo for further instructions."*

In any normal city, under normal circumstances it would've been almost impossible for a fugitive of Quinn's calibre to move around unobserved. Yet in these decaying streets and without heat or light, what was once a colourful and vibrant city was now deserted, dark and ominous.

Although he would never admit it, Quinn was nervous. In all his dealings, he valued obscurity. He liked the idea of doing business anonymously, never having to meet clients or ask questions. To him, the process was simple. He only needed to know who and where. He was never interested in the why. Two years earlier, Quinn's murder of a prominent Icelandic Volcanologist, Elín Gylfadóttir, brought him to the attention of an organisation, known simply to him as "*The Organisation.*" His only regular contact was with a man who spoke in a soft Italian accent and although they'd never actually met, he sensed that in the past, they'd perhaps had dealings at some point.

For Gylfadóttir's murder, his weapon of choice had been *Colodotoxin.* An incredibly expensive, but deadly, experimental toxin from the Middle East. Once administered, it would appear to the authorities that the subject was the unfortunate victim of a heart attack. Gabriel was particularly proud of that one.

Taking a deep breath in the cold, early morning air, Gabriel gazed across at the remains of the *Castel Sant'Angelo*, or Mausoleum of Hadrian. Upon walking around its perimeter, he was careful to avoid the restoration project and its neat piles of rocks which had been painstakingly organised into sections, marked with letters, *A117, B202* and so on.

An owl hooted across the river and Gabriel glanced at an unoccupied wooden bench that was to be the agreed meeting place. Then, turning away, he proceeded to crouch low out of sight behind a restored section of the stone wall. Once confident that he couldn't be seen, he reached into his pocket, pulled out his pistol, slowly attached its silencer and waited patiently for the client to arrive.

Minutes later and after rubbing his eyes, he looked up in surprise to discover that the bench was now occupied. The sitting man was of medium build and perhaps in his early sixties. Although his face was obscured, he could see that he was smartly dressed. Black trousers, leather gloves, a long raincoat and a matching charcoal grey *Borsalino Avalon Fedora.*

"My God he came…"

From his position behind the wall, Gabriel observed the man for a few moments before finally standing up. Then, taking deep breath, he raised his weapon and stepped out apprehensively from the shadows and moved towards the bench.

"Are you going to shoot me Gabriel?"

As the man removed his hat and turned to face him, Gabriel lowered his weapon and his mouth fell open in astonishment. It was the face of a man that he never thought he would see again. It was the face of his father… His natural father, Cardinal Jean Louis Bouchard.

"I knew it. I knew it was you all along."

Bouchard shook his head. "Yet you said nothing."

As he walked around to the front of the bench, Gabriel gritted his teeth in anger.

"You abandoned me and for what? To protect your precious church?"

Bouchard remained subdued, his voice quiet and unemotional.

"You're no fool Gabriel… you must have understood. I was a young priest on my first assignment in Belfast. I couldn't allow a scandal like that to go public. The church had to be protected."

As he listened to Bouchard, his anger now gave way to grief, as agonizing childhood memories flooded back, forcing him to stumble backwards, and fall on the bench.

"You bastard, you abandoned me and you left my mother to rot. They took me away, you know, into foster care… to give me the chance of a stable home. That was a joke, there was nothing stable about it."

Bouchard slowly got to his feet and sighed as he stood solemnly over his son. Gazing down he then placed a hand upon his son's shoulder. Suddenly Gabriel's distraught expression turned to horror as Bouchard unexpectedly lashed out with his fist in fury. The blow struck the Irishman with such force that it sent him reeling sideways, flinging him face down onto the ground in agony. As he landed, his pistol flew out of his hand and rested by the bench only a short distance from Bouchard's feet.

With warm blood oozing from a head wound, Gabriel turned himself over to face Bouchard with a look of panic as the man loomed over him menacingly with his pistol now in hand.

"What the hell…"

"*Idioto…*"

Gazing down at his son with repugnance, Bouchard snarled in anger. "Your mother was a whore and you are nothing more to me than a bastard."

"W… What, but…"

"You were given one task Gabriel, find out who had access to the symbols from the Scotsman and eliminate them. But you turned what should have been a simple kill in Copenhagen, into an international fiasco."

Wiping blood from his head, Gabriel sat forward and desperately tried to speak, "But… I…"

As he raised his voice, Bouchard gritted his teeth in fury. "The worst part Gabriel is that you brought that fiasco here, onto our streets, and into our church."

Suddenly Bouchard lashed out, enraged, kicking Gabriel hard in the stomach.

As the once powerful Quinn whimpered and writhed on the ground in agony, Bouchard stepped forward and raised the pistol threateningly. "My organisation can no longer tolerate your mistakes my son. The world is changing and a new order is rising. In this new world, he has promised us that the faithful will receive power and glory, but also that there is no place for weakness… and you my son, are so very weak."

"No. Please, father…Wait."

The two bullets struck Gabriel in the chest like a hammer causing his limp body to slump backwards onto the ground like a rag doll. For a moment, Bouchard glanced at his son's lifeless body unemotionally, before taking a deep breath and turning towards the Tiber where he raised the weapon once more and tossed it away into the river. Satisfied that his task was now complete, Bouchard turned and gave one final glance at his son's lifeless body before turning back towards Vatican City.

31

Saturday 22nd October - 6.50am EST –North Atlantic Ocean

37,000 FEET ABOVE the cold waters of the North Atlantic, a US Government chartered Gulfstream G550 jet soared smoothly across the early morning sky on its way from Rome to Groton, Connecticut. Inside the cabin, two of out of its three passengers slept soundly. Itss third, Professor Helen Moore, was restless. Having tossed and turned for most of the journey, she finally succumbed to her frustration and sat up. After briefly glancing out of one of the aircraft's signature oval windows, she took a deep breath, unbuckled her seat belt and climbed out of her seat. As she stirred, her companion Richard Quest woke and opened his eyes.

"What's the matter, can't you sleep?"

Now on her feet, Helen rubbed her eyes and shook her head. "Not really, my mind's racing. I can't seem to relax."

"Do you want to talk about it? We could always help ourselves to a drink. After all, we are on a private jet."

Smiling, Helen gave an enthusiastic nod. "That's about the best suggestion I've heard in days."

Unbuckling his seat belt, Quest stood and they both moved quietly down the cabin towards the galley. As they brushed past the sleeping CIA Agent Mark Reynolds, Helen whispered, "Do you think we should wake him?"

Observing Reynolds for a moment, Quest shook his head. "No, let him sleep, he needs the rest."

Seconds later the pair were helping themselves to two large glasses of *Glenmorangie* single malt whisky.

"I didn't know you were a whisky drinker Helen."

Taking a large gulp of the amber liquid she grimaced as she swallowed, "I'm not, normally. But let's face it things haven't exactly been normal, have they?"

Quest shook his head and swallowed a mouthful. "No, I suppose not."

Picking up their drinks, the pair sat at opposite ends of a small oak table and placed their glasses down.

"So, do you want to tell me what's really troubling you. Is it the attack again?"

As Helen glanced momentarily down the cabin, Quest sensed that this time it was not the brutal assassin occupying her thoughts, but something else.

"Not this time. To be honest, since we left Rome, I haven't really thought about him."

Taking his glass, Quest took another sip and returned it to the table. "Well that's good."

"I suppose."

"So, what is it?"

"I guess I'm just worried about the future."

For a moment, Quest was unsure how to respond.

Then after taking a deep breath he gave a nod. "Who's future, yours?"

Gazing at her, he remembered the first time they'd worked together. Two years earlier, in the small Scottish village of Alva. The pair had been brought together to investigate the unearthing of a mysterious black pyramid beneath an abandoned silver mine. Even more bizarrely, the pair were introduced to Dougie Allan, a man who claimed to have travelled from 1710 to present day.

Nervously swallowing another mouthful of whisky, Helen placed her glass down and shook her head. "No, everyone. I mean, look at what we've seen, what we've been through."

Smiling awkwardly, Quest fidgeted uneasily and then sat back. "But we survived and we'll go on surviving. Like Demarco said, we just have to have faith."

"I suppose so."

Shuffling forward in his seat, Quest's expression softened and he unexpectedly reached out and clasped Helen's soft hands and smiled warmly.

"Look, we've been friends for a long time and I promise you that everything's going to be alright."

Suddenly Helen's eyes widened and her lip quivered. "Don't say that Richard. No one can guarantee that…"

Grasping her hand tightly, Quest interrupted. "Look Helen. We're working with some of the best people here. Agent Reynolds, for one, and I'm sure that this Father Palovic in Dubrovnik and Father Demarco will do their best to come through for us."

Wiping a tear from her cheek, Helen nodded and gave an anxious smile, "Okay."

Swallowing his final gulp of whisky, Quest returned the glass to the table, took a deep breath, reached into his jacket pocket and retrieved the piece of paper containing the symbols given to him by Dougie Allan. After unfolding the sheet, the pair stared in silence at the image of the three interlocking rings with two horizontal lines through the centre.

"Perhaps it means that *Audi* will take over the world."

Quest Smirked. "As funny as that sounds, somehow I don't think that will actually happen. Besides, I already thought of that."

Helen's eyes lit up and she smiled broadly, for what felt like the first time in days. Then, glancing back at the symbols on the paper, she returned her thoughts to the topic at hand.

"Seriously though Richard, do you have any idea what these symbols represent?"

Quest shook his head and his smile fell away. "Not really, but from my discussions with Father Demarco we have to assume that like before they're somehow mathematical in nature."

"Mathematical?"

"Sure. It seems like a reasonable place to start. Per Reynolds' request, Demarco's already contacted Father Palovic in Dubrovnik and as this is his area of expertise, I guess we'll just have to wait and see what transpires."

Quest paused and then continued, "Anyway, for the moment we have our own puzzle to solve."

"We do?"

"Of course. The Sea Mist, remember? Or have you

forgotten why we're out here. Although I must be honest, I have a bad feeling about this."

Helen frowned. "I don't blame you, I'm not keen on the submarine idea either. But that said, I'm sure that…"

Raising his hand, Quest shook his head and lowered his voice to a whisper. "No, it's not that Helen. It's what I fear we might find that's troubling me."

32

Saturday 22nd October - 8.40am EST - Central Intelligence Agency, Langley, Virginia

ON THE THIRD floor of the George Bush Center for Intelligence, Deputy CIA Director, David Tyler, sat alone in his office, slowly sipping his first black coffee of the morning. After flicking through his daily copy of *USA Today*, Tyler placed the newspaper down, leaned back, and picked up a remote control. He switched the TV onto CNN and a solemn faced reporter appeared. As he watched, Tyler prepared himself for yet another barrage of bad news.

"...and with the Naples death toll still rising, Italian authorities believe that the chances of finding anyone else alive is remote."

Taking another sip of coffee, Tyler swallowed and continued watching the smartly dressed man as he moved on to the next story.

"In other news, the UNITY church continues to see its numbers swell despite growing criticism from international faith leaders regarding the church's beliefs. Earlier, the group's

North American spokesman, Brother Thomas Weyn, defended yesterday's announcement that the church is now not only seeking worldwide religious unity; it also seeks political unity as well. Brother Weyn also reiterated his recent announcement about the church's founder and supreme leader, known only as Michael, will make his inaugural appearance at the United Nations building in New York on Wednesday evening at 7pm. But what will Michael talk about? That is the question on everyone's lips. As the world cries out for direction, many believe that Michael and UNITY may just be the way forward. The event will be attended by heads of state from around the world, as well as a host of international scientific and religious leaders who are eager to hear what this modern-day prophet has to say.

With anticipation running high and every seat filled, the UN has taken the unprecedented decision to televise the entire event live, to a worldwide audience…"

Tyler's attention was suddenly diverted away from the broadcast as a knock sounded on his office door. "Come in."

As instructed, the door swung open and Jess Marshall, his personal assistant, strode confidentially across to where Tyler was sitting.

"Good Morning Sir."

Tyler smiled. "Good morning Jess. How are you today?"

Placing a green A4 folder down on Tyler's desk, the thirty something smiled. "Fine thank you Sir, I've a couple of items for you. The first from the Italian embassy informing you that Agent Reynolds and his party are on route to Connecticut to join the *Richmond*. The second, however, I think you'll find of particular interest."

"Really. Why?"

"Picking up the folder, Tyler proceeded to flick through its pages, suddenly stopping at a grainy black and white photo of what appeared to be the body of a familiar looking Irishman. "What the…"

"From the local police, a man matching the description of Gabriel Quinn was discovered this morning in Rome. It would appear Sir that he was shot several times."

For a moment, Tyler remained silent.

"That's good news isn't it Sir? I'm sure Professor Moore will sleep a little more soundly now."

Tyler rubbed his chin, frowned and leaned back in his seat. "Perhaps."

"Sir?"

"It's the first rule of assassination Jess. Kill the assassin. This puzzle has just become more complex than I anticipated."

"Is there anything I can do Sir?"

Tyler remained silent for a moment and then nodded, "We should inform Reynolds. Can you take care of it Jess? I'm sure that it will come as a relief to Professor Moore."

"Of course, I'll take care of it right away. Will there be anything else Sir?"

Tyler shook his head and gave his assistant a smile before she nodded, turned heel and left Tyler alone.

Pushing his chair backwards, Tyler got to his feet, turned to face the window and sighed. As he stared out into the early morning sunshine, his eyes began to suddenly brighten and his face began to morph into something hideous, something inhuman. Then, as he spoke, his voice transformed from the familiar into a raspy, throaty hiss. "My brothers, we need to meet. Events are progressing faster than I anticipated."

*

Friday 22nd February 1710 - Kenmore, Highland Perthshire, Scotland

Tom Duncan was running breathlessly through a thick, almost impenetrable forest. Behind him, although unseen, he sensed that the creature was closing in. Then, in an instant everything changed. Tom was free of the trees and found himself standing alone in lush open grassland.

Taking a moment to catch his breath, he gazed through the early morning haze towards the point up ahead where the tree line continued. Tom's expression suddenly turned to one of shock, as standing about 30 meters away was the familiar shape of his six-year-old daughter, Amy, crying and dressed in an uncharacteristically scruffy red dress, the distraught child suddenly caught sight of her father and bolted excitedly towards him.

However, her efforts appeared to be in vain and Tom's elation soon turned to horror. From behind the child, a sinister whispery smoke emerged and suddenly encircled her.

"Daddy."

Rushing forward in desperation, all Tom could do was watch in horror as in one horrific moment, both the child and the creature vanished into nothingness.

Gritting his teeth, Tom flung himself on the ground where the pair had been. Now alone and lying face down on the damp early morning grass, the hysterical father pushed himself up onto his knees and began to hammer the ground where his daughter had been. "No."

"Tom, wake up lad. You're dreaming."

"Huh… what?"

The nightmare was over and as Tom's eyes flickered slowly open and any lingering images of his daughter, the creature and the forest soon dissolved into nothingness. Now fully awake. Tom found himself back on the familiar shoreline of Loch Tay, gazing upwards at the concerned face of Dougie Allan standing over him.

"Are ye alright lad?"

Taking a deep breath, Tom exhaled and gave a weak nod. "It was just a bad dream, that's all."

"Well, all right then. Grab your things, it's time for us tae move on. I'll get the horses."

Within minutes, Tom had cleared the site and both men were now back on horseback and riding out of Kenmore, along the shoreline of Loch Tay, towards Fortingall.

"Can I ask you something Dougie?"

"Aye, of course."

"Do you think we'll actually find this key?"

Glancing out across the cold, dark waters of the loch, Dougie took a deep breath and sighed.

"Aye… I hope so."

"What do you think it's for? I mean, what do you think it does?"

As the horses plodded slowly along the loch side, Dougie suddenly turned and gave Tom an icy glance. A glance that made him feel very uncomfortable. Although Dougie didn't continue right away, Tom felt a shiver run over him and sensed that the Scotsman knew more than he was letting on.

"Dinnae worry lad, I have a feelin' that we'll ken soon enough."

33

Saturday 22nd October - 2.55pm CET - Dubrovnik, Croatia

FOUNDED IN 1225 by the Dominicans, or Black friars as they were known, Dubrovnik's magnificent priory is situated in the eastern part of the city, close to the inner Ploce gate where it merges with the city's strategically important stone walls. As one of the most important architectural parts of Dubrovnik, the priory's museum hosts major exhibitions of ancient artefacts and works of art for thousands of visitors who flock to the city each year. The priory prides itself with a total compliment of 12 monks, 8 pupils and 3 knights. 23 men who are dedicated, not just to their unyielding faith, but also for their love of this magnificent building and its historical treasures.

One of these monks is 72-year-old Abbot, Vladimir Palovic, who has been a faithful and devoted servant of the church for over fifty-six years. A man, who devoted his life to the study of ancient cultures and artefacts. A man who, nineteen years ago, met and inspired a young

Italian man to, not only take up the priesthood, but to also continue his studies in mathematics and science. This man was Antonio Demarco.

At the heart of the priory is the church of Saint Dominic. Built in simple, Gothic architecture the church is designed with a hall-like pentagonal Gothic apse, which is separated from the central area by three high, arched openings. The complex acquired its final shape in the 15th century, when the vestry, capital hall and the cloister were added.

Inside, the church is richly decorated with the most notable piece being an enormous golden Crucifix affixed to the central arch above the main altar. This is the stunning work of the 14th century artist, *Paolo Veneziano*. Below the crucifix are the mourning characters of Mary and St Joseph, depicted in the recognizable Byzantine-gothic style.

Just outside the church is the middle courtyard and at its centre lies a richly decorated stone well. For the monks, the courtyard is a like a small green oasis and in the summertime under the hot Dalmatian sun, herbs and flowers provide a soothing and relaxing atmosphere.

That is, of course, not to say that the city hadn't endured its share of sadness over the years. During the Yugoslavian war of the 1990s, the region had fallen under dispute, accumulating in not only damage to the city, but also to its population. Today though, any thoughts of war or conflict were long gone. Dubrovnik had not only enjoyed peace, but had also been fortunate in avoiding those terrible quakes two years earlier.

Today, inside the priory's small but functional library,

Father Vladimir Palovic rolled his eyes and glanced towards the door in annoyance, as from a distance, he could hear the recognizable sound of running shoes as they clattered ever closer along a nearby corridor. Moments later and as a knock came to the library door, the old man, placed his pen down and sat back with a sigh. *"Uđi, Saša."*

As the heavy wooden door swung open, Palovic raised his hand and motioned the young pupil inside.

"How did you know it was me Father?"

The old man smiled. "I always know when it's you Sasha. You, how shall I put it. You have a unique sound. How many times Have I asked you to stop running through the corridors? It's disrespectful."

"*U redu, Oče… Ispričavam se*, but it's arrived, the parcel that you've been waiting for from Rome."

Nodding in gratitude, the old monk beckoned the youngster inside, pushed back his seat and got to his feet. "Very well, bring it over here please."

The eighteen-year-old nodded and walked across to where the old man was standing. Then after handing him the brown paper wrapped parcel, stepped backwards. "Is there anything else I can do for you?"

"*Ne, hvala ti*, I'm fine."

Turning to leave, the youngster suddenly stopped in his tracks as Palovic called him back.

"You're not going to give up that easily are you Sasha?"

"*Oče…* "

"Surely you must be curious as to what's inside?"

For a moment, the pupil said nothing and then he slowly returned his gaze towards the old man. "*Naravno,* but I didn't want to presume…"

The old abbot smiled and beckoned the pupil to return to the room's large square table.

"Curiosity is not a sin Sasha. Come, let us see what this puzzle is and if we can help my friend Antonio solve his mystery."

As instructed the teenager returned enthusiastically to the table and began to tear at the parcel's wrapping. Once opened, he spread its contents out onto the table for the old monk to inspect.

"*Gledajte Oče* there's a letter. Would you like me to read it for you?"

Palovic nodded in appreciation and returned to the comfort of his chair, coughing and wheezing. *"Jeste li dobro Oče*? Do you need some water?"

Shaking his head, Palovic motioned the youngster to continue. "*Ne hvala, u redu sam*. It's just old age I'm afraid. Now, please read, if you don't mind."

Nodding, Sasha opened the envelope and unfolded the letter and began to read.

My Dear friend Vladimir,

I trust you are keeping well and thank you for agreeing to help decipher the enclosed symbols. As discussed on the telephone, I've enclosed copies of my research. Unfortunately, I cannot share their origins as this information is unknown to me and is apparently classified.

I do however understand that our work may be of vital importance to international security.

As mentioned, I've been working with two Scientists: A Doctor Richard Quest and his colleague, Professor Helen Moore. They believe, like myself that these symbols may have something to do with the increased tectonic activity around the planet, activity that has caused so much destruction.

I have taken the liberty of passing on your details to the British Government and I'm sure that either Doctor Quest or Professor Moore will contact you in due course. I have also provided their contact details along within my research.

Vladimir, as well as the symbol, I've another, more personal, matter that I wish to mention and

Without warning Sasha suddenly fell silent…

"Što je Saša, what's wrong?"

For a second, the youngster gave Palovic an uncomfortable glance, before folding the letter closed and placing it down onto the table in front of the old man.

"*Oprostite Oče*, but I think that the remainder of the letter might be best read by yourself. It appears to be somewhat… personal in nature."

At first, the old man said nothing, then leaned forward and gathering up the letter, and gave the youngster a nod. "*Naravno Saša*, I understand and thank you."

Moving towards the doorway, the young pupil excused himself. "If it's alright with you Father, I have duties to perform. May I be excused?"

"*Naravno Saša*, although I would ask for your discretion in this matter. I'm sure you understand."

With a respectful nod, the youngster opened the door and slipped away, leaving the monk sitting alone in the heat of the stuffy library. As silence fell, Palovic wiped his forehead and listened intently as a flock of swallows chirped noisily as they swooped and soared past the room's ageing sun shades. Within moments they were gone and

Palovic leaned forward with a renewed interest and began to read the remainder of the letter.

... Vladimir, as well as the symbol, I've another, more personal matter that I wish to mention and although it may sound ridiculous, I find myself in need of your counsel once more.

Over the past few months many of the clergy have, for no apparent reason, abandoned their posts at the church to join a new religious order called UNITY. Now you know that I am a rational man, but I feel that there is something amiss here. Even my friend's Father, Evan, and Father Bettany have vanished without even saying goodbye.

I tell you Vladimir it's not like them to just simply walk out and abandon their faith like this. There's also something else, the other morning when I was walking in the gardens, I felt as if I was being watched, but when I turned to look there was no one there. I know that you'll probably just think that I have an overactive imagination but I believe there's something going on here and I intend to find out what it is.

For now, I wish you all the best, my friend, and hope that you'll have better success with the symbols than I have. I look forward to receiving a progress report from you in due course.

Your Friend, Antonio.

Placing the letter aside, Palovic got to his feet and began to inspect the contents of Demarco's package with interest. Within moments, the entire surface of the table was covered with documents, drawings and calculations of all kinds. Then, as a knock sounded against the library's door, the old man's face turned pale in shock as he unfolded the final sheet and placed it down on the table.

The heavy door swung open and an anxious looking

teenager stepped into the room. "*Oče, jeste li dobro?* I knocked but you didn't answer."

"Huh... What?"

Running across to Palovic, Sasha placed a hand onto the old man's shoulder.

"Father are you alright? What's wrong?"

Gazing at the monk, Sasha glanced down at the paper to see an image of three interlocking circles with two horizontal lines running through the centre.

After a second, the old monk wheezed and stepped back. "*Ja... ovo sam već vidio...* "

"Seen what Father?"

"This symbol, I've seen this symbol before."

The old man suddenly darted forwards and began to shuffle wildly through the various documents, his eyes ablaze with a sense of urgency. "Što je to, what exactly are you looking for?"

Turning towards the pupil, Palovic placed both of his hands onto the youngster's shoulders. "*Odgovore Saša*, I'm looking for answers."

34

Saturday 22nd October - 10.30am EST - New York City

THERE'S AN OLD saying that you can walk past a painting a thousand times and never truly appreciate its nuances. Never seeing that vital element, that one piece of detail that sets it apart from the rest. Buildings can be like that also. Tucked unobtrusively away out of sight. You pass by them every day, yet you never truly know what's going on inside.

Nestled between a multi-story car park and a huge thirty floor tower block lies the unassuming East 53rd Street headquarters of UNITY. A church, which until two years ago, had a mere following of just 1800 souls. Today however, that number has mushroomed to over 1.2 billion worldwide.

To an outsider or non-believer, this highly secretive organisation is an abomination of all things holy. An increasingly powerful cult that ignores the traditional doctrines of Christianity, Islam, Judaism and Buddhism to follow the teachings of a man, whose followers consider to be a modern day prophet. A prophet who has seduced the public with his promises of wealth and power. Despite having never actually seen their leader, devotees continue to flock, despite the warnings from world leaders and even family members who are concerned as to where this blind devotion will lead. But to the faithful, UNITY is more than a religion and Michael is more than a prophet. To them he is a living God.

In a small, makeshift television studio on the building's second floor, UNITY front man, Brother Thomas Weyn, smiled with satisfaction as he completed his third interview of the day. As the small, red lamp on top of the television camera flickered off, Weyn took a deep breath and gave a nod towards the young reporter.

"How was that Miss Simpson? Did you get everything you need?"

The young reporter glanced briefly across at her cameraman for confirmation that he was satisfied with the material. After receiving a thumb, she exhaled and turned back towards Weyn and beamed with gratitude.

"Yes, thank you."

"Excellent. Well then, if you'll excuse me I have other matters to attend to."

Climbing to his feet, the tall, smartly suited man shook hands with the reporter and nodded to his equally smartly dressed assistant who followed him out of the room and into a corridor, closing the studio door behind them.

The pair made their way up a narrow flight of stairs in silence and entered a room with a small sign above the doorway which read "*The Red Chapel.*" Inside, the sparsely furnished room was adorned in a deep red colour, including its walls and plush carpet. Everything was the same blood red, all except for a few wooden benches and a large, polished white marble altar at the front of the room.

Entering, the two men walked down a small aisle and stopped adjacent to the altar.

"So, Brother Simon, you've been unusually quiet this morning. Is something troubling you?"

At first, the powerful looking young man said nothing. Then, turning towards the altar he cleared his throat. "I'm afraid I have bad news."

"Oh…"

"Gabriel is dead. It appears that he was killed by his Father."

Stepping forward, Weyn sighed heavily and nodded. "Yes, I've heard and although it's unfortunate, you have to understand that sacrifices have to be made. After all, even Abraham offered his own son, as a sacrifice to his god. We must be prepared to do the same for ours if necessary."

"But what of the Cardinal? Quinn was brought in to eliminate problems. Now it would appear that those problems remain, are you not concerned?"

Placing his two hands on the cold marble altar, Weyn gazed upwards towards a set of closed red velvet curtains and exhaled.

"Calm yourself Brother, it is of no concern. Bouchard is a loyal and trusted servant. He will not fail us."

Turning sideways, Weyn leaned forward and reached

out towards a thick, gold tasseled rope. As he pulled, the velvet curtains slid quietly open to reveal three large golden rings affixed to the wall above the altar with two horizontal lines running through the centre.

"Soon everyone will understand. Unity is the way. One mind, one body."

35

Friday 22nd February 1710 - Fortingall, Highland Perthshire, Scotland

FLANKED BY MOUNTAIN passes and forests of rich native woodland lies the ancient hamlet of Fortingall, or it's medieval name *Forther-cill,* meaning *"church of the fort' or 'upper land."*

Lying at the base of Glen Lyon, the region forms an area known as Breadalbane and is surrounded by what many believe are some of the finest prehistoric and archaeological sites in Scotland. For future archaeologists, it would be known as druid country as it contains numerous standing stones and circles. To those ancient Picts and Celtic tribes, these monuments were deeply spiritual and often steeped in myth and legend.

One of those stones lies just outside the village and as is known in its native Gaelic as the *Càrn nam Marbh*, or *'Cairn of the Dead'* which sits at the base of a large burial mound and was said to have been used as a 14th century burial plot for plague victims by an old woman who turned out to be the village's only survivor. Three hundred years later, it's not the rotting bones of the dead that local people remember. It's the stark image of that old woman riding away on a white horse which continues to send a shiver down the spine of anyone who should be unfortunate enough to find themselves walking past the stone on a cold moonlit night.

As the youngster casually strolled past the cairn, he stopped for a moment to watch a flock of irate crows fluttering and cawing wildly overhead on the lookout for scraps of food. Finally convinced that he was a lost cause, the birds turned eastwards and disappeared over a clump of nearby trees. Turing back to gaze at the tall protruding grey stone, the boy caught sight of the two strangers as they emerged on horseback over the brow of a nearby hill. Ever mindful of outsiders, the eight-year-old watched for a moment before turning and bolting towards home.

By the time Dougie and Tom arrived in Fortingall, any early morning haze had cleared and the sky was bright and cloudless. Riding towards the walls of the local church, Tom took a deep breath and smiled as a flock of starlings swooped and soared in perfect formation overhead. "Look at that. Don't you think that's just amazing?"

"Huh, whits that lad?"

"Starlings, don't you think it's amazing at how they can swoop in formation like that. My mother called it cloud dancing."

Without a response, Dougie continued riding towards the gates of the church.

"Wow, this is amazing to see it like this."

"Like what?"

Tom turned and grinned like a Cheshire cat. "Oh,

Dougie just look at this place, it's incredible. Just think about it, in years to come this'll be all gone. A fire will rip through the church. In fact, it's going to be so spectacular that the only thing to survive will be the bell. Hence the old saying *saved by the bell.* A new church was built in its place around 1900. The family and I used to visit here all the time."

As the horses pulled up to the outside the long church building, Dougie climbed down and tied his animal to a nearby fence post.

"Well laddie, I hope for your sake that you'll get tae visit it again. In the meantime, we need tae get tae work. Tie yer horse up while I'm awa tae find the abbot."

"Of course."

As Dougie rapped on the building's heavy main door, Tom climbed down from his horse, and as instructed, tied the animal to the fence post and waited for a response from inside. Moments later, the large door creaked open and a young monk, perhaps no older than 25, greeted the pair with a warm smile. Wearing a long brown and white cassock, the monk cleared his throat. "Good Mornin' Sir, can I help ye?"

Dougie nodded. "Aye my name is Dougie Allan and this is my friend Tom Duncan. Mr. Duncan here has a keen fascination in the history of yer famous Yew tree. We've made a wee trek fae Stirling in the hope that ye could possibly help."

As Tom joined Dougie in the doorway, the monk nodded warmly and smiled. "I'm sure that won't be a problem, but if ye'll kindly wait fae a moment I'll see what can be arranged."

The door reopened a short time later and the monk politely beckoned the pair inside. "Gentlemen, if you'll follow me this way please."

Upon entering the wood panelled entrance, the young monk led the pair down a short passageway with a grey stone floor and into a small sitting room where they were introduced to an elderly man in his seventies. "Father Thomas, may I introduce Mister Dougie Allan and Mister Tom Duncan. Gentlemen may I introduce you to the abbot of our small order, Father Thomas McRae. Father these twa gentlemen have travelled fae Stirling in the hope that you'll permit them tae see the tree."

Struggling to his feet, the old monk shook hands warmly with the two men.

"It would be our pleasure, but before ye go, ye might perhaps accept some hospitality? It looks like you twa have had a long journey. Perhaps we can even offer you a bed fae the night?"

Before Dougie could decline, Tom stepped forward, and to Dougie's annoyance, accepted enthusiastically on his behalf. "That would be very kind thank you."

"Excellent. Well then if you'll kindly follow Brother Daniel he'll see to all your needs."

After thanking the abbot for his generosity, the pair turned tail and followed the younger man out into the corridor, leaving the old man alone. As the door closed behind them, Tom was surprised at the expression on Dougie's face. Rather than him appearing happy about the abbot's offer of hospitality, he seemed frustrated and impatient at yet another delay.

Minutes later and the pair were in the church's small

kitchen, sitting around a square oak table with two bowls of hot soup.

Returning to the table, the monk placed down an additional bowl of fresh bread and two goblets of red wine for the visitors.

"There ye are gentlemen. If ye'll excuse me, I'll arrange some rooms fae ye. I'll be back shortly to show ye around."

With a mouthful of soup Tom nodded in gratitude. "Thank you."

Now alone in the kitchen, Tom swallowed another mouthful of soup before leaning in towards Dougie and lowered his voice. "Dougie, that was really rude. I thought ye'd be glad of a warm bed after sleeping on wet ground for two nights."

Gulping down a mouthful of wine Dougie slammed his goblet down on the table and wiped his mouth with his sleeve. "Tae be honest laddie I dinnae give a rat's arse aboot staying' the night. I've a task to complete and I plan tae get it done. Now if ye want tae help then that's fine, otherwise ye can bugger off back tae Alva."

Suddenly Dougie stood up and stormed away towards the kitchen door. "Dougie, wait a minute."

"I'm awa tae feed the horses, I'll be back soon."

Now alone, confused and becoming increasingly concerned about Dougie's erratic behaviour, all Tom could do was watch as the big man stomped away leaving him sitting bewildered and alone at the table.

*

Saturday 22nd October - 3.30pm EST - The Lincoln Memorial, Washington DC

"Four score and seven years ago, our fathers brought forth on this continent a new nation, conceived in liberty and dedicated to the proposition that all men are created equal.

Now we are engaged in a great civil war, testing whether that nation, or any nation so conceived and so dedicated, can long endure. We are met on a great battlefield of that war. We have come to dedicate a portion of that field, as a final resting place for those who here gave their lives that that nation might live. It is altogether fitting and proper that we should do this.

But, in a larger sense, we cannot dedicate, we cannot consecrate, we cannot hallow this ground. The brave men, living and dead, who struggled here, have consecrated it, far above our poor power to add or detract. The world will little note, nor long remember what we say here, but it can never forget what they did here. It is for us the living, rather, to be dedicated here to the unfinished work which they who fought here have thus far so nobly advanced. It is rather for us to be here dedicated to the great task remaining before us—that from these honoured dead we take increased devotion to that cause for which they gave the last full measure of devotion—that we here highly resolve that these dead shall not have died in vain—that this nation, under God, shall have a new birth of freedom—and that government of the people, by the people, for the people, shall not perish from the earth."

The Gettysburg Address – Abraham Lincoln - Thursday, November 19, 1863

After reading through Lincoln's Gettysburg Address for the second time, CIA Deputy Director, David Tyler, sighed and glanced up at *French's* magnificent seated sculpture of Abraham Lincoln before finally turning away. With the Memorial to his back, Tyler descended the monument's stone steps, walked past a noisy family and continued onwards down the left-hand side of the Reflecting Pool towards the Washington Monument.

The afternoon was cold, with a blustery wind descending from the east which whipped up leaves from nearby trees. Apart from the family and the occasional jogger, the area was unusually quiet for the time of day. Arriving at a wooden bench, Tyler brushed away a small clump of leaves with his hand, sat down and proceeded to open his copy of *The Washington Post.*

Before he began to read, he glanced out across the water and smiled inwardly as a small flotilla of ducks swam by. Returning his attention to the newspaper, he sat back and began to read the headline with interest. *"UNITY in Shock at Canadian Election Win!"*

Aware that he was no longer alone, Tyler looked up to see an elderly beggar approaching from his left, and as the man stopped by the bench, Tyler folded his newspaper away and placed it down as the man took a seat next to him. Unshaven and dressed in an old pair of jeans and a black parka jacket, the man glanced across at Tyler and with intense bright blue eyes and drew breath.

"These people confuse me brother. They are capable of such beauty and yet commit such atrocities against each other. They then attempt to justify their actions by building memorials and monuments. They crave peace, yet continue to plan for war and violence. I'm puzzled, we all agreed that this cannot be allowed to continue, yet you still object to what must be done."

Glancing outwards across the Reflecting Pool, Tyler drew breath and nodded reluctantly in agreement.

"It is not that I disagree brother. You know the prophesies as well as I do. If the warnings are correct, then he will return and mankind will be forced to make a choice."

"If they make the wrong choice, what then brother?"

For a second, Tyler remained silent before taking another deep breath and climbing to his feet. Fastening his coat, he picked up his newspaper and gave the memorial one final glance. "Then we proceed as planned."

36

Saturday 22nd October - 3.45pm EST - Groton, Connecticut

IT WAS IN 1872, the height of the American civil war, that the seafaring towns of Groton and New London would form the beginnings of America's first naval base. Nestled between the Thames and Pawcatuck rivers, these close neighbours would play a major role in US shipbuilding and naval history. By 1915, the New London Naval Base would officially become home to America's first submarine fleet and a year later would become its first Submarine Base. But it wasn't until 15 years later that in 1931 that the *USS Cuttlefish* was built as the first submarine built in Groton. Today, the main base occupies more than 687 acres and is home to more that eighteen attack submarines, the housing and support facilities for more than 21,000 civilian workers, active-duty service members and their families.

Cruising past numerous residential and military buildings, the black *Ford Expedition* sped quietly along

Crystal Lake Road and finally pulled into a large car park adjacent to the main base entrance.

"Doctor, Professor if you'll kindly step out and follow me, I'll arrange to have you signed in."

After glancing across at her colleague, Helen nodded at Reynolds, opened her door and climbed out of the vehicle. Once outside, the pair followed the agent across to a nearby guardhouse and disappeared inside.

Minutes later, and after undergoing a thorough security check, the trio emerged, each clutching a valid base pass. After returning to the SUV, the car pulled out of the car park, turned back onto Crystal Lake Road and sped away southwards.

"I thought we were going to the base."

"We are, but the boat doesn't leave until tomorrow morning so I've taken the liberty of arranging accommodations for you both at a nearby hotel."

Helen nodded. "I see."

Moments later and after a short drive along the highway, the *Expedition* turned left and came to a small driveway next to the entrance of a modern, but basic, looking two story *Navy Lodge* hotel. As Reynolds jumped out of the front seat, he opened the back door and motioned his two passengers out of the car.

"I'm afraid it'll be rather simple compared to what you're used to Professor, but I'm confident that you'll at least get a good night's sleep."

As Reynolds passed two bags to Doctor Quest, he slammed the trunk closed and returned to the car. "Wait, you're not joining us?"

"Unfortunately, no. I have to attend a short navy

briefing. Don't worry its quite routine. I'll catch up with you in the morning. In the meantime, why not get some rest. I've a feeling we're all going to need it."

*

Saturday 22nd October - 9.30pm CET - Vatican City, Italy

"Avanti…"

The polished oak wood door to Bouchard's office swung open to reveal a distressed and pale looking Father Antonio Demarco standing in the doorway. "*Antonio, stai bene amico mio?* You look dreadful, what's wrong?"

Sweating profusely and without uttering a word, Antonio glanced once around the room before slamming the door shut and striding across to where the cardinal was sitting. "*Mi perdoni, Sua Eminenza* but I need to talk to you."

"*Certo amico mio* come in."

With a concerned look, Bouchard climbed to his feet and motioned the priest to take a seat. As he did, Bouchard picked up a jug of iced water, poured two glasses and passed one across the table before returning to his seat. "*Ecco, bevi questo* and tell me what's troubling you."

Antonio gulped down a mouthful of water before placing the glass down onto the desk. "*Sua Eminenza, La prego, non mi giudichi.* I know that this'll sound ridiculous but I can't remain silent any longer."

"*Antonio,* it is only God who can judge you my friend and not me. So please tell me what is it that's troubling you."

With shaking hands, Antonio continued. "*Beh, dopo*

the events of the past few days, I sought to take solace in the library. To focus my attention on solving the riddle of Doctor Quest's symbols."

Picking up his glass, Bouchard took a sip of water and nodded. "Seems like a reasonable course of action, especially after that awful attack."

"Well, after our meeting in the church yesterday I was on my way back to the library and had the definite feeling that someone was following me…"

"Oh Antonio, *di sicuro non…*"

"*Sembra ridicolo, lo so.* But then later in the library, I was picking out a book and I turned to notice two priests at a nearby table staring at me. Once they realized I was watching them, they turned away in pretence. I know it was no coincidence."

"*Chi erano* these priests, did you recognize them?"

For a moment, Antonio fell silent before shaking his head in uncertainty. "*No… ma ad essere sincero*, there have been so many comings and goings, I don't know who they were."

"*Beh, forse* after the incident yesterday they were just curious bystanders. Is that not at least a possibility?"

Antonio fell silent as a sudden wave of doubt began to creep in. Then, as Bouchard looked on, Antonio shook his head, confident that it was not simply his imagination and what he'd seen had been genuine.

"*No Sua Eminenza, era più di questo.* If it was a case of simple curiosity I'd understand. But, if I think back a couple of months I was in the gardens and I could have sworn that someone was watching me."

Listening intently, Bouchard leaned back in his chair

and stroked his chin. "*Va bene Antonio*... let's say that for the moment that you're right and someone is watching you. I must ask to what end? I mean you're a priest, what possible reason would somebody be interested in you?"

"*E i simboli?* Perhaps they're making somebody nervous."

Taking a deep breath, Bouchard got to his feet, walked around to the front of the desk and placed a hand on Antonio's shoulder and smiled. "*Se questo è vero, Antonio* then I promise that together we'll get to the bottom of this."

"*Grazie Sua Eminenza... lo apprezzo.*"

"*Purtroppo* I'll have to leave you for the moment. I have a late supper engagement with Cardinal Randall. I can assure that you're safe within these walls. Now continue with your work and don't worry, I'll have a word with the Swiss Guard in the morning and see if they can help. *Che Dio sia con te, Antonio.*"

As he gave a weak smile, Demarco stood and shook hands with his friend. "*Grazie, Sua Eminenza.*"

As Antonio departed and the door closed, Bouchard remained standing in silence. A few seconds later and now confident that he was alone, his false smile slipped away and after returning to his desk, he retook his seat, calmly picked up his phone, dialled a number and waited for the call to be answered. A second or two later the line clicked and a man with an American accent answered.

"Yes."

"It's Bouchard. We need to talk..."

37

Friday 22nd February 1710 - Fortingall, Highland Perthshire, Scotland

AS THE DOOR to the chapel opened, Tom gasped as Brother Daniel welcomed the two men inside the medieval church. “So, this is our chapel.”

Although Tom had visited Fortingall many times with his wife and daughter, it was always to the church which was built in 1900. To stand here now in the original building, that was something truly special.

“Would you care to look around?”

Tom nodded enthusiastically. “Oh yes, I would very much.”

Motioning the two men inside, the young monk smiled. “Well, we have several fine tapestries in the vestry and the altar is medieval, over three hundred years old.”

“Really?”

“Oh yes but we have artefacts that are much older than that.”

“How interesting…”

“Perhaps after the evening meal Father McRae will

recount some of his stories for you. He's been here a long time and I can tell you, he's quite the historian."

"That would be appreciated."

"Of course, please take all the time you need. Our gardens are to the rear. That's where you'll find our famous Yew. But. If you'll excuse me, God's work is never done."

"Thank you, you've been very kind, please pass on our thanks to the abbot."

"Of course."

Left alone to explore, Dougie stepped away from Tom and began a meticulous inspection of a nearby statute. Tom, on the other hand, remained in the doorway to absorb the moment and take a slow deep breath. The result was glorious. A rich, musty scent filled his nostrils, almost like opening a chest of old library books, combined with the faint and unmistakable church aromas of beeswax and incense.

Standing upon the stone paved centre aisle, Tom could see an impressive stone altar placed in front of a magnificent stained-glass window at the far end of the church. In that moment, he realized that he wasn't just walking into an old church anymore, but walking into history itself.

"This is incredible, don't you think Dougie?"

Suddenly aware that Dougie hadn't responded, Tom's gaze now returned to the Scotsman, who appeared deep in thought beside another small statue.

"Dougie?"

"What? Oh, aye I'm fine lad, sorry what did ye say?"

Tom's expression turned to one of disappointment.

Not simply at Dougie's lack of interest for the church, but for also not sharing Tom's enthusiasm for the moment.

"I said, don't you think the church is amazing?"

"Oh, aye lad, it's grand."

As Dougie moved on to inspect a nearby painting of Madonna and Child, Tom returned his attention to the chapel's grey stone walls and its collection of ornamented paintings depicting the various stations of Christ's journey from persecution to ascension.

Then, moving to the head of the church, Tom paused at the small altar for a moment of quiet reflection before stepping back.

Other than the splendid window, altar and paintings, the remainder of the sanctuary was rather unremarkable. No elaborate decorations or carvings, just simple stone walls and wooden pews, nothing that would classify it as extraordinary. Returning his attention to Dougie, Tom cleared his throat and called out. "Are you sure about this place Dougie, it all seems pretty average?"

Joining Tom beside the altar, Dougie motioned his friend through a small side door which led to the rear the of the church. "Keep focused laddie and dinnae be fooled. There's more to this place than meets the eye."

Once outside, Tom trailed behind Dougie into a small courtyard and then out into a small garden. As the skies overhead began to darken and droplets of rain began to kiss the ground, Tom gasped in eerie recognition as the pair turned a corner and came face to face with Fortingall's oldest resident.

The Yew tree itself was huge, with an enormous ancient trunk which had been entwined by smaller, younger radices. To an observer, the tree looked twisted and gnarled, almost as if it was in pain. Roots had snaked and matted themselves around the base like a writhing, squirming nest of vipers. "That's incredible. it looks exactly as I remember it. A little healthier perhaps."

Walking up to the tree, Dougie stepped forward, reached out and grasped hold of one of its branches, "Healthier?"

"In the 1900's there was an increase in the numbers of day trippers and collectors who'd come by and literally hack whole chunks of the tree away, simply to gratify their curiosity. It became such a problem that fencing was erected to protect it."

"I see."

"So now that we're here, can you tell me more about this mission that we're on? I mean you still haven't told me what this key looks like?"

Gazing at the tree, Dougie paused before responding. "It'll resemble a wee black pyramid."

"You mean like the one we discovered in Alva?"

"Aye, but it'll be much smaller and cold tae the touch."

Sighing, Tom shook his head. "Talk about trying to find a needle in a proverbial haystack. Where on earth do we begin?"

Gazing up at the mighty tree, Dougie rubbed his chin for a moment before responding. "We're going tae need tools."

"For what?"

"Tae dig laddie, whit de ye think?"

Tom's expression suddenly turned to one of horror.

"You can't be serious? They'll never give us permission to dig here. It'll damage the tree."

Dougie growled before snapping back harshly.

"Who said anything about asking permission. We dinnae have time fae that. We have tae find that key at any cost. Now come awa, we'll return tonight."

*

The old priest was sitting by the fireplace, mesmerized, as he listened to the continuous rhythmic ticks of a nearby wall clock. Taking another sip of tea, the old man suddenly shuddered as a loud knock came to the door.

"Aye."

As the door swung open, Brother Daniel entered carrying a large leather-bound book.

"I brought the book you asked fae Father."

"Thank you, that's very kind."

Placing the book down on a nearby table, the younger man dipped his head courteously before stepping back to leave.

"Wait a moment Daniel. I was wondering how our visitors are doing?"

Stopping in his tracks the younger monk paused and motioned with his hand towards the adjoining church building. "They're exploring the church Father."

"I see. Is it still raining outside?"

The monk paused to glance through a nearby window, then, after a moment returned his gaze towards the old man. "Aye, it looks like we're in fae quite a storm."

Picking up his cup, the old man took another sip of

his nettle tea and held the cup tightly in his frail hands to keep them warm.

"Did ye invite them for dinner?"

"I did as ye asked Father."

"Good."

For a moment, Brother Daniel remained still and solemn, before returning his gaze towards the darkening skies. "Do ye think it's them Father?"

Returning his cup to the table, the old man sat back and wheezed.

"It's hard tae say. Only time will tell."

Picking up an empty teapot, the monk excused himself and moved back towards the door.

"I'll awa and mak ye a fresh pot Father."

As he departed, the old man nodded in appreciation and closed his eyes to meditate. Once shut however, he soon found his thoughts averting to the visitors and how he could prepare himself for the eventualities which may soon begin to unfold.

38

Sunday 23rd October - 6.25am EST - Groton, Connecticut

AFTER A NIGHT of unsettled sleep, Professor Helen Moore decided to get up and take an early breakfast, rather than lay in bed. Although the hotel was no Hilton, her room had been reasonably comfortable, albeit somewhat basic. This is, of course, apart from the annoyance of a faulty air conditioning unit which hummed intermittently throughout the night. Around 3am she had thought about calling down to reception, however in the end she decided to simply plug her ears with cotton wool and tolerate the situation.

She now sat in the hotel's small restaurant. Although to be fair, the word restaurant wasn't exactly the word she would have used to describe her current locale. A breakfast bar with a few tables and chairs would have been more accurate. Unlike, many military themed budget hotels she'd encountered over the years, stainless steel cutlery was nowhere to be seen as she munched through multi-coloured *Cheerio's* in a cardboard bowl using a flimsy plastic spoon.

Sipping her coffee, she looked on with interest as a rather bedraggled looking catering assistant shuffled across to a nearby television and switched it on. Moments later, the early morning peace and quiet was shattered by the drawling voice of a smartly dressed CNN news reporter as he delivered the morning headlines.

"If you're just joining us. The world was shocked this morning as the Vatican announced that Pope, Julius IV has died overnight. The progressive and much-loved Pope appears to have suffered a heart attack. A Vatican spokesman said that despite receiving medical attention, doctors were unable to revive the Pontiff after he complained of feeling unwell earlier in the day.

Messages of sympathy have begun to flood in from political and religious leaders around the world. In London, British Prime Minister, James Walton, said that he was saddened at the death of such a progressive and loved leader. Here in the United States, UNITY spokesman, Brother Thomas Weyn, also reflected his own shock and sadness, saying that despite being religious rivals, he was deeply saddened by the news and wanted to reach out to the Catholic community to offer support if needed.

Per Vatican sources, there are plans for 3 days of national mourning before any conclave can begin. But just who could replace such a loved Pope? Sources are remaining tight lipped. However, pundits are advocating that this man, Cardinal Jean Louis Bouchard, could be a front runner for the position. We'll of course bring you more on this story as events unfold.

In other news and staying with UNITY. It appears that the faith's influence knows no boundaries. Since the formation of its political wing, the Red Council, the church continues to make substantial gains in both regional and national elections. Only yesterday France, Germany, India and Poland became the latest countries to relinquish power in a series of stunning election wins by a promise of not only unifying faiths, but also political parties. The latest win now places UNITY in power in over 54 countries around the world.

In the face of this astounding success, many world and religious leaders continue to criticize UNITY, suggesting that it's not healthy for any one political or religious group to have such power. In contrast. UNITY's spokesman, Brother Thomas Weyn, disagrees. This is what he had to say…"

With her cereal almost finished, Helen leaned across, picked up her coffee and took a sip just as the screen flicked over to an interview in which a young female reporter was in conversation with a handsome middle-aged man, dressed in a smart charcoal grey suit.

"Brother Thomas, how do you answer the critics that have denounced your faith as nothing more than a cult and that religion should have no place in politics?"

"I can see how some might think that, Miss Simpson. However, you must remember our doctrine differs vastly from others in that, like our leader, it's alive. Now of course it's nothing new for a religion to be political. You must only look back throughout history to see the Roman Thirty-year war and the Crusades. If you want recent examples, we've had the Lebanese Civil War and don't forget the Israeli and

Palestinian conflict. All of which have cost millions of lives in the name of what… Faith."

Religion and politics have become a cancer which has caused nothing but division, chaos and conflict. UNITY aims to change all of that, one faith and one political party for peace and harmony for everyone, irrespective of gender, race, faith or creed."

"What about your critics who accuse you of simply riding on the back of those terrible disasters?"

"I think someone had to act, Miss Simpson. The events of the past few years have crippled this planet and wiped out nearly half of its population. Michael has ordained that it's inconceivable that humanity should continue in this way. Greed, hatred and war should be a thing of the past and after Wednesday it will be. This is the dawn of a new age. When the world meets Michael, everyone will understand that UNITY is the way. One mind, one body."

"Morning Helen."

Suddenly aware that there was now someone standing beside her, Helen placed her cup down and glanced up to see Richard Quest standing over her, coffee in hand. "May I join you?"

"Of course."

Placing his cup down, Quest pulled up an adjacent seat and sat down. "So, what's good?

"Huh?"

"Breakfast. What's good for breakfast?"

Glancing at her half-finished bowl of multi coloured cereal she grimaced. "To be honest, you might want to go for the bagel."

"You know I think I'll just stick with my coffee."

Swallowing his first mouthful, Quest leaned in closer and lowered his voice.

"We've received instructions from London. Whilst we are on board the *Richmond*, we're under the jurisdiction of the Americans. As such, we're to follow the directives of both the commanding officer and Mark Reynolds."

"Reynolds?"

Quest nodded. "I know, I guess we must see it from their angle. It's their submarine and to have civilians aboard when its operational is highly unorthodox."

"I suppose so."

Swallowing the last of her coffee, Helen nodded in agreement. "Have you had any luck with the symbols?"

Leaning back, Quest rubbed his eyes and shook his head. "Not really. I received another email from Father Demarco, he's continuing with his assumption that they are likely numerical in nature. But as to their meaning, well that's still a mystery I'm afraid."

Looking across at Helen's empty mug, Quest pushed his chair backwards and got to his feet. "Would you like another coffee?"

"Sure… that would be good."

Picking up the mug, Quest turned heel and headed away to a nearby coffee machine for a refill.

Now sitting alone once more Helen refocused her attention back towards the television news broadcast.

"With only 3 days to go, preparations in New York have reached fever pitch. With UNITY now being not only the world fastest growing religion. It's also now the largest.

Here in the United Nations Building, preparations

continue to ensure that Michael's broadcast will be carried without hitch to a global audience…"

"It's all a bit creepy, don't you think?"

Placing the now full coffee mug back down onto the table, Quest retook his seat and glanced at the television. "What do you mean?"

"Well, placing all your faith in some hokey religion with a leader that no one has never seen."

Picking up her mug, Helen sipped the warm fresh coffee and gave a sarcastic smile. "That's the whole point of religion, isn't it? Look at Christianity for example. Can we prove that Christ is the Son of God? Yet millions of people throughout the ages believe he is."

For a moment, Quest remained tight lipped as he glanced worryingly across at the television before drawing breath and continuing. "I agree, but you have to admit that it all seems a little unnatural. I mean how can this so-called religion become so influential so quickly. Not to mention this *Red Council.* I tell you It's a dangerous combination and just doesn't seem right to me."

Helen smiled. "Richard, you worry too much. Whatever happens, I'm sure that it will be all for the better. The past two years has been hell for everyone. Maybe we need a fresh perspective. Something to believe in again. Perhaps this Michael is the answer and perhaps not. Today and for the here and now, all I know is that in just over an hour, Reynolds is going to walk through that door and I'm not going to greet him looking like this."

Quest laughed. "Now is hardly a moment for vanity Helen."

Helen grinned, pushed back her chair and got to her

feet. "Perhaps you're right. I'll meet you back here in an hour okay?"

As she walked away towards an elevator, Quest took a deep breath, picked up a nearby newspaper and began to read.

39

Sunday 23rd October - 11.40am GMT - 10 Downing Street, London

BRITISH PRIME MINISTER, James Walton, stared glumly out onto the rather despondent looking gardens of Number 10 Downing Street, hoping that his day would somehow improve. Overhead, once promising early morning skies had been traded for an afternoon of heavy and seemingly persistent rain. Stepping back from the window, he exhaled with a heavy heart as he glanced down at his copy of *The Sunday Times* to read its main headline for the sixth time.

"Pope, Julius IV Dies age 74"

The news of the Pope's death wasn't the only story to sour his mood. As Walton's eyes shifted, his heart sank further as he re-read the sub-headline "*UNITY Sweep to Power in France & Germany.*" Turning away from the newspaper, Walton stood silently in the centre of the room for several moments. Gazing despondently across at his favourite portrait of Sir Winston Churchill, desperate for the old man to provide any guidance. But, with nothing forthcoming Walton shook his head in anxious disbelief at the thought of everything that this man, this legend had fought for was now slipping through his fingers like a crumbling handful of sand.

What could he do? Standing in silence he pondered over the portrait of the great man. His mind racing through endless scenarios and subsequent consequences. Should he attempt to seek an alliance with UNITY? Should he offer the British people a choice, a referendum, or was it down to himself and the Government to make that choice on behalf of the people?

Turning to his desk, Walton paused for a moment by a small drinks table before lifting a bottle of *Glenfiddich 12-year-old Single Malt Whisky.* Gazing at the bottle for a moment, he ensued to pour himself a generous amount.

Seconds later and now re-seated, he picked up the crystal glass, closed his eyes and downed its entire contents in one large gulp. As the warm amber liquid made its way downwards, Walton's attention was suddenly refocussed, as his desk phone began to ring.

Shuffling forward in his seat, he paused in order to recompose himself before picking up the receiver. "Yes."

"She's here Prime Minister, will I send her in?"

"Yes, please Lisa."

Placing the handset down, Walton slid his chair back and reluctantly got to his feet just as the door to his office swung open. Making his way forward, he gave a forced smile and extended his hand to welcome his Home Secretary, Anne Petrie.

"Anne it's nice to see you. I hope you are the bearer of good news?"

"Well, I'll do my best Sir."

Smiling with renewed self-confidence, Petrie shook hands and opened her leather handbag as Walton motioned his visitor to sit down on a nearby couch.

"Would you care for some tea?"

"No thank you Sir."

Pulling out a cream coloured A4 folder from her bag, she leaned forward and handed it to the Prime Minister who immediately opened it and began to sift through its contents. "This is everything?"

Closing the clasp on her bag, Petrie placed it down by her feet, sat back and gave a nod.

"It is Sir and as you'll see the security services have found nothing to indicate that UNITY's motives are nothing other than sincere."

Placing the folder down, Walton frowned, sat back and rubbed his forehead. "Perhaps so, but why do I get the gut feeling that this is wrong?"

"Sir?"

"Seriously Anne, where the hell did they come from? Two years ago, they were nobody and today, they rule half of the fucking world."

"James."

"I… I'm sorry Anne but I just want to know what the hell is going on."

Becoming increasingly agitated Walton climbed to his feet, walked back across to the nearby drinks table, picked up the bottle of *Glenfiddich* and unscrewed its cap.

"Care for a glass?"

As he proceeded to pour himself another generous

helping, Petrie leaned forward and shook her head disapprovingly. "It's a little early don't you think?"

After returning the bottle to the table, Walton retook his seat and gulped down a mouthful of whisky. "On an ordinary day, I would agree. This has been no ordinary day. I'm sorry but right now I need it."

Petrie leaned forward and gave a reassuring smile. "Of course, I understand that it's been a difficult day. It must feel like a weight on your shoulders, trying to balance what's best for the nation. You know, you automatically assume that UNITY is a threat. But what if they are not?"

"Anne please, not again."

"Prime Minister would you at least have the courtesy to hear what I have to say?"

Giving a sigh, Walton sat back and gave a reluctant nod.

"What if they are not the threat that you perceive? I admit it, I'm a member of UNITY and have been for the past year. So far, I've seen nothing to indicate that they are dangerous.

I have to be honest though, most of the cabinet agree with me in that we should at least sit down with them and have a conversation."

"What? You can't be serious?"

"James… I was never a religious person, but I admit, I've not just found a faith, but a calling. If you could just open your eyes and realise that Christianity, Islam and all those other dogmatic religions clinging to their outdated beliefs are based on what? Nothing but myth and ancient superstition. UNITY is offering you the opportunity to believe in something greater. Something more powerful and alive. You shouldn't turn away from it:

you should embrace it. If you don't, then there could be unfortunate consequences."

Gulping back the remainder of his whisky, Walton's eyes narrowed as he suddenly leaned forward. "I'm sorry Anne, but for a moment there that almost sounded like a threat."

Sitting back, Petrie smiled with conviction.

"It's not a threat, it's simply a promise. All I'm saying is that UNITY is coming. One way or another, the world is changing and we want you to be part of it. Just think of the opportunities James."

"Enough Anne."

Rising to his feet, Walton strode forward, stopped opposite Churchill's portrait and turned to face Petrie and raised his voice. "Anne, we've known each other a long time now, and in all those years I've never seen you like this. So willing to sell yourself out and abandon your principles. His generation fought and died for this nation so that we would be free from tyranny and oppression. I'm sorry, but I'm not going to throw those principles away simply because a group of religious fanatics want my seat in Parliament."

"But Prime Minister…"

"I said no Anne. However, we are a democracy. So I will allow you to present your case to the cabinet. Unlike you, I don't believe that they will agree with you and I'll prove that later his evening."

Bitterly disappointed with Walton's decision, Petrie's confident smile fell away and was replaced with a look of frustration intermixed with a tinge of anger. For the moment, she had lost, but in her mind this defeat would be short lived. "Yes, Prime Minister."

As she rose to leave, Walton suddenly stepped forward with a serious expression.

"Anne, one other thing. It seems clear to me that your heart is no longer in this job. I think you've let your new-found beliefs cloud your judgement. As such, I fear we have become incompatible. After the session, this evening I'd appreciate your resignation."

"Sir?"

"I'm sorry Anne. You can call it retirement or whatever you wish. I assure you the British people are deeply grateful for your many years of service and this will no doubt be reflected in the public announcement that will follow. That said, I'll expect your letter of resignation on my desk by tomorrow morning. Good day Anne."

As the Prime Minister turned away, Petrie gritted her teeth, the seething anger now rising inside her like a pot of boiling water. "Yes, Prime Minister."

Within moments, the door had opened and she was gone. Once outside, Petrie made her way down the staircase of number 10 and out of its famous black front door onto a rather damp and squalid looking Downing Street. The afternoon's heavy rain had eased and as she made her way past the security cordon, she stopped to compose herself. With anger simmering inside, she clipped open her bag, took out her cell phone and after punching in a phone number, waited to be connected. After a moment, the line clicked and was answered by a man with an American accent.

"This is Brother Weyn."

"It's Anne Petrie."

"Yes Sister. Were you successful?"

Composing herself, Petrie glanced around to ensure she wasn't being watched. "No, he wouldn't listen and I'm afraid he's also asked for my resignation."

"That's unfortunate. The others, does he suspect?"

"No."

"Then our time has come. Did you receive the parcel?"

"I did."

"Good. Remember Sister, UNITY is the way. One mind, one body."

"I understand."

Seconds later and with the skies clearing overhead, the call was over and Petrie put the phone away. Clipping her bag shut, she took a deep breath, turned left towards Whitehall and walked away with a fresh sense of purpose.

40

Friday 22nd February 1710 - Fortingall, Highland Perthshire, Scotland

AS AFTERNOON SLIPPED into night and the storm gathered momentum, Dougie and Tom had finished their evening meal and had moved to join the clergy huddled by the fireplace in the manse's small sitting room. Sitting opposite Father McRae and Brother Daniel, Tom stared into the fire, captivated by its flames, as its sparks crackled and danced in the room's semi-darkness.

Outside, the wind and rain whipped mercilessly against the church windows, reminding Tom that he was ever grateful for not having to sleep rough on such a wild night. Sipping on a hot whisky toddy, the old priest coughed once before placing his glass down onto a nearby table.

"So, Mr Duncan. I hope that your trek to our wee church was worth your effort?"

Glancing across at Dougie, Tom leaned forward and gave an enthusiastic smile. "Oh indeed, yes thank you Father."

Shuffling forward, Dougie mirrored Tom's gratitude. "Aye thank ye fae your kindness Father. That's a grand housekeeper ye hae. She's a braw cook, I may have tae steal her awa fae myself."

As he wheezed, the old man gave a fragile smile. "I'll pass on your thanks. I'm sure she'll be glad tae hear that."

As Dougie sat back, Tom turned to the abbot and cleared his throat. "Brother Daniel and I were chatting earlier. He informed me that you're quite the historian, is that right?"

Glancing across at his younger colleague, the abbot smiled sheepishly before picking up his glass and taking another sip of his hot toddy. "Well I dinnae ken aboot that Mister Duncan, but it's true I've a keen interest in history. Whit is it ye'd like tae ken?"

As the old man returned his glass to the table, Tom realised that this was his chance. An opportunity to ask the questions that he'd always wanted to.

"If I may, the story of Pontius Pilate. Do you know if it's true? I'd love to know your thoughts."

"Well for that story I'm going tae need a refill. Perhaps Brother Daniel would do the honours."

"Aye, of course Father."

As directed, the young monk climbed to his feet, walked across to the small table, lifted the whisky bottle and proceeded to refill the glasses of the three men. As each nodded in gratitude, Daniel finally topped up his own before retaking his seat. The abbot proceeded to reach downwards and picked up the large, leather-bound book brought to him earlier by the younger monk.

"Well, as ye can imagine, tales often become hazy over

time, but I'll do my best. This book is very old and contains what I believe tae be the truth behind many of those myths. It appears that in AD21 the Emperor Augustus did indeed dispatch an envoy to establish diplomatic relations with some of the important clans. At that time, there was a chieftain called Metellanus, whose stronghold was close by, near the head of Glen Lyon. Rumour has it, that it was a member of the delegation who fathered a child with a local woman and that this child, subsequently returned to Rome with its parents, was brought up as Pontius Pilate."

"But Father, surely this all just speculation?"

"Ah not at all, look here."

Opening the book, the priest flicked through its delicate hand-written pages. Then stopping on a page, he glanced up at Tom who was now standing above his left shoulder. "Right here look."

Gazing down in amazement, Tom looked on in wonder at the ancient painting. It depicted what appeared to be a Roman officer, a woman and a young child playing opposite the twisted trunk of the Fortingall tree.

"It's beautiful Father."

Smiling to himself, the old man wheezed and gave a nod. "Of course, lad. It also means that the history books are right. If these images are to be believed, then this is the young Pontius Pilate."

Suddenly Tom's eyes widened in shock as he recognised something in the painting. Something that he wasn't expecting. "Oh my God. Dougie, look at this."

Dougie sprang to his feet and strode across to where Tom was standing. "Whit is it lad?"

"Do you see anything familiar?"

Squinting in the semi-darkness of the firelight, Dougie struggled for a moment to see exactly what is was that Tom was looking at. “Nae lad, I canne see whit…”

Suddenly Dougie’s expression changed and his voice faded into silence. For the first time, he now understood exactly what it was that drew Tom’s interest. In the hand of the small boy sat the instantly recognizable shape of a small black pyramid.

“Father what’s this?”

Pointing to the pyramid the priest glanced briefly at his colleague and nodded. “We’re nae sure. It was apparently found by the child near the tree. But, as to what it is and what its purpose is eludes us I’m afraid.”

Despite his silence, Tom sensed from Dougie’s expression, that he wasn’t entirely happy with the priest’s explanation. Also, Tom was also now beginning to suspect that Perhaps Dougie wasn’t being entirely truthful either.

Stroking his chin, Father McRae wheezed as he rotated the book towards himself and briefly flicked through its pages before stopping at another striking image of a small Roman temple. The picture depicted a crowd of sobbing figures. Everyone looking upwards towards the figure of an elevated Roman senator who held aloft the miniature black pyramid in his hand.

“What does it mean… the pyramid?”

Leaning across to his small table, the elderly priest picked up his hot toddy, took a sip and shook his head. “Some believe that it means death Mister Duncan. Mythology suggests that it was the pyramid that somehow caused the plague here in the 14th century. Of course, that’s just speculation, there’s nae actual proof.”

Rising to his feet, Dougie stepped across to the fireplace and gazed pensively into its flames. "Do ye ken whit happened tae it Father… the pyramid I mean?"

Returning his empty glass to the table, the old man shook his head. "Nae really, most think that it was lost, others that perhaps it was taken to Rome. Some including myself believe that it's still here, buried somewhere in or around the church. Believe me though, I've tried looking for it, with no success, of course."

Watching the orange sparks dance in the twilight, Tom shivered as he caught sight of Dougie's mouth as it suddenly arched upwards into an unsettling smile. "Aye, of course Father."

41

Sunday 23rd October - 8.10am EST - US Naval Submarine Base, Connecticut

STANDING ON THE busy dockside, Agent Mark Reynolds gazed upwards in awe at the enormous grey hull of the *USS Richmond.* Powerful and deadly, the *Richmond* class of next generation nuclear-powered fast attack submarines were conceived in the early 90s as a replacement to an ageing cold war fleet of Los Angeles and sea wolf class attack boats. With an overall displacement of 8,100 metric tons and a length of 390ft (115m) the *USS Richmond,* remains by far, one of the most formidable weapons in the US fleet. Boasting a crew compliment of 15 officers and 123 men, the boat could run submerged for weeks, or even months, if required.

Whilst Reynolds hailed from a military family. He'd made the decision early in his career that, unlike his father, a navy life was not for him. Although grateful for the opportunity and despite a family disagreement, Reynolds concluded that a year in the navy was enough. Once discharged, he opted instead for a career in law enforcement and intelligence. After joining the FBI, he quickly progressed into the ranks of the Secret Service where he remained until accepting his recent position with the CIA.

Despite being early morning, the dockyard was a flurry of activity as the enormous submarine prepared for departure. Watching with interest as the *Richmond's* crew loaded the last of its provisions, Reynolds waited patiently by the black *Ford Expedition* for Moore and Quest to complete their paperwork. As he surveyed the boat's grey hull, Reynolds' expression suddenly turned to surprise as he caught sight of a mini submersible attached to the upper hull. Before he could enquire as to its purpose, his attention was drawn back to the moment as Doctor Quest tapped him on the shoulder. "Is everything in order Mr Reynolds?"

Turning to see Moore and Quest standing behind him, Reynolds nodded and motioned the couple towards the gangway. "Yes, I have your passes, and we're now free to board. Are you ready?"

Glancing nervously over his shoulder at Helen, Quest straightened up and gave a reluctant nod. "Apart from the odd claustrophobic thought. Yes, I believe we are."

Giving the pair a reassuring smile, Reynolds motioned the couple towards the gangway.

"Don't worry. After what you've both been through in the past few days, this'll be a piece of cake."

Moving past two heavily armed guards, the group stepped onto the gangway and were met by another two men: a middle aged black American officer in his thirties and a younger sailor in his twenties.

"Agent Reynolds, Doctor Quest, Professor Moore. Welcome aboard the Richmond. I'm Tom Dalby, the boat's XO. If you'll kindly pass your things over to crewman, Diogenes, here, he'll see to it that they're delivered to your assigned bunks."

As instructed, the trio passed their bags to the smartly dressed youngster who promptly turned heel and disappeared through a nearby hatch.

"Now if you'll follow me to the officer's mess, the Skipper has a few questions for you before we depart."

"Of course. Thank you."

After shaking the officers hand, Reynolds gave a reassuring nod in the direction of the two scientists before they awkwardly stepped forward towards the open hatch.

"Don't worry Professor, I can assure you she's a solid safe boat."

Moving inside, Helen uttered a cynical laugh. "That's what they said about the Titanic."

As the XO grinned and stepped forward, Helen glanced across at Richard for support, who returned his own nervous smile.

Once inside, the group quickly made their way down one level and through a series of busy narrow corridors to finally arrive at a door with the words "*Officers Mess*" embossed onto a brass plate affixed to the centre of the door.

Knocking twice, Dalby waited for a response.

"Enter…"

Promptly turning the handle, Dalby pushed the door open to reveal three awaiting officers seated around a rectangular oak dining table. As Dalby and the visitors poured inside, the men promptly got to their feet and the XO stepped forward to make introductions.

"Captain, I'd like to introduce Agent Mark Reynolds of the CIA... Mr Reynolds this is the Richmond's commanding officer, Captain Brad Butler."

Stepping forward, Reynolds smiled curtly before shaking hands with the elder of the three men. Although dressed in a similar khaki uniform to the two, the four stripes of gold insignia attached to his uniform radiated respect. Even as the man smiled, Reynolds couldn't help but feel intimidated, and rightly so, given the huge responsibility that this man bore.

"Mark Reynolds, I knew your father, Frank. I served with him a few years back in Hawaii."

"Yes Sir."

"Bad business. I'm sorry. He was a fine man."

Reynolds swallowed hard as a sudden image of his father surfaced from the back of his mind.

"He was, Sir. Thank you."

Almost two years earlier, Lt Cmdr. Frank Reynolds had been serving aboard the *USS Jimmy Carter* when a catastrophic tsunami hit the region, resulting in a trail of devastation across the South Pacific. Inopportunely for the *USS Jimmy Carter*, the sub had been undergoing a crew rotation in Pearl Harbour and had the misfortune to find itself at the epicentre of the quake. There were no survivors.

"As you've already met my XO, Tom Dalby, may I introduce my Chief of the Boat, Karssen Beck, and our Doctor, Lieutenant David Denatti."

Shaking hands with the two stern faced men, Reynolds,

somewhat uncomfortably began his own introductions. "Captain. Gentlemen, may I introduce Professor Helen Moore and Doctor Richard Quest. They've been seconded from the British Government to assist with our mission. They're smart people, and we're lucky to have them."

After shaking the visitor's hands, Butler motioned the group to take a seat. "Welcome aboard, please have a seat."

As the officers retook their seats, Reynolds shifted along to allow the two scientists to join him on the opposite side of the cramped table. Unlike the Captain, the other officers appeared to be much younger, and Helen sensed that the Executive Officer, or XO, appeared more open minded to having visitors aboard the submarine than the captain. As Quest scrutinised the other men's facial expressions, he couldn't help but feel that they were outsiders here and somehow trespassing on hallowed, naval ground.

"Doctor, Professor despite our qualms, I want you to feel welcome. Please understand that it's rare to have civilians aboard an operational submarine. Naval traditions consider it to be bad luck, especially under such… unusual circumstances. In fact, apart from a set of co-ordinates and a report of two missing fishing vessels, I have to ask why we're involved at all?"

An uncomfortable silence momentarily filled the room, before Helen Moore took a deep breath and leaned forward. "Captain, on behalf of the British Government I completely empathise with your situation. We live in unusual times. However, if you could've witnessed some of things we've seen, well to be frank they defy belief."

As she spoke, Helen experienced a sudden wave of emotion as memories of a past meeting in Alva with a man who claimed to be from the 1700s, the discovery of an enormous subterranean cavern beneath an abandoned Scottish silver mine and most shocking of all, the discovery of an ominous black marble pyramid and the terrible events which followed.

"Two years ago, we were exposed to something..." Helen's lip quivered and her voice suddenly faded.

As her head flopped, Quest leaned forward in support and placed a hand on her shoulder.

"I'm sorry, please forgive us Captain. The past few days have been very difficult."

Butler glanced at his three officers and offered a comforting smile. "Well, I'm sure there'll be plenty of time to continue this discussion once we're underway. In the meantime, my XO will get you settled into quarters. It's a little cramped, I'm afraid, and you'll have to rotate bunk usage, but I'm sure you'll manage."

Helen glanced at Quest and gave a weak smile. "Thank you, Captain."

As he climbed to his feet, the other officers stood to attention.

"XO once you've seen to the needs of our guests, please join me at the con. COB prepare the boat for departure. It's time that we got underway."

"Yes Captain."

As he opened the door, the Captain suddenly stopped in his tracks, reached into his trouser pocket and pulled out a small white envelope. Turning back, he handed it to Doctor Quest. "I almost forgot Professor, you received a couple of messages from London. Oh, and Mr Dalby can you please arrange for more suitable clothing for our guests?"

"Of course, Captain, I'll see to it right away."

After a firm nod, the Captain had departed, quickly followed by the *Richmond's* Chief of the Boat and the young Doctor who were up and away before Dalby could complete his sentence.

Now alone with the three visitors, the officer smiled and motioned them all towards the door. As they stepped forward, Helen suddenly raised her voice.

"Clothes?"

"Yes Professor, you'll each be issued with a set of coveralls and safety shoes for the duration of your stay on-board. Not the most flattering, I agree, but they're designed primarily for safety and practicality. They are vital, especially aboard a submarine. So, if you'll all kindly follow me. We'll get you settled in."

42

Sunday 23rd October - 7.30pm GMT - 10 Downing Street, London

AS THE RAIN finally eased above central London, British Prime Minister, James Walton, sat alone behind his desk glancing over his notes in preparation for his upcoming cabinet briefing. Leaning across his desk, he picked up an A4 sheet entitled *Anne Petrie Press Release*. After a short bout of coughing, he glanced once over the text, signed it and placed it into his out tray for processing. Leaning back in his comfortable black leather chair, Walton reached across his desk, picked up a TV remote control and flicked the TV onto the *BBC News* Channel just as the half hourly news bulletin was starting.

"This is Mark Rodgers with the latest news headlines from the BBC.

As the world comes to terms with the sad and sudden death of Pope Julius, a Vatican spokesman confirmed that the holy father died from a heart attack in his sleep during the early hours of this morning. As messages of love and support continue to flood in, Vatican authorities have made the unprecedented decision to re-open St Peter's Square tomorrow ahead of its planned opening in December. With repairs to St Peter's Basilica almost complete, the Italian Government has successfully petitioned the members of the Vatican council to allow the public to attend for three days of national mourning which is scheduled to commence tomorrow. This will be followed by a state funeral next Friday.

In other news, UNITY continue to gain support for its political aspirations, as this afternoon, the Russian government formally requested membership of the church's increasingly powerful political body, the Red Council. Upon accepting the country's request, UNITY spokesman, Brother Thomas Weyn, said that he was delighted at President Sergey Belanov's decision to take his country forward into a new age of peace and prosperity.

However, despite the UNITY's success there are still strong pockets of resistance from a small number of United Nations members. In response to their anxieties, Brother Weyn again repeated his message of peace."

"Although I understand and appreciate the delegate's concerns, I wish to reiterate UNITY's message of peace. Our world has undergone massive change. It's time to put aside centuries of mistrust and violence and come together as one people. This Wednesday evening at 7pm our leader, Michael, will share his unique message for the world. A message of hope, a message of UNITY."

"In anticipation of the upcoming events in New York, Brother Weyn also teased reporters with the promise of a major announcement planned for tomorrow afternoon."

"I don't want to spoil the surprise, but in anticipation of Wednesday's historical event, UNITY plan to share something

special and I can promise, you won't be disappointed. Unity is the way. One mind, one body."

"Prime Minister."

"Huh…"

Suddenly Walton's attention was diverted away from the news broadcast as his assistant Lisa Harkins stood sheepishly in the open doorway.

"I'm sorry to disturb you. I did knock."

Switching the television off, Walton coughed again and placed the remote back onto his desk, looked up and smiled warmly.

"That's all right Lisa, I didn't hear you."

Moving quickly inside the room, the young assistant strode over to the Prime Minister's desk, placed down an A4 folder and stepped back. "Do you want me to get you something for your cough? It sounds nasty."

"No thanks I'll be fine. What can I do for you?"

"Sir, I've just heard from the Americans. The *USS Richmond* has departed from Connecticut and your message to Professor Moore and Doctor Quest has been received."

Leaning back in his chair Walton nodded in mild satisfaction. "That's good news. I just hope they can find some answers."

"Yes Sir. The cabinet have also arrived for the meeting and they're waiting for you downstairs."

Walton coughed once again before gulping down a final mouthful of water. Then, placing his glass down, pushed back his chair and climbed to his feet. "Well then. I guess we should get going."

*

Sunday 23rd October - 8.55pm CET - Dubrovnik, Croatia

Though late October, the evenings in Dubrovnik could often still be warm and sultry. Within the walls of the city's magnificent 12th century priory, 72-year-old Vladimir Palovic was sitting quietly alone on a small bench trying to enjoy the tranquillity of the commune's private gardens. For over fifty-six years he had prayed with, and for, the people of Dubrovnik. Through good times and bad, he'd always done his utmost to deliver messages of positivity and hope. But it wasn't always easy, and sitting here now with his eyes closed, those meandering memories of the Yugoslav conflict soon began to creep back into his thoughts. Memories of dark times, where whole towns and families were pitted against each other. Sadly, like most conflicts, political power, greed and religious indifference were the root cause.

With his eyes still closed, Palovic drew breath and smiled inwardly as the sudden rush of rosemary and jasmine filled his nostrils and began to calm his thoughts.

As the old man exhaled and finally relaxed, he said a small prayer of thanks and was about to reopen his eyes. When he heard footsteps approaching from behind.

"*Oče,* I'm sorry to disturb you."

Recognising the voice, Palovic opened his eyes and smiled. "You're still running Sasha. I thought that we'd discussed this?"

The eighteen-year-old was the youngest of the priory's

six pupils, and per many of the elders, the most enthusiastic. His heart was in the right place. "*Da,* I'm sorry Father, but it's important. I think you should see this."

Leaning forward the old man rubbed his eyes and motioned the youngster to sit down next to him. "*Vrlo dobro*, please take a seat before you fall over."

The youngster sat down and began flicking through the pages of a large book. "Now my young friend, what's so important that you had to disturb an old man's prayer?"

As he stopped flicking through the pages, the youngster sat forward and pointed to the page.

"Forgive me Father, but after our conversation in the library, I decided to do some research on the symbol myself and I happened to come across this."

Placing the book onto the old monk's lap, the youngster pointed to an old hand painted picture of a knight, fighting a dragon by the sea.

After staring at the picture for a few moments, Palovic shrugged his shoulders and looked up.

"Žao mi je *Sasha* but I don't see anything unusual."

Rolling his eyes, the youngster shook his head. "It's the story of the Milini dragon. Come on Father, you must know this one?"

Palovic shrugged again and shook his head. "*Oprosti mi,* it's been a long time."

"*St. Hilarion* was an old man, a hermit who lived in Milini. One day he was out fishing in the bay when he witnessed a battle between two knights on Milini Beach. It's said that one of the knights was so fierce that he had the power to change his form. Firstly, into a giant snake and then a dragon."

"*Zmaj?* I think you're letting your imagination run away with you. Come on, let's go inside and have some tea…"

As Palovic gave a sceptical smile and began to rise, the youngster's expression turned solemn and he suddenly seized hold of the old man's sleeve and hauled him back down."

"*Sasha*!"

"Forgive me Father, but this is important. Look again."

The old monk exhaled and looked down once more. "All right. What is it?"

Flicking through the delicate pages, Sasha swivelled the book back towards his mentor and pointed at a smaller picture. A foreboding, dark-haired figure, dressed in dark armour and carrying a sword and shield.

"It's here, look at this Father."

For a moment, the old man didn't understand. To him, the picture simply looked like one of a thousand others that he'd seen many times before. Then his jaw dropped and Sasha knew that he understood. "Do you see it Father?"

"*O moj Bože*… Yes, I see it."

"The shield Father. Look at the shield. It's the same as the symbol, but how is that possible?"

For a moment, the old monk simply stared at the picture, astounded at the youngster's discovery. The markings on the knight's shield were indeed identical to the symbol that Antonio Demarco had sent him. Three circles with two horizontal lines running directly through the centre.

"*Ne znam Sasha*… I just don't know."

43

Saturday 23rd February 1710 - 2.40am - Fortingall, Highland Perthshire, Scotland

OUTSIDE, THE FEROCIOUS storm battered against the bedroom's two small, arched windows. Unable to sleep and despite Tom's earlier objections, Dougie decided to take this opportunity to explore the church and its grounds unaccompanied. Under the cover of darkness and using the storm to mask his movements, Dougie sat up, pushed back his blanket and swung his feet out onto the floor. After dressing, he collected his belongings and left the room. After quietly making his way down a narrow staircase, Dougie paused for a moment by the main entrance to ensure that he hadn't disturbed any of the house's occupants.

Once satisfied he hadn't, he made his way outside, walked through the nearby gardens and stopped outside an unobtrusive side entrance of the church. Once inside, he picked up a single burning candle and used it to ignite several others so that he could see. Once satisfied, he refocussed his attention towards the building's 12th

century altar and placed his bag down opposite. Gazing at the floor, he began to slowly and methodically examine each of the stone floor tiles around the base of the altar in detail. After several minutes, he dropped down onto his knees and gave out a sudden elated cry. *"Yesss..."*

Examining one unusually patterned tile, Dougie noticed that, unlike the others, this one had been deliberately carved with an almost familiar emblem. Bringing the candle closer, he proceeded to run his palm across its distinctive pattern. There could be no mistake. It was comprised of three interlocking circles of equal size, complete with two horizontal lines through the centre.

Reaching across towards his tool bag, he pulled it open, took out a large hammer and drew a deep breath. Then, seemingly oblivious as to the amount of noise that he was about to generate, raised the hammer, and proceeded to strike the tile with an almighty thud.

*

Sunday 23rd October - 8.10pm GMT - Cabinet Meeting Room, 10 Downing Street

As James Walton finally stopped coughing, he gulped down the last few drops of water and returned his empty glass to the conference table. With a final wheeze, he pushed his leather chair back and proceeded to stand. Once on his feet, he glanced around at the solemn faces of his ministerial colleagues and began to circle slowly around the table.

"We've known each other a long time and we've all

suffered. But I can't believe what I'm hearing here today, what you're proposing."

As he spoke, Anne Petrie, Walton's outgoing Home Secretary suddenly got to her feet and interrupted.

"James it's nothing personal. We hope you understand but…"

Raising his hand, Walton stepped forward and shouted angrily. "Anne, if I could at least be allowed to speak. You come in here, despite our earlier agreement and propose that we, the British Government align ourselves with UNITY. This group of religious fanatics. I think you're out of your bloody mind!"

Staring at the other smartly dressed cabinet members, Walton spluttered once more and continued. "Surely you must all see the madness in this proposal?"

With no response from the others, Petrie took and deep breath and shook her head in apparent defeat. "You see, it's no good. I told you he wouldn't listen."

Furiously banging his fist down onto the table, Walton shook his head and shouted irritably. "You're damn right I'm not going to listen. It's over, Anne. Now would you please leave, before I have you removed."

Despite his threat, and to his surprise, Petrie didn't budge. Instead the stern faced woman simply returned to her place at the table, glanced at the others and motioned them to stand. As they did, Walton's expression suddenly turned from one of anger to one of alarm.

"What is this, what's going on?"

Without responding, Petrie began to address the group. "My brothers and sisters, as you can see we've been reasonable. Now it seems we have no alternative."

As she spoke, Walton once again began to splutter and cough uncontrollably. “Brothers? Anne what are you talking about?”

As the increasingly uncomfortable silence continued, Walton’s heartrate quickened. In all his years in Government, he had never witnessed anything like this.

As he watched intently, a chill ran down his spine, and for the first time, his concerns morphed into fear. Petrie and the others appeared to be waiting, but exactly what for, was for the moment unclear. Reaching inside her jacket, Petrie suddenly pulled out a small empty glass vial and placed it down onto the table in front of her.

“What’s that? What’s going on?”

“It’s called *Colodotoxin* Prime Minister. It’s a rather ingenious substance, completely undetectable. You see, there’s a storm coming and he’s promised us not just power, but survival. Unfortunately, along the way, there must be… casualties.”

As he coughed once more, Walton raised his hand to wipe spit away from his mouth, and as he did, he suddenly reeled backwards in horror. His hand was not covered in drops of saliva, but with drops of blood. “What…”

Before he could complete his sentence, a sudden and agonising pain shot through his chest, almost as if an immense weight had been placed upon him.

“Argh…”

Without warning, Walton’s vision began to blur and as he stumbled back, his leg struck the table with a thump, causing him to collapse uncontrollably onto the ground in agony. “Help me… Anne please!”

It was too late. Stepping forward, Petrie unhurriedly

knelt beside the crumpled figure and offered the fading James Walton one final callous smile. "I want you to know that your country has nothing but the greatest of respect for you, Prime Minister, and that the circumstances of your heart attack will be thoroughly investigated."

"Heart… Wh… No."

Walton, gazed upwards in horror as Petrie rose to her feet and returned to her place at the table. Then, as he gasped his last, the group began a cold melodic chant in unison. *"We are one. We are one. We are one. Unity is the way. One mind, one body."*

44

Sunday 23rd October - 5.30pm EST - New York City

INSIDE THE UNOBTRUSIVE third floor room known only to its followers as the *Red Chapel,* UNITY frontman, Brother Thomas Weyn, was kneeling alone in quiet meditation opposite the chapel's small white marble altar. After taking a deep breath, the solitary figure pushed himself back upwards onto a seat. Gazing across at the nearby altar in mild satisfaction, he contemplated the events of the past 48 hours and attempted to justify to himself his part in the murders of British Prime Minister, James Walton, and the leader of the Roman Catholic church, Pope Julius IV. For the most part, Weyn never considered himself an evil man, but as a colleague once remarked, one man's evil is another man's salvation.

Born the son of a prominent Boston lawyer, Weyn initially followed his father into the family law firm. However, six months before graduation, he made the unprecedented decision not to take the bar exam. Thus, his father was furious and accused him of not only wasting his career but also the family's hard-earned money. Despite attempting to explain his decision, Weyn's relationship with his parents faltered and would never truly recover.

As Thomas continued to deliberate over his actions, he recalled an event that would became pivotal in his decision to join the UNITY church. He recalled taking a train journey from New York to Boston, where he underwent what could only be described as a life defining moment. A passenger who had joined the train in Hartford entered his carriage and proceeded to take a seat opposite him. As Weyn eyed the man, he found himself staring, with an almost insatiable sense of curiosity, at the man's unusual appearance. Dressed in a well-tailored black suit, the figure had an unusually pale, gaunt face and the most piercing pair of bright blue eyes that he'd ever seen.

As the journey progressed, the two men eventually struck up conversation. The stranger explained that he'd just arrived in the US and was in the process of forming a revolutionary new church, a church that he believed would one day change the world.

At first, Weyn didn't pay much attention to the man's ramblings, but as the train sped onwards into the night, he found himself becoming strangely mesmerised by the man's soft, seductive voice. By the time the train pulled into Boston station, Weyn found himself in the uncharacteristic position of wanting to know more. That was the spark and within a week he'd committed himself to help grow the church. Despite never seeing the man again, he was sold on his promises of power and wealth. It wasn't long before he began his crusade to engage large numbers of followers and the rest, as they say, was history.

"Forgive me brother, I didn't mean to disturb your meditation."

"Huh…"

With his attention broken, Weyn glanced upwards to see his smartly dressed assistant standing above him. Leaning back in his seat, Weyn smiled and acknowledged the man forward.

"That's all right. You have some news?"

Glancing once around at the sparsely furnished room, Simon nodded. "I received call from London."

"And?"

"It's done."

Rising to his feet, Weyn gave a satisfied nod. "That's excellent news brother. What of the others?"

As Weyn turned towards the door, the younger man nodded and joined him in the slow walk down the aisle. "The other six vials have been delivered. I suspect it won't be long before we hear something."

"Well then, I think we can safely proceed onwards to the next stage. Ensure the new ad is aired tomorrow morning. I want maximum coverage."

"Of course, Brother. I'll see that it's done."

"Good."

As Weyn grasped the door handle, the younger man suddenly reached out and placed a hand on his mentor's shoulder. "Forgive me, but there's one other small matter we need to discuss."

"What is it?"

"Rome. Bouchard has requested a replacement for Quinn. Apparently, he still has some… Loose ends that he needs tying up."

Weyn grimaced. "The fool should have thought about that before he pulled the trigger."

Simon nodded in agreement. "Yes, Brother."

"Very well. Tell him to clean up his own mess."

"Of course, I'll send the message right away."

*

Sunday 23rd October - 8.55pm EST - North Atlantic Ocean

Under the waters of the cold North Atlantic, the enormous grey hull of the *USS Richmond* glided smoothly and silently under the waves. Inside its steel shell, the boat's crew worked efficiently and purposefully like a well-oiled machine. With the evening meal over, Richard Quest was sitting alone at a table in the Officer's mess, surrounded by a plethora of books and papers. Placing his book on *Classical Religious Symbol's* down, he leaned back into his seat and rubbed his eyes. Even though the boat had been at sea for only a day, it felt like an eternity. As Quest picked up a mug of coffee, his thoughts were suddenly interrupted by a knock at the door.

"Come in."

The door swung open to reveal the young sailor who had been escorting Professor Moore through the sub's maze of narrow corridors. As the youngster stepped aside, a familiar face appeared in the doorway. "Excuse me Sir."

As Helen Moore entered the room and thanked the sailor, the youngster nodded in reply, stepped back and closed the door, leaving the couple alone.

"What's wrong? Couldn't you sleep?"

Taking a deep breath, Helen frowned before stepping across to where Quest was working and took a seat. "Not really. How on earth can anyone sleep on these things? You rest for four hours and then offer your bunk to someone else, I don't think I'll ever get used to this."

Quest smiled, pulled out a nearby seat for Helen and nodded. "You won't have to. It's only for a few more days."

As Moore took the seat opposite, she glanced across at the table and sighed. "It looks like you've made some progress."

Quest shook his head and refocussed his attention to his copy of *Classical Religious Symbols.*

"Not really. However, I am still convinced its mathematical though."

"Really?"

"Assuming of course, that its connected to the original symbol. Statistically, it must share some of its mathematical commonalities."

Helen looked puzzled.

"So, what you're saying… is that the solution is right here in front of us right?"

Quest smiled. "Exactly."

"So where do we go from here?"

Quest's smile fell away and his expression turned serious. "I sent a message to Father Demarco and his friend in Dubrovnik this morning with some ideas and…"

"…And what?"

"Well I guess I'm just a little disappointed that they haven't responded."

Smiling warmly, Helen squeezed Quest's hand in an

attempt to reassure him. "Hey, Rome wasn't built in a day. These things just take a little time, that's all."

As she spoke, her voice suddenly trailed off as a knock came to the door. "Come in."

As the compartment's, small steel door creaked open, a grim-faced Mark Reynolds entered, clutching a piece of folded A4 paper.

"Are you alright, Mr Reynolds? You look pale."

Stepping across to where the couple were sitting, the agent grimaced and reluctantly handed the sheet across to Quest.

"I'm sorry Doctor. I'm afraid I have some bad news."

45

Saturday 23rd February 1710 - 3:15am - Fortingall, Highland Perthshire, Scotland

"MR ALLAN, JUST whit the hell dae ye think you're doing?"

Dougie turned to see a young Brother Daniel standing in the doorway with a horrified expression on his face. Rather than providing the youngster with a reasonable explanation for his actions, Dougie simply ignored him and returned his attention to the altar. The young monk looked on in disbelief as Dougie raised his hammer in preparation for a second strike.

"Mr Allan, you must stop!"

It was too late. When the hammer fell, it struck with such force that it literally split the stone tile in two. As the monk shrieked out in protest, Dougie continued to ignore the youngster as if he wasn't there. Determined to stop this heinous act of vandalism, brother Daniel summoned all his courage and stormed forward towards the front of the church. Meanwhile, seemingly oblivious, to the teenager's approach, Dougie continued to remove the shattered tile and picked his way through the debris. In a moment of elation, he suddenly yelled out as he spotted his prize. A small wooden box buried within the debris. Grappling inside to retrieve the precious artefact, his attention was suddenly interrupted as the infuriated teenager grabbed his shoulder.

"Mr Allan... you must stop!"

Dougie was furious at being interrupted, during his moment of victory. In a wholly uncharacteristic move, he gritted his teeth, spun around, grasped hold of the teenager's throat and hissed. "Get awa fae me boy."

In one swift action, he heaved the bewildered monk clean off his feet and threw him across the floor. As the boy crumpled onto the ground, he wailed in pain as his leg struck the base of a nearby pew, causing his ankle to shatter in several places. Moaning in agony and with the prospect of a second blow forthcoming, Brother Daniel curled himself up in a panicky attempt to defend himself against the marauding Scot. As the seconds passed, the second attack never came. Instead, Dougie returned his attention to the small box beneath the altar.

Extending his arm, Dougie knelt, reached underneath the altar and pulled out the wooden box. Now in his hand, the box itself measured no more than thirty centimetres in length. As far as he could tell, it was almost completely smooth, apart from the front, which displayed a curious symbol. Three interlocking circles with two horizontal lines running directly through the centre.

Proceeding to dust off the remaining debris, he turned to the quivering teenager and stepped forward. "I'm sorry for your discomfort Brother, but I can assure you that it won't be in vain."

Wincing in agony, the trembling teenager's expression turned from one of shock into one of disgust.

"Y… You're insane."

Without responding, Dougie took a deep breath and prised the box open. As the cover peeled away, his smug, self-confident smirk melted away into one of shock and eventually into fury. Dropping the now worthless container onto the stone floor, he glared at the teenager in seething rage. Then, in a moment of sheer fury, he rushed forward, grasped the boy by the throat and bawled. "Where is it!"

*

As the storm raged outside and rain battered against the rooms small window, Tom's eyes flickered open. Unsure as to why he awoke to such a start, he immediately sensed there was something wrong. After a second or two, he threw back his woollen blanket, swung himself out of bed and proceeded to get dressed. Then, opening the bedroom door, he slipped quietly out into the corridor and quickly made his way downstairs towards the front door.

*

Meanwhile, inside the basilica, Dougie's nostrils flared with rage. Moving forward towards Brother Daniel, he roared. "I said, where is it?"

Blooded and bruised, the sobbing teenager began to crawl away in a frantic attempt to save himself. "Pl… Please, I… dinnae ken whit you're talkin about."

"Liar!"

As Dougie delivered another blow to the teenager's stomach with his foot, he turned, enraged, and swept his arm atop the altar, sending a burning candle, communion cup, bible and a heavy gold cross clattering down onto the stone floor of the church.

"Dougie!"

Swiftly whirling around, the Scotsman gazed towards the main entrance. Standing in the doorway, a bewildered Tom looked shocked at what he was witnessing.

"Dougie, what the hell's wrong with you? Have you lost your mind?"

For a moment, Dougie stared at his friend in silence, before turning towards the cringing teenager and snarled. "Stay back! This wee bastard has been lying tae us all along. One way or another I'm going tae get the truth oot o him."

With a look of utter abhorrence at his friend's behaviour, Tom closed the door and moved forward. "What? But he's just a boy."

Before Tom could complete his sentence, Dougie had already spun around and grabbed the teenager by the scruff of his neck and was now in the process of pulling him in closer. Now cheek to cheek, he scrutinised the boy's bruised face and hissed. "I'll ask ye once more. Where is it?"

"Pl... Please I dinnae ken whit you're talking aboot."

Dougie shoved the boy to the ground like a rag doll and snarled. "I've wasted too much time on this."

As he landed, Brother Daniel unexpectedly shrieked out in agony as his body began to twitch and spasm grotesquely on the ground, as if as an invisible electric current was being passed through it.

"Arghhh."

"Dougie! What the hell?"

Then, to Tom's revulsion, the boy's body slumped to the ground seemingly lifeless as Dougie now turned towards him with nostrils flaring like an angry bull. His eyes wide with hatred and fury. "As I said, I've wasted too much time on this."

The raspy voice that now spoke was new. Although it appeared to emanate from Dougie, his familiar soft Scot's accent had been replaced with a curious and disturbingly cold voice.

"What the hell…"

As a chill ran up his spine, Tom looked on in horror as the familiar shape of Dougie Allan began to transform, morphing into something hideous and frightening.

"Oh my God!"

Within moments Dougie Allan was gone and in his place stood a fearsome, cloaked creature. Its face pale and drawn with piercing, steely blue eyes.

"God can't help you here, my friend."

As its raspy voice echoed through the church, Tom stumbled backwards in fear and suddenly lost his footing, inopportunely causing him to trip and collapse onto the cold stone floor in pain. "Caius."

As the menacing creature edged closer, Tom looked on as its mouth abruptly curled upwards into a cruel grin and its eerie blue eyes glared directly down at him.

"Very good Tom."

"I don't understand. Where's Dougie?"

Before he could continue, Tom's throat suddenly began to constrict, almost as if an invisible force had grasped its hands around his throat and was slowly, but surely, tightening its grip.

"I don't know and frankly, I don't care."

B… but, no Argh…"

Gasping for air like a fish out of water, Tom endeavoured to edge away in a last frantic bid to escape the terrifying creature. But with each attempt, the tautness of the beast's grip around his throat simply increased to a point where he now could no longer keep his eyes open. Finally succumbing to nothingness, his last thought was "*Who's that?*" as another voice echoed through the basilica, "Let him go."

46

Sunday 23rd October - 9.20pm EST - 58 miles east of Sable Island

BELOW THE ROUGH waters of the North Atlantic, the enormous grey giant arrived on station to begin its investigation into the disappearance of the fishing vessel, *"The Sea Mist."* Below decks, in the *Officer's Mess*, a concerned looking Doctor Richard Quest glanced across a small table at Helen Moore, before re-folding a sheet of A4 paper and handing it back to Agent Reynolds.

"What is it Richard?"

Swallowing hard, Quest turned towards Helen and exhaled. "A message from Whitehall. Apparently, James Walton has suffered a heart attack and sadly passed away. Anne Petrie has been named as his successor."

Helen's eyes widened with a look of shock. "Oh Richard, I'm so sorry. I know you were friendly with him."

It was true, Quest had enjoyed a longstanding friendship with the Prime Minister. A friendship that had been defined in high school and then blossomed throughout his university years. While Walton had chosen to pursue a career in politics, Quest had been keen to follow his love of the sciences. After graduating, both men went their separate ways and it would be pure chance that years later they would be reunited at a charity dinner. After completing his PhD in physics with mathematics, Quest accepted a job as senior advisor in the Government's Communications Headquarters (GCHQ) in Benhall. It was there that Quest would later be introduced to a younger, but equally brilliant Professor Helen Moore.

"I can't believe he's gone. He didn't seem unwell at all the last time we met."

Reaching out across the table, Helen grasped hold of his hand.

"I guess you never know why these things happen. Sadly, there's nothing we can do about it. The Prime Minister gave us a task to complete and I think that it's our duty to honour him by seeing it through to completion."

Forcing his lips into a weak smile, Quest nodded and took a deep breath. "Of course, you're right."

Leaning back, Quest refocussed his attention back towards an anxious looking Mark Reynolds.

"Mr Reynolds? You still look uneasy. Is there something you're not telling us?"

For a moment, the agent awkwardly dropped his gaze before taking a deep breath and recomposing himself. "Actually, there was something I didn't mention."

"Oh?"

"As you are no doubt aware, UNITY has been growing in popularity at a startling rate."

As Quest gave a nod, it was now Helen who sat forward with curious interest.

"Of course."

"Well. It would appear that the British Government like so many, have made the precarious decision to join the *Red Council*."

Suddenly Helen's expression of concern transformed into one of alarm. "I'm sorry, I thought I just heard you say that our government has succumbed to a bunch of crackpot religious nuts."

"Helen..."

"What, I'm serious. That is what you're telling us Mr Reynolds, isn't it?"

Giving an uneasy nod, Reynolds walked across to the table and took a seat. "In our absence, these *crackpots* as you call them have become a formidable political power. They have literally won over the hearts and minds of the people. It's by no means simply the UK either, they've made considerable gains in over 50 countries. Officially, they boast over a billion followers. but authorities are now suggesting that it may be closer to two."

As Reynolds fell silent, Helen glanced across at Quest and scowled. "It all just seems a little fast, don't you think?"

"What do you mean?"

"Well, how can one organisation gain so much power so quickly? It's unnatural."

Reynolds shrugged his shoulders. "I agree professor, but just think about what's happened. There can't be a family alive who hasn't lost someone in those dreadful disasters. Perhaps it's simply a way for them to find some comfort in their lives."

Taking a breath, Reynolds climbed to his feet, glanced

down at the mountain of paperwork on the table before excusing himself and moving towards the door.

"Well, I can see you're both very busy. I'm sorry to have been the bearer of bad news. Now if you'll excuse me, I have a meeting with the XO. I'll stop by later and see how you're doing."

As Quest acknowledged the agent's departure, Reynolds opened the cabin door, and within seconds, he was gone, leaving the two scientists sitting alone at the table.

"Perhaps he's right. Helen."

"About what?"

"Perhaps it's simply our suspicious nature that's assuming the sinister in all of this. What if this UNITY is nothing more than they appear to be a godsend?"

Glancing down at the table, Helen picked up a copy of the symbol provided by Father Demarco. As her eyes surveyed the mysterious mark, she took a deep sigh and slowly exhaled. "I hope you're right Richard, I really do."

47

Monday 24th October - 4.05pm CET - Vatican City, Italy

AS AFTERNOON SUN trickled over the magnificent domes and spires of the newly restored St Peter's Square, Antonio Demarco sat at his desk in his small apartment feeling guilty. Not simply for failing to attend to his morning duties. But for allowing himself to succumb to his fears. The past few days had been challenging and finding strength had been an uphill struggle. After the sudden death of the holy father and a succession of unfortunate events revolving around Doctor Quest and Professor Moore, Antonio felt jittery. In the past, he would have simply sought out the counsel of his friend and mentor, Bouchard. But today, that was not possible. The Cardinal was busily preparing for the holy father's funeral and the upcoming conclave that would inevitably follow.

Picking up a glass of steaming hot espresso, the priest held it up to his nose for a moment to allow the aroma of the coffee to penetrate his nostrils. After taking a sip, he smiled to himself, not simply because the fragrance was strong and bitter, but because it was familiar and right now Antonio needed the familiar. As the warm liquid glided down his throat, Antonio reached out, picked up a TV remote control and pushed the on button. Moments later, the screen flickered to life and revealed a smartly dressed news reporter standing outside the United Nations building in New York city. Turning up the volume, the priest took another sip of espresso and leaned back to listen to the report.

"With only two days now until Michael's inaugural speech here in New York, both preparations and anticipation are running high. UNITY's Brother Thomas Weyn said the event will see leaders attend from all over the world. It will be history in the making. The big question on everyone's lips is, just what will Michael have to say?"

Staying with UNITY. Here in New York, Brother Weyn has announced that this evening, there will be services held in every local church worldwide to celebrate the upcoming arrival of a man whom many are already calling the new messiah."

"The church has also launched its new emblem. One which every member will be asked to exhibit in the form of a small tattoo. Not simply as an act of faith, but also as a symbol of peace and love for all mankind."

As the picture changed to reveal the symbol, Antonio practically choked on a mouthful of coffee in disbelief. Now on screen was the identical symbol that he'd been working on. The same three interlocking circles with the same two horizontal lines running through the centre. For a moment, time appeared to freeze for the astonished priest. As the picture flipped back to the reporter, Antonio picked up the remote control and pressed the off button.

As the picture turned to black, Antonio remained sitting, open-mouthed, as he glanced down at the piece of paper provided by Doctor Quest.

"*Dio Mio.*"

*

Monday 24th October - 10.45am EST - The White House, Washington DC

After attending an early press briefing, a fatigued President Hillary returned to the Oval office to gather his thoughts and prepare for an upcoming meeting with CIA Deputy Director, David Tyler. Glancing out of one of the room's large south-facing windows, the President watched with interest as two gardeners frantically attempted to gather leaves from the White House lawn. Their efforts being continually hampered by winds which whipped underneath their raked bundles, forcing the men to work harder.

Turning back towards the desk, the President took his seat and closed his morning copy of the Washington Post. After folding it neatly, he tossed it into a nearby waste paper basket. Taking his seat, he shuffled forward and was about to pick up the TV remote, when a sudden knock sounded on the door.

"Come in."

As the door swung open, Hillary was greeted by his personal secretary, Marjory Hicks. An efficient and an elegant New Yorker, Hicks had joined his administration team a year earlier. Once inside, she nodded and strode across to where the President was sitting.

"Here are the reports you requested Mr President."

"Thanks Marjory, anything else of interest?"

Nodding, the fortysomething year old placed the files down onto the desk and cleared her throat. "Well Sir, yes. Several things. Firstly, an invitation from the British Government to attend the funeral of Prime Minister Walton on Friday. Next, a request to meet the Brazilian ambassador and finally, a request from UNITY's Brother Weyn to meet for discussions."

"Discussions. For what exactly?"

Shrugging her shoulders, Hicks simply shook her head.

"I'm not sure Sir. If I had to guess, I'd say perhaps to see if the US will join *The Red Council*?"

For a moment, the President's eyes widened in horror. "You can't be serious?"

"Sir?"

"You think that I would sell his country to a bunch of religious lunatics?"

"No Sir. That's not what I was trying to imply at all."

As he raised his hand to object, Hicks fell silent and lowered her head in mild embarrassment.

"It's alright Marjory, everyone's entitled to their opinion. But for now, perhaps, we should get back to the business at hand. Could you please send in Mr Tyler at your convenience?"

Nodding politely, the assistant stepped backwards and headed for the door. "Of course, Mr President, right away."

After opening the door, she motioned to a smartly

dressed CIA Deputy Director to enter. The elderly Tyler rose promptly, nodded with gratitude and proceeded inside the Oval Office. Moments later, and after the door was closed, Hicks took a deep breath and shook her head in disappointment.

Once seated behind her own desk, Hicks took a moment to recompose herself before reaching down to pick up her small leather handbag. Once in her lap, she unclipped its gold-plated clasp, reached inside and pulled out her cell phone along with a small padded envelope. Glancing around to ensure that she was still alone, she opened the envelope and emptied out a small glass vial. Gazing at the innocuous object with a sense of nervous hesitation. Hicks appeared both daunted and repulsed by its simplistic ability to kill without a trace. Moments later, and as she placed the vial down, she took a deep breath, picked up the cell phone and dialled.

"Hello."

The familiar voice that answered was that of Brother Thomas Weyn. As she listened, the soft voice sounded calm and controlled. "Hello Sister, is everything going according to plan?"

Taking a deep breath, Hicks responded nervously. "I'm not sure about this brother, it seems very risky. What if I'm exposed?"

"Relax Sister, *Colodotoxin* is completely undetectable. He will look like all the rest, as if he'd simply become overworked. I can assure you it's quite painless. Hillary's death will be an enormous achievement for UNITY and for you personally. I promise that when Michael arrives, he will reward you."

As his words faded, Hicks gave a wry smile as images of wealth flooded into her thoughts. “Of course, Brother. I’ll see that its done right away.”

48

Saturday 23rd February 1710 - 3:35am - Fortingall, Highland Perthshire, Scotland

"I SAID, LET him go…"

As the storm raged outside, a solitary voice echoed throughout the basilica, drawing Caius's attention away from Tom's seemingly lifeless body. As the terrifying creature turned towards the voice, Tom suddenly coughed and spluttered in relief. His lungs beginning to fill with air, and as he slowly regained consciousness, his eyes flickered open.

Gradually refocussing, Tom could now make out the shape of the old priest, Father McRae, standing by the doorway at the far side of church. Too weak to shout out a warning, all Tom could do was look on in horror as the menacing cloaked figure moved ever closer to the old man. Surprisingly however, as it approached, the priest didn't flinch, and rather than flee, he simply smiled at the creature who now stood only meters away.

"It's been a long-time brother. I've been waiting for you."

As the old man wheezed, Caius drew breath and sneered. “I know.”

Glancing across at the lifeless body of Brother Daniel and then across towards Tom, the old priest shook his head disapprovingly.

“You didn’t need to kill the boy. He was innocent.”

“Innocent?”

Suddenly the creature’s blazing blue eyes bulged and its expression turned to one of resentment. “Innocent… he wasn’t innocent. He was as guilty as the rest of his filthy species. You said it yourself. They’re all guilty and should be removed. I’m simply speeding things up a little, that’s all. What’s the matter brother? Are you having second thoughts? I think that perhaps you’ve been living amongst them for too long.”

As the creature spoke, the old man gave a heavy sigh and began to walk slowly inside the church. “It’s true, I can’t deny it. I have become fond of them. They differ from other species and are capable of so much….”

“Yes, so much hatred, greed, and don’t forget the violence.”

The old man smiled and gestured towards Tom.

“Is that all you see? What about their music, compassion, faith? What about their love brother, does this not move you?”

At this point, Caius exhaled and gave a hollow laugh. “Ah love. I must admit, that’s my favourite. You see brother alongside love, comes devotion. Earn that along with faith and they can be manipulated like sheep.”

Suddenly Father McCrae’s expression turned solemn

and his tone turned threatening. "Brother, you were warned that it's forbidden to interfere."

Before the old man had completed his sentence, Tom's mouth fell open in disbelief as the priest suddenly began to fade and morph into an equally hideous creature.

"Oh, my god."

Now fully awake and noticing that the side door to the church was only meters away, Tom decided that this was his opportunity to escape. Pulling himself upwards, he began to crawl towards it. However, as he shuffled along the stone floor he caught sight of another problem. The burning candle which Caius had knocked off the altar earlier had hit the ground and its flame had ignited the edge of a thick velvet curtain. With billowing black smoke pouring into the basilica, Caius stepped towards his counterpart and barked.

"Don't be hypocritical brother, you've already interfered. We all have. For centuries, we've watched as their hatred and violence towards each other has grown. If they're not fighting in the arena, they're exterminating each other in the name of religion, race or politics. It's not that I disagree with the others, it's just that I see a different path for them, that's all."

Tom watched in disbelief as the two cloaked figures now began to circle each other like a pair of wolves, seemingly oblivious to the dangers of the fire.

"One in which they become your playthings?"

Caius suddenly stopped pacing, stepped forwards and sneered. "Precisely."

Glancing across at the burning curtain, the creature that was Father McRae shook his head with disappointment. "I won't let you do it brother. Whatever it is you're planning."

As the flames began to climb up the curtain, Caius looked over towards the body of Brother Daniel and licked his lips. "That's irrelevant for the moment. What does matter is what I came for."

McRae shook his head. "I don't have it and even if I did, do you honestly believe that I would give it to you?"

Huddled behind a wooden pew, Tom watched in astonishment as the two creatures glared at each other in preparation for what he now believed was an inevitable confrontation. Now noticing that the flames from the burning curtain were now dangerously close to his position. Tom found himself mesmerised, primarily out of a fear, but also out of obvious curiosity.

"No, but I think you're going to tell me where it is."

Glaring at his adversary in contempt, Caius snarled as a small, flickering white light began to emanate from between his fingers, followed by tiny sparks of electricity which popped and hissed in the semi-darkness.

"You're insane. I'm not going to fight you here."

Stepping forward, the creature pulled his palms apart to reveal a ball of pulsating light which began to flourish and expand. Sneering at McRae with a sense of ruthless revulsion, Caius raised the ball of electricity above his shoulders and hurled it directly at him. "Who said anything about a fight."

49

Monday 24th October - 4.40pm CET - Vatican City, Italy

SPRINTING ACROSS ST Peter's Square, Antonio Demarco rushed past groups of busy workmen, ignoring them as they hurriedly dismantled scaffolding and large swathes of plastic sheeting from around the newly restored *Maderno Fountain.* It had been decided by the Vatican hierarchy that a funeral service for the late holy father should take place within two days and thus, St Peter's Square would have to be cleared in order for the public to attend. Once through the *Porta Sant'Anna gate,* Demarco turned left past his beloved *church of Sant'Anna dei Palafrenieri* and continued past an astonished looking Swiss Guard who simply stood open mouthed as the Priest scuttled by, clutching an A4 brown envelope.

"La prego Padre, aspetti."

It was too late. Antonio was already past the guard and running at full speed towards the Vatican Library where he hoped his friend, Cardinal Bouchard, would be gracious enough to grant him an audience. Minutes later and after running up the stone steps of the *Archivio Segreto Vaticano*, Antonio arrived.

Sweating profusely outside the office of his mentor, Antonio took a moment to compose himself and exhaled slowly before knocking on the large door.

"Sì, avanti."

Responding to the invitation and familiar voice of his friend, Antonio swung the door open and as instructed, stepped in.

Inside, his expression turned to one of surprise as he realised that the Cardinal was not alone and was in fact engaged in what appeared to be a high-level meeting with several of his counterparts.

"*Oh mi dispiace Sua Eminenza*, I didn't mean to disturb."

As well as Bouchard, twelve other elderly cardinals were sitting around a large oak meeting table. Before Antonio had the opportunity to edge backwards and leave, Bouchard was on his feet, motioning the younger priest to come forward. "*Antonio, Va bene*, you're amongst friends here."

Nodding nervously, Antonio stepped forward and walked across the polished oak wooden floor towards his mentor. *"Sue Eminenze, credo che la maggior parte di voi conosciate mio amico, Padre Antonio Demarco."*

One of the elderly men, Cardinal Peter Randall nodded courteously and cleared his throat. "*Sì, infatti*, but why does he look so troubled?"

It was true. As the room fell silent, an anxious looking Antonio stepped nervously forward, placed his brown envelope down in front of Bouchard, who immediately reached over and picked it up. Moments later, it was open and after looking at the familiar symbol, Bouchard retook his seat and placed the document onto the desk. "*Dunque,* what seems to be troubling you my friend?"

"*Sue Eminenze*, haven't you seen the news this morning? UNITY have released an image of their new symbol."

Shaking his head, the Cardinal glanced over at several of the attendees seated around the table, before returning his attention to the three-circled symbol with the two horizontal lines running through the centre. *"No, ho paura di no."*

"*Sue Eminenze, non so come o perché,* but their symbol and this one are the same.

Suddenly, Bouchard's eyes widened. *Che cosa?! Di sicuro, deve essere una coincidenza?!"*

Antonio glanced around at the blank faces, placed his forefinger on the symbol and raised his voice. "*Sue Eminenze*, it's no mistake, they're the same. How is this possible?"

Suddenly Bouchard stepped forward, walked around to the front of the table and stood beside Antonio. Placing a firm hand on his shoulder, the Cardinal glanced awkwardly around the room, before lowering his voice and calmly motioning him slowly towards the door.

"*Antonio, amico mio*, the first thing we're going to do is not panic. I'm sure there's a perfectly reasonable explanation for all this."

"Ma, Sue Eminenze."

Now in the doorway, Bouchard pulled open the door and began to usher Antonio through it.

"I tell you what I'm going to do. Unfortunately, I must

finish our meeting, but I promise I'll call on you later and we can talk."

"Sì, certamente Sue Eminenze, grazie."

Delivering a nervous nod, Antonio departed, leaving a smiling Bouchard standing in the doorway. Once sure that Demarco was gone from the corridor, Bouchard's smile fell away as he closed the door. Taking a deep breath, he exhaled heavily and turned back towards the other cardinals. After gazing at them for several moments in silence, he proceeded to retake his seat around the table.

50

Saturday 23rd February 1710 - 3:55am - Fortingall, Highland Perthshire, Scotland

WITHIN THE WALLS of Fortingall church, the ball of effervescent white light thrown by Caius, struck the cloaked creature directly in the chest with such force that, as it exploded, it burst into a plethora of brilliant white and orange sparks. As McRae stumbled backwards in a momentary attempt to absorb the weapons energy, he took a deep breath, raised his hand and stepped forward. As he did, the remains of the spherical object surrounding him immediately began to dissipate and within moments it was gone.

"I told you, I won't fight you brother."

Fearfully watching the unfolding events from behind a nearby pew. Tom coughed and spluttered as he heard the distant shouts of "*Fire!*" coming from outside the church. In a bid to protect himself from inhaling more of the deadly black smoke now pouring from the fiery curtains, he placed the back of his hand across his mouth. Also, if things weren't bad enough, the smell had merged with the reek of the energy discharge to create a rancid odour, which made Tom gag as it violated his nostrils.

Glancing back towards the altar, Tom's expression turned to one of alarm as he watched huge flames now beginning to lick the wooden rafters of the basilica's medieval roof. With the remains of the curtains now collapsing and numerous portions of burning timbers falling down from all sides, Tom sensed that unless he moved from his hiding place, his life would be in jeopardy. So, without a second thought, he quickly closed his eyes, said a brief prayer and with all his strength, pulled himself upwards and stepped out into the aisle. Meanwhile, on the far side of the church, Caius stepped menacingly towards his counterpart and hissed. "You're weak brother. It doesn't have to be like this between us. Join me and together we could be invincible."

The cloaked creature that had been Father McRae shook his head in sombre displeasure. "You're delusional. You know our laws, we're not permitted to interfere."

Without a word, Caius suddenly spun around towards the horrified looking Tom Duncan on the far side of the church and snarled. "Look at him. Disgusting like the rest of his filthy species. You can't imagine how hard it's been for me to spend so much time with him. Perhaps I should just kill him now."

As he walked towards his foe, the second creature began to slowly morph back into the familiar shape of the old priest, Father McRae. Within seconds the metamorphosis had been completed and it was now the voice of the priest who spoke. "No, leave him alone."

"Then save him, and yourself for that matter. Give me what I want."

"Never. For you would only bring untold destruction with it."

As McRae's words faded, Caius cackled in mild satisfaction and again began to slowly circle the old man, like a wolf circling its prey. As he moved, a second ball of energy materialised between his fingers and began to crackle and fizzle in the semi-darkness.

"Then, as you die brother, know this. Humanity, like this world, is now mine and there's nothing you can do about it."

Before he could respond, the budding ball of white light that Caius was holding suddenly erupted into a blazing orb of orange which struck McRae directly in the chest at point blank range. Unlike the previous attack, this time the old man was hurled uncontrollably up into the air, only to come crashing down moments later onto the stone floor of the basilica, surrounded by a shower of shimmering orange and white sparks.

As the sparks dissipated from around McRae's body, he stumbled awkwardly forward, steadied himself for a moment and took a breath. Caius sprang forward, licking his lips in anticipation of one final attack on his nemesis. But this time, it was the old priest who had the upper hand. With incredible speed, McRae suddenly spun around and opened his arms wide. The wave of invisible energy that emanated from him was sudden and brutal. Striking Caius with such force, that he was flung twenty feet into the air. When he eventually crashed to the ground, the impact toppled over and smashed several of the church's wooden pews.

"Don't be a fool brother. You're aware of the prophecies. You can't win."

Rising from the stone floor like a deadly cobra, the furious Caius gave a hollow laugh and bellowed. "You're wrong brother. Don't you see. This is only the beginning."

With black acrid smoke now filling the church and burning roof beams crashing down from all sides, Tom decided to make a final bid for freedom. So, turning away from the nightmarish creatures, he made a sudden dash towards the safety of the basilica's side door. However, before it could be reached, the building and all its contents suddenly exploded into a brilliant white light. Moments later, Tom found himself surrounded in an eerie silence and engulfed within a blinding white light.

"What…"

51

Monday 24th October - 10.55am EST - The White House, Washington DC

PRESIDENT HILLARY AND Director Tyler sat opposite each other on either side of the Resolute desk in silence. After flicking through the classified report supplied by Tyler, the President placed it back inside its folder, leaned back and sighed. “Is there a possibility that you’re just being paranoid?”

Shuffling uncomfortably in his seat, Tyler shook his head. “No Mr President. Including the Pope, the Canadian Prime Minister and now the British Prime Minister. That’s eight unexplained, high-profile deaths in the past 14 days.”

“Unexplained?”

“All of them said to have suffered massive heart attacks.”

“So, how can that be unexplained? If the coroner’s reports all confirm that they died of natural causes, there is nothing to suggest anything sinister.”

Rising to his feet, Tyler began to pace anxiously back

and forth. "But it's not natural Mr President, don't you see?"

Taking a deep breath, the President also rose from his chair, turned towards the window and gazed out onto the White House gardens below. "So, let me get this straight. You're suggesting that there's an international conspiracy involving the assassination of prominent world leaders. Am I hearing you right, Mr Tyler?"

"Mr President you asked me to investigate UNITY."

Turning to face his Deputy CIA Director, the President shook his head and raised his voice angrily. "Yes, I did. But I didn't expect this bullshit. For Christ sake David, it sounds more like a plot from a spy novel than an agency report. I asked you to investigate UNITY and you informed me that they were squeaky clean. Now you're telling me what? That they could be involved in the greatest conspiracy in human history."

Tyler took a deep breath and exhaled. "Mr President don't you see, there's something out of place here? A religious organisation with political aspirations that appear to have no limits."

Turning back to his desk, the President shook his head. "Christ, next you'll be telling me that this whole thing is related to those pyramids or bizarre hooded creatures."

As the President retook his seat, Tyler stopped pacing and drew breath. "Well, what if they are?"

"What?"

"What if they are linked Mr President? What if there is a conspiracy to somehow attain global power. Are you really willing to take that risk and ignore my recommendations?"

The President remained silent, leaned back in his seat and frowned as Tyler returned to his seat opposite and gazed apprehensively at the President. "Mr President, I'm asking you this, not only as the Deputy Director of the CIA. But also as your friend. Don't attend Michael's inauguration in New York. Find some excuse... any excuse not to go and make it stick."

Suddenly, the President shivered, almost with a sense of fear, as he gazed across the desk at Tyler. For the first time, he sensed that there was something genuinely wrong. He'd known the man a long time and in all those years, Tyler had never taken a stance like this. Leaning forward, the President clasped his hands and placed them down onto the desk in from of him and exhaled. "Alright David. We'll do it your way. Go ahead and make the arrangements."

*

Date Unknown - Location Unknown

As Tom became slowly accustomed to the brilliance of the light and opened his eyes, he looked on in shock to discover that he was not alone. Standing a mere twenty meters away, the blurry image of the old priest, Father McRae, stepped forward into focus. With his worst fear now confirmed, Tom's first reaction was to turn and flee, but as he spun around to depart, the priest called out.

"Now Tom... what am I to do with you?"

For an instant, time appeared to stand still. Tom felt that he was momentarily unable to breathe, let alone speak. As he watched the outline of Father McRae take shape, his heart began to race and he started to sweat with fear. Although he had met the man, his mind was cautioning him that this was no man, it was a beast. Sensing that his could be his end, Tom closed his eyes and awaited the hand of fate.

"It's alright Tom, don't be afraid. You're safe now."

Taking a deep breath, he stopped, took a deep breath and turned around apprehensively towards the old man. "What's happening, where am I?"

The old man walked forward and gave him a reassuring smile. "I'm sorry, but I had to act. He would have killed you and I couldn't allow that."

"Who, or I guess I should ask, what are you?"

"That's a good question. It's a long story and a somewhat complicated one. We are known as keepers. We've been among you even before your world cooled and your race walked upright."

"You mean you're God?"

McRae shook his head and grinned.

"No, we are no more God than you. However, your species is only a very small part of a much bigger picture. For centuries, we've watched your evolution with concern. With each new generation, your species has become more violent and dangerous."

Tom stepped closer, looking confused. "Dangerous? To whom?"

Without directly answering his question, McRae simply sighed and continued. "All you need to know is that judgement was passed and a process was started."

"You mean the disasters?"

McRae nodded. "I didn't agree with that decision. Some

felt that humanity should be given another opportunity to recompense for its past transgressions."

Tom shook his head. "But not Caius?"

Shaking his head, the old man's smile dissolved and he groaned. "No. For reasons I can't discuss, he has been banished. His hatred and lust for power within our race have caused problems in the past."

"What problems?"

"It's complicated, but for one reason or another it appears he's targeted humanity and now your world is in great peril."

Eyeing McRae in apprehension, Tom opened his mouth to interrupt. Before he could speak, the priest continued. "I'm sorry Tom. I know this is a lot to take in, but if he does intend to enslave humanity, he will do it quietly and deviously. Subtly turning man against man and even fathers against their own sons."

Tom shook his head, raising his voice in alarm. "Then you have to stop him!"

The old man sighed and shook his head solemnly. "It's not that simple I'm afraid. You see, your civilisation has been given the unique gift of choice or self-determination. That, along with emotion is what drives you to tears when you listen to a piece of music, or the ecstasy you feel when you climb a mountain. Unfortunately, it's also responsible for your darker traits. Your ambition and animosity towards each other, simply because of colour, religion or language. These facets generate fear among you and it's that fear that drives your hatred and violence towards each other. It will be those traits that he will attempt to manipulate."

As he spoke, the old priest began to walk, and as he did, Tom followed by his side. “So, you're saying that we must do this, stop him I mean, by ourselves?”

McRae nodded. “Exactly. Right now, he is fashioning an army of followers to aid him in his grand vision.”

Tom stopped for a moment and raised his voice. “If that's true, what chance do the rest of us have?”

The old man suddenly pulled aside his cloak and hauled out an old, but familiar looking book and passed it to Tom. “Here. You'll no doubt recognise this from our earlier meeting? Think of it as an instruction manual.”

Staring at McRae, Tom appeared momentarily puzzled. “Instructions?”

“There's going to be a war Tom, and in a war, a general must gather his army. I need you to be my first soldier.”

“Me?”

“There are others out there who can help, but you'll need to find them. This book will help.”

Taking the ancient book from the priest, Tom gave a nod of gratitude and carefully began to turn its dilapidated pages. Moments later, he looked up in confusion.

“But, the language. I don't understand it. These symbols don't mean anything to me.”

Smiling, with a sense of newly found confidence, McRae placed his hand firmly on Tom's shoulder and smiled. “Don't worry, I'm sure you'll understand soon enough.”

Removing his hand from Tom's shoulder, the old man turned and abruptly began to walk away. As he moved, Tom shouted out in unease at the thought of being abandoned in the bizarre labyrinth.

“Wait, please don’t go. Don’t leave me here, I don’t know what to do. I need your help to get home.”

As he spoke, the silhouetted shape of the old man again began to change and morph. Moments later, the priest was gone. In his place stood the distinctive shape of one of the forbidding looking cloaked creatures.

“Don’t be afraid Tom. You are home.”

52

Monday 24th October - 6.55pm EST - 27 miles east of Sable Island

BENEATH THE MURKY waters of the North Atlantic, the crew of *USS Richmond* continued in its search for the wreck of the doomed sea vessel, *The Sea Mist.* Sitting at his station in sonar control, the 23 year old Petty Officer listened intently through his headset to the sounds of the living ocean. Searching for anything that might help solve the mystery of the fishing boat's unexplained disappearance. For most submariners, adventure was the attraction. Not for Matthew Woods. His career had been defined around sound. Ever since childhood in Pensacola, Florida he'd loved music. Listening to anything from a Mozart cello concerto to an invigorating Bruce Springsteen track. For Woods, the ocean was more than music, it was his own personal orchestra and as its conductor, he had to be able to separate the players from their instruments. Or in naval terms, the dolphins from the enemy.

Having been on duty for 3 hours, Wood's throat was becoming dry. Taking a deep breath, he leaned back in his seat and reached up to remove his headset. As he did, the soft sounds of the ocean suddenly changed. An extra sonar ping announced that there was something ahead. His first thought was that it was simply a fishing boat above. However, as the sound increased, so too did his interest. Reaching across, he turned up the volume on his console. The soft hiss of the ocean began to interchange with something else, a soft, but definite rhythmic hum.

As he listened intently, the lights suddenly flickered and he concluded that whatever this was, it was no vessel. The rhythmic signature was not a sound that he'd encountered before. Making the decision to follow procedure, he immediately sat forward and pushed his radio call button.

"Conn, sonar."

A moment later the radio crackled and responded as the familiar voice of the XO, Commander Tom Dalby.

"Sonar, Conn. What do you have Woods?"

"Conn, Sonar. New large contact ahead, approximately seven miles and closing."

*

For the XO, this was what the crew needed, although they'd only been at sea a short while. Finding a piece to the puzzle would provide a morale boost. "XO, Sonar. Can you identify?"

"Sonar, XO. No Sir, it doesn't appear to be a vessel of any kind… But it's big.'

"XO, Sonar, can you be more specific?"

For a moment, the radio remained quiet. Then Woods abruptly responded.

"Sonar, XO. Stand by."

Glancing to his right, the XO rubbed his chin and tutted just as the lights in the conn flickered once. "XO, Sonar, very well, standing by."

Giving a nod towards the *Richmond's* 33 year old Chief of the Boat, the XO took a deep breath as once more as the light of a nearby workstation flickered off and back on again. "What the heck? Chief of the Boat, dead slow ahead."

COB responded with an acknowledgement, stepped forward and cleared his throat. "Very good XO. Helm manoeuvring. Order dead slow ahead."

After carrying out the instruction, the young Helmsman nodded. "Aye Sir, reducing speed to dead slow ahead."

A minute or so later, the grey giant's propeller began to slow and as instructed the submarine began to reduce speed.

*

Whilst waiting patiently for the computer's analysis of the approaching object. Sonar Operator, Wood, continued to listen through his headset to the low rhythmic hum.

At first, he thought that it was possibly another submerged submarine, but as the minutes progressed, he concluded that it was something much bigger. As he leaned in closer to the instrument panel to increase the volume, the light above his workstation flickered and his display flashed up its result of the infrared and sonar scans, causing his mouth to fall open in shock. "Sonar, Conn."

After a moment silence the radio was answered. "Conn, Sonar. This the XO, what do have for me?"

For a moment, Wood simply gazed at the screen in awe, unable to find the words required to accurately describe what he was seeing. After fumbling with the microphone in his hand, he finally pushed the call button and responded. Sonar, Conn. Sir, I think you'll want to wake the Captain. I think you're both going to want to see this."

*

Monday 24th October - 6.55pm CET - Dubrovnik, Croatia

Sitting in solitude and surrounded by several flickering candles within one of the priory's small side chapels, Abbot, Vladimir Palovic meditated, while listening to the sound of rain drumming against the basilica's large stained glass window. Since he was a child, he'd loved the rain, not simply for its calming qualities, but also because it made everything feel clean. Having just finished reading a disturbing email from his friend, Antonio Demarco. The elderly Palovic was becoming deeply concerned about his friend's troubles in Rome. This, alongside the recent announcement of UNITY's introduction of a new logo that bothered him. A logo that bore an uncanny resemblance to the one provided by his friend. Sitting forward, the old man took a deep breath, opened his eyes, reached across and picked up a nearby book. Once in his hands, he flicked through its pages, until he stopped at the legend of *St. Hilarion and the Milini Dragon.* Scrutinizing the small painted picture, he glared at the knight's shield and rubbed his chin as a shiver ran up his spine.

"Jeste li dobro Oče?"

Turning towards the familiar voice in surprise, Palovic groaned. *"Sasha?"*

"Oprostite mi, but you were absent from evening meal. The others were becoming concerned and sent me to check on you."

As Palovic closed the book and placed it down, the pupil walked across to where the abbot was sitting and sat down next to him. "*Izgledate zabrinuto* Is everything okay?"

Palovic gave a forced smile. "*U redu sam Saša*, I suppose. I'm just worried about my friend, Antonio."

Noticing the book on the bench, Sasha sighed. "*Oprostite Oče*, but I see your looking at the book again and I wonder if you've told your friend of our discovery?"

As Palovic's head dropped, Sasha didn't need to ask a second time as the expression on the old man's face was clear. "*Ali zašto niste* Oče, it could be of great importance to him?"

Rising to his feet, Palovic placed a hand on the boy's shoulder and raised his voice. "Because my dear Sasha, there's something very wrong here. The knight's shield in the painting and this UNITY church. A faith that's risen from nothing and now one that ascends beyond even our own church."

"*Možda*, they're just lucky father."

"*Ne Saša*, don't you see that's impossible. True faith is cultivated over thousands of years. It takes time to nurture, with missionaries, books and learning. Whereas this so-called religion has appeared from nowhere in what, two years. How is that even possible?"

For a moment, the boy glanced across at the burning candles and shrugged his shoulders. "I don't know Father."

Palovic exhaled and began to quickly pace back and forth. "*Točno*. The UNITY symbol, the picture in the book and now my friend's troubles. I tell you my young pupil, I suspect that the coming together of these elements is no coincidence."

"*Ali* to what end father?"

The old man shook his head and then snapped his fingers.

"*Ne znam* but come Sasha, come and help me fashion an email to my friend. Perhaps an invitation to visit us here in the priory will lift his spirits and help us find some answers to our questions."

53

Monday 24th October - 1.40pm EST - 27 miles east of Sable Island

"THIS IS RICHARD Delaney reporting for CNN. These are the headlines for Monday 24th October. With less than two days to go before world is introduced to Michael, preparations at the United Nations are in their final stages. With invited guests including world leaders, scientists, religious leaders and even some monarchy. Security is running high. Of course, if you can't make it to the event in person, don't worry. CNN will be on hand to broadcast the entire event live from New York, starting at 5pm.

Staying with UNITY. Spokesman, Brother Weyn, has announced that any followers who have not yet received their faith tattoo are not to panic. Due to unprecedented demand, it was feared by some followers that they would miss the Wednesday midday deadline and fall out of favour with the church. However, Brother Weyn, has announced that the faithful should not panic and that anyone who wants to receive the blessing will be able to do so.

Finally, in Moscow, President, Sergey Belanov, today

announced that he was delighted that his government had voted unanimously to become a full member of the Red Council. He said the decision would end years of distrust and hostility between Russia and the west and would further aid UNITY's vision for peace and prosperity for all.

In other news…"

As the lights again flickered inside the *Officer's Mess*, Mark Reynolds picked up the remote control, pushed the off button and returned the device to the table. As the screen went black, Reynolds leaned back in his seat and sighed. "We picked up that broadcast about an hour ago. Events do appear to be moving faster than I anticipated."

For a moment, the two scientists simply sat facing each other on opposite sides of the table in silence, before Helen Moore sat forward with an increasingly confused expression on her face.

"I'll say. What about the United States? Have they joined this *Red Council*?"

Reynolds shook his head. "No, at least not yet anyway."

Taking a sip of coffee, Doctor Quest closed the book he had been studying and leaned forward with interest. "Mr Reynolds, this tattoo that the reporter kept referring to, what exactly is it?"

Suddenly Reynolds looked uncomfortable and his head dropped.

Glancing towards Quest with a look of concern and then back to Reynolds, Helen Moore sat forward and grasped hold of the agent's arm. "Mr Reynolds… Mark, what is it? Please tell us."

Swallowing hard, the agent looked up and pointed towards a nearby piece of paper and to the mysterious symbol written on it. The same three rings and two horizontal line symbol given to Doctor Quest by the Italian priest, Demarco.

"It's that symbol Doctor, that's the new UNITY symbol."

At that moment, Helen's face turned an unhealthy shade of pale and her lip began to quiver.

"B… But how can that be? Richard how is that possible?"

Releasing the agents arm, Helen's expression turned to one of dread as she ensued to cover her mouth with her hand. Then, appearing to be become nauseous, she quickly reached across the table for a nearby glass of water. After gulping down several mouthfuls, she placed the glass down and Quest leaned in closer to offer support. "Now, let's all just slow down here for a moment shall we. Helen nobody is suggesting that this is anything more than it appears to be, a coincidence."

Looking upwards, Helen's expression turned to one of horror, tinged with anger. "What! that's bullshit. Richard don't be so naive, of course there has to be a link."

Suddenly Helen's voice trailed away as a knock sounded and the door to the *officer's mess* abruptly swung open. Standing in the doorway was the boat's commanding officer, Captain Brad Butler, followed by a stern-faced XO, Commander Tom Dalby. As the two officers entered, the three civilians rose to their feet as a sign of respect.

"That's alright folks, please be seated."

As the Captain's low, gravelly, southern accent reverberated around the room, the XO stepped forward and placed an orange folder down onto the table.

"Okay Tom, do you want to bring them up to speed?"

Nodding respectfully, Dalby remained standing whilst the Captain joined the others around the table. Once Butler was seated, Dalby took a deep breath, opened the orange folder and took out several graphics.

"Yes Sir. Agent Reynolds, Professor, Doctor I believe we may have solved the mystery of the missing fishing boats. A short while ago we detected a large object on sonar. After carrying out an investigation, which included both sonar, thermal and 3D plotting, we believe this may be the culprit.

As the XO rotated the graphics towards the two scientists, Doctor Quest suddenly sat forward with an astonished expression. "Oh my God. Helen, it's a pyramid."

*

Monday 24th October - 7.55pm CET - Vatican City, Italy

Inside his small Vatican apartment, Father Antonio Demarco was uneasy, having read yet another message from his friend Vladimir Palovic. In the email, the abbot expressed deep concerns for his friend's wellbeing, as well as for his current state of mind.

Upon completion, Antonio decided to lay down on the bed to gather his thoughts. With his eyes closed, Antonio smiled inwardly at the kind invitation to visit Dubrovnik. It had been many years since he'd visited his friend, and Croatia for that matter. Perhaps a short vacation would help clear his mind and provide some well needed rest. As he began to dose off, Antonio was unexpectedly disturbed as a knock came to his door. Getting up off the bed, he ran his hand through his hair in a vain attempt to make himself look half presentable, before moving towards the door. "*Sì*, who is it?

After a moment of silence a familiar voice responded. "*Sono io, Antonio, Jean Luis.*"

On hearing Bouchard's voice, he took a sigh of relief before reaching for the door handle.

"*Certo, Sua Eminenza.*"

As the door swung open, he was greeted by a troubled looking Cardinal Bouchard who immediately stepped inwards and placed a hand on his young friend's shoulder. "Good evening Antonio. After our meeting earlier, I was worried and wanted to stop by and see how you were doing. I hope I'm not disturbing you?"

Nodding enthusiastically, Antonio stepped aside and welcomed the elderly Cardinal inside.

"*Niente affatto Sua Eminenza*, please come in."

Once inside, Antonio closed the door and invited his friend to take a seat by his desk. "*Prego, Si accomodi, Sua Eminenza*. Would you care for some tea?"

Shaking his head, the old man pointed eagerly towards a nearby bottle of red wine sitting atop a small side table. "Perhaps something a little stronger?"

Giving his friend a grin, Antonio picked up the bottle and proceeded to fill two glasses with the red liquid. After returning to his own seat, he handed one across to the Cardinal and took a sip from his own glass. "*Salute.*"

After gulping down a mouthful, the Cardinal set his glass down and breathed heavily. "So how are you my friend? I must admit I was a little concerned earlier."

Antonio gave an uneasy smile and shook his head. "*Mi perdoni Sua Eminenza*, it was simply the shock of seeing the similarity between my symbol and the UNITY logo. In hindsight, I'm sure it was just a coincidence."

Suddenly the cardinal's expression turned serious. Leaning in closer to Antonio, Bouchard lowered his voice. "*Ma,* what if it's not, my friend."

"*Che cosa*?"

"What if it's not your imagination and this is no coincidence?"

"*Cosa intende dire Sua Eminenza*?"

Taking a deep breath, the Cardinal reached across, picked up his wine glass and took another sip. After returning the glass to the table, he again leaned in closer. "Antonio, I didn't want to say anything earlier, but I too have noticed several priests acting strangely."

"*Davvero?*"

"For some time now I think I'm being watched. Some of the senior cardinals are even suggesting that the Catholic church should join this *Red Council*."

Suddenly Antonio's mouth fell open in shock. "*No. Non è vero*."

Raising his hand to temporarily silence Antonio, Bouchard took a deep breath and continued.

"*Sì* Antonio and there's more."

"*Che cosa, Sua Eminenza?*"

Bouchard now lowered his voice, almost to a whisper. Antonio leaned in closer to hear.

"The archives Antonio. I've just discovered that they've been broken into."

"*Cosa!*"

"*Non so* what they were looking for. But I must confess I'm beginning to feel a little uneasy myself."

Rising to his feet, Antonio began to pace anxiously back and forth. "Have you spoken with the Swiss Guard Eminence?"

Bouchard nodded. "*Sì and* they've agreed to increase security measures, in and around the Vatican."

"I see."

"*Dimmi una cosa amico mio*, this symbol of yours, are you any closer to discovering its meaning?"

Antonio stopped pacing and glanced at his friend, groaned in mild defeat. "*No, Sua Eminenza*. I've even sent a copy out to a colleague, but, like myself, he's had no success."

Bouchard appeared disappointed. "*È un peccato* my friend. I will continue to pray for your success."

Antonio nodded with gratitude. "*Grazie Sua Eminenza*."

As the Cardinal climbed to his feet in preparation to leave, Antonio suddenly stepped forward.

"*Sua Eminenza,* while you're here, I have a small favour to ask."

Bouchard nodded and smiled warmly. "*Certo Antonio, di cosa si tratta?*"

"*Mio amico* a Dubrovnik, has asked me to come and visit him at the priory and I thought that it would be an opportune moment to take some rest."

Placing his hand on Antonio's shoulder, Bouchard smiled broadly. "*Ecco* that's probably the best suggestion I've heard all day. Go ahead and inform your friend, I'm sure we can spare you next week."

It was as if a weight had been removed from Antonio's shoulders. Grasping his friends hand, he shook it warmly and smiled with gratitude. "*Grazie Sua Eminenza*, I can't tell you what this means to me."

Opening Antonio's door, the cardinal smiled and shook hands once more before turning to leave. "*Prego*. I'll continue with my investigation and I'll let you know if I discover anything of significance."

As Antonio waved goodbye, the door closed, leaving Bouchard standing alone outside Antonio's apartment. As his smile slipped away, the cardinal made his way down a nearby stairwell. Once outside and confident that he would not be seen. He reached inside his coat, pulled out his cell phone and proceeded to dial a number. Moments later the call was picked up. "*Pronto*."

"*Sì*."

"*Sono Bouchard*. I'm afraid we'll have to deal with this problem ourselves, begin preparations. It would also appear that my friend is planning a trip to Dubrovnik. Find out who he's talking to."

"*Capisco*."

As he ended the call, Bouchard took a deep breath, returned his phone to his coat pocket and strode silently away down a narrow side street towards his apartment.

54

Monday 24th October - 2.40pm EST - 25 miles east of Sable Island

THE *RICHMOND'S* CREW waited anxiously for news on the discovery of a mysterious underwater object. Since the captain and XO had become engaged in a meeting with the two British scientists, whispers had begun to circulate around the boat that something alien had been discovered. Although unsubstantiated, this rumour had naturally generated some disquiet amongst the crew. This was further heightened by the recent onset of an inexplicable phenomenon which had manifested itself in the form of flickering lights and irregular power losses, affecting several of the submarine's minor electronic systems.

Huddled around a table in the mess hall, six crewmen were engaged in a heated discussion as to what the object could be.

"I'm telling you Jackson, it's alien. I'll bet it's some sort of spacecraft and I'll bet it's responsible for all those ghost ships down there. They don't call this place, the graveyard of the Atlantic for nothing you know."

"That's bullshit and you know it. It's probably just a piece of junk."

"Well how do explain the lights and stuff. You've got to admit that it's pretty weird."

Normally, Michael Hays, a 19 year old junior technician from Boston, wouldn't have got into such a heated discussion. But today was no ordinary day.

"Pipe down Hays, next you'll be telling us it's all just little green men."

Before the youngster could respond, the room suddenly fell quiet as a nearby hatch opened and the intimidating shape of the *Richmond's* Chief of the Boat stepped into the room. The New Yorker, Karssen Beck, was an imposing figure with a formidable frame. The man appeared as if he would be more suited to fighting in a wrestling ring than serving aboard a submarine. Despite his shape however, he had a solid reputation for fairness and for being a valued member of the crew.

After walking up to a nearby food station, Beck collected a tray and helped himself to a couple of slices of pepperoni pizza and a side salad, before taking a seat at an adjacent table.

"Guys, don't stop talking on my account. I'll be thinking that you're talking about me."

As the lights flickered and the crew dispersed from around the adjacent table, Hays got to his feet and stepped across to where the chief was sitting.

"Chief, can I ask you a question?"

Tearing off a piece of Pizza and stuffing into his mouth. Beck rolled his eyes, gave a nod of approval and continued chewing as Hays cleared his throat. "The object out there. The men are suggesting that it's something alien."

Swallowing the pizza, the big man glanced up at the youngster and was about to answer, when the PA system crackled and burst into life. "Chief of the Boat, please report to the officer's mess."

Rolling his eyes in mild annoyance, Beck swallowed the remainder of pizza before wiping his mouth with a napkin and climbing to his feet.

"Son, don't be concerned with rumors, just deal with the facts. I promise, if there are any aliens out there. I'll be the first to let you know."

As Beck strode away, the youngster gave a wry smile and as the mess hall door slammed shut. He was now left alone and felt somewhat embarrassed. "Yes Sir."

*

One deck above in the *Officer's Mess*, Doctor Richard Quest glanced at Agent Reynolds before looking back to the Captain in dismay and shook his head. "Captain, you can't be serious. We've come this far, we must go on. We need to know what this thing is."

Shaking his head, Butler coughed once and raised his hand to cut Quest off. "I sympathize with your situation Doctor, but you need to understand mine."

Turning the orange folder around, he flipped through a couple of pages then turned it back towards the two scientists and tapped his forefinger on the page.

"This is a big boat and that trench isn't designed for a vessel of this size, Doctor. It would be foolhardy for us to even try. I refuse to put this boat in any unnecessary danger."

"Well what about divers then?"

As a knock sounded at the door, the boat's XO leaned forward and shouted "Enter."

As instructed, Beck stepped into the room and strode across to where the group was sitting. Nodding respectively at the civilians, he then turned to the Captain and saluted. "You wanted to see me Sir?"

"Indeed, I did COB, thank you. It would appear, that we're required to move in a little closer for our two scientist friends here to investigate the object. Now, as the boat is obviously too large to navigate through that trench, I suggest you ready the mini sub for launch."

Taking a deep breath, Beck nodded and pursed his lips.

"Do you want me to assign some men Sir, or do you have someone in mind?"

Turning to his right, Butler gave a nod towards the XO and then glanced across the table at the scientists and Mark Reynolds.

"No, the XO will take lead, if that's alright with you Tom?"

Delighted that the Captain had faith in his abilities, Dalby gave a firm nod. "Of course, Sir."

Then, turning to the civilians, Butler lowered his gravelly southern tone. "I'm assuming you all want to go?"

As the trio gave a silent, but enthusiastic nod, the Captain looked at Reynolds and took a deep breath. "Very well. Mr Reynolds, as you know, the mini sub has space for only six. Can I assume therefore, that with your Naval experience you'll not mind participating as a crew member whilst you're aboard?"

Glancing once at the two scientists, Reynolds shrugged his shoulders and gave a nod.

"No problem Captain."

As the Captain rose out of his seat to depart, the civilians followed the lead of the XO by also duly standing in respect. "Very good and while we're on the subject. My officer oversees the mission. For your safety and his, I ask you to all follow his instructions to the letter while you're on board. Is that clear?"

As the two scientists nodded nervously in unison, the Captain smiled and turned towards the door. "Thank you."

As the door opened, Butler tutted in annoyance as the room's lights again flickered momentarily.

"Oh, and that's another thing. Can someone find out what's causing these damn power fluctuations, it's beginning to get annoying."

As the Captain marched away, Dalby turned to COB, and as the two men's eyes met, the XO was confident that the problem would soon be investigated. "Absolutely Sir."

Turning inwards to the scientists, Dalby smiled and clapped his hands. "Well then. Tomorrow's going to be an interesting day."

55

Monday 24th October - 8.05pm EST - The White House, Washington DC

AS SHE WAITED for the President to complete his phone call with the Chinese Premier, Marjory Hicks, Hillary's personal secretary finished tidying her desk and prepared to leave for the evening. Before departing, she walked across to a small fridge situated in the corner of her office, took out a bottle of spring water and unscrewed its cap. Placing the bottle and cap down, she then strode back across to her desk, opened its top drawer and took out a small padded envelope. Glancing around to ensure that she wasn't being watched, she opened the envelope and produced a small glass vial. After taking a deep breath, she momentarily contemplated her next move with an obvious sense of hesitation. Then, slowly exhaling, she returned to the table, cautiously broke the vial's seal and poured its deadly contents into the water. As she replaced the cap, she gazed in awe as the toxin dispersed innocuously into the water without trace. Finally placing the empty vial in her pocket, she gazed at the bottle once more. Partly with a sense of culpability for her part in the murder of the President of the United States, but also with pride, knowing that Hillary's death will pave the way for the US to become a member of the *Red Council.*

Moments later and with the water bottle in hand, she approached the Oval office, gave a smile to the secret service agent stationed outside the door and then proceeded to knock. "Come in."

As instructed, Hicks opened the door and gave the President a warm smile as she strode across to the Resolute desk.

"Mr President, I'm sorry to disturb you. I was just on my way home and I thought you'd like some fresh water."

Wearing no tie and sitting with his sleeves rolled up, Hillary stretched his arms out wide and gave a yawn. "Thank you, Marjory. That's very thoughtful."

As she placed the bottle down on a small side table, she stepped in little closer.

"How was the call with the Chinese Sir? I hope it was productive."

Scowling, the President moaned. "Not really, the President informed me that China has, this evening, petitioned UNITY to become a full member of the *Red Council.* What the hell is happening Marjory? I tell you, I think the whole world's gone mad."

"I wonder, Mr President. Is it such a bad thing? I mean joining the *Red Council,* especially after what's happened in the world. Those terrible disasters and with so many dead."

Suddenly the President frowned and shook his head angrily. "Never. Not under my presidency. We've come too far, sacrificed too much to give it all away. I tell you I won't allow it."

As Hillary fell silent, Hicks stepped back and smiled. "Well Mr President I can see you've a lot to think about. If you don't mind I'll call it a day and say goodnight."

Taking a deep breath, the President leaned back in his seat and smiled. "Of course, Marjory I'm ranting. Forgive my outburst, it's been a difficult day. Goodnight."

"Goodnight Mr President."

As she turned and left the room, Hicks closed the door and her fabricated smile fell away. Stopping in the hallway for a moment to take a breath, she then gritted her teeth with fury, before muttering "Fool," under her breath and continuing towards the main entrance. Moments later and after saying goodnight to a secret service agent, she was outside, feeling proud that her action would soon change the course of history.

*

Tuesday 25th October - 2.40am CET - Vatican City, Italy

Lying in the darkness, Antonio's eyes flickered.

"Dio mio… Padre."

With an awful sense of dread growing inside him, Antonio quickly turned back towards the restaurant. Running back along the crumbling street, the air became dense with thick white dust and he narrowly escaped being hit by blocks of falling concrete and twisted steel from above. With his eyes stinging and gulping desperately for air, Antonio moved quickly through a sea of blooded and bewildered faces. In the thick of the chaos, all Antonio could think about was his Father. Whatever the issues that he had been between them were now gone. Antonio didn't care anymore – he just wanted to reach him, to be with him. He had to be alive, he just had to be.

Antonio felt like he he'd been running for hours, but it was only for a couple of minutes. As he approached the Ristorante Maria, the shaking had now subsided and the scene had become still once more. In front of him, the normally well-maintained family restaurant had been replaced with a grotesque pile of rubble, broken glass and twisted steel. In the silence, he screamed out *"Padre!"*

Moving slowly through the nightmare, Antonio breathed heavily as he laboured to lift tables, concrete blocks and heavy beams away. With each step taken and each dead body passed, his hopes of finding his father diminished. Standing still with a sense of helplessness and with his eyes filled with tears and stinging dust, Antonio stood amid the rubble. He lowered his head and began to pray. "Father in heaven if you can…"

"Antonio?"

The voice was weak, but there.

"Antonio…"

Yes, there it was again, *"Padre."*

Turning quickly, Antonio listened intently, desperately trying to home in on the sound. Then suddenly there he was, his father, just ahead lying on the ground covered in rubble. But as Antonio approached, his elation turned to sadness. Kneeling by his father's side, Antonio could see that his father's crushed chest lay beneath a hefty steel beam. With a heavy heart, he realised that even if he could conjure up a miracle to move the beam, his father would probably not survive. Taking out a handkerchief, Antonio began to wipe blood and dust off his father's face.

"*Padre…* I'm sorry, I'm so sorry."

Gazing up at his son, the old man wheezed and winced in pain. "D… Don't be Antonio. We all made our choices. As it happens, I made some bad ones and I'm sorry for that now. But, now you must, listen Antonio. The sym… symbols…"

As he wiped tears from his eyes Antonio shook his head and interrupted, "No… Father, don't worry about that now, just lie still. Help will be here shortly."

Gasping heavily the old man gave a weak smile and shook his head, "No. You listen, Antonio. Th… the symbols. Antonio, they're not symbols: They're numbers!"

Antonio held on to his father's hand for the last time as Pietro Demarco wheezed and took one final breath. "No…"

Suddenly Antonio's eyes flickered open and he sat up in bed perspiring heavily. For Antonio, the past two years had been arduous. After many years of suffering the wrath of his father for abandoning a potentially promising career in mathematics to join the church, Antonio had endeavoured to repair the rift between himself and his father. Despite his efforts, it soon became apparent that his father was not interested. That was until Antonio sought him out to ask his assistance in solving a mathematical mystery. The Puzzle came in the form of a mysterious set of symbols sent to him by a British government scientist. A puzzle which would ultimately be solved in the last few moments of his father's life. Since that awful day, Antonio had lived with the constant pain of remorse. Wishing more than anything that he could turn back time and bring his father back.

As a tear ran down his cheek and with a heavy heart, Antonio swung his legs out onto the floor. Sitting on the edge of his bed, he took a deep breath and was about to climb to his feet when he suddenly heard his father's words echoing through his mind. *"No. You listen Antonio. The symbols. Antonio, they're not symbols: they're numbers!…"*

"Numbers…"

Suddenly realising that he had the answer to the puzzle all along, Antonio quickly jumped up, slipped on his dressing gown and walked across to his desk. Once his laptop had been powered on, he brought up the photo of the 3 ringed circles with the 2 horizontal lines running through the centre.

"Wait. What if I'm looking at this in the wrong way?"

For Antonio, the phrase *the wrong way*, literally meant, *"the wrong way."* After his father's death, he recalled working on the puzzle in a nearby police station. At the time, he'd all but given up hope of finding a solution, when a sudden trick of the light stretched out the symbols into what appeared to be a set of binary numbers. "*What if?*" the symbols needed to be distorted in some way. Gazing at the symbol on screen, one thought did come to mind. Although he knew the basics of computing, photo manipulation was not his forte.

Then, Antonio had the idea of taking a printed copy of the symbol given to him by Doctor Quest. Opening the top drawer of his small desk, he reached inside and pulled out a torch. He had the idea that if he could somehow shine a light through the paper, it would produce shadows on the wall. By reproducing the result of that evening in the police station, he hoped that it would reveal something useful. As he gazed at the picture on screen, he reached across to a bottle of water and proceeded to pour himself a glass. After gulping down a couple of mouthfuls, he reached across for the folder from Doctor Quest. After opening it, he flicked through its contents looking for the symbol. After a few moments, he realised it wasn't there.

"Oh no."

Rolling his eyes in annoyance, he groaned, recalling that the last time he had it in his possession was in Bouchard's office. Concluding that he must have left it on his friend's desk, he decided that his best course of action would be to simply print out another copy. Pushing his chair back, Antonio leaned across his desk and switched on his printer. After checking the paper level, he returned to his laptop and clicked the print button. As he waited, Antonio reached for his glass of water and gulped down another mouthful, just as the printer began its work. As Antonio rose to his feet, the printer suddenly began to grind and screech as several sheets of paper became jammed.

"Damn it…"

Cursing the printer in frustration, he rushed across and pressed its cancel button several times. After several moments of impatience, the printer eventually fell silent and Antonio flipped open its lid and pulled out the miss-fed sheets. Without warning, he reeled back in shock, dropping the mangled pile of A4 sheets of onto the ground. He then knelt and reluctantly turned over the top sheet. As the image appeared, he abruptly recoiled in disbelief, placing his hand over his mouth in horror. The faulty print job had printed the symbol, but had grotesquely stretched and altered its shape. As Antonio picked up the sheet and took a deep breath, everything suddenly became clear. The extraordinary events, the disasters, the UNITY church and the symbol. A symbol that was no longer merely just three circles and two lines. But one which had been transformed into an image that now made perfect sense. There, before his eyes. The image denoted three simple identical numbers. Three numbers that for over two thousand years had personified fear and terror in the hearts of men. For these numbers would signify the end of days and the rise of the beast.

The numbers were 666.

56

Tuesday 25th October - 3.35am CET - Dubrovnik, Croatia

AT FIRST, THE knocking sounded like faint drumming in the back of his mind. But as Vladimir Palovic turned over in bed, he sluggishly began to regain consciousness and realised that it was coming from the door. As another knock sounded, the old man's eyes flickered open and within moments he was awake.

"*Da*… Just a moment."

Taking a deep breath, he grudgingly threw back his bed clothes, swung his legs outwards and switched on a nearby side light. As its soft yellow glow began to illuminate the small room, he got out of bed, wrapped himself in a dressing gown and put on a pair of slippers. Taking another breath, he then walked slowly across to the door, paused for a moment and turned the handle. As it swung open, Palovic shook his head in displeasure at being woken in the middle of the night.

"*Saša, što je, što se desilo?* Do you have any idea what time it is?"

Without responding, the youngster stepped forward with a grim expression. "I'm sorry to disturb you Father, but you have a phone call."

"A phone call?"

For a moment, the old man was slightly taken aback. Receiving a phone call in the middle of the night was not something of a regular occurrence.

"*Da Oče,* it's your friend from Rome, Father Demarco. He sounds rather upset."

Realising that the call was potentially urgent, Palovic nodded solemnly at his pupil and patted him on the shoulder. "*Ebbene Saša*, let's go and see what's troubling my friend."

Seconds later, and with Palovic's door closed, the pair strolled quietly down a long dimly lit hallway. At the top of a large staircase, the boy suddenly motioned the elderly abbot towards the library.

"In here Father, you can take the call in here."

Once inside the library, Palovic stepped across to a small side table, pulled out a nearby seat and proceeded to sit down. Then, taking a deep breath, he leaned forward, picked up the rather antiquated looking handset and placed it to his ear. "Hello. Antonio, Is that you?"

At first the voice on the other end of the line sounded shaky and emotional, but then the caller appeared to pull himself together.

"V... Vladimir..."

"Antonio my friend, what is it? Is there something wrong?"

After a short silence, Demarco began to speak.

"*Vladimir, il... il simbolo.* I think I've managed to work out what the symbol means."

Turning to his young pupil, the old priest smiled. "That's good news my friend."

"No, no... you must listen."

Palovic's smile slipped away as he realised that, from Demarco's emotional state, whatever he had discovered, it was not good.

"It's alright my friend. What is it? What have you found?"

"I began to think that perhaps I was looking at the symbol the wrong way. You know the wrong angle or perspective or something. I thought that I'd print off a new copy. But unfortunately, the printer jammed and then when I pulled out the paper, the result was right there, as clear as day."

As Antonio's voice began to tremble again, Palovic took a deep breath and slowly exhaled. "What was it Antonio? What did you see?"

For a few moments, the line remained silent, apart from the occasional crackle until Antonio could be heard swallowing hard. "*Numeri...* it was numbers."

As he listened intently, Palovic felt a sudden shiver run up his spine. Almost as if he knew what Antonio's next words were going to be. "What were the numbers my friend?"

Again, the line crackled and remained silent for a few seconds, until Antonio finally found his voice. "The mark of the beast. 666."

As the words left his lips, Antonio began to suddenly

fall apart and become hysterical. "Wh… what am I going to do Vladimir? I'm so afraid."

For some reason Palovic didn't fall apart. Instead, he took a deep breath, glanced across the table at his young pupil and sighed. "Antonio… Shh it's alright my friend. Don't panic. Does anyone else know about this discovery?"

"No."

"Alright. Now Antonio listen, this is what you're going to do. Tomorrow you're going to come to Dubrovnik and visit us here in the priory. You'll be safe here and we can work together to find out what all of this means. Will you do that for me, my friend?"

After another pause, Antonio recomposed himself and exhaled. "*Sì*, I'll come."

"Okay then, for now try and get some sleep. Once you know your travel plans, let me know and we will prepare a room for you."

Antonio gave a sigh of relief. "Ti ringrazio, Vladimir, I really appreciate it. I'll see you tomorrow."

"Goodnight my friend."

*

Tuesday 25th October - 3.50am CET - Vatican City, Italy

Sitting inconspicuously outside Antonio's apartment building in a small white van, two shadowy figures listened in as he finished his phone call with Vladimir Palovic. Dressed as workmen in white coveralls, the two men turned to each other as the call ended and grinned. Satisfied that they had what they came for, the taller of the two men slipped off his headphones and clicked the stop recording button on his laptop.

Reaching into his pocket, he pulled out a packet of cigarettes and took one out. After lighting it up, he glanced up at Palovic's apartment, and took a long draw on the cigarette. A moment later he turned to his colleague and exhaled. "È quello… that's the one. Let's go."

After tossing his cigarette out of his window, the tall man sat forward, and started the van's engine. Moments later they could be seen heading towards St Peter's Square, but after a sharp turn left, they had disappeared and were soon nowhere to be seen.

57

Tuesday 25th October - 5.35am EST - The North Atlantic, 18 Miles East of Sable Island

ONE AND HUNDRED and twenty meters below the Atlantic Ocean, the crew of the *USS Richmond* made its final preparations to launch its six person DSV or Deep Submersible Vehicle, *"Wanda."* Its mission was simple: survey and investigate a mysterious submerged canyon which supposedly contained a bizarre underwater pyramid and determine if it, or something else, was responsible for the sinking of two Canadian fishing vessels.

Inside the officer's mess, Helen Moore waited with her colleague, Doctor Richard Quest, for the *Richmond's* XO and Agent Mark Reynolds to return. Gulping down the remainder of her coffee, Helen rolled her eyes in annoyance at Quest's continual pacing up and down in the small room.

"Oh Richard, for God's sake will you stop pacing. You're making me dizzy, they'll be here soon."

Quest didn't like small spaces, especially those that involved being inside a small room where the lights kept flickering on and off. Even as a passenger in an elevator or on a plane, he would insist on taking the stairs or sitting in the rear of the aircraft, rather than in the more comfortable business class seats towards the front. Even now, before boarding the mini-sub or deep-submergence vehicle, he was already feeling nauseous and claustrophobic. "Helen, that's easy for you to say. It wasn't your brother who locked you in a wardrobe when you were six. Confined spaces are just something I have a problem dealing with, okay?"

Sighing, Helen nodded and responded with a softer tone. "I'm sorry Richard. I didn't mean to bark so harshly, come and sit down."

As Quest offered a weak smile and made his way back to the table and retook his seat, Helen patted him on the shoulder. "It's all right Richard, these people are professionals. There's nothing to be worried about. Besides, we must find out about that pyramid."

"Of course."

"Well then, are you ready?"

Giving her a feeble smile, he glanced across once more and nodded. "As ready as I'll ever be."

*

In the command centre, Captain Butler stepped forward and slapped his helmsman on the shoulder.

"All right Jackson, Helm right 15 degrees rudder, steady course 320."

At the navigation station, the young seaman nodded as he repeated the Captain's order. "Aye Sir, 15 degree's rudder, steady course 320."

"Conn, manoeuvring. Okay ease the bubble and slow to 5 knots."

"Aye Sir, easing the bubble. Reducing speed now."

Standing behind a large sonar screen in the command centre of the USS *Richmond*, Butler waited patiently to hear from his XO.

"XO, Conn. Okay Captain *Wanda's* prepared and ready to board our guests."

"Conn, XO Stand by."

As the lights flickered in the command centre, the Captain turned to Karssen Beck, the sub's chief of the boat and rolled his eyes angrily. "COB, I don't believe this. I thought my instructions were clear."

Shaking his head, the big man groaned. "We tried Sir. According to diagnostics. There's nothing wrong. Woods did report some unusual energy readings."

"What kind of energy readings?"

The New Yorker shrugged his shoulders, somewhat unsure as to how to respond. "Some kind of vibration Captain. But, what it is remains a mystery."

Glancing across at the planesman, Butler shook his head. "Very well, let's get the DSV away. Hopefully our scientist friends will be able to shed some light on all of this."

Beck nodded in agreement. "Aye Sir."

As the Captain nodded, Beck stepped back and was about to leave before Butler suddenly shouted out, "And COB…"

"Yes Captain?"

"Keep those civvies away from anything, sensitive, understand?"

"Of course, Sir."

Once away, Butler turned back towards the sonar station, picked up a nearby radio mic and pushed the call button. "Conn, XO. Tom, they'll be on their way up to you shortly and then it's up to you. Good hunting Commander."

After a moments silence, the radio crackled and Dalby responded. "XO, Conn. Thank you sir."

58

Tuesday 25th October - 5.40am EST - New York City

AS KALEIDOSCOPIC RAYS of early morning sunshine poured over the rooftops of the Manhattan skyline, a solitary figure was sitting in silence on a simple wooden bench inside a small chapel. Although not unusual in design, it did bear a striking blood red, colour scheme. The chapel's location however could also be described as a little unorthodox. Situated within UNITY's East 53rd Street headquarters, it was tucked away in the building's third floor and was simply known as *"The Red Chapel"*.

Dressed in a smart, dark grey business suit, Brother Thomas Weyn sat back, took a deep breath and respired. As his eyes refocussed on the room's marble altar, a door was unlocked from behind and a surprised voice spoke out. "Forgive me Brother. I didn't think anyone would be in here this early."

Climbing to his feet, Weyn turned to face his assistant and nodded. "That's alright Simon, I couldn't sleep so decided that a little meditation might help. Today is a big day after all, I need a clear mind."

Closing the door, the younger, but equally well-dressed, man stepped forward and made his way down to where his mentor was standing. "As I'm here now, I thought you'd like to know that the last vial has been successfully delivered to the White House. I hear that it's only a matter of time now."

Glancing at the younger man, Weyn gave a satisfied nod. "Excellent. Pass on my congratulations to Marjory, she has been invaluable resource. Once the President's out of the way, nothing can stop us. All the pieces are falling into place my friend. It will soon be our time."

As he looked up at the large golden rings of the UNITY emblem that hung above the altar, Weyn's assistant sighed and turned to face his colleague. "There's one other small matter that I should mention. I've just been informed that we had a security breach last night. Were you aware?"

As Weyn shook his head, Simon took position opposite and sighed. "Forgive me. I didn't want to distract you with such inconsequential matters, especially today of all days. It appears that a small group of teenagers broke into the back of the building during the early hours of this morning."

Turning to the younger man, Weyn's expression suddenly turned serious. "Really?"

"We're not entirely sure what they were looking for; they were quickly apprehended and are currently being held for questioning."

Taking a deep breath, Weyn exhaled. "I assume you don't plan to release them?"

With a surprised look, the younger man shook his head vigorously. "Of course not. They'll be dealt with accordingly."

"And the families, what have they been told?"

"Nothing for now. A security team is picking them up as we speak."

Turning inwards, the two men began walking toward the chapel's entrance.

"Good. Prepare an appropriate press release and ensure it makes the morning news."

Arriving at the doorway, the younger man stepped forward, opened the door and waited for his mentor to walk through.

"Of course, Brother, and the intruders. How do you wish them dealt with?"

Stepping through the doorway, Weyn closed the door behind him and paused for a moment.

"UNITY is the way. One mind, one body."

"Kill them."

*

Tuesday 25th October - 12.45pm CET - Vatican City, Italy

Inside his apartment, Antonio Demarco took a deep breath and after shutting and fastening a brown leather suitcase, he stepped back and gazed at it for a moment. Not simply because it was a suitcase, but because of what it represented. Not only had it belonged to his father, but it had also been many years since Antonio had left Rome. To depart in this manner disturbed him.

Despite his yearning to leave, Antonio felt a tinge of regret. Not only for his lack of courage in deserting his friend Bouchard, in this time of need; also at the thought of abandoning his beautiful church: *The church of Sant'Anna de' Parafrenieri.* His breakthrough in deciphering the UNITY symbol was just too important, however. He had to work with his friend in Dubrovnik to somehow convince the world that this seemingly benign organisation was hiding something sinister. After adorning a long raincoat, Antonio picked up his suitcase and glanced around the apartment one last time before opening the door and stepping outside.

Minutes later, he was out in the afternoon sunshine and heading towards St Peter's Square. Noticing the *Porta Sant'Anna* ahead, Antonio stopped for a moment to gaze at his beloved church before continuing past a colourful Swiss guard. After Antonio paused to say hello, the man returned the gesture with a courteous nod and a tilt of his hat. *"Buon pomeriggio, padre."*

Pausing at the base of the Basilica's stone steps, Antonio proceeded into the church.

Once through the scaffold filled entranceway, Antonio fought his way past several enormous sheets of thick plastic before finally emerging into Vignola's masterpiece. Placing his suitcase down, he proceeded to walk down the basilica's centre aisle before stopping in front of its large marble altar. Then, after a short pause, he genuflected and took a seat on one of the red, velvet covered pews. Then, lowering his head, he began to pray.

"*Salve amico mio*. I suspected that that I would find you here…"

"Che cosa?"

Turning his head, Antonio was shocked to see a concerned looking Cardinal Bouchard standing to the far left of the Basilica.

"Sua Eminenza. Mi perdoni, I'm sorry I would have…"

Raising his hand to silence Antonio, Bouchard stepped forward and smiled. "*Ti prego amico mio*, there's no need apologise. However, I must confess that I'm a little surprised to see you here. You seemed to be in such a hurry."

As Bouchard sat down next to Antonio, the priest reached inside his pocket and took out a crumpled sheet of paper. *"Mi perdoni*, but after seeing this I hope you'll understand."

"What is it?"

As Bouchard unfolded the sheet, his eyes widened as he gazed at the image of the distorted circles and two horizontal lines. However, this was not the same familiar symbol. It had been replaced by three undeniable representations of the number six.

"Stavo provando to print a copy of the symbol and well, you can see the result."

Placing his hand over his mouth in a genuine look of shock, Bouchard glanced up, first towards the Basilica's grand dome and then back at his seated friend. *"Oh Dio mio. Certamente*, how could have I been so blind to have missed this."

Taking a breath, Antonio placed a hand on his friend's arm to comfort him. *"Va bene,* but don't you see, Eminence, it all makes sense now. I was being watched,

I'm sure of it. The question is why? I sense it was because I was getting too close to the truth?"

Bouchard climbed to his feet and pointed towards Antonio's suitcase at the rear of the church.

"E per quanto riguarda la valigia Antonio, were you just going to leave without saying goodbye?"

"No Sua Eminenza. I just needed to find answers, I need to understand what's going on."

As the Cardinal exhaled, he began to slowly pace back and forth. *"Hai paura, Antonio?"*

Antonio nodded. *"Sì, certo che ho paura.* this whole affair has unnerved me."

As he stopped pacing, the elderly Cardinal retook his seat and lowered his voice to a whisper.

"Devo ammettere una cosa Antonio. You're not the only one who's afraid. Several of us are concerned about the goings on here."

"Davvero?"

Bouchard nodded and continued. *"Sì,* there are even whispers circulating that the holy father may have been Murdered."

Antonio's expression suddenly turned to one of horror. *"Assassinato*! But how?"

Bouchard glanced around nervously for a moment before continuing. "Poison."

"No!"

After a pause, the Cardinal continued. *"Sì, ma se e la verità,* we need to find evidence."

Sitting forward with interest, Antonio took a deep breath and slowly exhaled. *"Capisco Sua Eminenza,* but why not just inform the Swiss Guard?"

Suddenly Bouchard grasped Antonio by the arm and shook his head. *"No, no amico mio.* Don't you see, they could be involved to. No. This has to be done quietly."

Antonio nodded in agreement. *"Capisco Sua Eminenza."*

"Bene. Now, when were you planning to leave?"

Antonio turned towards the rear of the basilica and glanced at his suitcase. "Right away, Eminence."

As he released the priest's arm, Bouchard rose to his feet and motioned Antonio to walk with him. *"Vieni, facciamo una passeggiata amico mi*o and perhaps you'll grant your old friend one last favour."

As the two men began their slow walk down the centre aisle of the church, Antonio nodded.

"Certo Sua Eminenza, qualsiasi cosa."

"A group of us were planning to meet in secret this evening. Perhaps if you came along, you could show them your findings. I'm sure that this new information would help our cause greatly and at the same time we could provide you with our evidence. What do you think Antonio? Could you stay around for a few more hours?"

Glancing awkwardly down at his suitcase, Antonio took a deep breath before giving a reluctant nod. "*Certo Sua Eminenza*, just say where and when and I'll be there."

On hearing Antonio's response, Bouchard smiled broadly and clapped his hands. *"Eccellente Antonio.* I really appreciate it, now perhaps we have a chance of finding out the truth. The meeting will take place in the *necropolis*, by the tomb of St Peter at midnight."

"Midnight?"

"*Lo so,* but we couldn't take the risk of holding a

meeting during the day. There would be too many prying eyes."

"*Certo Sua Eminenza, capisco.*"

As he picked up his suitcase, Antonio offered a conciliatory smile towards his friend, before

Bouchard waved goodbye and Antonio turned back towards St Peter's Square and his apartment.

59

Tuesday 25th October - 7.50am EST - The North Atlantic, 18 Miles East of Sable Island

AS THE HATCH to the submersible clanked shut, a loud hiss indicated that the sub's skirt had begun to fill with seawater. Inside the cabin, the *Richmond's* XO, Tom Dalby, prepared his passengers for departure.

"Alright ladies and gentlemen, remember what I said. As we pull away you may feel a slight popping in your ears, but this is perfectly normal. Everyone okay?"

His passengers all raised their thumbs. All except Doctor Quest, who looked as if he was about to throw up. But then, after receiving a nod of encouragement from Helen Moore, gave a wry smile and raised a thumb. Alongside Quest and Moore, were two other passengers, Agent Mark Reynolds and a stern faced marine.

"Richmond, this is Wanda, ready to detach."

After a few seconds, the radio crackled and abruptly burst into life. "Wanda, this is Richmond, permission granted, good luck."

"Thank you."

After pulling down hard on a nearby handle, Dalby leaned back in his seat as the DSV detached and slowly glided away from the *USS Richmond*, like a fish riding in the wake of an enormous whale.

"Forgive me for asking Commander, but just how deep are we planning to go?"

Turning to Helen Moore, Dalby smiled. "About 1500ft Professor. We believe that what we're seeing on the scope may only the tip of the iceberg, so to speak. To fully investigate, we need to get down to its base. We can only do that from within the sea trench itself. That's why we're using Wanda here; the Richmond is just too big."

As Helen gave a nervous nod, she grasped hold of Quest's arm as the engine kicked in and Dalby titled the subs steering column downwards. The DSV responded and it began its slow descent through the gloom towards the ocean floor.

*

Tuesday 25th October - 8.00am EST - The White House, Washington DC

"This is Richard Delaney reporting live for CNN. These are the headlines for Tuesday 25th October. With just one day to go before the world is introduced to Michael, the United Nations in New York has confirmed that everything is now in place for what promises to be electrifying evening. With the guest list including, world leaders, politicians, scientists, religious leaders and celebrities, tomorrow looks to be something very special. Remember, you can catch the entire event here tomorrow, live on CNN.

In other news, UNITY, spokesman, Brother Thomas Weyn, said that he was shocked and saddened by a seemingly senseless attack on its headquarters in New York overnight. Police reports indicate that a group of teenagers attempted to enter the building with the intention of starting a fire. However, the alarm was quickly raised and UNITY security personnel were on hand to apprehend the group before any damage was done.

This is the fourth time in as many days that a UNITY facility has been attacked. When Brother Weyn was asked how he felt about the attacks, he simply said that he felt pity for those involved and offered them an opportunity to attend counselling sessions with the church, rather than face the legal repercussions. According to UNITY and despite the offer, no response has been received yet. UNITY is the way. One mind, one body."

President Hillary's attention was suddenly interrupted as a knock came to the door. Leaning forward, the President picked up a nearby remote and switched off the television.

"Come in."

As the door opened, Hillary's personal secretary, Marjory Hicks, strode into the room and smiled confidently. "They're ready for you in the Oval Office Mr President."

As Hillary pushed his chair back and got his feet, he noticed that Hicks was donning an unusual symbol on the back of her right hand. As he scrutinised a little longer, he concluded that it was a small tattoo, identical to the UNITY symbol that was recently announced. Three interlocking circles with two horizontal lines running through the centre.

"Don't you think you're a little old for a tattoo, Marjory?"

"Huh?"

Nervously covering the back of her hand, Hicks gave a cynical smile. "It's not just a tattoo Mr President. It's a symbol what UNITY stands for. Coming together in peace and…"

Raising his hand, the President shook his head and sighed. "That's alright Marjory, I don't need another UNITY lecture."

Walking forward, he proceeded to follow Hicks out of the room and into its adjoining corridor. Moments later, as the pair entered the Oval Office, the awaiting group climbed to their feet and spoke in unison.

"Good morning Mr President."

"Good morning ladies and gentlemen. I trust you're all well?"

The group murmured a response as the president strode around to the rear of the Resolute desk and the entire group sat down. Along with Hicks, the other members of the group included Jack Nelson: The President's Chief of Staff, General Mark Gates, Press Secretary: Laura Claiborne and CIA Deputy Director David Tyler. Leaning across the desk the President picked up a nearby bottle of water and proceeded to pour himself a glass.

"So, Jack, tell me what's so urgent that we had to schedule a meeting before breakfast?"

Leaning forward in his seat, the President's Chief of Staff cleared his throat. "Well, Mr President, it's about the invitation from UNITY to join the Red Council. They're waiting for our response."

As he listened, Hillary couldn't help but noticing that some of the group members were also sporting similar tattoos to that of his assistant. At first, he didn't think anything of it, but as his eyes surveyed the room, he began to feel progressively uncomfortable. Finally, after spotting the symbol on the back of the General's hand, Hillary found himself unable to stay silent any longer. "What's the meaning of this?"

Glancing around for a moment Jack Nelson looked puzzled. "Mr President…"

"You know damn well what I mean. What's with the tattoos?"

As the Chief of Staff fell silent, the military advisor, Mark Gates continued the conversation.

"It's for Michael, Mr President. It's in preparation for his big day tomorrow, we're only following instructions."

As he returned his untouched glass to the desk, the President took a deep breath and climbed to his feet. "What instructions, what the hell are you talking about? You're all representatives of the Office of the President of the United States, not some crazy group of religious hippies, I tell you I won't have this."

Having been silent through the conversation, Hillary's assistant Marjory Hicks glanced across at the poisoned bottle of water and solemnly shook her head. "What did I tell you general? I knew this would happen."

For a moment, the President looked confused. Before Hicks turned to face him.

"You couldn't just go gracefully could you Mr president? You had to make things difficult?"

"What the hell. What are you talking about?"

"The Red Council. Don't you understand what it could mean for the United States, for our world. No more conflicts, no more wars: just peace. Michael has promised us these things as long as we work together."

Observing the group, the President stepped in front of the desk and raised his hands in disbelief as to what he was hearing. "I thought our Government's position on this matter was clear. We don't engage with religious fanatics. But now you come in here and inform me that, without any debate whatsoever, the position of the United States has changed overnight. Now you want to risk everything we stand for by engaging in a mutiny. Have you lost your minds?"

With a glance towards Hicks and with lighting speed, General Gates suddenly drew his weapon and pointed it directly at the President.

"General, what the hell are you doing?"

Gates sneered at Hicks as he prepared to shoot. "What are we wasting time for here. He's never going to agree. We should just kill him and that'll be the end of it. UNITY is the way, Mr President. One mind, one body."

As Gates swallowed and prepared to squeeze the trigger, the room was suddenly filled with an ear-splitting sound and its contents began to tremble. Without warning, the General screamed as his eyes unexpectedly rolled over white and his arm began to wave and wobble uncontrollably back and forth. Watching on in horror, Hillary could see that it wasn't only the general who was effected. The entire group, aside from Director Tyler, appeared to be losing self-control. As the General's pistol slipped out of his hand and dropped harmlessly onto the floor, the bottle of water sitting atop the President's desk suddenly shattered.

As the group collapsed onto the ground, seemingly unconscious. The President, in expectation of being struck with exploding glass immediately closed his eyes and raised his arms into a defensive position. But instead of the sound of broken glass hitting the floor, the room became swathed in an eerie and almost deafening silence.

As he opened his eyes, the President reeled back in alarm. The Oval Office and everything in it had gone, evaporated into a blinding white void. As his eyes flickered and adjusted to the brightness, he drew breath and touched his face. Then, running his hand through his hair, he exhaled to be sure that he could still breath, feel and see. Finally, he placed his hand on his chest. His heart, it was still thumping, albeit somewhat rapidly.

"I'm alive!"

As his familiar voice echoed out through the chasm, another voice suddenly spoke out from behind. "Well of course you are, Mr President."

60

Tuesday 25th October - 9.40am EST - The North Atlantic, 18 Miles East of Sable Island

FOR THE PAST 24 hours, the *Richmond* had been experiencing a series of increasingly annoying electrical anomalies. Small glitches that, although on the surface didn't appear to be serious, had built up to a point where they had now begun to impact several other electrical systems. Despite having ordered a boat wide investigation, the Captain was still no closer to finding the source, never mind contemplating a possible solution.

Returning to duty, Petty Officer, Matthew Woods, apprehensively retook his seat in sonar control. After slipping his headset on, he tensely glanced around at his fellow crewmates. Their faces were as sombre as his own. After briefly rubbing his eyes, he rotated the fader on his headset upwards in the hope successfully analysing the bizarre rhythmic vibration emanating from the newly discovered underwater pyramid. As he listened intently for a few minutes, he eventually concluded that whatever was generating the sound, was not naturally occurring.

As the lights flickered once more, his attention was interrupted by someone tapping him on the shoulder. Woods turned and the Captain came into view. He pulled of his headset and straightened himself up. "Yes Sir?"

"Anything yet?"

Woods grimaced and shook his head. "Nothing conclusive Captain, only ideas at this stage."

Butler stroked his chin and gave a nod. "Well then, would you care to make an educated guess as to what we're dealing with, Mr Woods?"

After a few seconds, Woods took a deep breath and continued. "Well Sir, I don't think its naturally occurring. I mean, it could be something mechanical or electrical. Perhaps a generator of some kind."

Butler's eyes widened. "Could it be nuclear?"

Wood shook his head. "No sir. We haven't detected radiation of any kind. But, in terms of the sound itself, I can say that it's definitely not one that I've encountered before."

With a reassuring slap to the back, Butler exhaled. "Very well, keep me updated of any changes alright?"

"Aye Sir, of course."

The Captain's attention was suddenly diverted way from the sonar station, as a nearby radio burst into life.

"Captain to the Conn please."

Turning away from the sonar station, Butler made his way back up to the Conn. Once there, he stepped across to greet a solemn faced COB, who was standing by the radio operator with a document, entitled maintenance report (Alpha Shift). As the Captain arrived, COB extended his hand and passed the document across to the Captain.

"The maintenance report Captain. I'm sorry to say that whatever's causing these anomalies is beyond us. I've had every department undertaking a thorough investigation. According to the feedback, the board's completely green."

COB's voice fell away.

For a moment, Butler stood puzzled as to why his Chief of the Boat had suddenly stopped speaking mid-sentence. As the seconds ticked by, he observed that it wasn't just the New Yorker that had fallen quiet. The entire crew had fallen silent and then in an instant he realised why. The boat was vibrating. At first, it was almost unnoticeable. Then, as the seconds progressed, the tremors rapidly grew in intensity. Finally, and without warning, there was almighty bang and the sub suddenly lurched to the left.

"Holy shit!"

As crewmembers scrambled to regain their footing and equipment began crashing to the floor, the boat was suddenly plunged into darkness as its internal lights failed. Seconds later, as the emergency lighting kicked in, Butler scrambled towards the dive control position and barked out. "COB sound the general alarm."

"Aye Sir."

As the alarm screeched out, the young helmsman franticly attempted to stabilize the submarine by pulling back on the dive planes. However despite his best efforts, the diving control column had experienced a complete loss of power and the sub continued its nightmarish plunge downwards.

"Captain, it's no use. We have no power, she's passing 140 meters and I can't slow her descent."

As the boat continued to shake violently, Butler took

a deep breath grabbed a radio mic. "CON, Engine room. We need emergency power now."

As he released the call button, Butler turned to COB and yelled out. "COB Get down to."

Before he could complete his sentence, the lights were suddenly restored and as the Helmsman sighed, he pulled up on the dive planes and shouted out. "Captain, I have power."

As the engines restarted, a sigh of relief travelled around the room, and the Captain turned to COB and slowly exhaled. "Another malfunction?"

COB wiped his mouth and gave a single nod. "Certainly, looks that way Captain."

As the boat stabilized, Butler glanced around at the anxious faces of the crew and lowered his voice. "We can't stay down here like this; these glitches; are becoming life threatening. If it happens again, we might not be quite so lucky."

Nodding in agreement, Beck sighed and responded. "Agreed."

"Alright COB, let's prepare to surface the boat. At least then we can investigate in relative safety."

As he reached for a radio mic to give the instruction, COB's expression turned to one of concern. "But Sir, what about the DSV? Commander Dalby?

Abandoning a fellow officer was a choice no captain ever wanted to make. Given the circumstances, Butler couldn't risk the entire crew and his boat by remaining on a boat that was now experiencing potentially life-threatening malfunctions. For Butler, it was time to make the call. Taking a deep breath, he nodded. "The DSV will be fine. Dalby's more than capable and besides, they have more than enough oxygen. Once we've sorted out our problems, we'll come back for them."

"Aye Sir."

As he gave a nod, COB pushed the call button on his radio mic. "Attention all hands, prepare to surface the boat…"

*

Date Unknown, Location Unknown

As President Hillary's eyes gradually adjusted to the intensity of the light, the realisation that this wasn't a dream began to rapidly sink in. Taking a deep breath, he turned apprehensively towards the familiar voice. "You? What the hell is this?"

As the familiar figure of CIA Deputy Director, David Tyler, stepped into view, Hillary shook his head. This was a man he'd known for years. A man he trusted and now it seems that he was nothing more than an imposter. One who had not only fooled him, but one who had also fooled the nation.

"I'm sorry Mr President, this must be all very unnerving for you. If you'll allow me a moment to explain?"

What choice did he have but to hear the man out. What could he do? He was trapped in, Well, he wasn't entirely sure where he was. Choosing not to respond, Hillary simply looked blankly at the man and gave a nod.

"Forgive me Mr President, but your life was in danger. They were planning to kill you."

Hillary's expression turned to one of shock. "What?"

"It's true. The water bottle on your desk had been laced with a deadly toxin. No doubt the same poison that they used to kill the British Prime Minister and probably the Pope as well."

Reeling backwards, the President suddenly raised his hands and exhaled.

"You're telling me that they wanted me dead, Why? What would that accomplish?"

Tyler took a deep breath and stepped forward.

"The *Red Council*, Mr President, they want the United States to join them, and were fully prepared to kill you to ensure that it did."

"And this place? You? I assume that you are not really David Tyler, the deputy director of the CIA?"

Tyler smiled. "It's complicated. We've been amongst you for so long that we share your world right alongside you."

Hillary grimaced. "So, you're an alien?"

Tyler shook his head and grinned. "No Mr President. I'm no alien, but we do have the capability to change our appearance. We are known as *keepers*. I am one of only a handful, whose mission is to care for your world."

Hillary gave a hollow laugh. "Care? From what I've heard, you've tried to destroy our world. Billions have died and..."

Tyler stepped forward, raised his hand and sighed.

"It's true, Mr President. I can't deny any of those allegations. But it's important that you understand why. You see, humanity has become a highly destructive species, far more than any other we've encountered. You kill each other for religious, political, or territorial reasons... You even kill each other for sport.

In the beginning, your species was given a unique gift. A gift of choice and you've squandered it in the pursuit of your own self interests. So, a judgment was made and the process of removing mankind had started. It was supposed to take generations. But circumstances have arisen that have... Well, sped up the process."

Hillary looked confused. "Circumstances? You mean the disasters?"

"Not all of us agreed with the decision, Mr President. One of us has even attempted to use the process to advance his own self interests."

"In what way?"

Suddenly Tyler's head dropped and he sighed despondently. "His name is Caius, Mr President and like myself, he is also a keeper. But somewhere along the line, he became twisted and cruel. So much so, that he was eventually banished. Throughout our history, he has taken many forms and many names. Now for one reason or another, he has targeted your species."

Hillary shook his head. "Mr Tyler, I think you underestimate our resolve. If you know our history and I think you do, then you know that we'll fight back."

Tyler shook his head and groaned. "No, you don't understand Mr President. The war has already begun and you're losing. Even as we speak he's building an army. One that will do terrible things."

"You're talking about this *UNITY* group?"

Tyler paused for a moment before nodding. "In creating UNITY, Caius has successfully forged a weapon of unimaginable power. Although it's not a tangible object, it will do untold damage to your world."

Hillary shook his head. "I don't understand, what weapon? What are you talking about?"

"Devotion, Mr President. It's a very subtle weapon. But as he gains power, he will use it more deviously. Then, he will turn man against man and brother against brother. Finally, when he has enslaved humanity and has no more use for you, then he will kill you."

Hillary took a deep breath and began to pace back and forth. "So how do we stop him?"

Without warning, Hillary staggered backwards in alarm, as Tyler's face slowly began to change. Morphing into something grotesque.

"Oh my God!"

Within moments, the once recognizable face of CIA Director David Tyler was gone. His face, his clothes. Everything that he was, had dissolved away. In its place, stood a terrifying cloaked creature. Its hair as black as coal and its eyes blazing like two bright blue moons.

"Don't be afraid George. There are others out there, like you, who now know the truth. Work with them to defeat Caius. It is the only way to save yourselves."

As his words faded and the creature slowly melted into nothingness, President Hillary found himself standing alone surrounded by intense white light. "Hey… Wait don't go! You can't leave me here alone!"

61

Tuesday 25th October - 10.20am EST - The North Atlantic, 16 Miles East of Sable Island

FIFTEEN HUNDRED FEET below the surface of the North Atlantic, the DSV *Wanda* descended slowly through the gloom to arrive at the lowermost point of mysterious underwater pyramid. Taking a deep breath, the *Richmond's* XO, Commander Tom Dalby leaned back and reduced the submersible's speed, before reaching forward to push a button.

"Alright ladies and gentlemen, let's see what's out there."

As he released the switch, the sub's two front floodlights illuminated the ocean floor. As her eyes adjusted to the glare, Helen Moore leaned forward and gasped in amazement. "Look at that, it's incredible."

Dalby and his passengers gazed in astonishment at what now appeared to be a colossal wall of solid black marble, approximately 250 meters ahead. Shuffling excitedly in her seat, Moore tapped her colleague, Richard Quest on the shoulder. "Richard look. It looks like the one we encountered in Scotland, but on a significantly larger scale."

Turning towards his partner, Quest responded with a nod of agreement. "The surface certainly looks similar. Incredible."

Agent Mark Reynolds turned towards the scientists, cleared his throat and joined the conversation. "I can't speak for the one in Scotland, but I can say it's similar to the one I encountered in Iceland."

Turning back to gaze out at the floodlit sea floor, Quest groaned. "But if it is of the same origin, why is this one so big?"

Reynolds shook his head. "I don't know."

As the group deliberated, Commander Dalby turned back towards the console and picked up the radio handset. "I suppose we'd better check in with the *Richmond*. Let them know our status."

As he pressed the handset's call button, the others murmured in agreement. "*Richmond* this is Wanda, come in, over…"

After waiting for around 30 seconds, Dalby pushed the button a second time. "*Richmond* this is the DSV Wanda, come in, over…"

Again, with no response, Dalby waited for another 30 seconds before making one final attempt.

"USS Richmond, this is the DSV Wanda, come in, over."

Taking a deep breath, Dalby frowned and turned towards Reynolds exhaling. "Strange…"

"What is it?"

Turning towards Helen, Dalby shook his head. "It

appears that we have temporarily lost communication with the *Richmond*, Professor. There's nothing to worry about, this sometime happens. We'll stay down a little longer and try again in around 30 minutes. Beyond that, we'll head back up to the rendezvous point."

Helen suddenly turned to Quest and grimaced. "What about oxygen? It seems that we've been down here for a long time. Do we have enough?"

Before Quest could respond, Dalby grinned. "More than enough Professor. Have no fear, this little lady is equipped with the very latest technology including, its own oxygen generator."

"Oh well, that's good then."

As the submersible's engine began to rev once more, Dalby sat forward and pushed a lever which began to increase the DSV's speed.

"Alright then. As we're here I suppose it won't do any harm to explore a little."

As the DSV's engine throttled, Dalby's voice faded away in mid-sentence.

"What is it commander?"

Before Dalby could respond, the young marine who'd been sent to accompany the group nodded and turned to Quest. "We're not moving… Commander look."

He was right, even as Dalby attempted to increase speed, the DSV remained motionless.

"What do you mean, we're not moving?" Said Quest worriedly.

"Okay folks strap yourselves in."

Suddenly Dalby's tone turned serious and he again revved the small submersible's engine.

As the engine moaned, Dalby's face turned to one of confusion. "What the hell? I don't understand, the equipment's working correctly. We should be moving."

As his words fell away, Dalby's expression abruptly turned to one of horror as the submersible suddenly began to shudder. At first it was almost unnoticeable, but then as the seconds ticked by, it increased tenfold. Within moments the entire vessel and its five occupants were being shaken so violently that Helen Moore began to scream. "Oh my God, what's happening?"

*

Date Unknown, Location Unknown

For a second, Tom Duncan could have sworn that he heard voices. After pausing for a moment to listen, he staggered further forward, straining to hear anything that might indicate life. There was nothing. Nothing but a never-ending silence encased within the brilliance of an incessant white light. He was thirsty and it seemed that he had been walking for hours.

As he prepared to walk forward, suddenly it was there again. Was that a voice?

"Hey… Wait, don't go… You can't leave me here alone!"

This time, there was no doubt, he couldn't believe it. The voice, it was out there as plain as day. Swallowing hard, he turned and as he tried to speak, the only sound to emerge however was a dry raspy "Hello."

Firstly, there was no response, so he tried again. "Hello…"

Then out of the glaring light, there it was, a blurry shape at first. But as Tom moved in closer, the shape began to eventually gain form. It was a man. Yes, he was sure of it, it was a man.

"Hello…"

The figure turned towards him and began to walk forward some more. Tom could now see that the man was in his early sixties, dressed in a smart grey suit. "Oh my God, I'm back."

Then standing, about ten meters away, the elder man spoke. "Are you one of them?"

"Huh?"

"A keeper? Are you one of those creatures?"

As he spoke, Tom noticed that the man, whoever he was, had a North American accent. Gazing at his suit, Tom glanced down at his own attire. He was mortified that he was still wearing the same white ruffled shirt, bottle green waistcoat, a pair of dark tanned breeches, given to him by Mary Allan. Swallowing hard, he proceeded to step forward and shake the man's hand.

"No, are you?"

The older man shook his head and felt relieved. "No, but I've been introduced to one. I'm George Hillary, who are you?"

"Tom Duncan."

Suddenly Hillary's expression turned to one of recognition. "Tom Duncan, the Scotsman's friend?"

For a moment, Tom appeared confused. How could this stranger possibly know who he, and even his friend Dougie was?

"I'm sorry, but have we met before?"

Hillary smiled and shook his head. "No, Mr Duncan we haven't. But I know a lot about you. You see I'm George Hillary, the President of the United States. I've read all about you and your friend Dougie Allan."

At first, Tom thought that this had to be a joke. How on earth could this man be the President? Then, the he more listened, Tom concluded that, as outrageous as it sounded, perhaps there was an element of truth is his story.

"Well, Mr President, if that's true. How on earth did you end up here?"

Eyeing Tom's 18th century Scottish attire, Hillary smiled broadly and drew breath. "That's a very good question, Mr Duncan and one that comes with a story. However, considering your own outfit and looking at where we are. I suspect that your story will be as equally compelling as my own."

62

Tuesday 25th October - 10.45am EST - The North Atlantic, 16 Miles East of Sable Island

"OH MY GOD, what's happening?"

Below the surface of the Atlantic, Helen Moore shrieked loudly as the DSV *Wanda* unexpectedly listed violently to the left and began to shake more aggressively than ever. At the controls, Commander Tom Dalby desperately fought an upward battle to maintain control of the submersible. But as each terrifying moment passed, Dalby sensed that he had little choice but to order an evacuation. Swallowing hard, he reluctantly leaned across, gripped hold of a large black handle labelled "*Emergency Main Ballast*" and prepared to give the order to surface. "Stand by..."

Suddenly he fell silent as the mysterious shaking unexpectedly ceased. Before anyone had the opportunity to speak, the craft suddenly lost power and was plunged into an eerie darkness.

As Helen let out a scream and Quest grasped hold

of her hand in attempt to comfort her. "Easy now, don't panic."

Turning anxiously in his seat, Dalby reached towards a small metal box at the side of his chair. Once opened, he removed a handful of plastic glow sticks, and after snapping a couple, handed out one to each passenger.

"It's alright Professor. Keep calm…"

"Christ. look at where we are. We're going to die, aren't we?"

As the soft, yellow light of the glow sticks filled the cabin, Dalby turned to Moore and shook his head. "Please Professor, it's important that we stay calm. We have an emergency generator on-board which should kick in…"

Without warning, Helen shrieked again, as the entire submersible was suddenly engulfed within a blazing white light. The passengers covered their eyes, and the small craft began to shudder and slowly move towards the wall enormous black wall.

"What's happening?"

As his eyes flickered open, Dalby checked his instrument panel and glanced to his right in horror.

"We're moving, but that's impossible. We have no power."

Agent Reynolds leaned forward with a grim expression and barked out. "For Christ sake man, blow the tanks and get us out of here."

Nodding in agreement, Dalby quickly shifted himself around and grasped hold of the "*Emergency Main Ballast*" lever. Wrenching it downwards with all his strength, Dalby's face turned to dread when nothing happened. But then, after a loud thud, the submersible suddenly exploded into brilliance and within one single instant, the DSV *Wanda* and all her passengers were gone.

*

Tuesday 25th October - 5.00pm CET - Dubrovnik, Croatia

Sitting in his room, Abbot, Vladimir Palovic gulped down a final mouthful of tea before returning his cup to a small side table. The old man then leaned back and closed his eyes so that he could listen to the latest radio news bulletin.

"This is the BBC World Service, I'm Alison Holt reporting from London. Here are the news headlines. In New York. Final preparations are now in place for Michael's hotly anticipated introduction speech at the United Nations. With just over 24 hours to go Final invitations have been dispatched and security checks completed. Everything is now in place for what promises to be the event of the century. Here in London the New Prime Minister, Anne Petrie has announced that, in celebration, tomorrow has been declared a national holiday for the entire country. This evening in London, as with many other cities around the world, celebrations are being held in stadiums and conference centres everywhere. UNITY have also announced, that this will be a final opportunity for the faithful to receive the mark of peace before tomorrow's event. UNITY is the way. One mind, one body.

In other News..."

The abbot's attention was drawn away from the broadcast as a knock sounded at his door. Opening his eyes, Father Palovic climbed to his feet, switched off the radio and walked across towards the door.

Once unlocked, he swung the door open and offered a weak smile to a familiar visitor. *"Saša, izvoli, uđi."*

As then youngster offered a respectful nod, Palovic stepped aside and the sullen faced pupil entered the room. *"Oprostite na smetnji, Oče.* But I wanted to inform you that Father Demarco has failed to arrive at the airport."

As the door closed behind him, the old man retook his seat and frowned.

"Ah, shvaćam."

"The taxi driver telephoned and told me that he waited for over an hour in the arrivals hall. I suppose it's possible that he was simply delayed. Maybe he'll arrive on a later flight this evening?"

Palovic shook his head and grimaced. "*Možda,* but it's not like Antonio to miss a meeting like this. Something must have happened?"

As the abbot rubbed his chin solemnly, the youngster shook his head and stepped forward to offer consolation. "*Oče, nije dobro da* draw conclusions. I'm sure there's a perfectly reasonable explanation. Perhaps we could telephone or send him an email."

Taking a deep breath, the old man smiled, grasped hold of the youngster's hand and ensued to haul himself up. "*U pravu si, naravno Saša.* As you say, perhaps it's simply nothing more than a delay. Come, we'll go to the library and you can help me compose a message to my friend."

63

Date: Unknown, Location: Unknown

AS THE TWO men strolled through the seemingly endless blinding light President Hillary listened attentively as Tom described, in detail, his recent adventure in Scotland. He gave vivid detail of almost being hung as a suspected witch as well as a chilling confrontation with not one, but two of the sinister keepers. If it hadn't been for the timely and unexpected intervention of the second creature, Tom would have been killed.

"It sounds to me as if we're dealing with two factions here. In my encounter, the creature masqueraded itself as one of my most trusted advisors. In fact, in the end, it even saved my life."

Tom nodded. "It certainly sounds as if we encountered a similar being, but…"

The President grimaced. "What is it?"

"There is of course, one other possibility."

"Sir?"

"Well, we've learnt that they can change shape. What if

your Father McRae and my CIA director are actually the same creature."

Tom thought for a moment and nodded.

"I suppose it's possible."

Hillary turned towards Tom with a look of puzzlement. "What about the book he gave you? What does it mean?"

Tom glanced down at the book in his hand and shrugged his shoulders. "I'm not sure. Its written in a language that I'm unfamiliar with. I can only hope that if we get out of here, we can find someone who can translate…"

As Tom's words fell away, the President turned to check that he was okay. "What is it?"

"Look…"

Peering through the intense brightness, Tom sensed that the light in the void had somehow changed. It now appeared darker and more defined, like a distant horizon. As the two men gathered speed, Tom's heart suddenly leapt, as from out of the horizon, something began to rise upwards. Something he knew he'd seen before.

"Oh my God!"

"What is it Tom?"

Stopping in his tracks, Tom took a deep breath, glanced at the President and pointed towards the object. "It's hope, Mr President."

*

"Professor… Professor Moore, can you hear me?"

The voice spoke from somewhere in the back of her mind. Helen felt as if she was floating, drifting through nothingness.

"Professor…"

Hearing the voice for the third time, Helen suddenly opened her eyes and sat up gasping for air.

"Helen it's alright, you're safe."

"What…"

With her eyes half open, the intensity of the light surrounding her was so bright that she hurriedly raised her hand to shield her eyes from the overpowering light. Then peering through her open fingers, she glanced upwards to see four familiar and concerned faces looking down at her.

"Am I alive?"

Suddenly, one of the standing figures knelt and took hold of her free hand and smiled.

"Yes Helen, you're safe and very much alive."

"Richard."

Moments later and with her eyes now becoming accustomed to the brightness, Helen grasped hold of Quest's hand, and with further help from Agent Reynolds, took a deep breath and hauled herself back on to her feet. They were no longer on-board the *Wanda*. She, like the rest of the group, found herself engulfed within a seemingly boundless world of bright nothingness.

"What happened?"

Stepping forward, Commander Dalby cleared his throat.

"To be honest Professor, I'm not entirely sure. One minute we were in the DSV drifting towards the wall and the next we were here, wherever this is."

Glancing across at Quest, Helen grimaced. "How long was I out for?"

"About an hour."

Glancing towards Dalby, Helen suddenly appeared confused. "But where's the DSV and the *Richmond*?"

Dalby grimaced and shook his head. "I don't know. We attempted to recon the area, but had to abandon it. We can't risk separating anyone from the group, they'd easily get lost in this."

Stepping forward, Quest nodded in agreement. "He's right Helen. This all looks very familiar and if this is anything like the labyrinth we investigated in Scotland, can't risk being separated."

Dalby motioned the young marine forward and cleared his throat. "Hudson, it looks like your time has come. Proceed ahead of the group and ensure you keep your eyes peeled. I don't want to lose anyone, understand?"

The twenty something youngster nodded enthusiastically. "Absolutely. In which direction Sir?"

Looking towards Quest for guidance. The doctor nervously scanned around for a moment and appeared to casually point his finger straight ahead. "I guess at this stage it really doesn't matter. That way seems as good as any."

As Dalby cautiously nodded in agreement, the marine turned to his left, and as directed, stepped forward. As he moved, Quest glanced at Helen apprehensively and they joined Dalby and Agent Reynolds as they anxiously began their walk into the unknown.

64

Tuesday 25th October - 11.40pm CET - Vatican City, Italy

AS PERSISTENT EVENING clouds finally cleared above the skies of Rome. Frantic last-minute preparations for the late holy Father's funeral were now complete and St Peter's Square was quiet. Construction crews working earlier in the day had now departed. The square's Egyptian Obelisk, Maderno's Fountain, and several of the surrounding stone statues had been restored to their former glory. The builders had also done a semi decent job of removing any non-essential scaffolding and heavy equipment. So much in fact, that if a visitor with little knowledge of the recent devastation arrived in the square, they would notice nothing unusual. Of course, beyond the perimeter of the Vatican, much of Rome was still in pieces.

A short distance away, and sitting alone in his small apartment, Antonio Demarco sighed solemnly at the thought of missing his flight and disappointing his Croatian friend.

However, after his recent discussion with Cardinal Bouchard, he was convinced that he'd made the right decision. If there was indeed a plot by UNITY to take over the Catholic church, Antonio had, not only a moral, but also a spiritual duty to intercede and defend the faith. If what Bouchard said was true and he and several other Cardinals wanted to escape, then he had to help.

As Antonio finished compiling his response to Vladimir Palovic, he sighed and clicked send. Once satisfied that his message had gone, Antonio closed his computer, sat back and gulped down the last few drops of his tea. Once on his feet, he placed the cup down and took a moment to look around his room. Although small, it had been his home for many years and, as he glanced at his familiar wooden crucifix above his bed, Antonio sensed that change was coming. At this moment in time, he wasn't entirely sure how that change would manifest itself.

Although the apartment held countless memories, it also carried several heavy regrets. Including the wish that he could have resolved his outstanding issues between himself and his estranged father, Pietro. At the time, the man wanted little to do with him. In his mind, Antonio had ruined his life. Antonio saw his calling to the church as something that burned in him long before any thoughts of studying mathematics at University. In the end though, it was losing his father in that terrible earthquake that was perhaps a Godsend. As Antonio knelt over his dying father, something touched both men. Something that even today, Antonio could not entirely describe in words. Glancing over once more at his packed suitcase sitting by the door, Antonio suddenly had the inclination to pray.

So, without further thought, he took a deep breath and knelt beside his bed and closed his eyes.

> *"Lord Jesus, I come to you now as your humble servant. Give me the wisdom to not only seek out your guidance, but also your strength. If the church, myself and indeed my own faith are to be tested in the coming days,. I pray that your love will carry me forward.*
>
> *Father I also pray for my friends. Give them strength to seek out the truth. May you fill their hearts and minds with your love. Tonight Lord, I have so many questions, so many fears. I only hope that when this night is over, I will know not only your love, but also your truth. Amen"*

After concluding his prayer, Antonio remained kneeling for a few minutes. When finished, he re-opened his eyes, made the sign of the cross and climbed to his feet. After picking up his charcoal grey raincoat, he proceeded to unlock his apartment door. He then picked up his suitcase and stepped outside. After one final look around the apartment, he slowly exhaled and switched off his light. Finally, after locking the door, made his way down a nearby stairwell and out onto the street below. With one last glance upwards, Antonio inhaled the cool night air, pulled his coat collar up for warmth and moved off towards *Via Paolo VI* and the *Excavations Office* on the far side of St Peter's Square.

*

Date: Unknown, Location: Unknown

Even from a distance, the marblesque pyramid was colossal. With an estimated height of over 100 feet, it appeared to rise from the horizon like an enormous sea creature about to swallow up its prey. Tom speculated that what they were looking at, represented only a fraction of its true size. Under examination, its surface was comprised of some form of polished black marble. But as neither man could locate any cracks or blemishes, it became clear that this was unlike any marble they'd encountered before. As the President gazed upwards in wonder, he suddenly clasped his hands and shook them vigorously.

"Mr Duncan this… This is just incredible. I mean, I've read the reports, but to be here and see it like this. It's simply amazing."

As Tom murmured in agreement, the pair suddenly became aware of a sound. No, it was more than just a sound, it was a vibration. Low and rhythmic coming from the pyramid, almost as if it were alive.

"I read in the report that you and this Dougie Allan discovered a pyramid in Scotland like this one. Is that, right?"

Gazing upwards in awe, Tom smiled and nodded. "Yes, it looks very similar Mr President. In fact, I wonder…"

Taking a deep breath, Tom suddenly stepped forward and cautiously placed a hand onto the pyramids enormous black surface. "What do you feel?"

Tom took a slow deep breath and exhaled. "It feels cold and clammy, but I also feel the vibration from within, almost as if…"

Tom's hand began to tingle and glow, forcing him to instantly remove it and step quickly back.

"What is it Tom? What happened?"

Tom swallowed hard as he inspected his hand. "I don't know… I touched it and I felt…"

"Felt what?"

Glancing at the President, Tom frowned.

"My hand, its tingling. Almost as if someone was trying to make a connection with me."

As Tom slowly rubbed his hand, Hillary stepped forward and raised his hand to touch the wall.

"Mr President don't…"

Unlike Tom's experience however, the President didn't flinch or remove his hand.

"You're right. It is cold and I can feel a vibration. But it doesn't feel clammy to me, just cold."

As the President removed his hand and stepped back. Tom shook his head and stepped forward. "Perhaps it was just my imagination, I could have sworn…"

Placing his hand onto the pyramid for a second time, the surface suddenly appeared to give way and liquefy. For Tom, it felt almost like plunging his hand into a deep pool of water. Watching carefully, the President quickly stepped forward with a look of concern. "Tom, are you alright?"

The sensation was bizarre. The surface of the pyramid rippled and danced like water, but it didn't feel wet to the touch. If anything, it felt more like one of those plasma globes that often sits in teenager's bedrooms.

"Yes, I'm okay, it's incredible."

After a few minutes and satisfied that he'd experienced enough, Tom was just about to step back, when something unseen from within the blackness reached out and suddenly grasped hold of his hand. If that wasn't bad enough, a face suddenly appeared on the surface. Almost like a reflection watching him from under the gloomy surface.

"Holy shit!"

For Tom, the fright was like an electric shock forcing him to reel backwards and collapse onto the ground. Concerned for his colleague, Hillary immediately rushed across to where his hysterical friend was lying.

"Tom, are you okay? What happened?"

After re-composing himself, Tom took a deep breath and sat up, gazing towards the pyramid with wild eyes. "I… I saw a face looking out at me and then something grabbed me."

After a visual inspection, Hillary established that everything was normal, With no face at the wall and no change in colour, the pyramid's composition was just as before: an enormous wall of solid black. As he helped Tom to his feet, Hillary pointed to the wall and shrugged. "Well it seems alright now. Are you sure it wasn't simply your imagination playing tricks on you Tom? I mean it's been a while since we both had water."

Now back on his feet, Tom grimaced and glared back at the pyramid suspiciously. "No, I'm telling you, this was no illusion. There's something, or someone, in there."

65

Date: Unknown Location: Unknown

WALKING THROUGH THE nothingness was a disconcerting sensation for Helen Moore. Although she and Quest had experienced something similar two years earlier in Scotland, the experience was unnerving, almost like walking around a room blindfolded. The strength of the light was now so powerful, that it was impossible to know in which direction one was travelling. At least Quest and Moore had experienced a similar cavern before. The young marine, he was walking ahead and beginning to show real signs of stress and disorientation.

"We're dead, aren't we? I just know we're dead…"

Watching the youngster from the back of the group. *USS Richmond* Commander, Tom Dalby glanced nervously around and shouted out. "You're not dead Hudson, I can assure you of that."

As he spoke, the youngster suddenly stopped in his tracks and appeared to become wildly hysterical, his body shaking and tears streaming down his face. "What! Of course, we're dead, we must be. Just look at this fucking place. There must be a way out. Wait, what about this way…"

Without warning the youngster suddenly turned heel and ran off into the light.

"Hudson, Wait. For Christ sake, you'll get lost."

It was too late. Within seconds, his voice faded and the twenty-something year old was gone,

"Oh my God! we have to do something."

Without warning, Helen suddenly lunged forward to aid the teenager. But, before she could run, Reynolds sprang at her from behind and grasped hold of her arm to hold her back. "Reynolds! What the hell are you doing?! Let me go!"

Reynolds glanced across at an anxious looking Doctor Quest and shook his head.

"I'm sorry Professor, but the commander's right. We must remain together here. You run out there and we could end up losing you as well."

As Reynolds released Helen's arm, Quest stepped forward and lowered his voice. "He's right Helen. Besides, just because he's lost for the moment. That doesn't necessarily mean we won't see him again, he could still turn up."

Without another word, and after giving a sombre nod of agreement. Helen turned with the group as they turned back onto their original course and began walking forward.

*

After the two men completed their circumnavigation of the pyramid, Tom suddenly stopped, took a deep breath and groaned. "What is it Tom? You look troubled."

"I was just thinking about the face I saw. What if you were right and it wasn't one of those creatures. Perhaps it was someone trapped?"

For a second, the president appeared pessimistic, but then seemed to soften. "I suppose it's possible. After all, that's how this whole thing started."

Tom gave a look of confusion. "What?"

"There was a recent incident in the North Atlantic involving a fishing boat lost in a storm."

"Sounds ordinary enough. What's the connection?"

The president frowned. "What was unusual, Mr Duncan, was the distress signal sent by the captain just before his vessel sank. He reported seeing strange lights from underneath the water."

Taking a deep breath, Tom returned towards the pyramid and sighed. "So?"

"So, he and his crew vanished, Mr Duncan. Indeed, only yesterday I received a report that one of our submarines had arrived on station to begin an investigation. Now I know that this all sounds far-fetched. But what if you're right? What if the face you saw isn't one of those creatures at all. What if it's one of those fishermen trapped inside that thing?"

Gazing nervously at the solid black wall of the pyramid. Tom took a deep breath, slowly exhaled and stepped a closer. Once adjacent to the wall, he raised his left hand, glanced quickly back at the president and swallowed hard. "Well, I guess there's only one way to be sure."

*

Two Years Earlier - Midlina, Iceland

Dougie Allan leapt sideways away from the furious creature and bolted at speed towards the chasm. Standing by the remains of the Midlina Bridge, Caius watched in disbelief as Dougie raised his arm and flung the miniature black pyramid into the blinding light. A moment later, an explosion of brilliant white light ripped across the Midlina skyline and a massive energy wave erupted from the crater that lifted Dougie clean off his feet and into the air. As he crumpled onto the ground, he looked on with satisfaction as the black pyramid began to close.

"What have you done?!"

Caius was furious and Dougie knew that his fate was sealed. As he slowly turned to face his inevitable punishment, Dougie had already accepted the fact that he was probably going to die. So, without saying a word, he took a deep breath, closed his eyes and with an image of his beautiful wife, Mary in his mind, waited for the inevitable.

When nothing happened, Dougie slowly re-opened his eyes. Caius was standing about five meters away, but there was something different about him. Although obviously still seething at Dougie, he seemed somewhat humbled in manner, almost fearful perhaps. Then as Dougie raised his head to look around, he immediately understood why. From within the light of the pyramid, six cloaked figures were beginning to slowly materialise around him.

"Dougie..."

Suddenly remembering McArthur, Dougie spun around and ran across to where the badly burnt Alexander

McArthur lay. Kneeling beside him in the dust, Dougie looked down as the man coughed and spluttered, desperately trying to find the strength to talk.

"Dougie I'm sorry for involving you in this. I had… little choice."

As McArthur's appearance began to regress back to his original form, Dougie placed his hand on the creature's shoulder and shook his head. "It's okay lad, I understand."

"Wait, help me up. I want to see him."

Suddenly McArthur grabbed Dougie's arm and began to pull himself up so that he could see Caius. Watching the other six cloaked figures appear, McArthur wheezed, "It… It's over you've lost. Plea… Please reconsider, it's not too late."

With his head hung low, the apparently defeated Caius sighed. Then Dougie looked on in disbelief as the creature's mouth slowly curled upwards into that a familiar cruel smirk.

Then raising his hand, he gazed first at the emerging cloaked figures and then at the wounded McArthur and hissed, "You've won nothing Brother. This is only the beginning!"

Suddenly the ground shook and McArthur opened his mouth to protest. But it was too late.

The spot where Caius had been standing suddenly exploded into a shimmering vortex surrounded by brilliant white light.

Gazing at the light-filled turbulence, Dougie lowered his arm, glanced up at the six other figures and then at McArthur.

"He's getting away! Ye have tae stop him."

Spluttering, McArthur lay back down in the dust and wheezed, "For now, there is nothing we can do. There will be other chances."

"B… But what about you? I thought ye couldn't die."

Gazing at the others, McArthur winced in pain and gave an uneasy smile. "Th… this body can die, but what we are will live on. That's the foundation of all life Dougie."

Gazing down at the dying creature, Dougie desperately glanced up at the other cloaked figures, hoping, almost praying, that they would intervene. "Please, you must help him."

Met with no response, Dougie's gaze fell back to McArthur as the creature took a final breath and close his eyes.

"No! McArthur wake up… Please!"

As Dougie stared silently at McArthur's lifeless body, he swallowed hard, climbed to his feet and turned to the shimmering, but now dwindling, vortex of light and sighed. "I can't believe you're going let him go."

As he turned to address the group, one of the cloaked figures stepped forward and spoke. "Dougie, it was his request that we send you home."

Dougie had a sudden vision of being reunited with beautiful Mary and of being able to sit by his fire on cold nights or to walk through the flower filled glen in mid-summer.

It was a fine vision, but looking down at McArthur's lifeless body and across at the shimmering remains of the portal, he realised that he had now indivertibly become entangled in a war and that in this war, Caius had just won his first battle.

"If I go back now, he'll have won. I'd live, but I'd be living a lie. Knowing that he was still out there, I'm sorry but I can't let that happen."

"Dougie!"

Before the others could respond, Dougie suddenly bolted towards the shimmering portal and hurled himself into the dazzling white light. With a sudden burst of brightness, the portal closed behind him and Dougie Allan was gone. As silence fell on Midlina, one of the cloaked figures stepped forward and sighed. "Everything has transpired as I have foretold my brothers. The prophecy was correct."

*

As Tom pressed his hand against the icy black marblesque wall of the pyramid, he could feel his hand tingling as the wall suddenly began to liquefy. What was once solid, now resembled a vertical shimmering pool of dark, almost black water. Taking a deep breath, he plunged his hand in further. Standing behind Tom, next to the pyramid, a concerned looking President Hillary nervously stepped forward. "Tom, are you alright? I don't think you should get too close."

Although, to the president, it appeared that Tom had plunged his hand into water, Tom's senses were telling him something quite different. His hand didn't feel wet. In fact, it almost felt like the static you sense when rubbing a child's balloon against a woollen sweater.

"Weird, I could have sworn that something touched

me. Now I don't feel anything and whatever it was, now appears to be..."

Suddenly Tom's face turned to horror and he shrieked out loudly.

"Arghhh..."

"Tom what is it?! Are you okay?"

Before he could answer and pull his hand away to safety. Something grabbed hold of his arm and began to jerk at it violently. Convinced that this was more than energy, Tom yelled out loudly and thrust his free hand outwards towards the president, in a desperate attempt to request support. "Help me!"

Responding immediately, Hillary grabbed hold of Tom's free arm and attempted to pull him free. Unfortunately, his efforts seemed to be in vain, as whatever held Tom in its grasp was not keen to let go. As Tom shouted again, whatever held him unexpectedly changed form. In a single moment, it was no longer energy holding him. It now felt as if it was something physical, almost like a hand. As he turned, the wall suddenly began to morph again. But what initially began as a rippling black wall, now appeared foggy.

As the seconds ticked by, the haze cleared. Something large was forming within the wall's structure. Panic stricken and terrified, Tom screamed loudly, and frantically groped for the president's hand in a desperate attempt to pull himself free. Without warning, the wall of the pyramid suddenly gave way and exploded into a spinning tornado of light. In a moment of sheer panic, whoever or whatever was holding onto him, suddenly let go and came tumbling through the maelstrom. As the vortex finally snapped shut and the wall became solid again, an energy wave erupted, propelling Tom and the president backwards, just as the large shape of a man collapsed onto the ground.

With his heart pounding, Tom gasped heavily. Then, pulling himself up, he ran across to the figure and cautiously knelt beside him and took a nervous breath.

"Is he okay?"

From his kneeling position, Tom couldn't see the man's face, as he was lying face down on the ground. "I don't know, but I think it's definitely a man. Hang on."

Now up-close, Tom reached across to the man's shoulder and slowly hauled him over onto his back. Now with his face in full view, Tom suddenly gasped in disbelief as the figure became instantly recognisable.

"Oh my God! It's Dougie!"

66

Tuesday 25th October - 11.55pm CET - Vatican City, Italy

STROLLING THROUGH ST Peter's Square in semi-darkness, Father Antonio Demarco took a moment to acknowledge a young Swiss Guard as he passed by the *Piazza Protomartri Romani.* With a few minutes to spare before his meeting with Cardinal Bouchard, Antonio stopped by the *Campo Santo Teutonico* to briefly admire several newly planted flower beds, before taking a deep breath and turning towards the *Necropoli di San Pietro.*

As he approached the excavations office entrance, a tall dark figure unexpectedly stepped out from the shadows, forcing Antonio to jump in surprise. It took a few seconds for Antonio to identify the figure. Then as the man stepped into the light, Antonio sighed with relief as he recognised, Cardinal Bouchard.

"*Eminenza*, I'm sorry, but you gave me quite a fright."

As he stepped forward to greet his friend, Antonio could now see that Bouchard was no longer wearing his usual red cassock but was now sporting a smart grey business suit and charcoal grey trench coat. As Bouchard stepped slowly forward into the light, he took a deep breath and acknowledged Antonio with a wry smile. "Forgive me Antonio, but these days, one has to be careful. You never know who may be watching. Come, follow me. The others are waiting inside."

After Acknowledging Bouchard with a nod, both men turned towards the excavations office entrance and opened its large heavy door. Having stepped inside, Bouchard closed and locked the door behind him before motioning Antonio to leave his bag by the entrance. "You can leave your case here, my friend. It may be a little tricky to navigate the catacombs with a suitcase and you can collect it on your way out."

Giving a nod in agreement, Antonio did as he was instructed and placed his case down just inside of the stone entranceway. "Of course, *Eminenza.*"

Stepping forward, Bouchard pushed open a large glass door and motioned Antonio to step through first. As Antonio entered the necropolis, the cardinal followed behind and shut the door, leaving both men standing in a dimly lit underground passageway. As the pair slowly snaked their way through a maze of dusty Roman cobbled streets, Antonio suddenly tripped on a protruding cobble stone, causing him to stumble.

"Antonio, are you alright?"

Fortunately, Antonio managed to control his fall, and after a brief pause, he nodded in mild embarrassment before resuming their journey through the labyrinth.

Dating back to the first century AD, the *Vatican Necropolis*, or "*City of the Dead,*" is a little known roman cemetery where it is said the actual Tomb of Saint Peter lies. For Antonio, this experience was always special. He would often imagine himself walking on two-thousand-year-old Roman streets, wondering what life would have been like for those early Christians as they walked and worshiped in what must have been extremely harsh times.

"Tell me Antonio, what time is your flight?"

"5.45am, *Eminenza*. It's an early flight, so I took the liberty of booking myself into an airport hotel."

As the pair turned into a narrow passageway, Bouchard took a deep breath. "I see, and did you manage to contact your friend? I hope you sent my apologies for detaining you?"

Taking a breath, Antonio shook his head.

"No *Eminenza*, I haven't spoken to him personally, although I managed to send a message informing him of my new arrival time."

Walking behind the younger priest, Bouchard suddenly gritted his teeth angrily, before stealthfully reaching inside his coat pocket and pulling out what resembled a miniature syringe. After slipping it into the palm of his right hand, he pulled off its plastic cap and carefully slipped the needle between his fingers, so that it would not be easily seen.

"I tell you what, Antonio. After our meeting, I could have my driver take you to the airport if you like. If you give me your friend's number. I'll also make sure he's informed about what flight you're on."

Antonio smiled and shook his head. "Thank you *Eminenza*. I really appreciate that, but I wouldn't wish to put you to so much trouble."

"Believe me my friend, it's no trouble."

Suddenly Bouchard stopped dead and grasped hold of Antonio's arm.

"Antonio, stay still. You have a wasp crawling on the back of your neck."

"Really…"

Suddenly, Bouchard's hand moved like lightning, and in an instant, the needle struck Antonio in the back of his neck.

"Ouch!"

For Antonio, the shock of the tiny needle penetrating his skin felt like no more than an insect bite. But for Bouchard, this cold and calculated assault had been executed both perfectly and professionally. In a flash and with the deadly toxin now delivered, the miniature syringe was swiftly discarded and kicked aside.

In an effort to remove whatever had seemingly bitten him, Antonio stumbled and swiftly brushed the back of his neck with his hand.

"Are you alright? Did you get bitten?"

Stopping for a moment to catch his breath, Antonio turned to the concerned looking Bouchard and nodded.

"Yes it did."

"Can I see?"

Turning away from Bouchard, Antonio lowered his shirt collar so that his friend could inspect the wound.

"Well… it's an insect bite alright. It looks to me like a wasp sting. However in this low light, it's difficult to see. Are you alright to continue?"

Taking a deep breath, Antonio gave a nod and both

men turned and continued onwards, through the necropolis towards the *Tomb of St Peter*.

*

Date, Unknown Location, Unknown

As Reynolds, Commander Dalby and the other members of the group continued their journey through the never-ending labyrinth of light, Helen Moore stopped dead and grabbed hold of her colleague's sleeve.

"I'm telling you Richard, I definitely heard voices. Believe me, it's not my imagination!"

Richard Quest shook his head and sighed heavily.

"Nobody's calling you a liar Helen…"

His voice fell away as, for a moment, he thought he saw the light on the horizon briefly darken, almost like a shadow as it dances on the surface of a lake.

"What is it?"

Without responding, Quest stepped forward and called out to Agent Reynolds and Commander Dalby. "Hold on a minute, Commander."

A few meters ahead, Dalby and Reynolds stopped as instructed, turned and walked back to join the two scientists.

"Is everything alright Doctor?"

Straining his eyes, Quest focussed all his attention on one distant spot for a few moments before taking a slow, deep sigh. "Look! up ahead, there's something out there…"

It was true, the horizon had changed. What was once a

never-ending labyrinth of blinding light had transformed and as Quest and the group continued slowly onwards, Helen's mouth suddenly fell open. "Richard look!"

What was dazzling white light had now altered into shadow and within seconds the shadows morphed into a recognizable shape. A structure that Quest and Moore knew all too well. Joining the two scientists, Agent Reynolds suddenly stepped forward and spoke in shaky voice. "My God! It's another Pyramid!"

*

Wednesday 26th October - 12.01am CET - Vatican City, Italy

There was something wrong: Antonio couldn't quite put his finger on it, but for some reason he suddenly felt dizzy and unable to focus. At first, he thought that it was nothing more than the warm, muggy atmosphere of the necropolis. But as the seconds ticked by and his throat began to tighten, he now thought that perhaps he was having a bad reaction to his recent insect sting.

"We're a couple of minutes late, but I'm sure it won't be a problem. They're in here, just up ahead."

As the two men entered the small medieval chapel, known as the *Tomb of St Peter*, Antonio suddenly began to feel nauseous and extremely dizzy. Moments later, his situation worsened, when he suddenly stumbled on a protruding stone tile and collapsed helplessly onto his knees.

"Antonio, are you alright? Are you hurt?"

Sweating profusely and now in considerable pain,

the younger priest found himself unable respond to Bouchard's question. Lying on the floor, overcome with dizziness and nausea, all Antonio could do was to hope that his friend would come to his aid.

"Here, let me help you."

Lying on the uneven stone floor in a semi-conscious state, Antonio could now hear several muffled voices above. Although he could sense them, he couldn't accurately make out what they were saying. Then, without warning, he felt himself being hauled upwards and dragged along the stone floor. Where he sensed that he been brought into a larger room and was now being seated in a large chair.

"Antonio, can you hear me?"

"Huh…"

In an anxious bid to open his eyes, Antonio took a sudden intake of breath and with all his energy, pushed his heavy eyelids upwards. The scene that greeted him was not the one he'd been expecting. Rather than Bouchard and his cardinal's, gazing down at him, he was confronted by what appeared to be six sinister figures, all wearing black cassocks and long red hooded cloaks. Even more frightening, was that each of the figure's faces were obscured with an identical silver human face mask.

For a moment, Antonio thought that he was dreaming. Perhaps reliving some old childhood nightmare. But as the minutes passed and the soulless figures continued their cold gaze, he quickly realised that this was no dream.

An icy shiver of dread stroked the base of his spine, as Antonio gazed fearfully into one of the cold metallic faces and attempted to speak. Perhaps, he thought, just perhaps they could be reasoned with. But, despite his best efforts, he found that his body was just too weak and all that materialised were just a few low groans.

"Relax, my friend, there's no use fighting it."

"Huh?"

Suddenly, to Antonio's horror, one of the figures stepped forward and removed its mask. Unable to speak, let alone move. All Antonio could do was watch in disbelief as his friend and mentor, Bouchard, walked towards him and smiled coldly.

"It's called *Colodotoxin* Antonio. It's a remarkable substance, completely undetectable in the bloodstream. A larger dose would have killed you for sure, just as it did the others. But with just the right amount, it can invoke temporary paralyses."

As he listened to Bouchard's inconceivable admissions. Antonio's eyes frantically darted from side to side as he attempted to not only rise out the chair, but also find the words that would somehow persuade his mentor not to abandon Christ.

Bouchard ushered the group to step aside. As they moved, Antonio's expression turned to one of repugnance and disbelief. The tomb of St Peter, the very epitaph of the Roman Catholic church was a scene of destruction. What was once the holiest of the holiest, had been defaced. Its altar was now blood red in colour and above it, where a medieval cross once stood, now hung an enormous red flag. A flag of three interlocking circles which were intersected with two horizontal lines.

"You see Antonio, your beloved church is becoming part of something much bigger. Tomorrow Michael will change the world and we want to be part of it. Now of course, there will be those, like yourself, who'll disagree. But you can be assured they will be dealt with.

Bouchard, suddenly turned to face Antonio. "I have to admit that we even thought about asking you to join us, but somehow I suspected that your answer would be no."

As he moved, the injured priest's expression suddenly turned to one of terror as he spotted a momentary flash of light from a large knife that suddenly appeared in the cardinal's right hand. Then, as his eyes bulged with panic, the other masked figures stepped forward and formed themselves in a semi-circle around Antonio. Stepping menacingly closer, Bouchard raised the blade. "God said to *Abraham, take your son to the land of Moriah and kill your son there as a sacrifice for me...*"

When it came, the attack was swift and brutal. In one blow, Bouchard's knife struck Antonio's throat and for one single instant in time, neither man was entirely sure what had just happened. For Bouchard, the only evidence was a visible thin red line which ran along Antonio's jugular. For the priest, well, he wasn't even sure if the blade had struck him at all. The brightness in Antonio's eyes faded as if the very light within him had been extinguished.

As he began to cough and splutter, Bouchard quickly stepped backwards as Antonio's throat abruptly opened and a river of warm blood began to spill out onto his raincoat and then on to the ground. As Antonio's head dropped and his body slumped forward in the chair, Father Antonio Demarco took his final breath and within an instant, everything he ever was and everything he would become was gone.

After a minute of silence, Bouchard stepped forward and raised his arms in triumph. As he and the other five cloaked figures closed in and began to chant. "*We are one. We are one. We are one. Unity is the way. One mind, one body.*"

With one final glance at Antonio's lifeless body, Bouchard turned to the group and exhaled. "Now, my friends. We travel to New York, to embrace our destiny."

67

THE SCOTSMAN, DOUGIE Allan, was dreaming. He was sitting in the middle of an open wheat field with his beloved wife, Mary beside him. Above them, a warm afternoon sun shone down and a gentle wind blew and caressed the stalks of wheat, as they fluttered in the breeze like butterflies dancing wildly over flowers.

"Are ye alright, my love?"

Wearing a long red dress and white cotton bodice. With a voice that was as soft as silk, Mary made Dougie feel safe and complete.

"Aye, I'm grand lass. I was just thinking, we should come up here more often. The glen is so beautiful at this time of year.

Mary squeezed her husband's large hand, leaned across and gave him a kiss on the cheek. "Aye, it is, and tae be honest there's nae where else in the world I'd rather be right now.

Drawing breath, Dougie lay back and gazed upwards into the cloudless blue sky, before slowly exhaling. "Dougie…"

"Huh?"

Turning towards Mary, Dougie's expression suddenly turned to one of confusion. "Did ye hear that?"

Turning towards her husband, Mary shook her head. "Hear what my love?"

For a moment, he thought that perhaps he was hearing things.

"Nothing, I thought I heard a voice calling me."

"Dougie…"

"Argh…"

Without warning, Dougie suddenly felt as if something, or someone had grasped hold of his arm and was now pulling on it violently.

"What the…"

Then, in dismay, he turned to Mary and cried out as she began to melt away before his eyes.

"Mary, no!"

But it was too late. As he turned his head upwards towards the blue sky, the entire scene unexpectedly changed. The wheat field, the green glen and even his beloved wife were now becoming an intense brilliant white light. In a moment, the transformation was complete and Dougie's eyes flickered open.

"T…Tom… wh…whit the hell!"

For a moment, Tom didn't respond. After his recent adventure, he wasn't entirely sure that, this man was the real Dougie Allan or perhaps another imposter. But as he gazed into the man's eyes, he saw a spark. Something that he hadn't seen for a long time. It was a look that he remembered seeing after he and Dougie first met in Alva two years earlier. That look was one of vulnerability and perhaps even fear.

"Dougie is it really you?"

As his confusion slowly dissolved, the big man gave a disorientated nod. "Aye lad… of course it's me. Why wouldn't it be?"

Glancing at the President, Tom tilted his head and gave a sigh. "Alright, in that case, do you remember where it was the last time we met?"

"Whit?"

"Just answer the question Dougie… please!"

Dougie thought for a moment and gave a weak smile. "Aye, of course it was in Alva… at that flying contraption. The helicopter, I think they called it."

Glancing over at the president, Tom nodded with relief. "Mr President, may I introduce my friend, Dougie Allan."

As Hillary walked across, both men grasped hold of Dougie's arms and hauled him to his feet. Gazing at the kilted Scotsman, the president grinned broadly and extended his hand for the bewildered looking newcomer to shake.

"George Hillary, Mr Allan. You don't know what this means to me. I've heard so much about you. It's not every day you get to meet a 300 year old man."

"Oh, er aye… grand tae meet ye."

Now on his feet and looking around the expanse, Dougie's expression abruptly turned serious.

"Laddie, I've so much tae tell ye. Iceland, we're in trouble…"

Tom glanced down at the book given to him by Father McRae, and smiled. "It's okay Dougie, we know."

Dougie's expression suddenly turned to one of confusion. "Whit do ye mean, ye ken. How can that be?"

Glancing firstly across at the president and then back to Dougie, Tom placed his hand on the Scotsman's shoulder and gave a deep sigh. "That, my friend, will take a little explaining."

*

Wednesday 26th October - 8.00am CET - Dubrovnik, Croatia

"This is the BBC World Service. I'm Steve Grayson reporting live from New York, where the atmosphere is electric. The city's streets have been adorned with hundreds of red flags and banners displaying the gold UNITY symbol. Even the United Nations itself has had a makeover. Instead of flying the flags of the worlds 196 individual countries, the UN is now flying a single flag. This flag represents UNITY, one world, one people. Even though its only 3am here on the east coast, thousands of devoted followers have already begun lining the streets of Manhattan in anticipation of seeing Michael for the first time.

In other news, Police in Rome have begun an investigation into the discovery of a priest's body which has been discovered in a park, a short walk from the Vatican. Details are sketchy, Police have not released the name of the victim, nor have they said how he was killed. Police Commissioner, Mario Bertoli, said that the investigation is still in its infancy and at this stage nothing is being ruled out."

Sitting in a small private study, Saša, the priory's young Dominican pupil, suddenly leaned across and switched off the radio. After grabbing a copy of a newly printed email, he opened the study door and sped along the corridor like an angry bull running towards a red sweater. Moments later, and after climbing a single flight of stone steps, he rushed into the priory's small, but well-stocked library. As the door suddenly flung open, a startled Abbot, Vladimir Palovic looked up and dropped his book in surprise as the troubled youngster rushed across to where he was sitting.

"Saša! Polako moj mladi prijatelju, uspori. Slow down. You'll injure yourself."

After taking a moment to catch his breath, Saša nodded and slapped down the piece of paper in front of the elderly abbot. "*Oprostite Oče*, but you have to read this."

"Što je to?"

Pushing the sheet forward, Saša's expression turned to one of deep concern. "*Oprostite ali, molim Vas, samo pročitajte!*"

Giving a nod, the old man put his glasses on, picked up the email and began to read.

"My dear Vladimir

Please accept my apologies for not arriving yesterday as planned, but as mentioned, I'm deeply concerned with the seemingly unnatural rise of the religious group, UNITY. After deciphering the symbol, I feel that there are too many unanswered questions. I discussed my concerns with Cardinal Bouchard and he suggested that I should meet with him and other members of the deity who had similar concerns. Now, although this may be nothing more than a suspicion on my part. I sense that the Cardinal isn't being entirely truthful with me. However, as a Christian, I feel obliged to at least give him a chance.

I've attached all my research regarding the symbols to this email. You must see this material delivered to either Doctor Richard Quest or Professor Helen Moore. They work for the British Government and will know what to do. I also mentioned you to them, when I last met them in Rome, so they may attempt to seek you out.

Vladimir, I must also mention that Bouchard knows of our friendship and may try to contact you. Now, although my suspicions at this stage are nothing more than that, suspicions,

I would suggest that if you don't hear from me by noon tomorrow, you should consider leaving Dubrovnik for somewhere safer. At least while things settle down. In the meantime, I'm about to meet up with Bouchard and when finished, I've arranged to take an early morning flight to Dubrovnik. So, all being well, I'll see you tomorrow.

Your friend,

Antonio

After he'd finished reading, Palovic folded the paper in half, took off his glasses and gave a sigh. "*Hvala* for bringing this to me Saša."

For a moment, the worried looking youngster remained

silent before sitting forward and grasping the old man's arm. "*Oče… ja…*"

"Saša what is it… what's wrong?"

Swallowing hard, the young pupil lowered his head in sorrow. "*Oče…* A few minutes ago, I was listening to the news and I heard a report that a man's body was discovered in a park, close to the Vatican"

Palovic took a deep breath and shook his head. "*Prijetelju moj*, Rome is a big city, it could have been anyone. I'm sure that…"

Saša shook his head and raised his voice. "*Ne! Oče*, I'm sorry but the reporter said that the victim was… a Priest!"

Suddenly the abbot's face turned a deathly shade of white and he slowly began to shake his head in disbelief. "Žao *mi je Oče…*"

Climbing to his feet, the old man suddenly exhaled and began to restlessly pace back and forth. A minute later he turned to his pupil and groaned. "*Saša* my friend, I need your help.

"*Naravno Oče*, anything."

Ushering his young pupil closer, Palovic lowered his voice to a whisper, "*Saša*, go ahead and print everything from Antonio's email. Once you've finished, delete everything, understand? Everything."

"*Da Oče.*"

"Then I want you pack a bag…"

"A bag!"

Palovic nodded. "*Da…* and Saša, let's keep this between ourselves. There's clearly something amiss here, so, the fewer people that know the better."

Saša nodded and stepped forward, towards the door. "I understand, Father."

"Place all the information from Antonio into an envelope and bring it to me along with the book. Let's meet back here in about 30 minutes."

As the teenager moved towards the door, he suddenly stopped and turned back nervously towards Palovic and raised his voice. "Where are we going father?"

The old man abruptly fell silent for a moment and after taking a deep breath, responded.

"We're going to take a journey Saša. One that I hope will provide answers."

"*Oče?*"

"*Da, sine moj?*"

"Everything's going to be okay, isn't it?"

Gazing at his anxious looking pupil, Palovic stepped forward, placed his hand on the youngster's shoulder and offered a reassuring smile. "*Dragi moj prijatelju*, I don't know what's happened to Antonio. But, I believe that God would want me to seek out the truth. If, as Antonio suspected, there is indeed a conspiracy, we need to root it out.

Now, although I may not be as spritely as I once was in my youth. I am prepared to do this alone if necessary. However, if you could find it in your heart to help, it would be greatly appreciated."

Without hesitation, the youngster immediately stepped forward and offered a confident smile. "*Naravno Oče*, it would be an honour."

68

Date, Unknown Location, Unknown

AGENT REYNOLDS PULLED out his pistol, lowered his voice and ushered the rest of the group to get behind him. "I said be quiet! I'm telling you I heard voices. Commander, if you please."

Without saying a word, Quest and Moore followed the agent's instruction and moved to the rear of the group, whilst Commander Dalby gave a nod, drew his weapon and stepped forward to join Reynolds up front. As they moved, the enormous black Pyramid loomed over them. Towering above them, like a colossal bird of prey about to strike.

"…And what of this Father McRae, what happened to him?"

Although the source of the voice couldn't be determined through the overwhelming brightness, Reynolds sensed that from the volume of the conversation, that they were very close.

*

Suddenly Dougie raised his hand to silence Tom and the president, who immediately fell silent and relocated behind the big man.

"What is it Dougie?"

"Whisht laddie, I thought I Heard something…"

Without warning Tom suddenly yelled out in surprise, as two men in US Naval uniforms and brandishing pistols, suddenly emerged out of the light, shouting at them to remain still.

"Stay where you are! Don't move!"

"Whit the hell!"

As Dougie sprang forward into a naturally defensive position. Tom grasped hold of his friends arm and pulled him back.

"Dougie, don't! It'll be alright."

For a moment, Mark Reynolds couldn't believe his eyes. Staring at the three men in front of him in disbelief. He motioned Commander Dalby to lower his weapon and as he did, Reynolds placed his own weapon back in its holster and stepped forward with a look of suspicion on his face. "Mr President, is it really you?"

As Dougie and Tom stepped aside, Hillary walked forward and smiled.

"Yes, it is and thank you for not shooting us Agent Reynolds, isn't it?"

As Reynolds nodded, Dalby stepped forward, just as Professor Moore and Doctor Quest emerged out of the light.

"Agent Reynolds, please allow me to introduce Dougie Allan and Tom Duncan, who I believe…"

"Dougie!… Tom!"

Overcome with emotion, Helen Moore suddenly leapt forward towards the two men and instantly flung her arms around the big Scotsman and kissed him on the cheek.

"Dougie! I... we thought you and Tom were dead. I'm so glad to see you!"

As she gazed into the Scotsman's eyes, she suddenly remembered their first meeting two years earlier in Scotland. After being assigned as part of a team to investigate Dougie and his claims of time travel and encounters with fearsome cloaked creatures., the two scientists were thrown into a whirlwind of adventure, which led to the discovery of a bizarre black pyramid underneath a local silver mine. That discovery was only the beginning. What ensued was a race against time to find the cause of a series of catastrophic disasters which scarred the planet and left millions of people dead.

Startled at her sudden appearance and her outburst of emotion, Dougie uncharacteristically blushed and smiled warmly at the scientist.

"Easy lass, it's grand tae see ye too. Although tae be honest, you folks are the last twa people in the world I would hae expected to see in here."

As Helen released Dougie, she immediately turned to Tom and grinning, like a Cheshire cat, proceeded to walk forward and give him an equally warm bear hug.

"Mr Duncan, Tom, it's so nice to see you again. Are you alright?"

Drawing breath and feeling somewhat bewildered, Tom simply smiled and gave a nod.

"I am, Professor thank you. It feels like I've not seen you in years."

“Believe me, I know what you mean.”

After releasing Tom, Helen stepped back and Quest stepped forward. “It’s good to see you again Dougie… Tom, Mr President.”

As each member of the group took it in turn to shake hands, Commander Dalby walked up to the president and gave a salute. “Mr President. Commander Thomas Dalby, *USS Richmond*. Sir, if I may ask, how did you end up here?”

Glancing firstly at Tom and Dougie in their 17th century Scottish attire, the president’s smile quickly dissolved away as he stepped forward and addressed the Naval officer personally.

“It’s a long story Commander. Nevertheless, all I can say now is that I’ve been the victim of a mutiny.”

Suddenly Dalby’s expression turned to one of shock. “Sir!”

The president raised his hand and continued. “For the moment, we must put that aside Commander. In the here and now, the seven of us have something in common.”

Glancing at the group, Hillary took a deep breath and sighed. “I don’t know what that reason is. But I do know that every one of us here has experienced or shared an extraordinary moment. A moment that makes us special.”

As he addressed the group. Hillary now began to walk slowly around, gazing at each person as he moved past them: Dougie, Tom, Agent Reynolds, Doctor Quest, Professor Moore and finally, Commander Thomas Dalby.

“Think about it! Firstly, a fishing vessel disappears in the North Atlantic. Before it sinks, it’s captain reports seeing a mysterious light underneath the waves. As a result,

I find myself ordering an investigation. One which will eventually bring you to this place. Then, I hear that our two British scientist friends, Doctor Quest and Professor Moore, are almost killed in Rome by a crazed maniac."

After pausing for breath, the president then turned to Tom and continued. "Mr Duncan, you were also pulled through time and not only did you miraculously survive your ordeal, but also received that mysterious book into the bargain. A book that, at least for the moment, is confounding. Then, we have Mr Allan here. A man out of time, a man who's been pulled away from everything and everyone he's ever known or loved.

Finally, there's me, George Hillary. The President of the United States. A man who's own colleagues plotted against me. Prepared to commit murder, simply because I refused to join their fanatical religious group. A group that has arisen from nowhere and one that has become a major religious and political power in the world."

As the president's words faded, Tom glanced at Dougie and stepped forward, clearing his throat. "I'll be honest Mr President. I'm unaware of what's happened in the modern world. But I do know that if my encounter is anything to go by, this Caius creature is brutal, callous and has little regard for human life. In fact, if it wasn't for the actions of another, I doubt I would have survived."

The president nodded and glanced around the group before continuing. "It sounds to me as if we had a similar experience, Tom. Indeed, we're dealing with two distinct factions."

Having remained quiet until now, Richard Quest suddenly stepped forward. "I'm sorry to interrupt, Mr

President. Tom, you mentioned that you received a book. May I look?"

Nodding, Tom picked up the old book and handed it across to Quest. As the scientist began to flick through its delicate pages, he was joined by his colleague, Helen Moore, who looked on with curiosity. After a few moments, Quest closed the book and turned back towards the president. "You're right, I've never seen anything like it. Hopefully there will be a way to decipher it."

As the president nodded, Tom interrupted. "I hope so, because this Caius seemed very focused on locating the artefact and Father McRae mentioned that…"

With a look of disbelief appearing on his face, Dougie jumped forward. "Oh please God laddie, tell me that he didn't find it, did he?"

Tom shook his head and looked at Dougie in shock. "You know of him?"

Dougie nodded unhappily, as he remembered his encounter in Iceland. "Aye, I met the bastard alright. He's bad news I can tell you that. Ye can be sure that whatever he's got planned, it'll nae be good."

Tom's expression now turned to one of curiosity. "Dougie, do you know what this artefact might be?"

Taking a deep breath, Dougie nodded reluctantly. "Aye… I was told by Alexander McArthur, that's the name O' the creature that befriended me. He said that each of them has a key of some kind. I dinnae ken whit it's for exactly, but I ken it resembles a small black pyramid. Now, from what I've seen, it's very powerful…"

As Dougie spoke, the president glanced across at Mark Reynolds, who immediately stepped forward and interrupted the Scotsman in full flow. "Dougie. I have something to tell you."

For a moment, the Scotsman look puzzled. "Aye lad, go on then."

As Reynolds fell silent, he glanced awkwardly around the group for a moment before continuing. "I was there, in Iceland, that day. I was assigned as a bodyguard for President Bryant. I followed him out to the bridge and well, when I got there, what I saw was frightening to say the least. I just hid out of sight."

"Whit did ye see lad?"

As he spoke, images of the battle between the cloaked fearsome creatures suddenly began to replay in his mind. " I… I saw everything, including you comforting one of the dying creatures and your eventual escape through the portal."

Unexpectedly, a sudden rush of guilt swept over the agent and as consequence he sighed heavily and stepped back awkwardly, feeling ashamed. "I'm just sorry I couldn't help."

Feeling a sudden rush of sympathy for the man, Dougie groaned, stepped forward and placed his hand on Reynolds' shoulder. "Look laddie, dinnae feel bad, ye did the right thing. Besides, if he'd spotted ye, you'd be dead now."

Without warning, Helen suddenly rushed forward and grasped hold of Reynolds' arm. "Mr Reynolds, look!"

As they turned towards the light, there was an abrupt gasp from the group as the figure of a twenty something year old male dressed in US Naval uniform, emerged from the void.

"Oh my God, Hudson!"

Upon eyeballing the youngster, the entire group immediately turned heel and rushed across to where the marine was standing. Once there however, it soon became clear that the he was not entirely himself. The last time the young marine had been seen, he was in a severely distressed state. But now, having been lost for hours, he appeared calm and relaxed.

As Commander Dalby approached the youngster, he noticed that he was unarmed. In fact, upon closer inspection, he was not only missing his rifle, but also his gun belt, 9mm pistol and spare ammunition.

"Hudson, are you alright? What happened?"

Despite waiting, the marine didn't respond and at first. Dalby figured that he must be injured. But as time progressed and the other members of the group stepped closer, it was Doctor Quest who noticed that there was something different about him. His skin was unusually pale and his eyes seemed brighter than normal.

"Hudson, are you, alright?"

Quest suddenly stepped forward and without warning, grasped hold of Dalby's left shoulder and pulled him backwards to what he considered to be a safe distance. "I'm sorry Commander, but I don't think that's Hudson!"

69

Wednesday 26th October - 10.25am CET - Dubrovnik, Croatia

AS WARM RAYS of morning sunlight glistened over the iconic red tiled rooftops and grand spires of the old city, an unshaven taxi driver waited patiently by his car, as an old priest and a teenager placed their two bags into the trunk of his silver *Ford Mondeo*. Glancing back towards the stone steps of his beloved priory, Abbot, Vladimir Palovic drew breath and inhaled the sweet smell of Jasmine for one last time. He swallowed hard to fight back the tears, just as his young pupil opened the car door. "*Ne brinite, Oče*. Everything will work out, you'll see."

Grasping the youngsters hand, the old man wiped away a tear and then gave a weak smile.

"*Hvala*, my friend."

As Palovic climbed into the back seat of the taxi, Saša closed the door and walked around to the opposite side. `Then, after scrambling inside the car, the somewhat scruffy taxi driver shut his door, started the engine and slowly pulled away.

"Where to, Father?"

As Palovic briefly eyed his young pupil, he drew breath, glanced back towards the priory and sighed. "The airport please."

Within moments, the car's engine roared and the taxi sped away down a narrow side street, offering Vladimir Palovic and his young companion one final opportunity to glance back towards a life they'd known for so long. Facing forward, they both glanced at each other anxiously, knowing full well that they were both heading into an uncertain and potentially dangerous future.

"*Oče?*"

"*Da Saša.*"

"You seemed reluctant to talk about it earlier, but if may ask, where exactly are we going?"

The old man nodded and offered a comforting smile. "*Prijatelju moj*, we know the names of the two British Scientists that Antonio wanted me to meet. We also know that they were working with him on something that was discovered in Scotland. So, I thought that finding them would be a good place for us to start."

As the walls of the old city fell out of view, Saša nodded and leaned back. A moment later his expression suddenly turned to one of confusion. "*Oprostite Oče*, but where exactly is that?"

Turning to the youngster, the old man smiled and inhaled. "Why Saša, We're going to Edinburgh of course."

*

Wednesday 26th October - 3.55pm EST - New York City

As the remains of an afternoon rain shower finally dissipated, Brother Thomas Weyn joined Brother Simon and thirty or so members of the *Red Council* as they each sat in quiet meditation, within the walls of the *Red Chapel.* He appeared indifferent to the fanatical hysteria happening on the streets outside. Most of New York, as with every other of the world's major cities had been frantically preparing to celebrate Michael's arrival.

Outside UNITY's headquarters thousands had gathered, many carrying flags and banners, some with the words, *"We are One!"* embossed on them. Even the officers of New York's police department, were feverishly encircling the building, attempting to provide a ring of steel to ensure the safety of the *Red Council.*

With UNITY now in firm control of the US federal government, it had been decreed by Brother Weyn that all law enforcement officers must don the uniform of the new state. This black *Naziesque* uniform comprised of a formal tunic, trousers and a leather gun belt, containing either a The Beretta 92F semi-automatic pistol, or a Walther PP9.

For the customary police hat, Weyn ruled that all local or national emblems were to be removed and replaced with a single distinctive band of red ribbon around the brim of the hat, as well as around the sleeves of each jacket. Lastly, each officer would wear the gold emblem of UNITY, both as an insignia on his or her hat, as well as a badge, pinned to their jacket.

Inside the walls of the *Red Chapel,* Brother Weyn

exhaled, before slowly opening his eyes and climbing to his feet. As he rose, the other members of the group followed his lead and stood in quiet respect. Gazing into the faces of some of the most powerful people on the planet, Weyn felt a sense of pride and satisfaction as he glanced across at each member of the group. Cardinal Jean Louis Bouchard, UK Prime Minister, Anne Petrie, US General; Mark Gates and Russian Premier; Andre Vasiliev, were but a selection of the famous and powerful now standing humbly before him.

"Today is History! Today, my brothers and sisters, your lives and the lives of everyone around you will be changed forever. Your politics, your petty squabbles, your religion, race, creed and colour. Everything that has ever divided our world is over. From this day forth there is only UNITY, one world, one voice!"

Suddenly, the group raised their arms and chanted his words in unison.

"We are one!... We are one!... We are one!"

As the chanting subsided, Weyn took a deep breath, raised his hand and prompted the group to be seated. "Brothers and sisters, you have travelled far. You have overcome adversity amid difficult circumstances and have been asked to make difficult choices. For that, you have my gratitude. It is never easy to kill, yet many of you have done so. It is never easy to kill a friend, or a family member and yet again, many of you have done that also. All in the knowledge that the life you leave behind is nothing compared to the rapture which now stands before you. So, as we go from this place to welcome Michael, leave your old life behind and join me. Power, glory and riches will be yours for the taking."

Weyn's voice shrank away as the overweight, fifty something year old Russian premier, Andre Vasiliev, suddenly rose from his seat and interrupted the proceedings. "Excuse me Comrade, but may I speak."

Glancing briefly at the others, Weyn shrugged. "Of course, brother. You are among friends here. Say what you will."

"Your promises are hollow comrade. You say you'll deliver us riches beyond belief, yet, I've seen no evidence of this. Now, I have no problem with killing. I've been doing it most of my life. But I do expect to be paid for my work."

At first, Weyn remained silent. Then, glancing towards Brother Simon, he gave a single nod and Simon climbed to his feet, walked across to where the Russian was standing and ushered him to the side.

"Brother, I understand your concerns and as a gesture of good will, please follow Brother Simon and I assure you, he'll provide you with but a small taste of the riches that await you. I hope that this will prove my sincerity."

As a greedy sneer appeared on the fat Russian's face. The fifty something nodded in agreement and shuffled out into the aisle. Moments later and standing by the door of the *Red Chapel,* Vasiliev did as instructed and followed Brother Simon.

Once in the corridor, Simon closed the door and ushered the politician into an adjacent room. A room that contained only two things. A small wooden box, no bigger than a standard shoe box, sitting on top of an ornate white marble pedestal in the centre of the room.

"Mr President, this is for you and is a token of our gratitude."

Smirking greedily, Vasiliev licked his lips and sauntered across to the pedestal and picked up the box. "What is it? What's inside?"

Simon shook his head. "I don't know Sir, why don't you take a look."

Turning away from Brother Simon, Vasiliev licked his lips in anticipation, took a deep breath and, as instructed opened the box.

As he gazed inside the empty container, Vasiliev suddenly became enraged, now knowing full well that he had been deceived. "Why you…"

As he turned towards Simon in fury, his words suddenly evaporated and his expression turned to one of disbelief. The smartly dressed Brother Simon was now pointing a Ruger 22–SR pistol with matching silencer directly at his head.

"What is this?"

"Why Mr President, did your mother never teach you that greed was a sin?"

Before the he could respond, Simon pulled the trigger, ploughing a single shot direct into the politician's head. As the bullet struck, it sent him reeling uncontrollably backwards onto the ground. As he collapsed, Simon took a deep breath and calmly stepped across to where the fat Russian had dropped. Then, raising the pistol once more, proceeded to fire two additional shots into the body, firstly into his chest and finally another into his head.

"Goodbye, Mr President."

After a brief silence, Simon coolly walked across to the white marble pedestal in the centre of the room, opened the wooden box, placed his pistol inside and shut the lid. Moments later and after taking one final glance at the body, he stepped across to the doorway, switched of the light and exited the room.

70

Date, Unknown, Location, Unknown

AFTER RELEASING COMMANDER Dalby's arm, Quest and the rest of the group remained silent, waiting tolerantly for Hudson, or whoever he was to make the first move. However, as the seconds slipped into minutes, Dalby became increasingly inpatient and, in a shock move, lurched forward, took out his weapon and pointed it directly towards the youngster. "Who or what the hell are you and where is Hudson?"

At first, the creature didn't respond. Then as Dalby gritted his teeth, and his finger began to tighten on the trigger. His arm suddenly began to wobble and then a few seconds later it began to shake violently Finally it became so violent that he shrieked out in alarm, "What the hell!"

The group looked on in shock, as the officer's body appeared to fall into a sudden and uncontrollable spasm, forcing him to drop his weapon and collapse onto the ground.

As he fell, Helen Moore rushed forward and cried out in anguish. "Please don't hurt him, he was only afraid."

Glancing across at her, the creature immediately released Dalby and drew breath. "Why, I had no intention of hurting him Professor. But I am afraid, violence of any kind cannot be permitted here."

After rushing to Dalby's aid, Helen Moore took a moment to check that the officer was okay, before helping him up. Once assured, she stepped back as Quest moved forward.

"Who are you? I mean, you're not Hudson, are you?"

At first the youngster thought for a moment, smiled and then shook his head. "No Doctor, you are quite right. I'm not Hudson."

"Then who are you?"

Glancing at each of the seven, the creature nodded and smiled. "I have many names Doctor and have lived many lives. You, along with the rest of your species were never meant to know of our existence. But it now appears that fate has brought us together."

Glancing at Dougie and Tom, Quest drew breath and continued. "Fate? What exactly does that mean?

Stepping forward, the creature began to slowly walk amongst them, stopping occasionally to recognise each person. "You are all witnesses Doctor, all of you. All chosen to represent humanity in the war that is to come. The scientists, the military man, the politician, the accidental hero and the family man."

Suddenly, Quest look puzzled. "War, what war?"

Revolving around to face the group, Tom gasped in amazement as the boy standing in-front of him suddenly morphed into the shape of a familiar old priest.

"I already explained that to you Tom, don't you remember?"

"Oh my God! Father McRae?"

Seconds later, there was another gasp. This time by Mark Reynolds, as the creature stepped towards the president and transformed again. This time into the shape of the Deputy Director of the CIA, David Tyler. Finally, the creature stepped across to where Dougie was standing and changed once more. This time however, for the Scotsman at least, this was to be the most profound change of all.

"Oh my God!"

"Hello Dougie."

For a moment, Dougie stood dumbfounded as the familiar figure of Alexander McArthur now stood opposite, smiling at him. A man, who 300 years earlier had once held the position of mine manager in his home village of Alva. When he vanished, it was presumed by many, that he'd fled the village having first plundered the mine for its riches.

That was the spark. That was the day that Dougie was offered that damn job. A job that not only turned his life upside down, but also a job that would ultimately rip him away from the one person he loved most, his wife, Mary.

"But… you're dead! I saw you die."

Taking a deep breath, the creature smiled, placed a hand on his shoulder and shook his head. "No Dougie. As I said, we have many lives and sometimes interacting with us brings out the best in people and unfortunately it sometimes brings out the worst."

Returning to the centre of the group, the creature

paused for a moment before morphing back into its original shape of the young marine, Hudson.

"There is a war coming, a war that will rip your world apart. It is a war that many amongst you have called the *end of days*. By now you know the name Caius? Indeed, some of you have already met him. Yes, he is of my kind, but unlike myself, he was banished for his greed and lust for power. Right now, he has amassed an army. The likes of which your world has never seen before. He will ultimately seduce your people into slavery, before finally carrying them to the gates of oblivion itself, unless he is stopped."

Placing a hand on Tom's shoulder, the president suddenly cleared his throat and stepped forward. "Forgive me Sir, but if he is so powerful. How on earth can we defend ourselves, let alone fight him?"

After a moment, the creature nodded. "Mr President, to win a battle, you must first have soldiers. You people, along with others around the world are to be our seeds. We've already provided you with three weapons. Firstly, the book which you now have in your possession. This contains all the knowledge you 'll need for the dark days ahead."

"Secondly, as humans you were given the gift of free will. This is a most precious and powerful commodity and is something that can only be given, never taken."

Pausing for a moment the creature drew breath and turned towards Dougie and Tom.

"Finally, there is an object. A key, which I believe you're already familiar with. It is an object of immense power, that in the wrong hands, could end all life on your world. However, if used wisely, it could restore the balance."

Dougie glanced across at Tom and both men nodded in unison. Then Tom addressed the creature personally. "We understand, but if may ask. The book you've given us appears to be nothing more than gibberish. None of us can decipher it. How are we to understand its content?"

Glancing across at the two scientists and then again at Tom. The creature smiled perceptively and slowly inhaled. "The answer you seek is out their Tom, you'll find it. All you need is a little faith."

Without warning, the creature's image quickly began to dissipate. As it faded Tom rushed forward and cried out. "Wait! How do we get home? Please don't go!"

As the creature fused back into the blinding white light, it suddenly uttered five final words.

"Tom, you are already home."

Then, as it finally evaporated, Tom's head dropped in despair, when Dougie placed a hand on his friend's shoulder. "Laddie, look!"

Glancing upwards, Tom sighed in relief and, for once, his anguish turned to Joy. As above their heads a gaping hole appeared in the brilliance, almost like a crack in its very fabric. On closer inspection, it appeared to be the opening to a cave and as Tom glanced at a familiar looking pile of rocks and debris laying on the ground, he turned to Dougie excitedly and grasped his friend's arm with joy. "Dougie… I think he's right. I think we're back!"

71

Wednesday 26th October - 5.10pm EST - New York City

AS THE LAST of the afternoon's sunlight slowly dipped below the Manhattan skyline, huge crowds that had been waiting patiently outside the Offices of UNITY suddenly surged forward and roared in jubilation as Brother Thomas Weyn and other members of the *Red Council* emerged out of the modest 53rd street office block. As large numbers of uniformed police officers began to frantically clear a path through the crowd, he waved enthusiastically as a fleet of black limousines pulled up and Weyn and his entourage pilled inside the vehicles. Once secure, the cars pulled away amid cheering crowds and within moments, they were gone. Speeding away towards East 42nd Street and to the home of the United Nations.

In the first car, Brother Weyn and Brother Simon sat quietly in the rear, whilst the driver up front did his best to slowly navigate through the crowded streets. Glancing across at Brother Simon, Weyn cleared his throat and broke the silence. "Are you alright Brother? You seem troubled."

Simon turned to Weyn and offered a nervous smile. "Not at all, I was just wondering…"

"Wondering what?"

Looking down at the small UNITY tattoo on the back of his hand, Simon took a deep breath and continued. "I was wondering, how we'll recognise Michael? I mean no-one has ever seen him and I've been responsible for generating the guest lists. We've produced 2440 badges for the event and not one has been generated for Michael. Aren't you concerned that he'll be denied entry? That could turn out to be rather embarrassing."

Weyn pondered the question for a moment and then laughed.

"Don't worry my friend, exactly how Michael arrives is inconsequential. I can assure you that when he shows up, you and the whole world will know."

Feeling slightly ashamed at asking what he considered to be a stupid question, Simon shook his head and leaned back. "Of course, Brother, I understand."

Turning once again towards his deputy, Weyn drew breath. "I sense it's something else…Ah, let me guess, it's Vasiliev isn't it? You object to the killing?"

For a moment Simon shuffled uncomfortably in his seat. Then, he turned to Weyn and shook his head. "Not at all, the man was a pig, he deserved to die. It's just that given today's circumstances, I would have preferred something subtler than a bullet to the head."

Glancing downwards at Simon's UNITY tattoo, Weyn nodded in agreement.

"As would I Brother. However, I sense that that's not really what occupies your thoughts."

Simon reluctantly smiled. "You're right as always. To be honest, I'm concerned that we still have a number of loose threads."

"Such as?"

Simon groaned. "The press continues to generate stories of resistance. I've just learnt that our offices in Manchester and Berlin were damaged yesterday."

Weyn's eyelids rose and he then leaned back and exhaled. "I see. Well then, tomorrow morning, we'll despatch our own security forces to those locations to investigate and, if necessary, arrest any suspected conspirators."

Simon nodded. "Of course, Brother. There is also one other small issue that I need to bring to your attention."

"Which is?"

"During my conversation with Bouchard this morning, he stated that he had some concerns regarding a Vatican priest, Father Demarco. Apparently, he'd been liaising with two British scientists, A Doctor Richard Quest and Professor Helen Moore.

"What kind of concerns?"

"They'd been working with Demarco on decrypting an unusual set of symbols which were apparently discovered in Scotland."

Weyn rolled his eyes and took a deep breath. "You know Brother, this is all very interesting but…"

Simon raised his hand, cutting Weyn off in mid-sentence. "Forgive me for interrupting Brother, but you don't understand. Perhaps if I show you one of the symbols, then you will." As Simon overturned his hand, to reveal his tattoo. Weyn's eyes widened, as he now understood, as to which symbol his colleague was referring to."

"Now, according to Bouchard, Demarco is dead and no longer a problem. But afterwards, I had another conversation with General Gates. He explained that only a week ago, the Deputy Director of the CIA had personally sent an agent out to work alongside our two scientist friends, apparently to investigate an incident off Sable Island."

As the enormous United Nations building came into view. Weyn took a deep breath and turned towards Simon and lowered his voice. "Listen Brother, in a few hours you'll have all the resources you'll need. I would like you to personally handle this investigation."

"Me?"

Weyn nodded. "I want anyone who's come into contact with that Symbol and any of its associated translations brought to me. Use whatever resources it takes, do you understand?"

Simon nodded in acknowledgment. "Of course, Brother. I'll see that its done."

*

5.55pm EST - United Nations, New York City

46 year-old Richard Delaney had been a reporter all his life. The son of an esteemed New York lawyer, Delaney graduated from the *University of Florida* and his first job was as a junior reporter for the *Miami Herald.* With two years' experience under his belt, he swiftly moved up the ranks. Gaining positions in such coveted publications

such as, *The New York Times* and *The Washington Post*. But it was his first job with CBS that really ignited his passion for TV journalism. After losing both of his parents in those horrendous disasters two years earlier, Delaney moved to New York to take up a role for CNN.

Now, being the kind of person who considered himself open minded, Delaney never succumbed to the UNITY idea of world peace. Not that he was sceptical in any way, but simply because he had no interest in religion. In his opinion, he simply didn't believe in one almighty power which controlled his destiny. However, he firmly thought that everyone had the right to their own opinions. So if they, like his brother, wanted to run off and join a crazy religious cult, then good luck to them. For him though, his work was as close to any religion out there and being the first person to break a story, now *that* was the holy grail of them all.

As the first of the black limousines pulled up at the front of the United Nations building, there was a sudden flurry from the press and the group suddenly surged forward. All desperate to get that first interview with the car's occupants. Looking towards Bill Grierson, Delaney's fifty something, chain smoking cameraman. He gestured his finger towards the car as a silent directive for Grierson to move into position. As the car stopped and Grierson raised his camera. The limousine's driver climbed out of the vehicle, walked around to the back of the vehicle and opened its rear left-hand door. As Brother Weyn and his assistant climbed out, there was an almighty roar from the crowd and Delaney leapt forward in anticipation of asking the first question.

"Brother Weyn... Brother Weyn if I may? Richard Delaney, CNN."

As camera bulbs flashed frenziedly around him. Delaney's adrenaline spiked as his prize unexpectedly responded by turning towards him and stepping forward. "Good evening Mr Delaney."

Delaney beamed with delight, feeling smug that had been successful in hooking the biggest fish of all. "Brother Weyn, we're live on CNN. Sir if I may ask you a few questions?"

Weyn took a deep breath and nodded enthusiastically, "Of course."

"I, like many others wonder how exactly this Michael will manifest himself tonight and, more importantly, what he plans to say in front of a global audience. Perhaps you could offer us some insight?"

Weyn smiled. "To answer your question Mr Delaney, I have to be completely honest. The truth is I simply don't know. I do, however, have faith. We currently live in a world in which religion, politics, war and greed have torn us apart. Tonight, in just under an hour, I have to believe that Michael will change all of that."

"One more question if I may. Can you comment on the reports that several UNITY church's and offices have been vandalised in recent days? Also, perhaps a word or two on the rumors that anyone involved has mysteriously disappeared."

Suddenly Weyn's smile fell away and his expression turned more sombre. "Mr Delaney, with respect that's the most ridiculous accusation I've ever heard. These people are nothing more than terrorists. Thugs who are trying to undermine the valuable work we are trying to do…"

Suddenly Delaney interjected. "If that's the case, perhaps you can comment on the rumors surrounding your security services and of the suggestions that they have been overly heavy handed?"

Taking a breath, Weyn suddenly glanced towards Brother Simon and nodded.

"Mr Delaney, I don't know anything about the missing people. However, I can assure your viewers that they have nothing to fear. UNITY is attempting to create a peaceful utopia and I'm sure you'll agree that in this new world, security and stability must be maintained. Now, if you'll excuse me…"

Before Delaney could respond, Brother Simon suddenly intervened, allowing Weyn to step aside. As he moved, Weyn's smartly dressed assistant stepped ominously closer, blocking Delaney's path for a few uncomfortable moments. Realising that his broadcast was still live, the reporter took a deep breath and swiftly turned back towards his cameraman and continued.

"So, there you have it. In just under an hour, the world will be introduced to Michael and I, for one, can't wait. Now back to Jack in the studio for the headlines…"

As the camera's red light flickered off, Delaney scrutinised Bill Grierson's stern expression. "So, what did you think?"

Grierson stepped forward, shook his head and frowned. "Honestly? I think you're fucking crazy. You can't go on live TV and accuse Weyn of being a Nazi stooge. At least not tonight."

Taking a deep breath, Delaney groaned. "Maybe so, but Bill don't you sense it? There's something wrong, I just know it."

Turning towards the United Nations, the two men proceeded to join the horde of reporters and they began to slowly file inside the building. Dropping his cigarette on the ground, the overweight Grierson shook his head, stepped on the cigarette and continued onwards.

"Richard, I think you're just looking too deeply into this whole thing. You need to relax, I'm sure that in an hour, we'll know everything."

As the line of journalists slowly shuffled towards the security checkpoint, Delaney took a deep breath and groaned, "That's what I'm afraid of."

72

Wednesday 26th October - 11.40pm GMT - Alva Gen, Scotland

AFTER SPENDING A miserable hour and a half scrambling and crawling through tight rugged passageways, Dougie, Tom and the rest of the group finally emerged out of the silver mine at the foot of Alva Glen. Fortunately, the entranceway itself was protected by an old rusting gate. With very little effort Dougie, Tom and Agent Reynolds soon had it forced from its hinges and lying on its side. As the trio strode over the gate and out into the cool night air. They were followed by Commander Dalby, President Hillary and, finally, an uncomfortable looking Doctor Quest and Helen Moore.

"Where are we?"

Taking a deep breath, Dougie turned to Professor Moore and smiled. "Tom was right lassie, we're back in Alva."

Brushing herself free of dust and cobwebs, she glanced towards Quest and tilted her head. "I can see that, but, *when* exactly are we?"

Suddenly Mark Reynolds abruptly stepped forward and

cleared his throat. "When we should be Professor! Look. I have a GPS watch and it tells me that the date is Wednesday 26th October and the time is 23.45pm.

Suddenly President Hillary stepped forward, looking confused. "I'm sorry, I didn't quite get that. Are you telling me that we've just travelled thousands of miles and that we're now in Scotland?"

Glancing across at Dougie, Reynolds nodded. "Yes Sir, I am."

"Unbelievable!"

As the group brushed themselves down, Dougie stepped across to where a bewildered Tom was standing. "Are ye alright laddie? Ye look a wee bit befuddled."

Overcome with emotion, Tom swiftly took a deep breath and swallowed down hard in attempt to fight back the tears now welling up in his eyes. "I'm home… I never thought I'd get back."

Dougie gave a strained smile. "Aye lad, you're a lucky man."

"Suddenly, Tom realised that his own anguish was probably nothing compared to the torment that his friend was now feeling. After all, yes, he was home and no doubt within a very short time, he would be reunited with his wife. But for Dougie, he was still a man out of time, still lost 300 years into an unknown future.

"I'm sorry Dougie… I didn't mean…"

Slapping his friend on the shoulder, Dougie grinned. "Now, dinne ye worry aboot that laddie. I'm sure, as you once said to me, all of this'll be fae a reason."

Suddenly the president stepped forward with an anxious expression. "Wait, did you say that it's Wednesday? If that's the case and we're in Scotland, that means that we're 5 hours behind the US."

Reynolds turned towards the president and sighed. "That's correct, sir. So, what?"

The president rolled his eyes. "So, Agent Reynolds, that means that in just 15 minutes, UNITY is going to introduce the world to this prophet of theirs, Michael. My God, they're at the UN right now."

Stepping forward, Commander Dalby shrugged his shoulders. "I don't understand Sir…"

Suddenly Hillary's tone turned from frustration to one of anger.

"Commander Dalby, don't you see? This group have killed Presidents and Prime Ministers all over the world. They've cleverly positioned themselves to not just to become a global power, but *the* global power. We're not just dealing with a group of religious fanatics Commander, we're dealing with a well organised plot for global domination!"

A flustered Helen Moore suddenly stepped forward and raised her voice. "Jesus Christ! We have to warn people, before it's too late!"

Grasping Helen's arm, Doctor Quest suddenly interrupted. "Wait! Look Mr President, we must be careful here. We must assume that if this group does have control over world governments, they also control the police, or even worse, the military."

Dalby nodded in agreement. "He's right Mr President. We have to be careful."

Helen glanced across at Tom and interrupted. "Tom, if we could get to your house in time. Then perhaps we could alert the media and warn people. I mean, surely not everyone has been turned."

Pondering Helen's suggestion, the president turned to Tom and took a deep breath. "Can it be done Tom? Could we make it in time?"

Looking upwards across the glen, Tom shrugged his shoulders. "It would be tight but, yes, we could certainly give it a try."

Dougie sprang forward and shouted enthusiastically. "Well alright then. In that case what the bloody hell are we waiting for? Let's go!"

*

6.50pm EST - General Assembly Hall, United Nations, New York

As CNN reporter, Richard Delaney, stepped into the lavishly decorated United Nations General Assembly Hall, he gazed around in awe and then turned to his cameraman, Bill Grierson, and shook his head.

"Well, we're in the belly of the beast now, Bill. Are you ready?"

Looking around the packed room in astonishment, Delaney had never seen so many people crammed into the normally 1800 capacity hall. The podium area at the front of the room was gone and in its place sat a large white marble table, with three high backed seats. On either side of the podium area, there were thirty seats, reserved for members of the *Red Council*. Even the room's iconic UN wall plaque had been removed and replaced with the UNITY symbol. As Delaney took his seat in the press area, he took a deep breath and lowered his voice. "Weird layout, the place looks more like a church than a conference hall."

With the voice of a producer screaming in his ear to get started, Bill Grierson signalled to his reporter to get ready to broadcast. As the camera red light flickered on, Grierson gave a thumb up and Delaney began his broadcast.

"Good evening, this is Richard Delaney reporting live from the United Nations building in New York City. Tonight, we participate in a moment of history that even your grandchildren will look back on. For the next hour, we join billions of viewers and listeners from all around the world as we welcome a man that has been referred to as a modern-day prophet. Indeed, some are even calling him the new Messiah.

In just a few minutes, Brother Weyn will formally begin the ceremony to welcome Michael. The atmosphere both inside and out on the streets is electric. Just looking around the hall tonight, absolutely everyone who's anyone is here.

As well as every member of the Red Council, we have presidents, royalty, religious leaders and even celebrities from the world of stage and screen."

From below where he was sitting, Delaney could see that two large doors had just swung open and a procession of sorts had started. Two lines of *Red Council* members, each garbed in long red robes began a slow walk into the hall. For Delaney, the most alarming element of the outfit was the sinister, identical silver face mask that each man was wearing.

"So here we go, the doors to the hall have opened and a hush has befallen the audience. As confirmed, the proceedings will begin with a procession of the Red Council. As they come into the hall I can see that each member is wearing, what I would

say is, a rather grand and striking set of red robes along with an unusual face mask."

As the procession progressed gradually down the centre aisle of the hall, around half of the attendees rose to their feet and dropped their heads as the entourage passed by. Glancing, somewhat bemused, at his cameraman, Delaney assumed that the audience members who remained seated were, like himself, not currently members of the UNITY faith.

As the procession reached the head of the hall, each member of the council took his or her assigned seat on either side of the large marble desk. As the standing audience members retook their seats, two solitary figures remained standing. Turning towards the UNITY symbol, both figures raised their arms and then spoke out loud. "Unity is the way. One mind, one body."

Without having to be prompted, many of the audience suddenly uttered the response in unison.

"We are one mind, one body."

"So, with the procession over, the two remaining members are now making their way around to the rear of this rather grand white marble table…"

Suddenly the last two figures reached up and in a perfectly co-ordinated move, detached their identical face masks and placed them down onto the table in front of them.

"So, with their masks now off, UNITY church spokesman, Brother Weyn, and his assistant, Brother Simon, will now address the assembly."

As the room descended into a hush, Brother Simon bowed firstly to the assembled audience and then to his superior before taking his seat. Now alone at the podium, Brother Weyn took a deep breath and opened his mouth to address the waiting audience.

73

Wednesday 26th October - 11.52pm GMT - Alva, Scotland

AFTER CAREFULLY SCRAMBLING down a nearby hill, Dougie, Tom and the remaining members of the group scuttled through the glen as if they were being chased by a crazed madman. Unused to such physical exertion, Helen Moore and Richard Quest remained at the back of the line, panting and wheezing in a desperate bid to keep up with the rest. With only minutes before Michael's appearance, Dougie, Tom, Mark Reynolds and Commander Dalby were firmly out front when they finally made their way out of the glen and onto Brook Street.

The evening itself was quiet, with very little traffic and few signs of life. As the group arrived onto Stirling Street, intersecting the two sides of Alva, Tom suddenly stopped and clutched his chest, breathing heavily. "I... I don't think I can go on..."

Waiting a moment for the others to catch up, Dougie

ran back to his friend, grabbed his arm and shouted out. "What! Dinne stop now laddie, we're almost there."

With his chest almost bursting, Tom gasped heavily and gave Dougie an unenthusiastic nod before continuing. Minutes later and after crossing the main street, Tom led the group down a deserted looking Queen Street, before finally recognising his own house which now stood only a few meters away. As he approached the building, Tom found himself overcome with emotion. His eyes welling up with tears and his heart leaping at the thought of being reunited with his family. Stopping outside the property's iron gate, he took a deep breath before lifting its latch. Swinging the gate, he looked up at the house with a sense of nostalgia, as if he hadn't seen it for years.

As the other members of the group arrived, Dougie stepped across to where Tom was standing and patted his friend on the shoulder. "Are ye alright laddie?"

Swallowing hard, Tom gave a heavy sigh. "I don't know… it's all seems so strange, to be suddenly ripped from your life and then find yourself thrust back into it."

Dougie smiled. "Aye… it is."

Taking a deep breath, Tom briefly glanced around at the group and sauntered up to the door. Moments later, he rang the bell after and after receiving no response, proceeded to press the button a second time. After one final knock at the door, he turned to the group and shrugged his shoulder. "That's weird, there seems to be no one home. They must be out or something."

Finally, as an exhausted Helen Moore and Doctor Quest came gasping through the gate, an Impatient Mark Reynolds stepped forward and spoke up.

"I don't suppose you have a key, do you Tom?"

Tom thought for a moment and then he remembered that there was indeed a spare key, that he and his wife, Jane, used for emergencies. Without waiting for any further response, he rushed over to a small stone wall beside the house, lifted a rock and sighed in relief as he picked up a familiar looking brass *Yale* key, which he then proceeded to unlock the door with.

"Thank goodness it's still here."

A moment later and the entire group, huddled through the main doorway and were now in the process of making their way into Tom's living room.

"Quickly, it's almost time."

Glancing at an ornamental clock sitting atop the rooms pinewood fireplace, the president suddenly barked out the time, as Tom quickly picked up a nearby TV remote control, switched the television on and flicked the channel over to CNN.

Gasping and exhausted, Helen Moore collapsed down onto a nearby couch before glancing up at her colleague, Richard Quest. "Did we make it?"

"I don't know."

As the TV flickered into life and the image of a packed United Nations building filled the screen, there was a sudden gasp from Quest as he spotted the enormous, but familiar, UNITY logo hanging on the wall in the main chamber.

"Oh my God! Helen look at the symbol, it's identical to the one that Father Demarco was working on."

As Tom rushed to increase the television's volume, the

president abruptly asked everyone to hush. "Shhh, let's hear what's going on."

"If you're just joining us, we're here in the United Nations building in New York, with only minutes to go before Michael's introduction. We're first going to hear from UNITY spokesman, Brother Thomas Weyn."

As Weyn stepped up to the podium. The camera shot changed, initially to display a view of the audience and then focussed on members of the Red Council. In one shot, the camera fixated in on one of the unusual silver masks, Helen suddenly shivered and broke the silence.

"What's with the creepy masks, that's just weird."

Now at the podium, Brother Weyn took a moment to gaze around the room and then took a deep breath before his voice boomed into the microphone. *"Unity is the way. One mind, one body."*

Again, without any prompt, the audience quickly responded, speaking in unison. *"We are one mind, one body.*

"Brothers and sisters, for centuries we've lived in a world of harmony and beauty. But humanity has contaminated that dream, with its greed and its desires. With its destructive lust for violence. For centuries, even your religions have talked of peace, but secretly condoned wars. Violence has become the norm for the world. When UNITY came to power, I swore to you, citizens of the world, that we would change and tonight, I'm going to keep that promise.

May the blessings of Michael be with you all."

74

Wednesday 26th October - 7.00pm EST - United Nations, New York

INSIDE A PACKED United Nations General Assembly Hall, News reporter, Richard Delaney, looked down from the press gallery with curiosity, as Brother Weyn stepped back from the podium and acknowledged his colleague. As instructed, Brother Simon stepped up to the microphone, took a deep breath, raised his arms and addressed the audience.

"Unity is the way. One mind, one body."

After a brief silence, the assembled audience responded with a mountainous chant. *"We are one mind, one body.*

"Rise and be recognised."

In a slightly unnerving moment, Delaney and his cameraman Bill Grierson watched as each member of the *Red Council,* along with most of the assembled guests, immediately got to their feet and raised their right hand. Initially confused by the gesture, Delaney motioned Grierson to focus in on the audience with his camera.

With the image of a man's hand now in shot, Delaney quickly realised that people were displaying their tattoos.

"I'll be honest folks, I've been a reporter along time and I don't think that I've ever seen anything like this. In what now appears to be a display of loyalty to UNITY, each member of the audience is being asked to display their tattoo, no doubt as an act of affiliation."

Glancing at his cameraman, Delaney nodded and continued.

"From our vantage point here, in the media gallery, I can see that just over a third of the audience are still seated. I can only assume that, like myself, these rather confused looking folks are not members of the club either."

"Unity is the way. One mind, one body."

Again, after a brief pause, the audience responded in unison. *"We are one mind, one body.*

As he listened to the chanting audience, Delaney surprisingly found himself shivering, almost as if an icy hand had just stroked the back of his neck. Looking down at the seemingly detached faces in the crowd, he suddenly had the impression that there was something wrong. Although not entirely sure what it was. He simply felt as if that there was something different about these people. Their faces, which until recently were filled with excitement and joy, now seemed emotionless, empty and almost mechanical in nature. After bowing to Brother Weyn, Simon returned to the table, picked up his own silver face mask and put it on. Afterwards, and in perfect unison, the thirty members of the *Red Council* climbed to their feet, stepped forward and divided themselves into two equal rows. Finally, and despite having received no instruction, one row relocated to the left-hand side of the hall and the second moved to the right.

"It appears that we are now only moments away, as we move into the final stage of the ceremony. The members of the Red Council are taking up their positions in preparation to welcome Michael."

After stepping across to the marble table, Brother Weyn picked up his own face mask and after a brief pause, walked across to the podium.

"Unity is the way. One mind, one body."

As before, the audience again responded in unison. *"We are one mind, one body.*

"Yes, we are. Today you are free. Free of hatred and free of anger. Today I release you from your meaningless lives. Today I release you from envy and from greed. Today the people of the world will truly become one. One mind, one body…"

"We are one mind, one body.

"Yes, we are one mind, one body. But the body is impure. There are those among you who are not part of the body. So, beginning tomorrow, every country, every city, every home will be purged, until we are pure, until we are at peace."

As his words reverberated throughout the hall, many audience members could be seen fidgeting and whispering unnervingly to each other in their seats. In the press gallery above the main hall, CNN reporter, Richard Delaney, and cameraman, Bill Grierson, glanced at each other tensely. Then, as Brother Weyn donned his own eerie silver mask, he stepped to the right of the podium and raised his arms, and, again stepped forward to the microphone.

"Kneel!"

As Simon stepped back, Delaney watched with curiosity at the entire hall of assembled guests as they swiftly shuffled forward in their seats and got down on their knees as instructed. As an unnerving silence filled the room, there was a sudden gasp of astonishment as a small shimmering light appeared at the back of the hall and began to float forward, towards the front of the room.

"We are one mind, one body. We are one mind, one body. We are one mind, one body." Refocussing his attention towards the camera, Delaney took a deep breath and continued his commentary.

"This is incredible. I don't know if you can see this. What appears to be a small light has just appeared in the centre of the hall and... wait a moment, there's something happening..."

As the light finally came to rest in the centre of the hall, there was an almighty gasp from the crowd as the hall suddenly began to shake and the shimmering globe exploded into a plethora of white light. Within seconds, the light began to twist and contort in on itself. With the sound of his producer screaming through his earpiece to have Delaney restart his commentary, the reporter raised his microphone and made a further brave attempt to describe what he was seeing.

"I don't quite know how to explain what I'm seeing. The light now appears to have changed. What started as a small sphere, now seems to have transformed itself into an opening or portal of some kind."

As the hall shook and various light fittings flickered intermittently. Delaney glanced down from the balcony and out into the audience. Bizarrely and despite the commotion, he was surprised to see that most of them were still on their knees, with their heads bowed.

"*With the audience still on its knees...*"

Suddenly Delaney's voice tailed off as the shimmering portal suddenly began to pulsate.

"*Wait... something is happening. Yes, I can see something emerging from the light.*"

Delaney and his cameraman watched wide eyed, as the shimmering light began to fade, leaving, what now appeared to be a shadowy mist floating in mid-air above the assembly.

"*We are one mind, one body. We are one mind, one body. We are one mind, one body.*"

Within seconds, the silhouetted figure began to slowly descend downwards towards the front of the hall. As it moved, its shape began to gradually solidify, until finally the outline of a cloaked figure could now be seen standing in the centre of the auditorium. As it came to a halt, it turned towards the assembled audience, who again began to chant loudly.

"*We are one mind, one body. We are one mind, one body. We are one mind, one body.*"

With news cameras now converging on the hooded figure, Delaney could see that, although it was the approximate height, weight and shape of a man, there were elements that were different. Its face, for example, had sunken, drawn in cheek bones, vivid blue eyes and abnormally pale skin. For a moment, the figure remained still and motionless, until suddenly it took a slow deep breath and began to gaze around the room.

From the right-hand side of the podium, Brother Weyn and Brother Simon stepped forward. Moments later, each man knelt on one knee in front of the cloaked creature and dutifully bowed their heads. "Welcome Master, the people stand ready to serve."

Glancing over the audience, the creature took another breath.

"They do this by their own accord and of their own free will?"

For Delaney and his cameraman, the creature's voice was unusual, cold and almost raspy in nature. It was not the kind of voice Delaney had come across before, neither would it be one that he would soon forget. Suddenly, both Brother Weyn and his assistant climbed to their feet and stepped back.

"They do Master."

As the creature gave a nod of satisfaction, Brother Simon abruptly stepped across to microphone and addressed the audience. "Stand and be recognised."

As before, the UNITY members of the audience immediately rose to their feet and as before raised their hand to exhibit their tattoos. As he nodded, the creature suddenly glanced up towards the large unity symbol and raised his hand. "Then it shall be so…"

Unexpectedly, the room began to shudder and shake. Light fittings attached to the ceiling began to flicker and swing from side to side. Then, without warning, people began to scream uncontrollably as the three-circled symbol hanging on the hall began to transform. Frightened, non-UNITY members suddenly started to leave their seats and pile into the aisles. Some even began moving towards the exits in sheer panic. As a speechless Delaney looked down on the chaos from the gallery, he now found himself beginning to panic a little. Suddenly, he spotted a video close-up of a woman's hand and in that instant, he immediately knew the cause of the panic. The tattoo on the woman's hand, just like the hanging wall symbol was undergoing a transformation. But unlike the wall, her tattoo appeared to be moving independently, underneath the woman's skin. Almost as she was being branded with a hot iron from beneath.

"*This is impossible… the symbols, they're moving by themselves…*"

As the circles and lines on the wall began to move, so too did the tattoos on people's hands. Within seconds, the symbols' final transformation had taken place and as the screams lessened, there was a sudden gasp from audience. The UNITY symbol that hung on the wall was no longer exhibiting three circles and two horizontal lines through the centre. It now revealed three numbers in tight formation. The same three numbers that each member of UNITY now bore as a brand on the back of their right hand. For Delaney and his colleague, the true horror was that the three numbers were now exposed as 666. The mark of the beast.

75

Thursday 27th October - 1.15am GMT - Alva, Scotland

Huddled around the television, the seven gazed at each other, shocked at what they'd just witnessed. Turning away from the screen, Helen placed her hand over her mouth and shook her head in disbelief. "What's wrong with those people? Surely, they've got eyes, Jesus, get out of there!"

Dougie shook his head and interrupted. "Don't you see, it's too late for them."

Turning to Dougie in horror, Helen suddenly raised her voice. "What do you mean too late? Are they blind, why don't they just run?"

Dougie glanced at the others and groaned. "Because he has control of them and…"

On screen, the tension in the conference hall mounted and the group watched as a small number of non-UNITY members made their way towards the exit. As he watched, Mark Reynolds suddenly shouted out and brought Dougie and Helen Moore's attention back to the live broadcast.

"Wait, look!"

*

7.19pm EST – United Nations, New York City

As an unnerving silence gripped the packed press gallery above the United Nations General Assembly Hall. CNN reporter, Richard Delaney, glanced nervously across at his cameraman, Bill Grierson.

"I'm not quite sure how to describe what I'm feeling right now. But one thing has become clear, this Michael character is not quite what we expected. Wait… something's happening, the two lines of Red Council members are now moving towards the front of the conference hall and lining up on either side of Michael, Brother Weyn and Brother Simon. I must say folks that I, along with the many other members of the press core are finding these images disturbing."

Observing the front row of the conference hall, Delaney watched with curiosity as the current President of the United Nations, Nigerian, *Ishan Oreke,* suddenly climbed out of his seat and strode towards the front of the assembly. As the camera zoomed in on the smartly dressed president, Delaney took a deep breath and watched nervously as Oreke approached Michael's position.

"Hold on… now I see something happening at the front of the hall. Ishan Oreke, the President of the United Nations is out of his seat and is now making his way up to the front."

Moments later and in full view of the assembled audience and television cameras, Oreke raised his hand, stepped forward and addressed Michael and Brother Weyn directly. "Brother Weyn, what is the meaning of this? What have you done to these people?"

Peering down at the smartly dressed president, Weyn took a deep breath and scorned. “Why, Mr President, I’ve done nothing. Everything you see is of their own free will.”

Suddenly the fearsome creature took a step towards Oreke, it’s face pale and gaunt with eyes blazing like fog lamps. “You are a President?”

Oreke swallowed hard and gave a nervous nod. “I am Sir, of the United Nations, and you? You are Michael I presume?”

Looking at the man’s unblemished right hand, the creature looked across at Brother Weyn and gently shook its head. “Michael… I forget. I have so many names…”

For a moment, the president appeared confused. “What do you mean, many names?”

Watching the man like a spider as it lures an insect into its web, the creature simply sneered.

“I see you are not one with the body?”

Shaking his head, the president gave a hollow laugh and responded angrily. “If you mean this ridiculous regime of yours, then no Sir, I am not of the body. I’m putting an end to ridiculous charade. Brother Weyn, please escort this gentleman and your group out of the chamber immediately. Otherwise, I’ll have no choice but to have you ejected by force.”

Without providing Michael or Brother Weyn with an opportunity to respond, Oreke immediately turned heel and marched off angrily towards the exit. However, before he could reach the centre of the room, many audience members suddenly clambered out of their seats and proceeded to block his path. Turning towards the assembled UNITY leadership, a bewildered Oreke cleared his throat and raised his hands to object. "What's the meaning of this? Brother Weyn, ask your people to step aside otherwise I will..."

Suddenly, Ureke's voice trailed off and he unpredictably began to splutter uncontrollably, almost as if something had become lodged within his throat. Seconds later, Delaney and his cameraman watched in dismay from the gallery as Oreke suddenly placed his hand to his ear. After removing it a moment later, his face turned to horror as he discovered that his hand was now covered in blood.

Suddenly panic stricken and overwhelmed by dizziness, the president screamed in agony as he began to tremble and convulse. Within seconds, his bloodied face had become twisted and contorted. Turning towards Michael, Oreke stumbled on a nearby chair leg and inadvertently crashed down onto his knees in agony. "W... What have you done?"

Watching the blood-soaked president squirming in agony on the floor, the cloaked creature's expression abruptly turned from apathy to one of fury, as it clenched its fist.

"I'm fulfilling a prophesy Mr President, one that was written a very long time ago. This is my time and I've waited so very long for it. I'm afraid your United Nations is no longer needed, and as it would appear, neither are you."

Finally, Oreke shrieked in anguish as his body began to tremble and spasm uncontrollably. Within moments, his clothes and the surface area around him were splattered with blood that was now spewing from his nose and ears.

"Arghhh...."

With one final powerful spasm, the President took a final breath and Ishan Oreke, the Nigerian president of the United Nations, was gone. With his lifeless body slumped on the ground, the packed conference hall suddenly erupted into panic and the thousand or so non-UNITY guests suddenly rushed desperately towards the rear exit.

"Jesus Christ… I don't know what just happened, but the UN president is dead. A complete state of panic has erupted here and I can see that all the non-UNITY members are now flooding towards the rear exit and… What? Hold on, I've just been told that all the doors have been locked by security. Oh my God!"

At the front of the hall, the hooded creature calmly turned towards Weyn and Brother Simon and hissed. "It is time, kill them all."

Nodding once, Weyn immediately stepped forward to the podium, took a deep breath and addressed the room. "We are one mind, one body."

After a moment, there was an almighty unified response. *"We are one mind, one body."*

Upstairs in the media gallery, Delaney's ongoing event commentary had now ceased. Despite a prompt from his cameraman, he, like his colleague was now genuinely afraid. Watching a nearby TV monitor, Delaney couldn't believe what was happening downstairs. One half of the audience appeared to have become emotionless automatons. The other half had fallen into a sheer panic, with people screaming and scrambling over each other, desperate to find a way out.

"The body is impure. There are those among you who are not part of the body."

"The body is impure..."

Observing the chaos, Weyn turned toward the members of the *Red Council* and motioned them to stand. A second later, the group of sinister red cloaked figures were now standing in a single line. Then, as Weyn ushered them forward, their sinister face masks glimmered with the bright lights of the conference hall. Upstairs in the gallery, Delaney's heart pounded as he and Bill Grierson grabbed their jackets and rushed towards a nearby exit to make their escape.

Inside the hall Weyn took a deep breath and once again coolly addressed the audience. "The body is impure. We must purge the unclean amongst us. Kill them!"

At first, the UNITY members remained calm and almost expressionless. Then, without warning, all that changed. Serenity and composure were quickly replaced with what could only be described as expressions of unadulterated rage.

"Kill!"

In what could only be defined as a scene from *Dante's Inferno*, Brother Weyn, Michael and the other members of the *Red Council* watched coldly as the scene exploded into brutal mayhem. Weyn's followers turned on the audience like a pack of vicious wolves.

Men and women began to attack each other using not only their bare hands, but also makeshift weapons including furniture and glass bottles. Within moments, blood curdling screams began to echo around the chamber as victims were ferociously beaten to death.

*

Fleeing the UN media gallery through an emergency exit. Reporter, Richard Delaney, and his cameraman, Bill Grierson, frantically rushed down a rear stairwell, desperate to escape the frenzied bloodletting that was taking place inside the conference room. As the pair ran down the stairs, they prayed that their plan would be enough to get them out of the building alive. However, as they turned a corner, the pair were suddenly startled by two New York police officers who appeared to be searching the building.

"Oh, Thank God officer, please can you help us?"

For a moment, the officers simply looked at the two men. Then suddenly, one of the men drew his weapon and pointed it directly at the reporter.

"Whoa easy! We're unarmed It's not us you have to worry about, it's the crazy shit's going on inside…"

Suddenly Delaney's voice fell away and to his horror, he noticed that one of the men had three small enflamed sixes on the back of his right hand.

"Oh my God!"

Glancing at his colleague, the officer smirked coldly. "Look Larry, two more of them."

Turning back to Delaney, the first officer nodded. "Look Larry, you know this guy. It's Richard Delaney, you know the famous news guy."

"Oh yeah, maybe we should ask for an autograph."

As waves of panic swept over Delaney and his colleague, the two men began to slowly edge backwards up the stairwell, hoping above all else that perhaps they might be blessed with freedom.

Regrettably, as the officers slowly edged towards them, Delaney now sensed that this situation was only going to end one way.

"Nah, I never liked him anyway."

Now nauseous and physically shaking with fear, Delaney made one last attempt to reason with the officer. "Please, you're a police officer. You have a duty to protect..."

Without warning, the two officer's insincere smiles dissolved away and in those final few moments of his life, all Richard Delaney could see gazing back at him, was nothing more than cold dark hatred.

76

Thursday 27th October - 12.40am GMT - Alva, Scotland

UNABLE TO WATCH the harrowing images any longer, Mark Reynolds decided to act for the greater good and picked up the remote control and switched the television off. As the awful pictures of blood soaked bodies and carnage faded, he looked around at the pale faced members of the group. Each of them clearly traumatised by what they'd just witnessed.

"I think I'm going to throw up…"

Pulling herself out of Quest's arms, a nauseous looking Helen Moore placed her hand over her mouth and suddenly bolted out of the room.

"Helen…"

Rising quickly from his seat, Richard Quest excused himself and proceeded to follow. A few minutes later, he reappeared and retook his seat next to the US President, George Hillary and *USS Richmond* Commander Tom Dalby. "I think she'll be okay."

Suddenly Dalby took a deep breath and groaned. "Well I'm not, Jesus Christ, did you see that?"

Suddenly the President sat forward and cleared his throat. "We have to call somebody, we have to put an end to this madness, Tom can I please use your phone."

Suddenly an exasperated Richard Quest climbed out of his seat and raised his hand to object.

"Gentlemen please, with respect Mr President, right now we can't do that."

"Why?"

"Right now, UNITY is solidifying their hold on our world. What we've just seen on screen didn't just happen in New York. I'll bet you it happened, or is happening everywhere. It's like what Dougie said, these people haven't simply been seduced, they've chosen to follow this path. The moment they did that, well, that was when they lost their souls."

Suddenly, the living room door swung open and a shaky looking Helen Moore stepped back inside the room. As she entered, she apologised as Tom rose out of his seat and offered it to the professor. As she sat down, Tom turned to the group and sighed. "Look, Doctor Quest is right. Who are we going to call? Right now, the only people I trust are the ones in this room. We've all come a long way and we knew this day would come. It's just come a little quicker than expected, that's all. Like Father McRae, or whatever he was, said we have to have faith and work together."

Dougie climbed out of his seat, stood beside his friend and addressed the group. "Aye, Tom's right. Remember whit happened to us in the mine. We've been brought together tae fight this bastard and from what I've seen, they're others out there like us. Perhaps it's time fae us tae stop running and to start fighting back."

Suddenly Helen yawned, and Quest gave a nod and spoke up, "Well, there's one thing for sure. Right now, we're in a safe place. There's nothing more we can do tonight. But tomorrow is another day."

The President glanced around at the others and nodded in agreement. "I agree. From what I've seen here tonight, it appears we've lost the first battle. So, if the war is to continue tomorrow, we clearly need to rest and regroup."

"Hang on, I have an idea."

Tom excused himself and walked across to a small oak cabinet. "I wonder if…"

Once opened, he rummaged inside for a moment, before taking out a bottle of *Dalmore* malt whisky and several glasses.

"I just remembered, I got this bottle of whisky a long time ago. I was keeping it for a special occasion and… well it would appear that this might fit the bill. After handing a glass to each person, Tom opened the whisky. Then, beginning with Dougie, Tom proceeded to pour a generous helping of the amber liquid into each person's glass. After placing the bottle down, he beckoned everyone to stand.

"Mr President, perhaps you would care to make the toast?"

With a glass of whisky in hand, George Hillary looked around at the six other solemn faces in the room and raised his glass. "I guess that after all the awful things we've been through, and what we've seen tonight, there's really only one thing we can toast."

As the group raised their glasses, Hillary took a deep breath and offered a sombre nod. "To the war..."

EPILOGUE

Friday 28th October - 8.25am GMT - Alva, Scotland

TOM DUNCAN WOKE to the sound of a heavy rain shower as it drummed against his bedroom window. As his eyes slowly opened, Tom stretched out his arms, pushed back the duvet, swung his legs out onto the floor and pulled himself up into a sitting position. Looking around the familiar bedroom was, at first, emotional. Even being back home seemed like a miracle, especially after what he'd been through. Looking across the room to a nearby side table, he caught a glimpse of an old photograph. It was a picture of himself, his wife, Jane, and his daughter, Amy, taken just a few weeks before her fifth birthday. Even though it was only a photo, just being able to see his wife's image again was special. Her soft blonde hair and blue eyes, and that smile. He always told her that her smile could break a thousand hearts.

She was always the strong one, the daring one. Always taking the initiative, he loved that about her. When his father suddenly died, she was the one who arranged the funeral. Jane was like that, nothing was ever too much trouble. Looking once more at the photo Tom smiled inwardly. It was nice to be back, despite the awful circumstances. He hoped and prayed that his girls were somewhere safe and out of danger.

Sitting on the edge of his bed, he pondered waking the others. But, after recalling that it was well after 3am when they finally went to bed, he thought that he should let them sleep a little while longer. Climbing to his feet, Tom suddenly caught a glimpse of the phone beside his bed. Gazing at the device, he wanted so much to call his wife, to tell her that he was alive and that despite the horrors of the previous night, he brought hope. However, he had vowed to Dougie and the others that no calls should be made. But having her image in his mind and being in such proximity to the phone was too much of a temptation.

Finally giving in, Tom picked up the receiver and held it in his hands. As he caressed it, crazy thoughts suddenly began to circulate. Thoughts like what if she didn't want to see him. Perhaps she was angry at the way he abandoned her. Christ, what if she thought that he was dead and married someone else. Then again, Tom recalled his promise, no phone calls. This was ridiculous, it was his wife and daughter for Christ's sake. Looking at the phone once more he took a deep breath and swallowed hard. He had to know, he had to know if they were alive and safe, he had to make the call.

*

8.50am GMT - Arthurs Seat, Edinburgh, Scotland

Jane Duncan had always been the outdoor type. Hiking was in her blood. So, when she had the opportunity to visit her parents' home in Edinburgh, she loved to walk up Edinburgh's famous *Arthur's Seat.* Sitting majestically above Edinburgh's famous Royal Mile and Princess Street is Holyrood Park. The park's pinnacle is Arthur's Seat, an ancient volcano, that sits 251meters above sea level. Apart from offering locals and tourists alike amazing views of the city, it's also the site of a large and well-preserved hill fort. Which is one of four, dating back around 2000 years. After the disasters of two years ago, tourists however were now very rare. Today apart from herself and Wallace, her energetic golden retriever, Jane was completely alone. Dressed in a navy blue *North Face* waterproof jacket, woollen gloves and a white woolly hat, she stood for a moment by the old fort and took a deep breath. After a short pause, she was about to call the dog over, but she was distracted as her cell phone suddenly rang. Reaching inside her jacket, she fumbled with the phone for a moment before pushing the answer button.

"Hello."

*

For a moment, Tom couldn't believe what he was hearing. A soft Scottish voice that he thought he'd never hear again.

"Hello, Jane."

For a moment, the line remained silent and then she responded. "Tom, oh my God is that you?"

Smiling inwardly, Tom took an emotional breath and

swallowed. “Yes, it is. I wanted to call you and tell you that we’re back.”

“I’m sorry, we’re back, who’s with you?”

As his eyes began to water, Tom exhaled. “It’s a long story and I’ll tell you all about it when I see you. Are you okay? Where are you?”

For a moment, the line went quiet and then she continued. “I’m in Edinburgh. My Mum and Dad moved from Stirling about a year ago. I’m just through visiting them. Where are you?”

Glancing across at his wife’s photo, Tom smiled to himself. “I’m in Alva, at home. Is Amy with you?”

Again, another short pause and then she continued. “She’s at my parent’s, but she’s fine. We were to come home tomorrow, but I see those plans changing now.”

Tom smiled. “I missed you…”

Listening intently to her voice, Tom heard her take a deep breath. “I missed you too. I’ll be home later so you can tell me all about it.”

Wiping a tear from his cheek, Tom swallowed hard and a took a deep breath. “Okay, I’ll see you later.”

“Bye for now… We are one mind, one body.”

As the line clicked and the call ended, Tom’s face suddenly turned to horror as his wife’s final words began to replay over in and over in his mind.

“*We are one mind, one body…*”

“Oh, my God!”

Lightning Source UK Ltd.
Milton Keynes UK
UKHW012222140221
378769UK00001B/211

9 780993 020247